The Kingdom Chronicles Vol. 1

A King's Quest

A. V. Wedhorn

A King's Quest

All Rights Reserved © 2005 by Helm Publishing
and the Author, A.V. Wedhorn

No part of this book may be reproduced, or transmitted in any form or by any means, graphic, electronic, or mechanical, including photocopying, recording, taping, or by any information storage retrieval system, without the permission in writing from the publisher or author.

Helm Publishing
Senior Editor: Dianne Helm
Head Cover Artist: Vin Libassi

For information address:
Helm Publishing
3923 Seward Ave.
Rockford, IL 61108
815-398-4660
www.publishersdrive.com

ISBN 0-9760919-5-X
Printed in the United States of America

Acknowledgments

To Dianne Helm for giving me my shot and to Bridgette for telling me it would happen.

Prologue

The Night of Sorrows

An explosion tore through the still night air of the peaceful palace, shredding it with so much force and sound that it shook the entire building right down to its foundation stones. All heads jerked upright at the sound and every eye in the royal birthing room except for the queen, who was in the throes of labor, turned in the direction of the horrific noise.

King Dorian Salidor's handsome face went rigid with fear at the sound. He was already worried half to death about his lovely wife lying on the bed, the birthing of the twins seemed to be taking a lot longer than what he thought was necessary. Now it sounded like the rest of the royal palace outside of the birthing room was being attacked.

Glancing at his protector, the knight champion Bertravis Liolbane and his new personal battlemage Colin Lightbringer, the king made a split decision. He commanded the battlemage to find out what was going on outside the throne room.

Grabbing his red oak mace staff, Colin raced out of the birthing room in a blur of black and gold.

Then, facing his champion, who also wore a worried expression etched upon his face, King Dorian ordered him to stand fast by the door and to check on the other two knights standing guard in the hall outside.

The tall stern faced Krannion knight commander and champion of the royal family, moved towards the door and slowly opened it, his hand tight on his proctors' sword hilt.

The ringing sounds of swords on swords and metal on metal signified a battle being fought outside. The sounds of it filled the birthing chamber. A look of alarm flashed on the champion's face when he saw no sign of the knights stationed outside of the door. He found them a moment later farther down the hall with Colin Lightbringer attempting to hold off a horde of what looked like Terian northmen being led by a tall blond haired man with ice-cold blue eyes from reaching their chambers. At least they had the help of the battlemage.

Two loud wails behind him split the air. The knight champion and royal protector thought he saw a slight smile cross the face of the blonde haired man leading the group as he looked in his direction and redoubled his efforts against Colin whom he appeared to have singled out personally and was fighting one on one.

Bertravis Liolbane slammed the thick oak door to the birthing room shut and quickly slid a thick iron bolt in place, locking them in. Turning back to the dark curly haired king that he was sworn to protect he said, "Sire it appears that we are under attack from a force of Terian invaders."

"Terians!" King Dorian Salidor's astonished voice said, "Here in the palace, this far south, are you sure Bertravis?"

"That's what they looked like sire," the knight champion told him in a grim tone, "They appear to be coming here to this very room! Help me block this door! We need to hurry and get the rest of your family to the escape passageway in your chambers before they arrive."

The Krannion knight champion turned and saw Lady Alice, the queen's mother, holding the second of the newborn babies in her arms and the queen holding the first.

As the knight and the king started to grab furniture and pile it in front of the door, he called out to the ladies in waiting to get the queen and the new born heirs out of this room and into the royal bedchambers.

Lady Alice bent over the queen and said something into her daughter's ear and for a moment the new mother looked distraught and shook her pretty head fervently no, then she stretched out a hand towards her second baby in her own mother's arms.

In a commanding low voice, the Lady Alice said something else and the queen reluctantly took what appeared to be a baby into her arms from her mother and allowed the first one to be given to one of her maids. Then all of the maids set out carrying the weakened queen towards the royal bedchambers.

The sounds of the fighting outside the door grew louder and closer, then in an instant it was over and an eerie silence was all the other two men heard as they still continued to pile up the furniture in front of the door.

Seeing that there was nothing else left that they could put in the way of the invading soldiers the king and his champion turned to face each other, both praying to their individual gods that they had bought enough time.

It was then that they heard the rich baritone voice that sounded familiar to them both outside the door say, "So they are in there then."

A cold imperious sounding voice answered the first in a hiss, "Yes."

Both the king and the knight looked at each other in relieved surprise glad at hearing the sound of the king's younger brother Lord Vargas and his wizard outside of the door. Their next words turned their blood to ice as they heard the kings fourth and only surviving brother say loudly, "Cyadine, destroy this door immediately, we have to hurry up and kill them and the newborn heirs before they can escape the castle."

The sound of a wizard's incantation being cast caused the two men to race out of the birthing chamber and run towards the royal bedroom where the others were fleeing.

The maids led the queen through a side room that was used as a wardrobe closet and into a narrow escape staircase that led down deep into the bowels of the castle, straight to an underground chamber and river that flowed beneath it.

As the king and his champion ran into the bedchamber, Bertravis noticed that there was no sign of Lady Alice or of the birthing rags that she had been clutching to her chest. He didn't have time to worry about her though at that moment as the king spun back to him and demanded that he give up his sword to him.

"What!" shouted the Champion, grabbing the leather wrapped hilt tightly in his hand, "Sire, have you taken leave of your senses?"

"Give me your sword, Bertravis Liolbane," the dark haired king ordered as he withdrew a leather-fighting glove out of his pants pocket and slipped it onto his left hand.

The knight protector and champion stared directly into the king's own dark blue eyes, tightened his hand over his swords hilt and for the first time ever refused an order saying, "No Sire, I will not. You and your family are my responsibility, you are to be saved and kept alive, I will die here now to protect you and yours, as is my sworn duty. Go on with the women and the children to the boats below, please Sire."

The king eyed the taller man with the dark eyes, standing in front of him and ordered again in an almost desperate voice. "Give me your sword Bertravis Liolbane and go ensure the safety of my family, they must be saved, I will stay here and buy you the necessary time," the king eyed the knight with a deadly serious expression on his face and in his dark blue-eyes, "You know that I am more than capable of doing this Bertravis. My children must survive to inherit my throne. Promise me on your own honor that you will see to it that they escape and survive to take the throne and crown again someday."

As he finished saying this, the door to the birthing chamber disappeared, it simply vanished into thin air and the men behind it began to remove the piled furniture that had been placed in their path.

King Dorian's eyes were still pleading with the knight and finally with a tear in his eye, the protector of the royal family withdrew his proctors sword and gave it over to his king, who gave it a few swings to test its balance and weight, then Bertravis Liolbane quickly knelt and swore at his kings feet that he would see to the safety of his family or die trying.

The king of the fourteen kingdoms nodded, then turned grim faced towards the approaching men, he stood in the narrow opening of the escape way with the silver proctors sword in his hand and hoped that he could kill enough of the men charging at him to give his family time to safely get away.

With hot tears spilling out of his dark eyes, the knight champion and royal protector turned and fled down the stairs towards the underground chamber after the queen and her babies, vowing to fulfill his promise to his king or die trying.

Part One

The Telling

Chapter 1
The Beginning

The setting sun glinted brightly off of the rapidly spinning dagger's blade as it flew through the air, towards the face of the dark haired young man standing by himself at the edge of the wood line. Mere inches before actually hitting him, the dagger struck an invisible magical wall and bounced off harmlessly into the underbrush surrounding the young mans feet.

Damien Daverge newly robed and newly graduated battlemage, fresh out of the academe for mages in Westlake, allowed a slightly nervous smile to play across his lips. He was glad that the shield spell he had cast about himself before actually revealing his presence to his attackers had worked outside of the academe's classrooms and out here in the wilds even if it was against a not so formidable enemy.

Of course he was a fully trained battlemage, having spent the past six years of his life at the mages academe in

Westlake, in a highly disciplined and rigorous environment. Under excruciatingly difficult conditions, he learned the arts and skills of his chosen craft and acquired his black and gold robes.

Now things were for real and he was facing off by himself against eight orcs armed with rusty swords and battered clubs, with the idea of his blood in their eyes. Understandably this at first caused him to be a little nervous and he had felt a few pangs of anxiety.

The actual dagger thrower was only one member of a band of eight orcs gathered around their campfire dividing up loot from a farmhouse that they had raided earlier in the day.

Damien and his traveling companions had discovered the remains of the farmer's family tortured and mutilated in their fields and had set off after the group seeking vengeance.

Orcs are sly, cunning and somewhat intelligent humanoid like creatures, large, with grayish green skin standing about six feet tall usually with yellow piggish eyes snout-like noses and boar like tusks that protrude up out of their lower lips. Orcs are cowardly when encountered alone, particularly when outnumbered, in confrontation, they tend to shirk away, but will attack on the sly whenever able. At times when they are found in large groups, like this one sitting here in the clearing around the fire and the numbers are on their side, they tend towards courage. Especially, when they see only one lone young man in the wilds, step out of the woods near their camp, far from civilization, or any other means of help, with no type of visible weapon showing other than what appeared to be a simple walking staff.

Grabbing their weapons and brandishing them high over their heads, three of the orcs charged towards the battlemage in a headlong rush.

A lot more confident in himself and in his abilities

now, Damien allowed a slightly larger smile to cross his lips. This was going to be easy, almost too easy. Then he remembered the farmhouse that these vile creatures had raided earlier in the day and about the family that they had slaughtered and the smile slid off of his face like water off of oil treated leather. As his dark blue eyes hardened into hard cobalt chips, Damien unleashed the second of the spells that he had prepared for this confrontation.

An explosion of bright light erupted from his outstretched hand and a bolt of silver lightening streaked out across the field in a vicious tendril of twisting electrical energy. A sizzling, crackling hiss filled the air. The speeding bolt smashed into the leading orcs chest, the magical force of the lightenings energy driving straight through its body, leaving a gaping cauterized hole in its wake where the orc's chest had been. The silver bolt continued on to engulf the other two charging orcs behind the first, in it's sizzling crackling fury.

Screams of pain echoed briefly throughout the clearing from the other two, before the bolt finished consuming them with its energy. It left nothing but sizzling husks and charred leather lying in the grass surrounded by crackling tendrils of electrical energy that writhed around the smoking remains like little silver snakes.

The remaining five orcs stopped short in their charging and started whispering amongst themselves in a huddle for a moment.

Damien could tell that they hadn't expected the lightening bolt by the way that they kept throwing furtive and frantic glances in his direction and then over to the charred remains through their narrowed yellow pig like eyes.

After a moment the orcs all moved again. This time they fanned out in an arms length line and started to advance a lot more cautiously towards him.

Two very loud, warlike ferocious screams erupted

from the tall grass behind the orcs, catching them completely unaware. Jumping in startled surprise, the remaining five orcs spun around to face this new threat that was now attacking them.

A tall lean man carrying a long sword in one hand and a formidable looking deadly spiked mace in the other was the first to reach them. Right behind him was a squat muscular, dark reddish brown bearded, barrel-chested dwarf with a slightly off-center long strip of white hair in his beard that ran its entire length from an old scar on his chin. He was armed with a very large axe hammer, an evil looking weapon that was both a hammer on one side and a wickedly notched single bladed axe on the other.

Both had been hiding in the tall grass behind the orcs and were now charging with their weapons in hand. The first man to reach them was Damien's adopted father's blademaster, Travis Longblade. His head was as bald as an egg and traced with numerous scars. His face looked like it had been carved from mountain stone, with deep-set eyes and a crooked nose, which had been broken in more than a few different places. This face may have once been a handsome one, but through the course of time and life, it had become toughened and hard edged. A look from the deadly blademasters dark eyes could usually set lesser men to scurrying, but it wasn't the look on his face that caused men to feel wary around Travis Longblade, instead it was the way that the dangerous man moved and carried himself that set him apart from the others.

Slightly over forty years old, Travis Longblade moved with a predator's grace, quick to strike and even quicker to kill if he deemed it necessary. It was this that caused other men to be fearful. No one really knew all that much about him, his past was sort of an enigma around Castlekeep and Damien had always suspected that there was a lot more to Travis' story than what he or his adoptive father was telling. All that he knew for certain about the blademaster was that Travis had fought in the pits as an arena slave for many years and had even more scars covering his body than what was currently showing on his head.

That was until his adopted father, Lord Richard Daverge, had seen him in the slave pits and had at once without question bought him from his owner, freed him from his bonds and had hired him as his blademaster and as a tutor in weapons and combat for him and his sons. That was about ten years ago, now Travis was in charge of all of Castlekeep's military forces and served his adopted father without question. At this moment, he was serving as an escort to bring Damien safely home from Westlake.

Without even thinking, Travis used both of the weapons in his hands like living extensions of his own body. Whirling into the orcs like a dervish on a rampage, Damien watched from across the field as the blademaster deftly ducked under the swing of one rusty sword that had been aimed at his head and brought his own sword in his left hand across his body and across the orc's stomach. In one swift motion the keen edge of the blademasters sword cut through the creature's abdomen, easily disemboweling it. A bloody spray filled the air accompanying the long swords stroke and the orcs entrails fell out onto the ground where it stood, viscera looping about its feet until it collapsed dead.

Following the momentum of his first strike, Travis kept spinning to the left. As he straightened back up out of his ducking crouch, he brought the mace in his right hand around at head level in an arc that carried the sharpened spikes into the neck of another orc. The deadly spiked mace tore completely through the second orcs unprotected throat ripping it out, effectively killing it. All of this happened so fast that the second orcs body didn't even realize that it was dead and it just stood there for a few moments spurting blood out of its throat all over the green grass in a bright red rainfall, before it also collapsed.

Damien's other companion was a little less tactful than the skilled blademaster, not quite being the swordsman or showman with his two weapons. Nevertheless, he was still deadly and made quite an impression, literally.

Abandoning reason, Kendle Stonebreaker charged headfirst into the battle, his short thick legs and arms churning like windmills in a storm. Dropping his head low, he drove his shiny steel skullpiece directly into another surprised orc's midsection with a thunderous crash that was accompanied by the sound of its cracking breastbone and the shattering of its ribcage. The heavy bodied dwarf drove straight through the first orc with his own powerful body, knocking it over with his weight and driving it backwards onto the ground. Still using the momentum that he had built up during the charge across the clearing, Kendle continued his forward motion. Rolling into and out of a somersault across the top of the fallen orcs body, he brought his axe hammer up into a two handed overhead smash and with one mighty swinging motion, dropped the flat head of the powerful weapon down onto a second orc's skull. The heavy weapon crushed it like an eggshell sending bits of blood and brains flying everywhere in a gory mist.

The last remaining orc having seen four more of its companions killed in the time it took to draw two breaths, dropped its own weapon and fled across the clearing, running towards the cover of the woods.

"Should I stop him?" yelled Damien from the other side of the clearing, as he pointed a glowing finger in the direction of the fleeing orc.

"No!" ordered Travis in a commanding voice. "Let it go!"

"What!" roared the reddish brown bearded dwarf in anger. Bringing his axehammer up into throwing position, he spun back to face the tall blademaster. "Why?" he demanded, the heat of the battle still sounding thick in his voice. "So that it can go out and slaughter another family of innocent farmers?"

Even Damien was a little stunned at the announcement and fixed the blademaster with his own questioning cool look.

Like all of his dwarven kind, Kendle hated orcs with a passion bordering on fanatical. Damien knew Travis was not very far behind the fierce dwarf in his own feelings for the vile creatures and between the two of them, the blademaster and the dwarf had taken the act of simply killing the creatures and refined it into an art form, with each always striving their hardest to out do the other with deadly flamboyant gestures.

"No," said Travis again in a manner that allowed no disagreement, his dark eyes locking with Kendle's own reddish brown ones, "We let it go," the blademaster said firmly, "so that it can warn others of its kind about what happened here today and hopefully that will scare them off from attempting another raid on Gaderian soil and killing more farmers."

Kendle shook his head in annoyance, not liking the idea of letting any orc live. Begrudgingly, he nodded, mumbling, "Maybe you're right Travis, but I still think we should have killed it."

Turning away from Travis, the dwarf rounded on Damien smiling, the momentary burst of anger already quickly fading away from his face and voice. "So what do you have the score at now?" he demanded cheerfully, "Who wins this round?" and he waved a thickly calloused hand in the general direction of the orcs dead bodies laying about the clearing.

"I'm not really sure," said Damien rubbing his chin thoughtfully, looking at both of them. "Travis definitely gets credit for the disemboweling of the first orc and for tearing the throat out of the second with his mace was quite a nice touch, but," Damien said eyeing the blademaster a bit dubiously when he saw a gleam start to glow in the other mans dark eyes, "it was against orcs," an almost criticizing tone filled his voice, "and almost anyone with a little bit of skill could do that. Now Kendle on the other hand," the young battlemage said and threw a smile at the dwarf, "turned himself into a dwarven battering ram, which was unique, followed it up with a somersault and the crushing of another orcs skull after rolling out of the somersault, I would say that yes Travis, you do get points for class and style, but Kendle gets credit for ingenuity and creativity," Damien now smiled at the blademaster, who now was giving him a dubious look in return, "And since at the end," the young battlemage continued as he shook his head at Travis, "you did let one go, I think I'll give this round to Kendle."

"Ha!" blurted out the dwarf in a victorious manner as he gave the blademaster a wide triumphant smile. "I told you that he would make a good game judge."

Travis waved his hand at the dwarf as if he was shooing off an annoying fly and almost smiled, something the stoic blademaster rarely ever did. Looking over at Damien, he rolled his eyes adding. "Yes but we all know how blood thirsty and battle hungry you mountain dwarves are, anyway."

"Hmmph!" snorted Kendle through his nose causing his long reddish brown mustaches to flair outwards for a moment, "I'm not a mountain dwarf, I'm a hill dwarf."

Actually Damien thought to himself, Kendle was both, but that was a different story for another time.

The dark reddish-brown haired dwarf with the long white stripe in his beard knelt down next to one of the dead orc's bodies and began cleaning the blood and brains off of his axehammer, using the orcs filthy tunic as a rag. "You're just a sore loser Travis," Kendle stated matter of factly toward the blademaster.

Travis rolled his eyes again at Damien who just smiled

back. Then the blademaster also began to clean his sword and mace with another orc's tunic.

Since he hadn't used any sort of weapon other than his magical abilities, Damien started checking the other orcs bodies for anything worth any sort of value. If he found something, he would turn it over to the blademaster, who would in turn make sure that it made its way back to any other surviving relatives of the massacred farmers.

"So," Damien asked after he had finished rummaging through the dead orcs pockets and not finding anything at all. "Are we going to continue on towards the city for a while, or do you think we should just take over their fire and stay here for the night?"

Travis looked up into the sky and studied the slowly setting sun for a moment before he answered. "No, we'll continue on for a while longer, who knows what type of predators the smell of all this blood and cooked meat might bring out and I'd rather not spend the whole night fighting and chasing off wild animals, when we could be sleeping."

Damien saw the wisdom in the other mans words and nodded. The three went back into the woods and retrieved their mounts from where they had hidden them out of view from the orcs and started off again.

Two hours later as the sun was starting to sink below the wood line Travis held up his hand in a small clearing next to a river and announced, "Here would be a good place to spend the night."

All three dismounted and in following the same daily ritual that they had been using for the past week, Damien and Kendle headed off into the woods to gather firewood while Travis went about unpacking their gear, checking out the horses and setting up the camp.

"How long Kendle," Damien asked once they were in the woods and away from Travis, "do you think it will take us tomorrow, before we reach the city?"

"If we leave early enough in the morning and keep at it

we should be able to make it by midday," the dwarf answered as he bent over and picked a dead branch up off of the ground and stuck it with the others he had gathered.

"Just in time then for the beginning of the harvest festival."

"Yes and it should be a good one with you returning from your long absence," Kendle answered, "I'm sure your father prepared some special events to mark your homecoming. Why are you asking, did you have any other plans? I would have thought," said the dwarf eyeing him questioningly, "that you would be entering in some of the competitions maybe like the staff or something, eager to try out your new battlemage skills against some adults, rather than just children?"

Before he had left for Westlake, he had been one of the cities finest children with his staff and had won several competitions using it during the festival times.

"I don't know... maybe," answered Damien, shrugging his shoulders nonchalantly, trying to appear disinterested. It wasn't time yet to let Kendle or Travis know about his real plans for the festival and as disinterested as he was trying to appear, he was very much awaiting the tournaments but not just in the staff, he had other plans for competing, unknown to both the dwarf and Travis and also hopefully his father.

Kendle eyed him again, this time a slightly suspicious look crossed his round ruddy bearded face, "I've never known you to shy away from any chance Damien at showing how good you are at something, I mean you look like you could hold your own and you have always been exceptionally good with your staff. As a child you were better than many adults I know with the exception of maybe Abraim, your father's chamberlain."

Kendle was right of course. Damien knew the dwarf was aware of how rigorous the training was for battlemages and he could indeed hold his own. He intended on showing everybody that in the tournament of cities championships. He was officially representing Westlake as their city champion, but he hoped no one in his family would find out. They were concerned of the possibility of severe injury or that he might be accidentally killed.

Killings in the tournaments were actually few and far between, but accidents did occur sometimes and before the clerics on duty at the tournaments could heal the unlucky contestant, they died. Damien had no intention of letting anyone stop him from competing this year. He should have competed in the past three events but he wasn't allowed while enrolled in the academe. This year he wasn't enrolled in the academe any longer and it was being held in his home city. Unbeknownst to anyone in Castlekeep, he was favored to win it all. There was no way he wasn't going to compete.

Turning away from Kendle so that the dwarf couldn't see his face, he said. "Come on, we have to get this firewood back to Travis before he misses us." then he set off, back in the direction of their camp with the dwarf trailing along behind him wondering what it was that Damien wasn't telling him.

A.V. Wedhorn

Chapter 2
Memories

    After dinner they set guard times and since Damien had the first shift he watched as the other two men went to sleep.
    Finding an uncomfortable tree and using his pack as a pillow, he propped himself up against it and settled in for the next three hours of his watch. He wondered to himself as he studied the stars and moons overhead, blinking and shining in the black nighttime sky, what kind of reception he would get once he returned home. He hoped that his return didn't stir up to many old feelings of resentment amongst his family members. He was the adopted son of the Highlord of Castlekeep and the named third son of the house. Damien had been the son of Richard Daverge's huntmaster, who was killed by a wounded boar on a hunt. While saving Lord Richard from certain death, he died before they could get him to a healer.
    According to his adopted father, Lord Richard asked

what he could do to repay the huntmaster for saving his life and Damien's father whose name was Allyn Woodshorn had asked if he would take in his newborn child and raise him as his own. This act of kindness that Lord Richard sworn to had caused a lot of problems for him while he was growing up in the castle. According to the laws of the land, a ruler can only name three heirs to a house and since Lord Richard had named him third over his own true third son who was bastard born but was still his real third son and a legitimate heir from his mistress of over twenty-years, Lady Ianna Rynall, there had been a lot of hatred between himself and Thaedrann, Lord Richard's true third born son.

Lord Richard also had two other sons from his first wife who had died during a plague that had swept through the city twenty-five years ago. They were named Berus and Kevis and were both about six years older than himself and Thaedrann. It hadn't bothered them at all, that his father had adopted him, but it had bothered his mistress, who for some reason, he wouldn't marry even after she bore him a son, just a day after the hunting accident. Lord Richard had chosen him over that son as he had promised and hadn't even claimed Thaedrann as his own, even now twenty years later.

Lady Ianna had always hated him for this and had poisoned Thaedrann's mind, telling him that Damien had stolen his birthright and inheritance. Being both bigger and stronger he had tortured him and beaten him up daily. Until Damien had discovered magic and the staff, Thaedrann had made his life hell, torturing and beating the child daily.

Unknown to any, his father's chamberlain Abraim, had taken it upon himself to teach him a little of the staff after one of Thaedrann's beatings had gone a little bit too far and he had limped around the castle for almost two weeks. It was actually Travis' job to teach Damien about weapons and how to use them but Travis who had never been defeated while fighting for almost ten years in the slave pits against some of the dirtiest fighters in the realm and who was almost a legend in Castlekeep had been defeated once by Abraim during a disagreement about weapons and their uses when they had first met. Damien had accepted the owlish eyed old man's offer of help.

Magic had came to him a couple months later while he had been watching Balthazar Tolarus, his fathers hawk faced advisor and wizard, one day in his study doing a simple cleaning spell. He had imitated the spell and cast it perfectly, much to the wizardly advisors amazement. He had discovered that he had a gift for learning, anything he saw done or learned. He could either repeat it or do it after memorizing it. He also had a memory gift that allowed him to recall anything he saw or learnt perfectly in his mind.

Along with his strong magical ability, this gift had gotten him accepted into the mages academe for study as a battlemage once he had turned fourteen. Balthazar had taught him all that he could as a minor apprentice in Castlekeep and had asked his father to send him to Westlake for training, saying that he had a gift like few others he had ever seen. Since the hawk-faced advisor was one of the most powerful and respected wizards who was not an archmage at the academe, in the entire fourteen kingdoms, Damien was encouraged to go.

Lord Richard had steadfastly refused and the pair had gotten into a huge argument over it.

He had been living in the castle for fourteen years and Damien had never known them to ever disagree, except for the one time about his best friend Logan Longshadow being allowed into the castle. This time the pair had ended up sending him out of the chamber hall while they continued to rage and argue vehemently with one another. He never, even to this day found out why his adopted father had argued about him leaving what he called the safety of the city and the protection of the castle, but somehow Balthazar had won out and Lord Richard had relented by allowing him to go to Westlake for battlemage training.

Battlemages are a selected group of individuals who practice magic and also serve as soldiers for the realm in its elite regiments and units as a counterforce to the Tua-latin War Wizards.

The requirements for becoming a battlemage are to first and most importantly, be able to work the arcane energy of creational magic without the assistance of any sort of spell components, books or aids. All mages can cast some sorts of spells without the need for books or components, but a battlemage is a person who has been so gifted that like the Elvynn people he or she needs no aids in working any sort of magic or at least wizardly magic.

Once long ago all forms of magic could be cast as one through the use of creational magic, like that which the Elvynn still use. When humans and the other races decided to rebel and escape the tyranny of their Elvynn masters who had enslaved them since the creational of the planet Tyrus, during the wars of power after the age of might, they had all foresworn the use of creational magic that had once held them as prisoners and slaves with the exception of battlemages.

The Elvynn were the first of all the Tyrus races and are more in tune with the planets own natural arcane energies. They can still practice creational magic but now only on their own continent and not in the lands of humans, dwarves and halflings. There are only a few Elvynn left in the human lands or the forsaken lands as they call them, but these Elvynn have also foresworn the use of the creational magic unless on the sacred grounds of Talathandria, the ancient and destroyed Elvynn capitol deep in the forests of Myramoor surrounded by the Edgemoor swamps. Talathandria had been cast down by the gods during the Endwars. The gods had stepped in to aid the other races in throwing off the bonds of oppression and to stop the Elvynn from destroying the planet itself. Creational magic can also be used in Westlake while studying at the academe during battlemage training. Humans can still cast creational magic through the use of special talismans and weapons without having to be battlemage trained. But these are extremely rare and hard to find. However, a battlemage doesn't need such things unless it is to cast clerical magic. For the most part though, creational magic was taken away from humans as payment to the gods for helping to free them from their Elvynn slave masters. This was a pact made to last for two thousand years, long enough for the humans and other races to establish their own nations and defenses against their former Elvynn oppressors. After that time and the banishment was over, things would revert back to normal and all races would regain the full use of their abilities, both Elvynn and the lesser races. To most human minds the memories of the pact itself had fallen away into the sands of time and the exact dates forgotten. To the Elvynn though who can live as long as six hundred years or sometimes longer, it had only been slightly over three generations past.

A battlemage can't cast clerical magic because it is a blessing given to each worshipper by their deity unless he possesses a talisman. A high-ranking battlemage can cast most types of druidic magic, but only in a limited form.

The second thing that an applicant for the academe's battlemage training needs is the physical abilities required to be a soldier and the right mindset.

All mages possess strong mental abilities to focus and concentrate, but a battlemages mind is honed to the point that he or she shouldn't be distracted during combat or warfare by anything and can make lightening fast decisions in the heat of battle regardless of the circumstances or conditions around them. All battlemages are taught in every form of combat, physical, mental and magical.

Most practitioners of magic including the Elvynn conclave of the Tua-latin, their creational war wizards, would prefer not to undergo the sort of physical training that becoming a battlemage requires, preferring instead to just rely solely on only their magical abilities.

Damien was only one of thirty-five of his classmates who managed to graduate out of the hundred that had tried. He excelled in both parts and all who were with him were taught by the academies battlemasters and archmages how to use all of their abilities to maximum effect.

The training that a battlemage receives at the academe makes them a step above most other magic users in some respects. The only other thing close to a battlemage in both fighting and magical abilities that he knew of in this realm at least, are the all male warrior clerics of Dar, the god of justice and morality, who strive to enforce and uphold the laws of the realm, known as the hands of justice.

The archmages at the academe believe in learning combat wizardry and magic through combat so they created the illusionary dome, it simulates all types of battlefields and situations in order to better prepare a battlemage student for war like environments.

The dome is a huge building located in the center of the academe and it is the only building that is solely restricted to battlemages and forbidden to other students. The stones of the building are enchanted with an antimagic nullifying spell that allows for all types of magic to be cast inside of the dome without allowing any to escape and harm anyone else. Even though the events in the dome seemed very real, he had always known in some sense, that they were all illusionary and that the arch mages wouldn't have ever let him or any of the other students with him actually die in the simulated battles and training sessions.

Westlake, home of the battlemage training site, with its tall walls and ivy-covered buildings was an independent city separated from the rule of the rest of the fourteen kingdoms and the capitol city of Kallamar, under the laws of the academe only.

The archmages who ruled and taught there were also the leaders of the city. With only one exception, if there was a problem that the mages council couldn't solve it fell into the capable hands of the supreme archmage, the half Elvynn leader Siraethiel Shanasar, the most powerful wizard in the entire Kallamarian realm.

People from all over the realm and even a few from outside of it including some from other countries and continents came there to learn and study, even some of the Elvynn creational war wizards.

Students of magic especially came to Westlake to study and learn their craft at the academe. Mages of all types even druids, clerics and shamans come to use the library located there, being as far as Damien knew the largest one on all of Tyrus.

Only the students though are restricted to having to stay in the academe itself or at least in the city of Westlake, everyone else who visits can come and go as they please.

There is only one rule while on the school grounds, unless you are a battlemage in training, inside the illusionary antimagic dome or while practicing, there is not to be any sort of fighting of any kind. All people meet in peace and leave in peace, any violation of that rule is punishable by death.

His unique learning and magical abilities that had gotten him accepted in Westlake were a gift, but in some ways they had also served as a curse.

He was, thanks to the powerful Balthazar's tutoring and his gifted memory, well beyond the scope of most of the other students at his level. This and the fact that he was also a noble's son made a few of his fellow less talented students jealous of his abilities even though he never acted like a lord's son or put on any sort of airs. He knew he was not really and truly a Lords son anyway, he was just the adopted son of a woodsman who had saved his lords life and who had just been lucky enough to have been given a special privilege.

The other students hadn't seen it that way and he had in fact paid a stiff price for his gift and his adopted birthright while attending the school in the beginning. At least until Trakiko Matsuri, his Esian battlemaster had started training him in special warfare, combat and tactics. Then the playing field at the academe had been leveled a bit.

Once while out for a weekend excursion in the city by himself, which was how he usually was a lot of times, a few of those same fellow students along with a couple of older ones had caught him alone. Away from the watchful eyes of the academies mages and teachers, they took it upon themselves to impress upon him physically what happens to noble's sons who embarrass other students with his abilities, by beating their example into him.

Against two or three of his assailants without his staff, Damien was confident that he might have been able to hold his own, he had been after all raised as a lords son and had had numerous lessons in combat and fighting from one of the best pit fighters in the realm and one of its toughest dwarves also and maybe if he had had his staff in hand, he might have been able to handle four by himself, but that wasn't how it had happened and when the odds were six to one against you, you took a beating.

Damien though had way too much of that Gaderian pride that people from his part of the realm are famous for. He couldn't allow the six students who had took it upon themselves to teach him a lesson about why rich nobles sons shouldn't best all of the other students around him including those that were a year or two ahead of him to break his spirit with a just a single beating. Or else it was that he was to stubbornly stupid to admit when he was defeated.

Kendle his dwarven companion had a saying that he had remembered as he sat bruised and bleeding in the dust and dirt of that alleyway in Westlake.

You accept your loss and admit defeat and possibly lose yourself and your pride. Or you accept your loss, live to fight another day and figure out why it happened so you can plot revenge against your enemies and grind them into dust the next time you meet.

He had followed the dwarf's advice, decided on the latter and plotted revenge. Every day after that, he redoubled his efforts in his classes at the Academe learning his magic and when the classes were over, he started going to the Arena pits and began studying the fighter's combat techniques, in hopes that he could learn their moves by using his unique learning ability to gain even more of an advantage in his fighting classes.

The idea for this had actually came from Travis in a round about sort of way. His father's blademaster was one of the best fighters Damien had ever seen and once he had told him that all he knew about real fighting, he had learned during his time as a fighting slave in the pits against fighters who were fighting for their lives rather than just their honor.

So Damien spent all of his free time at night studying these fighters, night after night during his first six months at the academe. He quickly learned what worked and what didn't. Also he learned as he watched that a man or woman possessed all sorts of natural weapons and the ones, who knew how to use them all, quickly defeated those that didn't. Another lesson he learned was that a lot of fighters who held a weapon in their hands forgot about those other natural weapons and concentrated solely only on using what was in their hands.

A fighter who could use a weapon, plus his other natural weapons like elbows, knees, feet, fists and head along with his weapon, had a distinct advantage over those that didn't.

He studied the hand-to-hand combat fighters the most

and learned quickly that the dark haired, yellow skinned Esian fighters from the farlands to the east were the best fighters in the pits. He attempted numerous times to try to get them to teach him their fighting styles, but was always turned away every time. None of them wanted to teach him anything because he was a non-Esian and for the most part theirs was a closed society. Finally after weeks of trying with no success, he decided to purchase a book about Esians customs and culture, which had some of their fighting methods in it, from one of the exotic booksellers in the market. A monk of one of the many religious groups, had lived there for nearly twenty years and had put all that he learnt about the far away place, down in writing. If, Damien had thought to himself at the time, nobody was willing to train him, then he would, like always, just have to learn it himself.

Each individual student is assigned a battlemaster according to his or her personality and abilities. Everyone in his class but him had already been assigned their battlemaster and that had caused him a little bit of worry, but not enough so that he forgot about his plans for revenge and stopped his own studying and training. It wasn't that hard to forget either, not with the taunting from the other students who had taught him their lesson.

Every day after his magical classes and studies before he would go to the pits, he would take the book he purchased and go to an out of the way meditational garden. There he could practice alone what was in his book and also what he had learned from the fighters in the pit the night before.

Damien smiled fondly into the darkness as he remembered his own battlemaster, Tiko was a frail looking, thin, wizened and wrinkled old fellow, with a bald head and barely noticeable tufts of wispy white hair sticking out from behind his ears, a pale wisp of a beard graced the old mans chin that was so sparse that it almost seemed funny and he was probably the oldest looking man Damien had ever seen. His whole face was a mass of wrinkles and in spite of the white hair, he was an Esian.

He remembered thinking at that time when he had first met the old man assuming he was probably one of the many easterners that the academe hired to help run the place and serve as servants and had in fact ignored him so as not to interfere with his duties whenever he saw him.

He was practicing like he always was, when he noticed the same old gardener who always seemed to be in the garden whenever he was looking at him. That day though instead of raking and pruning the plants, he was sitting instead, cross-legged at a far end of the garden meditating.

For the first time out of all of his visits to the garden he actually took notice of the old man.

Having set out his book, he had started to practice punching and kicking when the old man opened his hazel colored eyes again looking at him and he had began to laugh and snicker occasionally as he watched what he was attempting to try and do.

Something far off moved in the woods and brought Damien's mind snapping back to the present time, instantly alert. Eyes probing and ears listening, he searched the black darkness with his senses using his magic to probe a little farther out than a normal human could. Not seeing or hearing anything, he allowed his thoughts to drift back to that day in the academes gardens when he had confronted the old man about his laughter.

Turning to the laughing old man sitting on the grass, red faced and panting he had asked, in an irritated voice. "Don't you have anything better to do around here, like some work or something, anything other than sitting there laughing at me while I practice?"

In a singsong like voice accompanied by an atrocious accent that was almost not understandable, the old man asked. "Why do you study fighting arts out of a book or at the arena pits, instead of in the classes with the other students?" his mouth was smiling as he asked, but Damien had seen something in the old mans almond shaped hazel eyes that told him that this was more than just a simple question. The hazel colored eyes were studying him with such intensity, that unconsciously he had taken a step back away from the old man's penetrating piercing stare.

"Why should I tell you?" he had said stiffly still feeling irritated by the old mans mocking laughter and the fact that the direct stare made him feel slightly uneasy, maybe even a little afraid.

"Why!" had snapped the old man again, this time in a commanding voice, the smile had vanished from his face and the almond shaped hazel eyes were staring even more intently at him and it had felt as if they could see right through him. Damien remembered that he had felt both transparent and vulnerable under that intense stare and for some reason, he had known at that moment that he should tell the truth to this old Esian with the piercing stare.

Forcing himself to meet the old mans penetrating eyes with his own dark blue ones, he had taken a moment to arrange his thoughts and he told the old man the whole story of his life before coming to Westlake and about what had happened to him with the other boys since he had arrived here and that as of yet he hadn't been assigned a battlemaster.

Once he was finished, the old man had studied him for a moment longer before he had replied.

"Aaah now I see." then he nodded his balding head before continuing, "Revenge is a powerful emotion that burns deep into the soul. One must be careful of it lest it overwhelms one with its fury and destroys him or scars him for life."

His sing songy accent was terrible and Damien had had to concentrate hard to decipher what it was he was saying at first.

Then the old man had startled him by jumping to his feet with a quickness and grace that belied his ancient age. In a move that looked awkward to Damien since most esian's were always bowing to each other, he had held out his hand to Damien and waited until he shook it, then introduced himself as simply Tiko.

"You come here tomorrow and I teach you how to attack and defend yourself properly," the old fellow had told him.

"You!" he had said in startled exclamation, "How are you going to teach me anything, I'm sorry but you are way too old! I can't learn from you."

The old mans hazel eyes had changed from contemplation to one that glinted with quiet amusement for a moment before he spoke next and it was as if he knew some untold joke.

Over the years with Tiko, he had learned to recognize that look on his battlemasters face as one he should watch out for or avoid altogether, because it usually meant trouble for him or whomever else it was directed at and also it was usually accompanied with a lot of pain.

"Do you think that as a fledgling battlemage in training, that you with all of your magical ability and spells could win a battle against one of the too old archmages up there in the academes towers?" he had pointed with a long painted nailed finger up at the main building.

He had looked at the old man bewilderingly, then in a derisive tone said, "No! I wouldn't stand a chance, they would destroy me instantly with the amount of power that they can wield."

"And yet," the old man responded, holding up his finger as if making a point, "you choose to learn your art of magic from those same too old men. So why do you assume that another little old man couldn't teach you something else, another type of art? Do you think all other old men are too feeble and weak to do anything without magic?" he paused for a moment and let his words sink in, then the old man had added, "Never confuse age with strength or power, the elvynn did that once and it almost destroyed them and the entire world as well."

"That's not what I meant." he had told the little old esian feebly in an attempt to redeem himself.

The old man had waved off his attempt and said. "The first lesson of esian fighting arts as with magic is to never underestimate your enemy, or the power that they wield, if you do that it will almost always lead to certain defeat." The old man paused and considered him again thoughtfully with his hazel colored eyes, then stated, "We won't wait till tomorrow though, today, I test you today instead and I will teach you first lesson, okay."

Damien remembered that he had looked at the old man in puzzlement and had wondered at the time whether or not the fellow might have been a little light in the head, maybe he had his head touched by the gods fingers a little, deciding though to humor him, he had agreed and said. "Okay, teach me then."

"You do know," the old man had asked as he had moved in front of him with the amused look glinting in his eyes. "How to attack an opponent don't you?"

Damien remembered that he had nodded yes and the old Esian had said. "Okay then, you try to hit me with any part of your body anywhere on mine in an attack." he had gestured at his whole body with his long nailed hands "as hard as you can and all I will do is try and stop you, okay?" he had chuckled a little after this and then added, "Then we switch and I get to try and hit you while you defend against me."

"Are you sure? I wouldn't want to hurt you."

"Attack!" the old man shouted forcefully, in the same commanding voice he had used earlier.

Not really wanting to hurt the old man he threw a series of half hearted punch's and kicks at the small old esian, never once did he even come close to the old man, who simply moved left and right, easily avoiding his simple attacks.

When he had stopped to catch his breath, the old man had just given him a look of disgust, snorting. "You attack like little girl! Again!" the old man had said derisively.

Feeling a small bit of anger flare up inside of himself at the old mans condescending and disgusted tone, he threw everything he had into his next attack, deciding that touched in the head or not he was going to let the old fellow have it. As Travis had taught him and using what he had learnt in the pits watching all of the pit fighters, he came at the old man again this time in a furious assault. From all angles and in all directions he attacked and everything that he threw at the grinning old man missed, all of his punches and kicks never even came close to hitting the old fellow. His head had dropped momentarily towards the end and he remembered something he had seen a red headed female fighter do a few nights ago in the pits and tried it now. He had feinted with his hands and body towards the old mans face then he had shuffle stepped quickly with his feet and kicked out with one and just like the other night in the pit when he had seen the female fighters opponents reaction, the old man did the same and he dropped one his of his hands in order to block the incoming kick that wasn't there, instead Damien hadn't kicked towards the body or legs like he had seen others do, the shuffle step was a feint and he lashed out with the toe of his other foot and caught the old man on his ankle with the surprise move.

The old Esian hadn't fallen to the earth like the female fighters opponent had done several nights ago, but he had leapt back out of his range and had said enough. An almost pleased expression showed on his wizened face and hazel eyes at being hit.

"Better!" he had said, giving him again the same

amused look that he had given him earlier.

"Now I get to attack you and you have to defend against me okay, are you ready?"

He had nodded yes and Damien knew that he would never forget what had happened next. Suddenly he had found himself flying through the air of the garden, blasted off of his feet by a powerful blow to his chest and all of the breath in his lungs exploding from him in a whoosh. He landed hard on the soft grass, flat on his back, gasping and coughing as he tried to suck the air back into his lungs. An incredible pain filled his chest and black specks swam in front of his eyes.

Once, as a child he had been kicked in the chest by a horse in the stable, what he had felt then had felt similar to what he had felt after the little old fellow had hit him.

A shadow had fallen over his face blotting out the sun as he had checked his ribs with his fingertips, probing gently for any broken ones, amazed that they were all still intact. He had looked up into the shadow and found the old mans wrinkled face and mischievous hazel eyes staring down at him from above.

In that same atrocious accent, the old man cackled, "You didn't defend. Lesson number two, never forget lesson number one. Don't ever underestimate your opponent" then he had laughed again in a shrill cackle.

Damien groaned again whether in pain or at the old man's old joke, he wasn't sure.

"Tomorrow you be here again at the same time and I will teach you how to attack and defend properly. Not like little red headed girl who kicks people in ankles." Then he had bowed once again and left him lying in the grass of the garden.

He had gone to the garden the next day and every day after for the past five and a half years. Every moment that he wasn't studying magic with his teachers in the academe, after it was made clear that Tiko wasn't a servant, he was with the old Esian battlemaster learning martial arts, warfare, tactics and strategies to compliment his magic. Tiko had made it clear to him that he had been singled out by the academies masters to learn special warfare tactics.

Over time, the old Esian had become more like a second father to him than a teacher. He taught Damien about other things besides just warfare and martial arts, like respect, responsibility and loyalty. Also, he taught him to keep an open mind about everything, to use any kind of tactic, trick, or strategy that worked, whether it was in martial arts, battle, magic or just plain every day life.

Tiko, like all of the other instructors at the academe believed in hands on training in real life activities, so he would set up scenarios and situations for him both in learning and in fighting by making him compete in the pits himself. The fighting in the pits progressed along with his lessons and as he learned more from his battlemaster the more he won in the pits. The more he won, the more his popularity increased amongst the locals until he became a city favorite, then the city champion. Once he had asked Tiko why he was doing so much fighting and the old man had told him 'as you learn your spells you then cast them right, well it's the same with fighting as you learn to fight then you fight.' It had been this way for the past five and a half years until the other night.

Two weeks ago, the night before Travis and Kendle had arrived in Westlake, Tiko had summoned him down to the gardens where they had first met. He had gone down there expecting another practice session and was somewhat surprised to find his battlemaster kneeling in a meditative state in the center of the small garden like when he had first come to him for training, but this time he was situated on a large mat decorated with intricate designs from his homeland and burning fragrant candles set all about him in a semi circle. A large bundle, a teapot and two cups were also on the mat. Next to him was his prized fighting staff.

The ancient battlemaster was wearing a black as night silk kymono and the look on his closed eyed face was one of stern faced solemnity. As he had approached, without even opening his eyes, Tiko motioned for him to kneel in the spot opposite him on the mat.

When he had knelt in the spot to where Tiko had pointed, the old mans hazel eyes opened and he had spoke, "I have taught you all that I know about martial arts and battle skills, there is nothing more that you can gain from my instruction that you won't gain through your own life's experiences. This," He had said gesturing to the mat and everything on it, with a wrinkled hand. "is a celebration of your passage out of childhood and into manhood. You," his wizened hazel eyes locked into Damien's dark blue ones, "must never use what I have taught you for evil purposes, it would be both a disgrace to you and a dishonor to me. You must be a champion of justice and a defender of the weak, or else you will fail in life. Do you understand?"

"Yes, I understand."

"In my country it is custom during the rites of passage into manhood to exchange gifts." Tiko reached out with his hand, down to the ironwood staff that lay at his side and picked it up, tracing its length with the fingers of one of his hands, he took and held it out towards Damien with his head reverently bowed.

Damien remembered now as he reached and fingered the staff lying next to him, that he had gasped audibly and had shaken his head no at the same time that his battlemaster had offered him the prized weapon.

It was a black iron wood staff with rotating handgrips about a quarter of the way up from each of its notched ends. The weapon wasn't just a staff, it was a masterpiece of Esian craftsmanship, made over a thousand years ago by a master weapons smith for one of Tiko's ancestors, it had been handed down for centuries from father to son and father to son and now Tiko was offering the prized weapon and family heirloom to him as a father would offer it to his son. The staff could withstand almost any amount of damage because of the ironwood that it was made out of. Ironwood was one of the hardest substances on the planet, but that wasn't all. Hidden inside the staff itself were two long razor sharp blades, that, when the grips were turned to the left they would shoot out of either end making the five foot staff a deadly weapon with a foot long blade at it's ends which locked in place. Turn the grips to the right and instead of locking into place the foot long blades shot free with an amazing amount of explosive force, becoming projectiles that could pierce armor or knock a man from a horse. He had personally once found out how surprisingly effective the hidden blades were. Once during a weapons session only a few months back he had mistakenly thought that he had finally gotten the better of his wily old battlemaster and had started to move in for the kill, when Tiko had turned one of the bracers to the left and one of the double edged blades shot out into place and nearly tore through his own throat. If Tiko had wanted it to, it would have.

Now the battlemaster was holding out the staff with both of his wrinkled hands, ceremoniously saying. "I offer you this staff as a gift in hopes that you will use it as your own and I ask that you accept it as a gift from a father to a son."

Damien had shaken his head no, rather fervently telling the old Esian that although he loved him like a father, there was no way that he could accept the weapon. "That," he had told the battlemaster "is to be for your own sons, to be passed on to members of your own family."

Tiko had given him a withering look of resignation. "Do I look," he had said as he waved his ancient wrinkled looking hand up and down at his own old body, "like I'm going to be fathering any more sons again or live long enough to train them, once they come of age? No!" Came the hard answer to his own question, "I have only trained three other students before you since my exile from Esia thirty five years ago. Two of those go unnamed, one after he had completed all of his training on the night before he was supposed to graduate was cast out of the battlemage order and asked to leave the academe by the headmasters and not allowed the right to wear the robes of a battle mage due to unfortunate incidents, which was a shame. Other than you, I have never seen another individual so gifted for both battle and magic in my entire life. He might be the only person I know even more powerful than you. My third student died soon after leaving here in Kallamar, the capitol city, in a battle trying to save the old king and queen from their Terian assassins. I had vowed after them never to train another student until you came along. You have turned out to be less like a student and more like a son to me. You are the closest thing I will ever have to another one again in my life time," tears had welled up in Tiko's hazel eyes as he had said this and he held out the staff again, "Please accept my gift for the reasons that I'm giving it to you."

He had taken the proffered staff reluctantly and had placed it at his side.

Tiko then smiled a wide pleased smile, one that was so wide that it caused the wrinkles on his face to hide his delighted eyes.

Next Damien was handed the second object that was lying on the mat. It was a kymono much like Tiko's own except that it had been made in the colors of a battle mage, black silk, with edges trimmed in gold with one gold stripe on the lower sleeve which identified him as a fully trained battlemage of the first slash. Also embroidered on both of the sleeves were two elegantly stitched roaring tigers that exactly matched the same ones on Tiko's own silk sleeves and on the staff. They symbolized his ancient family crest back in his homeland.

"That," Tiko had said pointing to the Esian character on the front of the robe and on the staff. "Identifies you as a member of my own family. Should you ever be in my old homeland and in need of help of any sort, just find someone with that same character on their house or clothes and you will have whatever you desire." Tiko had never talked about his past but Damien knew without having to be told that he had once been somebody very important in his country before his own exile and banishment.

Every other Esian in the academe and in the city all deferred and bowed to the old man whenever he passed by almost like he was an Emperor or something. All of the Esian fighters who once had shunned from teaching him now tried to help him at every opportunity by offering advice.

They had then drunk the tea finishing the ceremony. A few days later he had left with Kendle and Travis for home.

He fingered the ironwood staff once again, of all the weapons in which he had learned under Tiko's tutelage and there had been many the staff was the one with which he felt the most comfortable. Maybe it was just the fact that he had learnt it as a child or maybe he just didn't feel the bloodlust that sword use entailed, he wasn't really sure what it was that made him feel the way he did, but he was certain in his mind that wielding the double ended weapon gave him a distinct advantage over most opponents.

It might be different against someone of Travis' skill, whose blademanship and ability with the mace or any other weapon that he held in his hands was perfect, on a scale with the legendary Krannion knights of the east and south. Against almost any other opponent, using a sword or any other kind of weapon, he knew that he stood a more than decent chance at winning. He had acquired this confidence in the arena pits back in Westlake, where for the past three years he had been the city's champion. And, if for some reason his fighting skills failed him he always had his more powerful magical abilities to fall back on.

Chapter 3
Castlekeep

The next morning Damien awoke feeling a foot prodding him in the ribs, stirring him up out of his sleep. He opened his eyes to see Travis standing over him. Wiping them with the back of his hand, he heard the blademaster tell him to start helping Kendle with the tearing down of their camp since they would be leaving within the hour. His muscles felt sore and cramped from sleeping on the cold earth. In following his normal morning routine he quickly did a few stretches to loosen and warm up, then he gathered up his stuff and went off in search of the dwarf.

All packed up and the fire doused, they moved off into the early morning mists that filled the small wooded clearing. About mid morning they reached the edge of the woods that marked the true beginnings of Gaderia's borders and Damien's homeland.

Rich fertile farmlands, vineyards and orchards filled

the fields that were his home. A long wide winding road stretched out in front of them disappearing off into the distance on either side as far as the eye could see.

The highwayman's trail as it had once been called led west straight to Castlekeep and east along a less direct route all the way to the capitol city of Kallamar. It was expected at this time of the year to be crowded. Merchants and Traders were on their way to the merchant's bazaar, held in the city every year during the harvest festival celebration.

Once per year Castlekeep held a massive bazaar during the harvest festival, where merchants came from all over the realm to sell their wares without having to pay any taxes for that week. It has been said that if you can't find an item during the bazaar in the merchants market at the harvest festival in Castlekeep then it probably didn't exist.

The harvest festival was a weeklong celebration of the Wilderness Wars from which the city of Castlekeep was originally founded. Once per year all of the farmers and growers would bring in all of their goods in for sale. Most of the goods brought in were fruits, vegetables and fine wines, which were shipped out from the cities harbors to ports all over the rest of the realm.

Damien noticed that there was a difference to the road today. Instead of the normal amounts of merchant wagons and carts, there was an extraordinary amount of people as well as families carrying items, pushing carts and riding in wagons stuffed full of what looked like all of their possessions headed west.

Two hours of weaving in and out of carts along the highwayman's trail and they finally topped a hill that overlooked the city and for the first time in six years Damien looked down at the place he used to call home.

The first thing he saw was the reflective shining blue surface of the Eversea Ocean, even from this distance Damien could tell that the city's harbor was filled with ships. Hundreds of masts dotted the water with spots of white, giving the bright blue water a speckled looking appearance.

"Almost home now," Travis said from the saddleback of his horse as he faced the other two.

Kendle looked up at the sun and rubbed his belly with one of his thick hands. "If we hurry, we can make it there in time for the midday meal."

Damien and Travis both exchanged glances then looked at the dwarf with amazed expressions on their faces.

"What?" protested Kendle, innocently shrugging his shoulders and holding out both of his calloused hands.

"How is it that you can be hungry again?" Damien asked him. "You ate all of your breakfast, what was left of ours and what was left out of our rations."

"I'm a growing dwarf," Kendle told them cheerily, a wide smile on his round bearded face.

Travis smiled at the dwarf as he added, "Yeah, round and wide."

Damien burst out into laughter and Kendle shot both of them glowering looks as they began their descent down the hill towards the city.

Castlekeep was the largest city of the seven western kingdoms in the realm. It sprawled along the coast of the Eversea Ocean, stretching out for miles and miles in all directions. One could actually see the city's progress by the walls that surrounded it. They looked like stairs leading in towards its center. The castle, for which the city got its name, was a massive fortress that sat high on a cliffs edge overlooking the ocean, dead center, everything else sprawling out from around it. The fortress had extremely thick stonewalls that towered over everything else. On its battlements if one looked, the guards could be seen on patrol, even though there hadn't been a war in almost three hundred years. Not many forces would dare attack the intimidating fortress or its many-walled city.

To the north you could just make out the Iron Peak

Mountains' snowy tips as they shone white against the clear blue sky. The mountains were home to the three dwarven cities Silverstone, home of Kendle's uncle, the dwarven Iron king Devlin Bonebreaker, High Hill and Stonebridge. All three traded precious minerals, armor and weapons with Castlekeep in exchange for food, meal, salt and the rights to ship out their goods to the rest of the realm. Kendle's father Edrynn Stonebreaker was the fourteen kingdoms trade ambassador for the dwarves. He traded for both races, hill dwarf and mountain dwarf.

Castlekeep was the only self-sufficient city in the entire realm. It didn't lack for anything, or need for anything and could survive without goods from any of the other cities in the realms. On the other hand, all of the other cities depended upon Castlekeep because of the food that was provided from its harbors and across the highwayman's trail.

What Damien saw as he topped the hill shocked him and he spun round in his saddle to face the blademaster and the dwarf in open mouthed wonder. He could see how the city had grown since the last time he was here but that wasn't what he noticed first.

Seas of thousands were camped outside of the cities massive walls, the likes of which the young battlemage had never seen. There were so many tents put up and wagons encircling it that for a moment it looked like the city was under siege from a marauding army. Damien thought that they looked like refugees from a war, but as a battlemage and a new member of the realms military he would have known if there were any wars being fought in the fourteen kingdoms and there were not. That was going to be part of his new duties.

After completing their training in the academe, all battlemages were required to spend another six years in the military defending the realm that coincided with the length of their training, so he certainly would have known if a war was taking place in the realm. The only enemy that could possibly be attacking Castlekeep would be the Terians to the north. Westlake or a few of the other mountain cities like Embry would be one of the first cities on their list due to its location and he was sure that it wasn't the Elvynn who were banned from war against the lesser races.

"What is all of this?" he asked gesturing at the sea of people camped outside of the city, "Who are all of these people and what are they doing here camped outside of Castlekeep's walls?"

"That," the dwarf said waving his hand at the masses, "is the result of the new tax laws created by our esteemed Royal Regent and ruler, Lord Vargas Salidor," a somber solemn tone filled his voice.

Lord Vargas Salidor was the ruler of the Kallamarian realm and presided over all fourteen of the kingdoms. He wasn't king because he was the fourth son of the old king before his older brother King Dorian Salidor had died. According to custom only three people per noble family house, can be named as an heir. When his third older brother, the past king, Dorian Salidor, his wife Ellanor and their newborn twin children were killed by Terian northmen who had invaded and attacked the royal palace in Kallamar the capitol city twenty years ago, Vargas, being the sole remaining surviving heir of the royal family took over, but also being the fourth son, couldn't be named king. In order to preserve the bloodlines, he became the royal regent until his own son, Seth Salidor, turns eighteen and takes over the throne and crown as the next true king of the realm.

Damien looked at the dwarf, still a curious expression on his face. "I don't understand? What do you mean all of these people here are the result of the new tax laws."

Westlake was an independent city, an exception to the realm. Proclamations made by the royal regent didn't affect any of its citizens, so he hadn't heard about any new tax laws being put into effect.

Kendle's face grew even more serious and his voice grew so hard it sounded as if he could grind stone with it, "Vargas passed some new tax laws that raised the cost of making a living so high that a decent being can either afford to make a living or feed his family but not do both and any who refuse to pay are being arrested and executed. Everyone from nobles to commoners are being killed as traitors to the throne and crown, so thousands of people have fled from the east and are coming west."

"I still don't understand," Damien's brow furrowed as he considered the dwarf's words, "Why are they coming here? Aren't we still a part of the realm and subject to its laws and royal decrees?"

"We are or at least we were until a few days ago," said Travis, giving the dwarf a reproachful look, the expression on the blademasters face made it plain that he thought that Kendle had said too much.

Sensing something terrible here, Damien realized that what he was hearing might be the beginning of a civil war between east and the west. Such a thing hadn't happened in almost a thousand years, not since the Highlord battlemage, Voriaa Sarr. "What exactly are you saying Travis?" he asked the blademaster.

The blademaster turned in his saddle and faced Damien. "Your father, his uncle," Travis gestured at Kendle who simply shrugged, "and the other six western Highlords have declared themselves to be exempt and have become tax free states, refusing to abide by any laws that they consider unlawful or unjust that are being passed by the royal regent."

Damien's eyes grew wide and then wider as he balked at hearing this, neither of the two had said anything about this during the whole weeklong trip home.

"That," Travis informed him, "is why so many people are here camped outside of the cities gates and around its walls."

"And if you think this is a lot," added Kendle waving at the camped out masses, "you should see how many are inside the city itself."

Damien considered what he was hearing and calculated it all in his head just as he had been taught to do in the academe by Tiko and his face paled a little at what he figured he was going to hear next. "What does this mean for all of us? I'm sure that Lord Vargas isn't going to let the realm crumble to pieces around him or fall into chaos while he rules especially right before his own son Seth takes the throne and becomes king is he? What actions is Vargas going to take? I mean regardless of all of this and whatever my father and the other western highlords are thinking, he is still the royal regent and the rightful ruler of Kallamar, at least for a little while longer."

Travis heard Damien's words and whipped his body around in his saddle angrily. "Vargas!" the blademaster snapped as he spat the name with so much venom, that it almost sounded like a curse. Rage flashed in his eyes, his face went hard as stone and the scarred hands gripping the reins of his horse turned white knuckle hot, trembling with anger. "That man!" Travis said in a voice suffused with anger, as he glared at the two of them. "Is no more the legitimate ruler of this land than you or me is!" and both Damien and Kendle could see that the blademasters whole body was shaking with barely concealed fury.

"In fact," Travis continued his voice thick with rage, "Vargas is nothing less than a filthy murderer who deserves to be killed and the gods willing he will someday be made to pay for his crimes against the throne and the crown." As the blademaster finished the angry tirade, his voice had taken on a deadly dangerous sounding edge. It almost sounded to Damien as if Travis wanted to be the one that did so. Then he slapped his reigns hard against his horses' neck, causing the animal to jump ahead of the other two in startled surprise, where he continued to ride by himself for a while.

Surprised at the unexpected outburst from the blademaster, Damien raised his eyebrows in astonishment, "What in Tyrus brought that on?"

"I don't know," answered Kendle, equally astonished at Travis' reaction. "I've never seen him act that way before. I mean Travis has always been a little bit sad or surly and he's stern but I don't think I've ever seen him outright angry especially like he was just then."

"I would say," offered Damien, "he definitely has no love for the royal regent."

Kendle's eyes followed the blademasters back as he rode on, considering Damien's words, "And I'd have to say I agree with you on that."

After a while Travis slowed down a little bit and allowed his other two companions to catch up with him. Both could sense by his actions that he didn't want to talk about the earlier outburst, so they rode the rest of the way to the cities main gate in complete silence.

The massively thick double iron bound black oak gates which marked the cities main entrance had been thrown wide open for the harvest festival and the guards stationed at them were allowing everyone to enter the city without any hassles at all. But Damien's trained eyes noticed that even though the guards weren't stopping anyone, they were still keeping a watchful eye on all who passed through. Every once in a while when one would think that they had seen something suspicious or odd they would make a quick glance upwards to a spot above them high up on the cities wall to an unseen watcher. Damien noticed that the guards looked upwards at their mysterious master as they approached. Then they did something they hadn't done before and stepped out into the flow of human traffic directly in front of Damien and his companion's horses, lowering their pikes menacingly the sharp glittering steel heads effectively barring their way into the city.

"That's right, stop them, called out a high-pitched voice, from above them, far up on the cities wall, "we don't want any overpaid mercenaries, scruffy looking dwarves or charlatan magic users inside our fair cities gates."

All three of them reigned in their horses and Travis gave the guards a look that would have struck them dead if it could have. The three guards looked uneasily at each other as they realized who the older man was. Quickly glancing up to the place where the high-pitched voice had come from, their eyes fell uneasily back to the blademaster who commanded Gaderia's military.

A wiry looking old man with silver gray hair shaved close to his skull climbed out from a place high over all of their heads and dropped lightly to the ground. A pleased look of amusement showed clearly on the old man's features.

Damien felt a wide grin crawl across his face as he recognized the thin little man who now stood in front of them.

The gatekeeper who had ordered them stopped was Simon Mullen, his father's own spymaster and commander of the ears of the city. Damien considered why Simon was here at the main gate to the city. Thinking about what Travis and Kendle had told him was going on in the realm with his father and the rest of the western Highlords rebelling, Damien decided that the spymaster's presence here was not just a mere coincidence. More than likely the wily old man had stationed his people at all of the entrance ways to the city, monitoring everyone who was entering and having the ones that they considered spies or a problem followed and watched. Taking a quick look around at the others around the entrance way, he spotted several beggars dressed in rags against one of the cities walls with cups in their hands, none of them seemed to be doing much begging and all were stationed in a place where they could see both the gate and Simon.

Confirming everything was okay, the old spymaster shooed the guards out of the way and led the three men off to one side out of the flow of traffic entering through the gate. Simon confirmed his thoughts once he got them alone and said to Travis that he had found a few Krannion knights entering the city and a few more of Vargas' own spies at the gates. Travis told him that he would pass the information onto Lord Richard after they arrived at the castle.

Krannion knights were the protectors of the east and south. Along with Darian clerics, they helped protect the people of the realm and were sworn to uphold the laws of the kingdoms. The knights did not possess magic like battlemages or the warrior clerics of Dar, but they were still outstanding fighters who were of noble blood and lived by a strict code of valor, honor and duty. The people of the realm loved the knights who served as their protectors and heroes.

Thanking Travis, Simon then turned to study Damien with his grayish-green eyes, "How was the academe?" he asked as his eyes roamed over the young battlemages body, "Did they teach you how to keep from setting your hair and face on fire with your magic?"

Kendle laughed and jabbed Damien in the ribs with his elbow playfully and even the hard faced Travis laughed at this. It was the first expression of emotion the blademaster had shown since the unexplained and unexpected outburst of anger on the hill above the city.

Damien pursed his lips together in a sour smile and said, "I think I can manage well enough now."

When he had first learned of his abilities he'd been attempting to light a fire with his magic for the first time. He succeeded in burning all of the long black curly hair off of his head, including his eyebrows.

"Lad," Kendle said still chuckling good naturedly as he

deliberately smoothed out his own eyebrows with his fingers, "I don't think that you will ever live that one down."

Damien directed the still somewhat sour look on his face in the dwarfs' direction and Kendle's chuckling became a fit of laughter.

Still examining him, Simon reached out grabbed a hold of the young battlemage upper bicep and gave his arm a squeeze.

"I'd say that they did more than just teach you some magic while you were away at the academe.

"Trust Simon," Damien thought to himself, to see the things that everyone else would normally miss. It was one of the reasons why he was the head spymaster in the west.

"Your muscles feel hard like a warriors and you carry your staff like one who knows how to use it now. I'd say the Academe definitely changed you some. We will have to stop calling you lad. It appears you've grown into a man while you were away."

Both Travis and Kendle looked at Damien for a moment as if they'd just realized the differences that they had missed during their trip and nodded in agreement with the spymasters' words.

"I believe you might be right," said Travis, giving him a more appraising look.

"The academe does make sure that you are physically ready for just about everything," Damien stated modestly and then added. "What good would an out of shape battle mage be in the heat of a battle or a war?"

"Hmmph," snorted Kendle, "War, shmore, are we going to go into the city now? Or are we going to stand here all day blabbering like a bunch of old women with nothing better to do? I for one have a pint of ale waiting for me somewhere in the city and I intend on finding it."

Seeing the city he was speaking of was too crowded to ride even his small horse into, Kendle handed the reins to a guard and stomped off. Travis did the same and followed behind, Damien shrugged his shoulders at Simon. "I should be going too, take care."

"You too Damien and by the way," the old man said his eyes glittering as he flicked Damien's staff with one of his fingers and whispered in a voice only loud enough for the young battlemage to hear, "good luck."

Damien eyes widened a little in surprised shock, he thought that Simon was referring to the tournament but he wasn't sure, he had done all he could to keep his name from being mentioned on the rosters and had even used an alias, calling himself Damien D'Lavernge.

Forcing himself to keep his voice level and trying not to reveal the anxiety that he was feeling, he asked, "What do you mean?"

Simon gave him a direct look and said evenly, "You know exactly what I mean."

Knowing the game was up where the canny spymaster was concerned, Damien smiled, "Thanks! But please don't tell anyone else, it's supposed to be a secret."

Simon nodded in agreement and said that his secret as all secrets in Castlekeep were safe with him unless his father wanted to know.

With a final wave, the young battlemage hurried off on foot after the other two, wondering how the spymaster had found out about the competition. But he shouldn't have been so surprised. It was said that if there was a hole in the wall of a building or a window opened that, Simon had an ear to it, listening to what was being said.

Multicolored banners and decorations were strung throughout the streets giving the city a celebrative feel. Some announced events going on throughout the week. Damien even saw several that announced the tournament of cities championships.

The sounds of songs and laughter filled the streets. The festival seemed to still be a joyous occasion, despite the more than unusual masses of crowds inside and outside the cities walls. Normally a few thousand people lived here, but now there were several thousands of people filling the streets and the city seemed ready to burst at its seams.

People from all walks of life, from beggars dressed in rags to rich merchants dressed in silken robes walked side by side. There were also numerous amounts of acrobats and entertainers displaying their skills to the crowds on every corner of every block.

Damien saw numerous city watch squads patrolling the streets ensuring that the peace was being kept. He didn't envy the watchmen their jobs at all. With all the extra people in the city and on the streets, partying and celebrating, they had their hands completely full.

Screaming merchants and vendors also added to the chaos in the streets. It took him several moments before he was able to catch back up with the blademaster and the dwarf.

Somehow, the crowds sensing their purpose, parted for them. Several merchants and storeowners shouted "hello" and "hey" at both Travis and Kendle, recognizing their faces, none of them recognized Damien, though, so no cheerful greetings were forthcoming. Even some members of the city watch waved friendly greetings at the pair, which they returned in kind.

Following the main street through the city the three made their way into the market square also known as the bazaar or merchants market which was located in the center of everything. The large open air square was huge, at one time it had been staging grounds for the entire castles army, now it was the main city's marketplace, three of it's sides were occupied by building and streets, the fourth was filled by the huge castle from which the city derived its name. The massive fortress, with its high stonewalls, battlements, tall turrets and parapets towered over every other building in the city.

Selling every type of merchandise in the realm vendors were yelling and screaming as they moved through the aisles of tables and stalls filling the merchants market. Travis ignored them as he led the group past the various stalls so intent and focused was he on reaching the castle.

Damien on the other hand, who hadn't been home in over six years gawked at everything as if it was brand new to him.

He heard a sound that he knew instantly as they made their way through towards the center of the square. The clash and scrape of weapons told him what was ahead of them.

The arena pits or just the pits as they are commonly called were located in the center of the square and served two purposes, first providing entertainment for the masses with gladiatorial-like games and the second purpose of the pits was to settle disputes, or differences between two parties or people who had disagreements or arguments. During festival times or celebrations, fighters come from all over the realm to compete. Any differences that needed to be settled in the pits remained settled, any recriminations taken by the losing party against the victor is a crime punishable by death.

Once a challenge is called, the two parties enter onto the sand. The person challenged has the right to choose armed, unarmed, or even magical combat but only if both fighters have the ability. There are only four ways out once one has entered the pits sands, by death, by unconsciousness, by surrender, or by being physically unable to continue due to injuries. A pit judge watches the fighters to make sure that none of these rules are violated. The festival was famous for its tournaments and contest in which a skilled fighter could win numerous prizes of gold. Fighters came here from all over the realm for just that reason. This year was the biggest tournament of all in the west, the cities tournament of champions in Castlekeep.

"Travis," Damien shouted loudly, trying to be heard over the screaming voices all around them, "can Kendle and I go see who is fighting today?"

The blademaster turned his dark eyes towards him and almost refused, but at seeing the eager light shining in Damien's own dark blue ones, decided to relent. "Go on, but don't be to long about it, your father will be eager to see you," then Travis turned and fixed Kendle with a long hard stare. "No fighting, no trouble and nothing stupid Kendle. I want you both back at the castle quickly, don't dally around too long."

The dwarf looked at Travis, an expression of pure innocence showing on his face. "Who me?" he asked, "Would I do anything of the sort?"

"Just don't, Kendle, no trouble." echoed Travis. Again he said it in a stern voice as he shook his head from side to side irritably much to the dwarf's amusement, who grinned wickedly at Damien.

Kendle was a well-known and well-respected fighter in the city. Even though he was short, the dwarf's body was also thick and wide. He was as strong as an ox and his compact frame was as hard as the rocks he mined. With lightning fast reflexes and a knack for taunting and irritating opponents to almost astonishing levels of rage with his comedian like antics, he was a crowd favorite whenever he entered the pit and they always cheered loudly for the dwarf. In the whole city there was only a few people could best him. Travis was one of them and Kendle knew better than to disregard the blademaster's warning.

With a final parting glance that bespoke trouble if they disobeyed, Travis continued on his way towards the castle. The pair smiled at one another and began to push their way through the crowds towards the stands.

Damien actually had his own agenda for wanting to go to the pits. It did not involve actually watching the fights at all. His real intent was to see the fighter charts posted near the main pit. Maybe it could be considered vanity, but he really wanted to know where he stood in the standings charts against other competition in the tournament.

After a lot of pushing and shoving, a few well-placed elbows, a couple of stepped on toes and several murderous glares from the fierce dwarf, which also included him fingering the hilt of his many notched axe hammer, they finally made their way close enough that Damien could see the charts. He was third place in the standings out of fifty competitors. He had not expected to be placed so high but he was pleased nonetheless. A couple moments later the pair were overlooking the edge of the main pit into its sand arena.

A fight had just finished. The victor was still standing in the sand and tears stained the man's face as he looked down at the still dripping bloody sword in his hand. Some of the pit cleaners were carrying out the body of the other man whom Damien assumed was his opponent, more cleaners were laying out fresh sand covering up the spilt red bloodstain that marked the fallen mans place.

The victor was an odd looking sort of fellow with both sides of his head shaved close to the skull and a long narrow strip of brown hair splitting the center. He was impossibly skinny also, but judging from the wiry body and the fact that he had more than a few scars decorating it, Damien assumed that he could take care of himself. So intrigued by the sad almost melancholy look on his face was Damien as he watched him leave, that he didn't even notice the next opponents step into the pit or at least until Kendle gave him a hard jab in the ribs saying. "Well, well, look there," A nasty sounding tone filled the dwarf's voice and his usually jovial eyes turned hard as mountain stone. "It looks as if the fat man's fighting. He's not supposed to be doing that any more." The dwarf's voice had a menacing edge in it.

Without even looking, Damien knew who it was, even

though he had been gone for six years. Sure enough, there he was, moving across the sand.

"Remember Travis' warning Kendle, no fighting and nothing stupid." Damien warned the fierce dwarf, stopping him with a light hand on his shoulder as he had started to step up to the edge of the pits lip and began to unsnap the axe hammer hanging at his side.

Kendle stared down at the other man in the pit for a moment then grudgingly lowered his hand and nodded his head, "You're right Damien, of course nothing stupid and no trouble and no fighting. I gave Travis my word, but you know he's not supposed to be fighting."

The man Kendle was referring to was a giant, standing a little bit over seven feet tall, with arms and legs the size of small trees and a chest that was as thick as an oaks trunk, named Uligar Rothe. He was actually a retired fighter, having quit the pits a few years back, just before he had left for Westlake. As far as Damien knew Uligar hadn't fought since that retirement had been forced onto him.

Before that, the large man had been a fierce competitor in several competitions and had even won more than a few. His body bore the purple scars of those past battles, but that wasn't what drew ones attention whenever people looked at the big man now. It was his horribly disfigured face, Uligar never was considered a handsome man but at one time he hadn't looked as bad as he did now. His face was a ravaged mask that barely resembled anything human, disfigured from a mass of criss crossing scars that decorated it and the remains of his half torn ears were tattered shredded stumps of flesh. The big man had taken to wearing his once short hair somewhat long, which served to hide his disfigured ears, but nothing could hide the devastating scars that covered his face.

Damien was shocked by the man's condition. What had once been a body that had rippled with large muscles was now one that age and too much drink hadn't been kind to. The muscles and girth of the giant chest had now turned to flab and had slid down to his belly, still though the size of the man was indeed impressive. The stumps of the ragged ears could still be seen poking out from beneath the somewhat long hair. Damien cast a sideways glance over at Kendle who was looking at the same thing, grinning an evil little grin.

No beast had attacked Uligar Rothe's ears or given him the horrible scars that covered his mutilated face, instead the marks had been put there by a certain ferocious bloodthirsty reddish bearded dwarf, bent on vengeance against the large man over a matter of honor.

He had never learned the actual reason for the attack on Uligar by Kendle, but he knew it had had something to do with a dwarven maiden who had ran afoul of the large man during a drunken rage after a lost match.

Whatever happened after that was left unknown to any but Kendle, the dwarven lady and Uligar. The angry dwarf had publicly challenged the man to the pit and what was left of the large mans face and ears were the work of the vengeful and angry dwarf, along with his banishment from fighting in the pit.

Kendle noticed that Damien's eyes were on the giant man's ears. He flashed him the same evil smile, then he reached down and gave one of the pouches at his belt a little shake. It supposedly held the remains of one of Uligar's ears. The dwarven female, whom Uligar had molested, had the other in a pouch by her side.

Damien shook his head then he gave exasperated smile to Kendle and then both of them broke out into a fit of laughter.

The crowd gathered around them started cheering louder as Uligar started circling the pit, waving his massive arms up and down high in the air in an attempt to incite their fervor. He ran around in circles for a few rounds then he froze in place. All of the color drained out of the giant's face as he stopped directly in front of Damien and Kendle and turned his gruesome countenance toward them. Somehow amongst the masses of people, he had spotted the white striped, reddish bearded dwarf in the stands and had stopped moving. The dwarf locked eyes with the large man momentarily before Uligar started going back around the pit again waving his arms. This time though he seemed to be doing it a lot less enthusiastically than before.

Chapter 4
The Cleric

While the pair in the stands had been studying Uligar's deteriorated condition, his opponent had made its way out onto the sand and stood alone, not doing anything in the center of the pit except for following the big man with its head and eyes. Nobody could tell anything about the big mans opponent because whoever it was had draped themselves in a long brown peasants cloak that hid the features under the darkened shadow of its cowl pulled low and covered its whole body all that could be told about Uligar's opponent was that whoever it was, the figure wasn't even half the size of the big man.

Despite the noontime heat, the figure still hadn't removed its long cloak and Damien wondered why in the world would anyone wish to keep their identity hidden, he thought as he studied the figure who stood about the same height as himself, maybe whoever it was disfigured or hiding something.

Kendle was trying to get the attention of one of the bet takers when he heard Damien and several others in the crowd gasp loudly in surprised shock and quickly turned back to the pits to see what had occurred below on the sand.

The well traveled dwarf, who thought he had seen just about everything in the pits and about the rest of the realm also now felt his own eyes grow wide with surprise at the sight of Uligar's uncloaked opponent.

The figure standing in the center of the pit had undone and removed its cloak in a swirl of cloth and now stood there uncovered in the suns bright light.

Damien felt his jaw go slack and his mouth dropped open at the sight in the pit, he cast a sideways glance at Kendle and noticed that the dwarf's expression matched his own stare of wide eyed amazement.

"My, my," said the dwarf still staring, "I don't think I've ever seen one of those before," he stopped speaking for a moment then added in an amazed tone. "By Garns teeth, I don't think I've ever even heard of such a thing or at least not in the past thousand years since the battle queen. I didn't even realize such a thing existed and I've traveled almost everywhere."

A young woman stood there revealed under the unshed cloak that now lay on the ground at her feet. She was very beautiful Damien noticed and was also about the same age as he was, with short curly strawberry blond hair that shone like burnished gold under the noontime sun, her slightly muscular arms and legs were tanned a golden brown and she watched Uligar circle around the pit through sky blue eyes that never left her opponent. It wasn't the fact that she was a woman fighting in the pit that had caused the gasps, women fought almost as much as men in the pits, nor was it her strikingly beautiful good looks. It was instead, what she was wearing under the long homespun brown cloak that had caused all of the people in the stands to have gone eerily silent despite Uligar's excited waving.

The young beautiful woman with the short curly strawberry blonde hair was adorned in the gold and black colors of a cleric of Dar, the god of justice and morality. Their colors were actually similar to those of a battlemage but were more gold than black. Clerics of Dar were all men and like Kendle said there hadn't been a female cleric of Dar seen in the realm in over a thousand years since the battle queen Ellanine Salaris. They were the religious equivalent of a battlemage, instead of relying though on magical energies for their spells they relied and drew upon the strength of their own dedication, faith and how much their god favored them in granting their powers. Also unlike battlemages who started their training at age fourteen and only spend six years under the tutelage of the archmages and battlemasters learning their magical, military and fighting skills, most clerics of Dar are born into their order and spend an entire lifetime devoted to learning and perfecting their abilities. They are also considered the hand of the law and insured justice throughout the fourteen kingdoms.

Damien knew a little about the order and realized that if she was not in the monastery in Muldar, located in the far eastern section of the realm and judging by her age, which seemed similar to his own, he figured that she was on what the clerics of her militaristic order called their ministries. Clerics of Dar went out from their monasteries for a period of ten to twenty years and served as wardens and protectors of the peace throughout the realm, some even served as administers of justice in some of the larger cities. Their monasteries were in almost every major city in all fourteen kingdoms and they worked usually closely with the ruling lords of every region they were in. They also preached to the masses about obeying the laws of the gods and their rulers.

The symbol of two crossed hammers with a sword in

between, a medallion of mythryll, a metal known to have magical properties, gleamed like molten silver as it swung and reflected back the suns rays, identifying her as one of Dars own, as she continued to circle in one spot, her eyes always facing towards Uligar.

Damien could see that the medallion and by the way that she moved, knew it must belong to her, unless she had somehow killed a cleric and stolen his medallion.

"What do you think, who is going to win?" asked Kendle, glancing over at him, while he was still looking at both fighters intently. Usually Kendle preferred to rely on his own instincts when it came to fighters he was choosing to place his gold on.

Studying them like Tiko had taught him, the young battlemage looked over at the dwarf, a slightly surprised expression on his face at the unexpected question. and then said, "the girl."

"Why?" asked the dwarf, looking at him speculatively. "Tell me some reasons."

"Uligar," Damien offered, "is a very experienced fighter, with lots of fights and wins, but look at him, even with his great size and strength, he's out of shape and even he knows it, it shows in his eyes, he has had a very wary look in them ever since she removed her cloak and I think that he might even look a little scared."

"And the girl?' asked the dwarf, eyeing him intently as he fingered he gold in his pouch.

"She is ready. Look at her stance, she has her arms held loosely at her sides but she is on the balls of her feet and there is an air of readiness about her, kind of like a coiled snake about to leap into motion at any moment. She also has some experience about her, she's not a stranger to fighting and neither does she seem intimidated by Uligar's size. Besides," Damien added a shake of his head. "If she really is a cleric of Dar, which is the religious equivalent of a battlemage, then unless he manages to get his hands on her, he doesn't stand a chance in there with her, she'll destroy him."

Kendle looked at Damien and gave him a nod of approval. He stuck his hand up in the air motioning for one of the bet takers that was moving through the crowds to come over, "That's exactly what I was thinking too, good job." then the dwarf added under his breath almost too low to be heard. "Maybe this will teach him another lesson about why he shouldn't mess with women." Even though Kendle wasn't sure what had instigated the fight he was certain without a doubt that Uligar deserved to get what was coming to him.

Before Damien could begin to question him about the statement, the dwarf began talking to a bet taker that had sidled up to him and was counting out gold coins.

Whatever it was that had happened between the dwarf and the other pit fighter must have been very bad. Damien knew, Kendle went by the live and let live philosophy that was common to almost all dwarves who lived outside of the dwarven cities, way of thinking, unless it involved matters of honor, revenge, family, or clan and wasn't known to harbor a grudge for long.

The pit judge stepped down into the pit sands and began to explain the rules of combat to them. Since the female cleric of Dar was the one who had been challenged, it was up to her to decide what type of combat it would be.

Damien was a little surprised when he saw her unsnap her hammer at her side and place it on the stairs, opting for open handed combat with the massive man rather than using a weapon against him. It didn't seem to bother Uligar, in fact the big man began to clench and unclench his ham-sized hands in anticipation of connecting with the cleric. If he did so, regardless how out of shape he was or how good of a fighter she was, the fight would be over quickly.

The pit judge waited for their nods of approval

showing that they understood the rules. Then he raised his hand high in the air between the two fighters, held it there for a moment and slashed it down yelling, "Begin!" as well as jumping quickly out of the way.

With a speed and quickness that belied his massive size, Uligar Rothe charged the pretty female cleric, in a bull like rush, intent upon finishing her and the fight off quickly as quickly as possible.

It was a very good tactic considering his large size and the speed in which he moved, it occurred to Damien that it showed how seasoned a fighter the large man really was. Uligar didn't want to give the Darian cleric time to mount a proper defense or time to strike him before he could grab her and hopefully finish her.

The girl must have anticipated some sort of attack of this type by the big man because she stepped sideways, darting quickly out of the way the moment he took his first step. Uligar's massive body crashed heavily into the pits wall with a loud audible thud.

The giant man staggered backward, reeling a little with a confused dull expression covering his scarred face as he stared groggily at the wall in front of him in disbelief. When he realized that the female cleric wasn't there smashed to a bloody pulp against the stone, he shook his head and turned just in time to receive a mighty blow from the female cleric's fist. Using Uligar's knee as a lift she had placed her foot on it, lifted herself high into the air and as he turned she threw a straightforward punch to the side of the large mans head.

Uligar convulsed with the blow and his eyes rolled back into his head showing their whites as he crashed heavily to the earth, unconscious. Such was the force of the impact of the blow that the female fighting cleric of Dar delivered to the scarred mans temple.

Damien's trained eyes noticed immediately though, that the small female cleric had pulled what could have been a killing blow to Uligar's temple short. She had put only enough power in her punch to render the man unconscious rather than killing him, like she easily could have. This action spoke about her character. He quickly glanced over at Kendle who had also noticed the short blow and was shaking his head in disgust.

"She should have killed him," rumbled the dwarf in a voice that was so low Damien almost missed it.

Several moments later Uligar crawled back up onto his feet and shook his head, trying to clear the cobwebs. He looked sort of surprised to be alive and that she had spared his life, when she could have easily killed him ending the fight.

He stepped towards her. This time however, as their eyes met he gave her a combatants nod of appreciation and he moved a lot more cautiously. Deliberately wary now, Uligar realized that he had underestimated the woman's abilities and didn't intend upon doing it a second time.

"Bet he won't try that again anytime soon," Kendle said, finishing with an evil little laugh.

Blood dripped off of the big mans chin, from a gash somewhere on his forehead. Using one of his large hands, he wiped the flow of blood away from his eyes.

Bouncing slightly on the balls of her feet now, the young female cleric waited for Uligar to recover and returned the nod with a slightly lopsided smile. The large man advanced towards her again and the two began circling each other.

Damien watched, fascinated by the young woman's movements as the real fight began. She was definitely very skilled and extremely well trained. It showed in her efficiency. Watching her cat-like reflexes, with little expense of energy, he hoped that she wasn't one of the competitors in the cities tournament. If she was, he would definitely have to take some time to come out and study her tactics against some of her other opponents. "Know your enemy and study them carefully" came Tiko's sing songy voice into his mind.

Uligar was also now studying her a lot more carefully than before through his crafty little eyes. He feinted some, throwing a few short punches to test her reflexes then threw out a long looping punch with his left hand, deliberately slow in another feint. Counting on the fact that she would try to slip to the right and evade the slower punch he threw a second much more powerful blow with his right at almost the same time, turning his hips and putting all of his massive size and long reach behind it.

But again she wasn't there, knowing that the power in the big mans punches would more than likely kill her if she tried to go toe to toe with the giant powerful man. The female cleric of Dar ignored the feint, knowing it for what it really was and took a step backwards. Bringing herself up on one foot, she cocked her other foot and held it ready.

Uligar planted his weight on his right leg when he struck out with his other real punch. The big mans large fist barely missed the female cleric's head and for a moment Damien thought that she had misjudged the distance of the large mans long reach as her short curly hair swayed slightly in the wind that followed the punch.

Already committed to his attack, there was no way that Uligar could have avoided what happened next. The female cleric saw his weight settle on his lead leg and at the exact moment that the punch swept by her head before he could recover, she pivoted her body and drove the heel of her cocked foot straight out and into the side of Uligar's right kneecap with all of the power that she possessed.

A loud bone crunching crack filled the stands with the impact of her striking foot, accompanied by a spray of blood that filled the air as the bones from Uligar's shattered knee tore through his skin.

The large man let out an animal-like scream of pain as he toppled to the earth clutching at his broken leg with shaking hands.

"Yes!" Damien shouted excitedly, throwing his fist high up into the air, along with everyone else as the rest of the people in the stands also erupted into cheers. Those cheering quickly stopped though as they watched what happened next.

The female cleric wasn't smiling as she looked down onto her defeated opponent, instead she had a somewhat sad expression on her pretty face and was shaking her head slowly from side to side. Kneeling down next to Uligar who was wailing plaintively, almost like a wounded animal, she bent over and took his torn and shattered leg in her small hands.

The large man visibly flinched as she touched him and looked up at her, a pained filled fearful expression on his mutilated face. She must have said something reassuring to the big man because the fearful look faded replaced instead by one of thankfulness as she started to pray over his shattered leg and destroyed knee.

A golden glow enveloped her hands in soft warm light as she placed them on Uligar's shattered and bleeding leg, the glow spread out from her hands and encased his entire leg with its light. If there were any doubts about her being a true cleric of Dar, they were quickly dispelled as the crowd watched the bones of the large mans shattered leg knit back together, followed by the mending of the torn ragged skin. When the cleric's hands stopped glowing and she removed them from Uligar's body, there wasn't a sign at all of the injury, not even a single scar remained behind.

Uligar looked up to her gratefully and she held out a hand helping him back up onto his feet. He gingerly took a few steps, then smiling a wide smile he grabbed the female cleric up in his large hands and hoisted her high up into the air over his head as the victor. The still silence in the stands erupted into an earsplitting deafening roar of applause.

The large man placed her back down grinning and she gestured him on towards the exit, while she looked up into the stands, her sky blue eyes shining fiercely.

She stood that way for several long moments, then she raised and lowered her arms in a gesture designed to quiet the loud crowd.

Damien couldn't take his eyes off of the young woman while she waited on the crowd to quiet, for some reason, it wasn't anything passionate of that he was certain, even though she was clearly very beautiful but he could feel something else in her as he looked at her. She must have felt his eyes on her somehow, because oddly enough she turned her head around in his direction and when their eyes met for a brief moment, he felt some sort of connection slip into place inside of him. As if she knew him in some way, she gave him the same sort of quizzical look, but then quickly nodded and smiled, which he politely returned.

Kendle also noticed the exchange and asked curiously, "Do you know her?"

"No," Damien answered, a puzzled expression on his face. "But I feel as if I should."

Finally the cheering crowd went silent and calling out in a loud voice she said, "An injustice was done here and now it's been corrected. Next time you wish to pick a fight with someone, don't make somebody else fight your battles for you. Try and take care of them yourself." Her sky blue eyes were locked on one single man standing amongst a small group of men wearing uniforms.

Every one of the heads in the stands turned to see who she was addressing, including Kendle and Damien.

The young battlemages dark blue eyes narrowed into slits, instant dislike appeared upon his features. Even though he hadn't seen the other man in six years Damien recognized the large young man immediately.

A tall golden haired young captain in the city watch stood across the pit from him, surrounded by his men glaring down at the female cleric with a hate filled cold look.

"Thaedrann." Damien hissed like a curse coming out of his mouth.

Kendle heard the name and groaned. He now placed a restraining hand upon Damien's own shoulder as he took a step towards the edge of the pit. "Remember what Travis said Damien," Kendle reminded him, "No trouble, no fighting and not to do anything stupid."

"I remember exactly what Travis said," Damien echoed, giving the dwarf a mischievous half tilted grin. "He told you not to do any of those things, he never said anything to me." Then he continued stepping forward up to the edge of the pit.

The dwarf knew that from that lopsided grin that there was definitely going to be trouble here.

Eyeing Thaedrann across the open expanse of the pit, Damien took a closer look at his old nemesis. Thaedrann had definitely grown bigger, he could tell even from this distance that he was well over six feet tall and most certainly outweighed him. Like him, Thaedrann had also let his hair grow long, in much the same manner as their father and a lot of other Gaderians. Damien could tell he was a very good-looking man with a handsome face and green eyes like his mother's. The young battlemage knew that Thaedrann was very vain about his looks. Women found his handsome features along with his impressive physique that he had inherited from his father very attractive. Thaedrann knew this and took advantage of it.

From here he could also see the bars of a captain in the city watch on the epaulets of Thaedrann's uniform. This was the man who had made his life as a child a living hell torturing him. Damien realized that deep inside, he still harbored a lot of bad feelings for Thaedrann, for all the embarrassment and pain he had caused him over the years.

Taking a deep breath Damien yelled mockingly over

the sounds of the crowd, using a bit of his magic to amplify his voice so as to be sure that he was heard.

"What's wrong Captain, can't the city watch handle their own battles, or do they always have to find someone else to fight for them." As all the heads in the stands spun in his general direction. Damien added, "Everyone here knows though that they have always had a little trouble handling the ladies."

Kendle muttered something incomprehensible and shook his shaggy haired head in dismay at Damien's bold words.

The crowd around the pit suddenly went quiet in stunned silence. Everyone craned their necks as they tried to see who had said the audaciously bold words, knowing the challenge in them was very clear.

The group of watchmen along with their captain whipped then heads around, all of their eyes searching for the source of the insult.

Thaedrann's eyes found Damien's for the first time in six years He knew that the large man recognized him instantly as his eyes widened slightly, then narrowed hatefully.

"Well, well," Thaedrann called out scornfully, "if it isn't little Damien, fresh from Mage School in Westlake! Shouldn't you be hiding somewhere with your nose in a book or something?"

The crowd around the pit laughed and turned once again in his direction. The young battlemage only smiled and shook his head, saying. "Can't handle one woman by yourself huh? Do you have to always have somebody else try to take care of them for you? Or," Damien said with a knowing smile on his face as if he knew the answer to his next question and he looked about conspiratorially at the crowd around him, playing up to them a little as he had seen Kendle do hundreds of times before, "is it true that you've always had a bit of trouble in the manly area of taking care of your women?"

The crowd erupted into raucous howls of laughter and jeering, all of it directed at Lord Richards bastard son.

Thaedrann not used to being the butt end of anybody's jokes, glared angrily at Damien through his slit-like emerald green eyes, hints of menace clearly showing.

The large man considered the returned Damien as he wasn't really sure what to make of the young battlemage. He was trying to figure out what it was that had so changed the young ward who he'd tortured and harassed as a child into the young confident man who was challenging him so openly here and now in front of half of the cities residents. He was a captain in the watch, a man not to be mocked in any sort of way, especially in front of people who were supposed to respect and fear him and obey his orders. Thaedrann also realized he was losing face in front of his own men, who were even now looking at him with slight jeers on their own faces. Rage bubbled up and seethed inside of his body, just under the surface of his skin and Thaedrann knew that he couldn't let this sniveler's insults go by unchallenged.

Snarling like an angry beast, he grabbed the bottom of his captain's tunic and lifted it up and over his head then tossing it down to the ground at his feet.

The women in the crowd squealed with delight at the sight of the handsome, young, blond haired captain's huge muscular chest and well-defined body. Thaedrann was definitely Lord Richards' son, possessing the same type of powerful physique, rippling with muscle.

With a venomous look in Damien's direction, he walked forward to the pits edge and jumped down. Thaedrann dropped the fifteen feet down into the pits sand and landed with a soft thump as easily and gracefully as a large cat.

The crowd around the pit now went eerily silent, as Thaedrann, his green eyes shining with menace still crouching catlike with his legs spread wide and one hand on the ground and his long golden hair fanned out over his muscular shoulders, waved his other hand in a beckoning motion at Damien as he looked up saying, "Come on down little mage, if you have the courage to back up your bold statements."

Damien tilted his head slightly sideways in a cocky manner then looked over at Kendle saying as he smiled his trademark half tilted mischievous smile. "It would seem as if I have been challenged."

Giving the young battlemage a grim look the dwarf answered. "It would seem so. Do you think that you can handle him? Thaedrann's a dangerous adversary, Damien, he's brutal, bloody, vicious and mean He usually tries to maim the opponents he doesn't like, permanently."

Seeing the pair huddled close together at the pits edge above him, Thaedrann called out in a loud mocking voice, "Don't worry Damien," and he smiled a wide vicious looking smile. "I promise I'll make this quick, a two hit fight, me hitting you and you hitting the sand!"

The semi silent crowd erupted into cheers and jeering howls again. Damien could tell by the crowd's enthusiasm that Thaedrann was a favorite, like Uligar before him. He recognized this because they had cheered for him in much the same manner for the past couple of years back in Westlake every time Tiko made him fight during his training.

All he had to do was steal Thaedrann's applause and audience and that would take some of the wind out of the arrogant mans sails. Damien gave Lord Richards' bastard a wry look as it became clear to him that there was more than just a fight going on here, this was also going to be a game of one-upmanship. He already saw a weakness in Thaedrann's glowing green angry eyes, if he could make Thaedrann angry enough to lose his temper, the fight would indeed be a short one. He could hear as plain as day again

Tiko's voice in his head saying, "An angry man or woman who lets his emotions control them rather than they control their emotions has already lost the fight. Anger is the mind killer, destroyer of reason and the thought process." For the first year of their training Tiko had always found numerous ways to anger and taunt him deliberately, teaching him how to control his emotions rather than the opposite. Kendle also was an expert at taunting opponents, irritating them beyond the bounds of reason. Between the two of them Damien figured he had learnt enough from the pair to push more than a few of the proud Thaedrann's buttons. So, why not start now?

He began by laughing, a long and loud drawn out condescending laugh at the other man in such a derisive manner that the crowd once again fell silent, then in an another deliberately loud offhand manner he said to Kendle as he passed him his fighting staff. Thaedrann's face he noticed was already started changing colors.

"Here hold this for me please, I'll be back in about a minute to retrieve it."

Kendle, shot the young battlemage a warning look and not understanding Damien's intent or his actions, then clamped a hard hand onto Damien's wrist and he whispered in an emphatic voice loud enough for only Damien to hear. "Don't play games with him lad and don't underestimate him, I'm warning you, even though Thaedrann is an arrogant hot headed fool, he is a veteran at this and he was well trained by both me and Travis."

Damien casually looped his wrist under and to the outside of Kendle's grip and pushed against the dwarf's wrist with his fingers. Without any effort he dislodged the strong dwarf's tight grip, saying to the suddenly shocked Kendle who didn't quite understand how the battlemage had gotten free from him.

"Stop underestimating me Kendle," Damien said fixing the dwarf with a hard look. Then he relented and the look softened some as he continued, "I have to do this if I ever want to be able to hold my head up with any sort of dignity in this city or with my family again and have peace within myself as well." As he said the words, he didn't feel any sort angst towards the other man any longer. Gone were the feelings of hatred that had flared up at the sight of the other man but he also knew that it was still time for this to end between the two of them here and today.

Kendle sniffed loudly in exasperation through his bulbous nose, which set his long mustaches quivering, but he also nodded in agreement. Damien was right. Travis wouldn't see it that way, but he understood.

"Well lad," the dwarf said with a slow roll of his reddish brown eyes, "as my father Edrynn always says go in then and fire him up," and he grinned at Damien.

The young battlemage returned the grin with one of his own half tilted smiles and said. "Don't worry about me Kendle." He cleared a space by spreading out his arms and motioned for all the people around him to step back away from the edge then he looked over, down to where Thaedrann stood waiting, "It's him you should be worried about!"

Kendle shot him another dark glare, but Damien ignored it as he reached into his pocket and drew out an old piece of old sweat stained corded leather, which he used to tie back his long curly black hair. If it was in his face while fighting, it would be a distraction. He had learned early on that loose flying hair could be used as a weapon. Once back in Westlake, one of his very first opponents had used his own to smash him headfirst into a pit wall.

Reaching down Damien gripped his own shirt to and pulled it up over his head, revealing his body honed by years of hard practice in martial arts and physical exercise combined with the rigorous training of the battlemage school. Corded muscles rippled on his lean frame and the same women who had earlier squealed when Thaedrann had removed his own shirt now showed their delight at the sight of his body. While he was not as heavily muscled as Thaedrann whose body possessed a lot of power and strength, Damien's hard muscled, whip cord like frame was built for speed and quickness and one could sense the power in it.

Kendle whistled softly at the sight of Damien's uncovered chest and back, though it wasn't the hardened muscles though, that had drawn the dwarfs' attention. Instead it was the numerous well-healed scars that covered his chest, arms and back, of all shapes, sizes and designs. The scars testified to his time and prowess in the pit.

"Hells teeth lad!" Kendle cursed in startled astonishment, "Where did you get all of those?"

Without turning around, he said over his shoulder, "I've been around the pit a few times myself, in fact, I've been the city champion in Westlake for the past two years, in both hand to hand combat and weapons combat."

Damien turned back to the dwarf, showing traces of a smile that didn't quite reach his dark blue eyes. "When I asked Travis if we could see who was on the fighting charts for the tournament, that wasn't true, I actually just wanted to make sure that they had spelled my own name correctly. I'm not just here for a reunion with my family Kendle, I'm here to compete and hopefully win the cities tournament and I'm third on the list out of fifty."

At hearing all of this, Kendle felt his eyes gape wide and his mouth fall open.

"So stop worrying about me, you can check the lists if you want to. Besides," Damien added mimicking Kendle's own evil grin of earlier. "This is revenge." then he turned away and went over to the pits edge. Before the dwarf could offer any more protests he bent straight over at the waist, placed his hands at the edge of the pits lip and gripped it tightly with his fingers, thinking about the deliberately showy entrance that Thaedrann had made, he decided to make his even better. Shifting his weight up on to his hands he did a complete handstand, then using a tiny bit of his magic he propelled his body high up into the air, did a compete flip accompanied by a twist so that he was facing Thaedrann from high up in the air, then with his arms outstretched along side his body he used his magic to lower himself slowly down onto the sand, he landed softly with a flourish and then after a deep bow to the cheering crowd, he smiled a pleased grin at the other man.

Chapter 5
Revenge

Heat rose from the hot sand in shimmering waves as the noontime sun beat on it like a blacksmith pounding on hot iron. The pair stood about ten paces apart facing each other, their piecing gazes locked.

Damien noticed that Thaedrann's face had gone slightly redder after his dramatic entrance and he thought to himself, "good!" hoping to irritate the large man's pride even further, as their eyes locked, he deliberately winked.

Seeing the wink thrown in his direction, Thaedrann bristled even further with rage, at being mocked and at being outdone by someone who he considered his inferior. He was after all a part of Lord Richard's own blood, the actual son of a Highlord and not just the adopted son of a peasant ranger named an heir on a promise for having saved his father's life. Without waiting on the pit judge to enter, the blond haired man started to take steps towards the smaller man, but was stopped by a sharply spoken command.

The pit judge stepped down into the arena and motioned Thaedrann back towards his own side of the sand.

Damien deliberately sat down on the hot sand and removed his traveling boots. He would also fight in his bare feet, just like the cleric in the previous fight had done. Even though the sand was burning hot, he hardly noticed it through the hardened soles of his calloused feet.

Thaedrann called out contemptuously as Damien had started to remove his shoes, "The odor from your feet won't help you win this fight, you do realize that don't you?"

He ignored the comment and tossed the boots over to a corner in the pit, far out of the way, then scrambled back onto his feet. "Nor will the stench emanating from your mouth help you. He tossed back and watched Thaedrann's face go livid.

"Are you ready now?" came his angry reply.

Damien nodded and stepped over to the side of the pit judge, Thaedrann did the same on the other side.

This was his place, regardless of the location. Whether it was in Westlake or Castlekeep it was still the pit and after having fought in it so many times before, to be here felt more of a homecoming than the city above him did. He knew that all he had to do was to discern the weaknesses of the man in front of him and exploit them just like Tiko had taught him in the Academe. Thaedrann had already given that much away to him.

As the pit judge explained the rules to the two combatants, the crowd had grown eerily silent, somehow sensing that this was more on a more personal level. Even the bet takers had stopped moving amongst the people in the stands, none were sure whether they wanted to lay any odds on the outcome of this fight.

Betting on Thaedrann was almost always a sure thing and they would have felt comfortable in their wager, but

Thaedrann's opponent wasn't like most other men. He was a fully trained battlemage, trained in all kinds of combat and in all kinds of tactics. Many people gathered in the stands seemed reluctant to part with their money betting against him. Already a lot of them had lost more than a few gold pieces in the last fight, having chosen Uligar over the pretty female cleric of Dar.

Someone in the crowd must have been from Westlake and recognized him as the city champion because the next sound heard in the silence was a loud yell. "For the pride of Westlake."

Damien grinned a sly wide smile and bowed deeply to the stands again, he threw a salute in the general direction of the voice that had yelled. Now all of the people in the stands erupted in screams for Westlake and the cities name echoed all about him and Thaedrann.

"What's this all about?" Thaedrann growled irritatingly when he had finished saluting.

"Didn't you know?" Damien asked innocently, "I'm the Westlake champion, representing the city in the tournament of city champions in both hand to hand and weapons fighting." Then he looked over to the pit judge and identified himself, asking as he did so, "Would Thaedrann would qualify as a good display of skill?"

The pit judge now saw the trap that the other arrogant young man had allowed himself to be led into. He fought to hide a smile as he said that indeed Thaedrann did qualify a skilled opponent.

All fighters in the cities tournament had to fight what was called a warm up match against a suitable opponent to show that they were indeed capable and able to fight. Damien chose then, since he had been the one who had been challenged, for hand-to-hand combat. He knew there would be other fighters in the stands who would also be watching this bout with interest, especially now that his name was echoing through the air. He didn't want to give away too much about himself to them.

Thaedrann blanched slightly at Damien's words about the championships and a flicker of doubt showed briefly in his green eyes. He hadn't known who the Westlake champion was, but he did know that he was a hands down favorite to win the whole tournament.

"Yo...You're," he stammered momentarily, before he caught himself and snapped his jaw tight, fiercely biting off the words he had been about to say. Instead the blond haired man changed his expression to one of smirking condemnation and said, "Yeah, right," in as condescending a manner as he could manage. Thaedrann felt an uneasy feeling begin to stir in his stomach and wondered for the first time whether or not he might have bitten off more than he could chew. He knew about battlemages and their abilities. The man in front of him certainly wasn't acting like the old Damien that he had tortured and embarrassed as a child. Damien's calm, steady dark blue-eyed gaze unnerved him slightly.

Damien saw the look that had filled Thaedrann's eyes when he heard who he was and decided that now was the time to drive the barb in even deeper saying in a voice only loud enough for the blond haired man to hear. "Remember what you said, this is only going to be a two hit fight, me hitting you and you hitting the sand." He stressed the 'me hitting you' part.

Thaedrann gave him a blustering sneer, which Damien chose to ignore, instead focusing on steadying his breathing and centering his internal energies. He knew Thaedrann was right handed and would probably lead with that hand, He knew that he could stand toe to toe with him for a while, but eventually the larger mans strength would begin to take a toll on him.

The judge was almost finished explaining the rules to both of them. Damien shifted into a ready fighting stance, placing his right foot forward, turning his knee slightly inward to protect his groin, dropping his head a little to protect his throat and raising his left heel for springing forward and backwards. His right hand would be his attacking hand and his left would be the deflector, he doubted that Thaedrann was enough of an opponent that he would actually have to switch stances from left to right for speed and power purposes, using his ambidexterity. He wanted to try and keep from showing this to the other more skilled opponents he would face in the tournament later on.

Thaedrann, like Uligar who had fought before him, liked to use his size and appearance as a threat, so his stance was one of aggressive confidence. Kendle was right, Thaedrann was very well trained and more than likely this brashness was a ruse designed to throw him off.

The pit judge finished explaining the rules but before he could even finish dropping his arm between the two men, Thaedrann threw out his right arm in a lightening fast lunge-punch with all of his weight behind it, as he stretched out, hoping to catch Damien off guard before he could react. It was a favorite tactic of his and usually it worked.

Not today. Damien saw the surprise attack coming and expecting it to be a right handed punch, quickly shuffle stepped sideways and slipped out of its range. The larger man had put every ounce of power into that surprise punch in hopes of living up to his boast of the fight only lasting for two hits. But with no opponent in front of him to absorb the impact of the lunge, his momentum carried him forward and he stumbled slightly, off balanced and almost tripped onto his face. With the speed of a cat, Thaedrann quickly got his feet back underneath him and then unlike Uligar who had fought before him and had been caught by the surprise blow to the head from the female cleric while his back was turned, whipped his other arm about in a full circle, his fist whistling through the air behind him in case Damien had tried to attack him from behind while he was off balance. If Uligar had countered with the same move in the earlier fight, he might not have been struck unconscious by the blow to the temple.

Many opponents would have been hit by the blindly fast backfist thrown by Thaedrann, but Damien wanted the fight to last. Thaedrann completed the spinning turn only to find the battlemage standing about five feet from him smirking at him condescendingly and wagging a single finger up in the air at him from side to side as if he were scolding a wayward child, making a few tsk-tsk noises to go along with it.

Thaedrann's handsome face turned purple with rage, his eyes glowed with green fire. He felt his blood begin to boil inside of him like liquid fury at being mocked by the smaller man whom he had always considered his lesser. The once silent crowd now began to howl and jeer again but this time it was at the young handsome blond haired man who was being scolded.

Damien dropped into ready stance and waited for Thaedrann to come again, he knew he would. The handsome man's pride was wounded and he had to make amends. That was another lesson of Tiko's, one that had taken him who also had a lot of pride a long time to learn.

The larger man had not anticipated how fast the smaller mans reactions would be so now Thaedrann sized Damien up in a slightly different light. Seeing him waiting he realized that he really did have a challenge here Thaedrann adjusted his tactics as Travis and Kendle had taught him. He charged at Damien with a loud roar in almost the same manner as Uligar Rothe had done in the previous fight. Damien watched the charge coming and was preparing to dart out of the way sideways again, maybe to the left this time, when instead of diving at his body and trying to pin him into the wall with his weight, Thaedrann dove low towards his feet with his long arms outstretched wide attempting to cut off any attempt at escape to the sides.

Damien reacted instinctively and leaped forward, high into the air towards the center of the pit a split second before Thaedrann caught his feet with his strong hands and arms.

The two men missed each other completely. They flew by one another, one passing underneath and the other passing above, like acrobats performing in a traveling circus.

Damien stretched out his hands in front of him, tucked and rolled himself up into a ball, doing a somersault as he struck the sand coming back up onto his feet.

Thaedrann, wasn't as lucky as the young battlemage, his headlong dive carried him headfirst towards the pits wall. Before he could get his hands back in front of him, he crashed face first into the stonewall with a heavy hollow sounding thud.

So hard was his impact with the wall that a cloud of mortar dust blew out from between the stones seams settling down on Thaedrann's inert unmoving body like a fine white mist. He lay there in the sand unmoving for a minute before finally pushing himself off his stomach and crawled, trembling up onto his hands and knees. Blood flowed freely out of his mouth, dripping down onto the sand where it splattered in little red explosive bursts. Using the back of his hand he wiped the blood away from his mouth.

"You move well!" he said to Damien in a low guttural voice as he regained his feet, his green glowing eyes locked on him.

Damien wasn't paying attention to Thaedrann or his compliments. Instead his attention was focused on an item that seemed out of place on the golden brown sand of the pits floor. Something gleamed brightly in the sunlight at the base of the wall near Thaedrann's feet. A moment later he realized what it was and the vengeful battlemage felt both of the corners of his mouth turn up in a wide smile as he shook his head up and down appreciatively. It definitely would serve to help fuel the blond haired man's anger even further.

The large blonde haired man saw both the triumphant smile on Damien's face and the nod. He wasn't sure if this was some type of ploy by Damien to distract his attention for an attack but he decided to take the risk. He quickly glanced downward at the sand to see what it was that held the young battlemages attention. A single almost glowing white tooth lay on the bloodstained sand reflecting back the noontime sun. Thaedrann put a hand up to his mouth, realizing then that it was one of his.

He saw the satisfied smile on the face of the other and his own features twisted violently. All sense of reason and wariness fled Thaedrann's green eyes as they locked on Damien's own and he said in a voice of absolute grim certainty. "Playtime is over mage, I'm going to kill you now! Of that you can be absolutely certain!"

The large man exploded into motion then, furiously kicking and punching at Damien, from all angles and levels in an attempt to overwhelm him with a furious ferocious assault.

Damien had been a little concerned about this type of attack because of the training that the other man had received. But compared to the lightening fast attacks that he had suffered under for the past five and a half years during his studies with Tiko and the numerous assaults he had faced from a variety of very skilled opponents as champion in Westlake, Thaedrann's attacks were weighted and slow. He almost knew what the other man was going to do before he did it. Using his arms, shoulders and legs, he either turned or parried all of the blows harmlessly aside, directing the force of their momentum to where it couldn't possibly hurt him.

After a full minute or so and gasping for breath, Thaedrann took a step back and let out a scream of pure animal like rage and frustration at having all of his attacks diverted and thwarted by Damien. Never had he ever faced such an opponent. An unpleasant flicker of doubt surfaced in the back of Thaedrann's mind causing him to pause, thinking silently to himself, "I should have been done with this weakling by now." Gone were the murderous glares, in the green eyes, replaced instead by ones of fear and desperation.

Damien looked hard at the other man and he nodded. They both knew that a lesson had been taught and learnt here today. With a hint of steel sounding in his voice, he beckoned Thaedrann on saying only loud enough for him to hear, "Let's finish this."

Until then the battlemage had yet to launch any sort of attack of his own against the other man. Thaedrann now stepped cautiously forward with his defenses in place this time and a fearful look in his green eyes. Damien reached deep inside himself and centered all of his energies just like he had been taught, focusing on the inner power that ran through his body. One thought kept flashing through his mind as he did so and that was, Thaedrann's comment about the fight only being a two hit fight. He could not believe how big headed and arrogant the other man had become during his long absence. It was time for his two hits. Channeling all of his internal energies in his body into his hands, he caused his inner power to become an extension of his own striking power.

Thaedrann decided that since it was impossible to hit the smaller faster man, he would instead use his own strength and overpower him with brute force.

That was the other thing that Damien had earlier decided that he would have to watch out for when he had evaluated Thaedrann.

Acting like he was going to attack again with his fists, he faked two punches at Damien's head then tried with his large hands instead to circle his waist and lock him in with his powerful arms. He might actually have succeeded, but the young battlemage had other plans to end the fight with a special attack of his own.

Thaedrann's mighty arms and powerful hands closed on empty air as Damien kicked out both of his feet and dropped low with both of his legs stretched out in a split to both sides of his body.

The unexpected move dropped his torso and head down below Thaedrann's waist level, bringing his eyes and hands even with his groin. Now he attacked! Using all the power that Damien could muster, he struck, driving the palm heel of his open hand upwards into Thaedrann's testicles.

The force of the blow accompanied by the power of his own being lifted the large blonde haired young man completely up off of his feet. Air exploded out of Thaedrann's lungs in a wretched gurgle of pain. Quickly Damien hopped back up onto his feet and looked at his opponent.

Thaedrann's face went completely white. His emerald green eyes had rolled somewhere up into the back of his skull and he staggered about, moaning in pain, hunched over clutching at his groin with both hands.

Moving so that he was in front of the other man, Damien drew his arm back, set his feet under him and struck again, this time driving the flat of his palm into Thaedrann's face and nose, shattering it and smashing it flat, sending blood flying. The impact from the second blow sent Thaedrann's large frame flying through the air across the arena pit until he crashed heavily onto the sand, on his back several feet away. His crumpled form wasn't moving at all now and two small trickles of blood ran out of his broken mouth and nose.

"No woman, at least for the length of the harvest festival, will look becomingly upon Thaedrann's bruised and broken features," Damien happily thought to himself.

Even Healers took breaks during festival times and charged extremely heavy prices for their services, so unless Thaedrann paid out a lot of gold, he would have to let his face heal naturally. He would be reminded every day for the next week at least by the pain of the lesson. Pride and arrogance should never be brought to a fight, it violates Tiko's first rule, never underestimate your enemy.

Damien knew that the fight actually shouldn't have been allowed to go on as far as it had. The pit judge should have stopped the fight when he had rendered the larger man unable to continue with the disabling groin shot. Like the rest of the crowd that had fallen into stunned silence, the judge just stood there not moving, surprised by the speed and quickness that Damien had used when he had finally decided to attack and dispatch Thaedrann. Snapping his mouth shut, the judge raced out into the sand, grabbed Damien's hand and threw it into the air announcing him the victor.

The crowd exploded into cheers and yells, coins from the stands fell down all about him like a shiny rain as the people showed their approval of the fight. He started to move towards the stairs that led out of the pit, when he felt a strange sensation as if someone was studying him intently. Turning around in a slow circle, he scanned the stands, looking with his dark blue eyes. The female cleric of Dar with the sky blue eyes and short curly strawberry blonde hair gave him an approving nod. Then she turned and melted back into the crowd.

Kendle, met him halfway up the stairs, as he was coming down and handed him a sack in passing, saying, "Come on lad, what are you doing, you can't leave all that gold and silver behind, you well earned it." then he went down into the pit and bent over picking up the gold and silver coins that littered the sand, Damien sighed loudly, knowing the dwarf would not let him leave until they had collected every coin and went back down to help.

Kendle looked at him, his face flushed with excitement, "By Garns teeth, where in the world did you learn to fight like that? I've never seen anything like that in my entire life!"

Picking up the coins, Damien shrugged and said, "They don't just teach magic to battlemages while they are training you at the academe."

"I'd say not, so where did you learn how to fight like that?" Kendle asked again, seeing that Damien was trying not to answer the question.

Damien gave in and proceeded to tell the dwarf all about Westlake and Tiko as they left the pit. Laden with two large sacks of gold and silver, they hurried off towards the castle.

Castlekeep was a prosperous city. This was reflected both inside and outside the castles grounds. His adopted father, Lord Richard, had spared no expense in decorating it for the festival.

A massive moat filled with water, separated the keep from the rest of the city. Damien glanced down into the dark water as the pair made their way across the drawbridge. The decorative floats and lanterns that filled it gave the moat's black waters a colorful and festive appearance. The keep itself and the walls were actually two separate structures with gardens and courtyards between them. Stone walkways ran throughout the grounds and colored lanterns hung throughout. Though they were not lit yet, they would be by this evening and the grounds would look sort of magical. The outer walls of the castle that protected the keep were sixty feet tall, ten feet wide and even though it was festival time Damien could see the members of the ever present sentinel guard manning their posts on the walls. All of them were dressed in shining festival armor with gleaming chain mail and steel headpieces that reflected brightly in the sunlight. Their cloth surcoates were a bright blue with a silver trim and were emblazoned with the Daverge family crest, a silver-striking falcon with outstretched talons. The courtyards surrounding the massive keep were filled with numerous buildings, all of which had a purpose to keep the castle running smoothly. There was an inner keep with its high walls, tall turrets, spiraling staircases and large halls and chambers were where Damien, his family and the rest of the keeps inhabitants lived. Every building inside of the keeps massive walls had been decorated with gaily-covered streamers. With nods thrown to the guards across the courtyard the pair made their way through the large arched entranceway that led into the keep. Even though the guards might not have recognized him, Damien thought to himself, they did recognize Kendle's red and white striped beard.

The entry hall that led into the main audience chamber was lined on both sides by ancient suits of armor. Damien nodded to an unknown servant who was removing dust from them in preparation for the night's ball and feast. Legends told that these were the ancient rulers of Castlekeep and that if the outer walls of the keep ever fell to invaders these suits could be brought to life and help defend the rest of the castle. Both passed out of the hall of rulers and into the massive main throne room or audience chamber as it was called now. Damien was surprised by the amount of activity in the room. Numerous lavish tapestries of great battles hung from the massive high walls. Sunlight poured in from large windows set high in the ceiling, illuminating the whole chamber in golden hues. A myriad of blue and silver tiles covered the floor depicting the House of Daverge crest. Two very large fireplaces, almost tall enough for a man to stand upright in, occupied both ends of the room. The throne that Lord Richard conducted business from had been moved to a corner. Very long tables, each about six feet wide and about twenty feet long were covered with white tablecloths. Numerous piles of dishes glistened in the sunlight. Servants scurried everywhere putting the final touches on all of the decorations before tonight's guests arrived.

Damien saw a troupe of acrobats and jugglers warming up in a corner. Bards and minstrels were tuning up their instruments and an orator was preparing a spoken tale.

Oblivious to all of the room's activity was Lord Richard Daverge, Highlord of Castlekeep, his advisor and wizard, Balthazar Tolarus and Travis. The three men were huddled at one of the tables farthest from the activity. With their heads close together having a hushed conversation to low to be heard by anyone else in the room. Damien saw an opportunity for a little mischief and quickly cast an ears spell, hoping that he could listen in and overhear the words being spoken. But as quickly as he cast it Balthazar's head shot up, his hawkish eyes darted about the large room quickly looking for the source as he used his own magic to disrupt the spell. His rich brown eyes fell on Damien as the originator of the spell. A wide smile crossed his face as he recognized the young man who at one time had been his own apprentice and whom he hadn't seen in six years. He turned to alert the others at the table to their presence but Lord Richard knew something was up already at the way Balthazar's head had sharply jerked upwards a moment ago.

A pleased look of delight lit up his proud face. He got to his feet and went around the table. Quickly crossing the room, the Highlord of Castlekeep enveloped Damien in a large bear hug, welcoming him home loudly in his baritone voice. Lord Richard held his adopted son out at arms length and examined him, his steel gray eyes showing warmth and love as he regarded his adopted ward.

Balthazar was right behind his Lord and he too gave the young battle mage a hug, welcoming him home. Travis hadn't bothered to rise when they had come in. Instead he stayed in his chair, scowling at Kendle and the large bags that they both were carrying in their fists.

Age, Damien noticed hadn't been unkind to his father or Balthazar. Both looked a lot like they had when he had left them six years earlier. His father had always been an imposing figure and at age fifty-five he still seemed so. Standing straight at the same height of six and a half feet tall as Thaedrann, but with wider, broader shoulders and a more muscled frame, he still looked like he could break almost any man in half with just his hands alone. A little bit of age showed on his face and Damien thought he saw a few worry lines around his steely gray eyes. There also appeared to be some sort of tension in them too. He still radiated a sense of both command and power that drew others to him and made him the ruler of Castlekeep and Gaderia.

Balthazar stood slightly behind his adopted father as they all looked at each other. His hawk like face with its piercing brown eyes and hooked nose seemed to have aged some too while he was away. His rich brown hair was now shot through with a few streaks of gray that Damien didn't remember from before he left. He was a slight man with a lean build, adorned in his red velvet robes, trimmed in silver that named him an advisor to nobility and gave him also a sense of power.

Though Balthazar, like his father didn't need the robes of his office to let others know that he was powerful, it seemed to ooze from him somehow and couldn't be overlooked. His was that of the magical power sort rather than the commanding kind.

"Travis here has informed me that your journey here was mainly uneventful but that you did do a fine job on some orcs with those spells of yours." Lord Richard said.

Damien started to answer but Kendle abruptly cut him off.

"Spells, hells." The dwarf said, his face still looking excited. "You should see him fight." Kendle bowed and swept his calloused hand out at Damien elaborately.

"Young Damien here is representing Westlake as its champion in the seven cities tournament and is one of the favorites to win."

The three men all looked at the young battle mage with arched eyebrows. "And," the dwarf continued, drawing their attention back to him, "he took out Thaedrann in the arena pit with only one punch."

"Excuse me?" Lord Richard asked curiously eyeing the two of them, "What fight?"

Damien started to answer, but once again the excited Kendle cut him off as he began to vividly describe every sequence of the fight in loud detail so that anyone and everyone in the giant hall could hear his telling. He ended by trying to do the splits in an imitation of Damien's but only succeeded in falling on his face during the attempt, which caused everyone to laugh.

There was an angry scraping noise of wood on stone as Travis thrust his chair back and stood up, his face dark with suppressed anger. He eyed Kendle and the fierce dwarf noticeably swallowed under the hard gaze.

"I thought," the blademaster said, still staring hard at the dwarf, "I gave you explicit instructions about no fighting." Frustration was clearly evident on Travis' features at having been disobeyed.

"You did, you did." answered the dwarf, stepping back a few steps away from the blademaster's angry look.

"You told him." Damien cut in interrupting the angry blademaster, fixing the same look that Tiko always used on him when he wanted attention. "You didn't tell me though and I needed a warm up anyway for the tournament." That statement and the look brought Travis up short and he blinked in stunned surprise.

A deep booming laugh erupted from Lord Richard as he listened to and watched the confrontation, "He's got you there Travis." his father said still laughing.

After a moment, even Travis laughed slightly. "I guess

your right, but I still think the two of you well knew what I meant."

Lord Richard motioned his blademaster back into his seat, "These things happen between men," then he asked seriously, "Is Thaedrann okay?"

"He'll live," answered Kendle, "but he definitely looks a little worse for wear right now."

"Okay then," said his father now looking at Damien admirably, "I'm glad its finally settled between you two on even ground. Why don't you go on and get ready for the festival dinner and ball? There will be plenty of time for us to socialize later, but guests are already arriving."

Damien nodded his head yes, embraced his father again and with a smile to Balthazar, he stepped out through one of the room's many exits towards the corridors that led to his chambers.

The sights and smells in the corridors of the ancient castle brought back many thoughts and memories of his youth from before he had left for Westlake. All of these swirled into his mind as he went towards his chambers in the abandoned west wing of the castle. He had chosen this location because it kept him far away from Thaedrann.

Approaching a thick iron bound door with the Daverge family crest on it, Damien stopped short. Taking a deep breath and letting it out slowly, he concentrated briefly on the spell he wanted, placing his fingertips on the door he cast the incantation. A bright yellow light flared out from the center of the door in the shape of a magical glyph. Damien felt relieved, he knew now that the wards he had placed there years ago to keep out intruders like Thaedrann was still in place. If anyone beside himself had attempted to enter the room while he was gone, unless they dispelled the magical ward they would have received a nasty shock. That the glyph was still in place, meant that no one had disturbed his room. Glyphs and wards were magical drawings, usually put in place as protective devices such as the one that he had used.

The one on the door was a glyph of an electrical nature that would give anyone attempting to open the door without removing it or saying the password to disable it, a rather nasty jolt. Damien said the words to a second spell and a pale blue light spread out from his fingertips, running the entire length of the door, until it was encased completely in blue light, then as quick as they had appeared both the blue light and the glyph winked out leaving nothing but bare wood behind. Damien reached for the door knowing that as it opened he had truly returned home.

Chapter 6
The Seeker

The rat faced fat man studied the scraggly bearded face of the young man fighting in the pit, so intently that his beady little eyes began to water.

Almost twenty years had passed since he and about thirty other seekers loyal to the throne and the crown had had this man's face burned into their mind's eye through the use of blood magic, an almost forgotten and forbidden use of creational magic.

Cyadine Syndell, the Royal Regents wizard and advisor had used the forbidden magic with the purpose of finding this young man in front of him under any circumstances and if any of them did, they were to report back to the capitol city of Kallamar as soon as possible.

The rat faced man's name was Ferris Molkae, he was the secretary to the Royal ambassador of Kallamar, the ex commander of the realms military, now retired who was stationed here in Castlekeep.

He had been in the bazaar shopping for a few items. Passing close to the pits he had noticed the unusual silence of the crowd and had stopped to see what was going on, his incessant dignitary's curiosity getting the better of him.

Ferris pushed and shoved his way through the crowd until he reached a space in the stands where he could see what was going on below him.

Thaedrann Rynall, Lord Richards' bastard son was in the pit below and from the look on his face and the redness of his complexion, the secretary could tell that he wasn't too happy. Ferris looked for Thaedrann's opponent and found a young man that stood up from where he had been sitting on the sand doing something. The instant that the secretary's eyes saw the face of the long curly haired young man with the dark blue eyes and the scruffy uncut beard who was Thaedrann's opponent, he felt his heart lurch in his chest as the long dormant blood magic burnt into him by the royal wizard flared to life in his veins like a fire filling his insides. "It's him," he said before he could stop himself and wiped at a cold sweat that had erupted from the pores on his forehead with the back of his hand. Thinking to himself, "God's be damned! After all of this time searching, I am the one who found him."

He could tell that the face was slightly different but no one he had never seen had ever caused the magic to flare up and act the way it was now.

The Royal wizard had assured him along with the rest of the seekers that they would know the one they were seeking the moment they laid their eyes on the person even if they were wearing a disguise or had somehow acted to conceal their features using magic. Such, Cyadine had told them was the nature of the blood magic.

Turning, Ferris grabbed the arm of a young man standing next to him rather forcibly.

"That young man fighting in the pit down there," he shouted at the young man next to him, unable to control himself as the magic coursing through his insides seized him, "Who is he?"

"Excuse me!" said the skinny young man irritability as he jerked his arm out of Ferris' grasp and glared at him hatefully.

"Five gold to you sir." Ferris said urgently, he could feel the magic in his veins boiling now, it coursed through him like a hot liquid fire and spittle flecked and foamed at his lips. "If you can tell me who that is fighting in the pit?"

The skinny man with a funny hair style who had fought in the earlier fight before the female cleric held out his hand palm outstretched and waited until Ferris counted out five gold marks from the pouch at his side and put them in his hand before answering.

"That sir," said the young man as he pocketed the gold, "is Lord Richards bastard and second commander in charge of the city watch, Thaedrann Rynall."

Ferris' rat like face went an angry shade of red and his beady little eyes almost turned the same color as he snapped angrily at the other man. "Not Thaedrann, you stone dumb oaf! The other one, moron!"

The other mans eyes glittered dangerously for a moment as he considered whether or not he should hit this insulting fat man, then decided it wasn't worth the trouble, striking a royal secretary might get him thrown in jail for the entire length of the festival. Instead the skinny young man with the hard eyes, thin face and funny haircut held out his hand once again saying, "That information will cost you another ten gold marks."

"What!" roared Ferris angrily, purple veins began to show on his face. "I just paid you five marks."

"That," said the skinny man with a self-satisfied smile "was for the other man. For the information on that one," he pointed at the dark curly haired youth in the pit, "from me will cost you."

Ferris shoved his hand back into his pouch and

withdrew another ten marks and thrust them into the other man's outstretched palm.

The young man gave the Secretary a sly look and answered his question as he pocketed the gold. "I don't really know who he is."

Ferris' whole face now really went an angry vivid shade of purple and the veins that showed earlier now threatened to pop as they bulged outwardly.

"But," the Skinny man cut in before the secretary could protest. "Somebody said he was a newly trained battlemage just out of Westlake and that he arrived here with him." he pointed, indicating a dark reddish haired dwarf with a white stripe running slightly off center the entire length of his beard.

Ferris noticed the slightly worried expression etched on the dwarfs face. As secretary to the royal ambassador he was expected to know just about anyone with any sort of title and a little about all of them. This was especially important right now with the possibility of a civil war breaking out between all of the fourteen kingdoms over disputes of Lord Vargas' new tax laws. He immediately recognized Kendle Stonebreaker standing at the edge of the pit, nephew to Devlin Bonebreaker, ruler of the Iron Peak dwarves to the north and son to Edrynn Stonebreaker, the semi ruler of the southern hill dwarves. Judging by the look on the normally unconcerned dwarf's face and the fact that the young man in the pit was a battlemage wearing their colors of black and gold, he assumed that the man who set the bloodmagic on fire in his veins must be Damien Daverge, Lord Richards ward and adopted son, the third heir to Castlekeep. How interesting! He is fighting Lord Richard's bastard son. He had never met the Highlords third son, he had left for the academe before he had been moved here as Dalmar's secretary. Ferris knew a lot of things, namely that Lord Richard's blademaster and the dwarf had been sent to Westlake to retrieve his third son from the Academe of mages, where he had just graduated and escort him home.

He was the one that the seekers had been tasked to find. Ferris wished he had found this out years ago. It would have saved him a lot of time searching all about the city.

Being in Westlake also explained why none of the other seekers had ever found him before. The mage's city was the one place where no seekers had been tasked to search. Someone infused with bloodmagic might have been discovered and that might have led to probing questions about how they had been enspelled with the forbidden magic.

An overwhelming desire to report what he had found seized and filled him with such a sense of urgency that after one more last look at the young man in the pit, Ferris turned and left the stands almost at a run, pushing and shoving people rudely out of the way as he went.

The battle scarred, thin-faced young man watched him leave and a curious expression filled his eyes as he looked from the two young men in the pit fight below and back in the direction that the secretary had fled. What was so important about Lord Richards adopted son that it would cause a royal secretary from Kallamar to pay fifteen gold marks to a complete stranger just for the lads name? Maybe he would have a few members of his newly earned mercenary band look into keeping an eye on this mage also. "One never knew," Kyle Wyndin said to himself, "where a bit of profit could be made."

Ferris used his bulk to clear a path through the milling crowds in the bazaar. Once he was through them and out onto open roads, he burst into a waddling run.

Dalmar Ariaas' royal ambassador's estate was located on the outskirts of the cities center. It set in amongst some rolling hills far from the rougher neighborhoods of the inner city or by the docks.

By the time that Ferris reached the stone gates of the grounds and the guards that kept out intruders, he was red faced, panting heavily and on the verge of collapsing in the middle of the street. Gasping for breath, he ordered the guards to open the gate. Then he barreled past them and on into the manor house. Grabbing a servant by the collar of his tunic as he passed by, he yanked the man to a stop and demanded to know where Lord Dalmar was. After he received his answer he rudely shoved the man out of the way and hurried off in the direction of the ambassador's personal study.

Lord Dalmar Ariaas was an ex soldier of almost thirty five years of service, he had close cropped gray hair, a military and stately bearing that he hadn't left behind when he became a royal ambassador. Even though he had been out of the military for almost seven years he still looked and acted like a soldier. He had been hand picked by Vargas to be an ambassador to this region for those same reasons.

An ambassador who once was the commander of Kallamar's fourteen armies and a hero of the realm would have a better chance of getting things done, here in the west. Every noble family here had a member in some branch of the military, rather than some pompous ass that was given the post as a sort of gift for services to the throne.

Dalmar was actually friends with Lord Richard Daverge and the other six Highlords of the western cities. Most of the western lords over the course of several years have developed a dislike of all things from the capitol city. Lord Richard was the only one who had stayed completely loyal to the royal regent until a month ago when he urged the rest of the western highlords to rebel and become tax free states and had the Ambassador deliver the message.

When Ferris burst into his office, the royal ambassador was reading his invitation for this evening's festival ball

A King's Quest

and banquet. The sight of his secretary was astounding. The man was red faced, panting and in dark sweat stained robes.

"I... I found him, milord, I found him." Ferris yelled loudly at the ambassador, "I found him."

Dalmar looked at his secretary, annoyance and irritation crossed his face at the unexpected interruption, he set down the invitation he had been reading and glanced over at him standing in the doorway to his office. Ferris was blabbering something unintelligible.

"Found whom Ferris?" Dalmar asked, his irritation quickly changed into amazement, he would have never thought it possible that his secretary could ever expend as much energy as it looked like he was doing now. Ferris had always put forth only as much as was necessary at any given time, now it looked to him like the fat man had been actually running.

The royal ambassador leaned back casually in his large chair and stared at his secretary until he finally fell silent. Ferris began to speak again as if he wasn't able to control himself.

"Milord, you do not know this, but I am a seeker for the court, set on a task by the Royal Regent himself and his advisor. I have found the person that I was tasked to find and now I have to get to Kallamar as soon as possible. We have to notify the royal advisor Lord Cyadine right away."

Dalmar studied his secretary for a moment wondering how important one man could be that he should have to jump at the mere mention of his secretary finding him. "Tomorrow," he thought to himself, "it'll wait until then." and he told Ferris so then added. "Today all I intend to do," he said holding up the invitation bearing Lord Richards blue and silver crest, "is to go to the festival ball and enjoy the events."

Ferris' beady eyes narrowed slightly at this and he studied Lord Dalmar for a several moments before deciding that he was indeed serious and was going to delay his departure. The secretary reached into his robes and withdrew a scroll case bearing the Royal seal of Kallamar, a flying dragon breathing fire in a circle of gold and set it on the table, pushing it across towards the royal ambassador.

"Open it milord." Ferris intoned, "and all will be explained."

Dalmar studied the worn looking scroll case, cut its flaking seal with a fingernail, opened it and pulled the parchment out of its case. With both hands he unfurled yellowed parchment and laid it out flat on the table in front of him so that he could read what it said. After he was done his face went stark white with rage. "Is this thing for a real?" Dalmar asked coldly, stabbing the parchment in front of him with a finger and looking at his secretary with flat eyes and an expressionless soldier's face.

The secretary shrugged his shoulders, "I don't even know what it says m'lord, I was just told to give it to anyone who tried to delay me in passing a message to Lord Cyadine or the Royal Regent Lord Vargas."

Dalmar studied his rat-faced secretary for a few moments as he tried to decide whether or not he was lying. Deciding that his secretary was too much of a coward and too afraid of him personally to ever try anything as bold as that, he slid the document across the table for him to read.

> To Whomever this may concern
>
> The bearer of this document is on a dire mission for the safety of the throne. Any and all members of the realm who read this document is to give whatever help necessary the bearer of it requires no matter what the request is. Any and all who fail in providing the bearer of this document whatever help they need to complete their mission will be

put to death for treason against the throne and crown. By the order of Lord Vargas Salidor, Royal Regent of Kallamar and ruler of the fourteen kingdoms.

Now, Ferris read the parchment, his eyes going wide as saucers, then he reread it again and his wide beady eyes narrowed as his face took on a more cunning and feral expression, much more akin to his own nature. Smugly he said eyeing the royal ambassador, "It would seem m'lord that we won't be waiting till tomorrow to deliver my message after all, will we?" in a haughty voice he added, "Rather I think we will be delivering it right now, in fact, immediately!"

Dalmar glared coldly at Ferris through his gray eyes, weighing the man who stood in front of him and the parchment that he clutched in his fat fist, after a few moments of consideration reached a decision.

Speaking in an icy tone that seemed to chill the room by several degrees, the ex marshall of armies asked. "What is in that document right now that could keep me from removing your head from your shoulders without anyone knowing the better of it, just for disobeying me?"

The smug and sneering expression melted off of Ferris' face as fast as it had appeared. He wondered whether or not he had pushed the ex Marshall of the military too far Usually, Dalmar was not a man to try to bend to your will that often, his iron core usually resisted such efforts. Ferris' feral like eyes bulged and he croaked weakly. "W..What about you m'lord and your oath of obedience and fealty to the throne and the crown? Would you also betray those?"

Dalmar thought about this for a moment. He was a military man, regardless whether or not he had a post that he wanted and he didn't take his oaths of allegiance or any other part of his duties lightly. Loyalty was a part of his nature as a soldier. No matter what he thought about the man who ruled or of the advice he got he still had sworn an oath of fealty and he knew he would do what they required no matter how much he disliked it.

"Besides milord," Ferris said, once he saw that he wasn't going to lose his head and that his words had struck home with Dalmar. "Lord Cyadine assured me and the thirty other seekers with me that if any of us turned up missing under any sort of unusual circumstances that he would know of it and launch a full investigation into our demise. I am sure that if he thought he had any reason to suspect you milord," an almost derisive tone crept back in behind the secretary's words as he emphasized the word you, "he wouldn't hesitate one moment in removing your head from your shoulders. Besides you do have that new wife and lovely newborn baby that he would probably choose to make pay as well."

Dalmar's jaw clenched so tight that a tic began to spasm on his cheek at hearing the words. Knowing that the threat, however subtle, was also the truth. He had never liked his secretary and had always considered him a pig. His words proved it to him. He also knew that his secretary was probably right, it would be just like Cyadine to have placed some kind spell on his seekers if one of them died, the royal adviser and wizard was one of the coldest and most calculating men Dalmar had ever met, even more so than many of his generals he commanded while he had been in the military. There wasn't any love at all lost between the two men and Dalmar knew also that his secretary was right in saying that Cyadine wouldn't hesitate in removing his head or his family's heads.

He glared at the secretary a final time before saying in a flat voice, "All right, we will do things your way, Ferris, for now." Then he stood up and moved out from behind his large desk, leading the way out of his study and into an adjoining room with Ferris trailing on his heels like a

A King's Quest

trained puppy.

A large object stood alongside one of the other room walls and was covered over by a giant blanket. Dalmar went over, grabbed one of the blankets edges and yanked it off, revealing a large ornate and intricately rune carved silver mirror underneath, reflecting both his and Ferris' images in its cold surface back at them. The large ornately designed mirror was a magical mirror of walking, it allowed a person to travel through its surface to another mirror of the same type in a different location through the use of a magical phrase which activated both mirrors. You had to concentrate on where the other mirror was located to pass through. The only bad thing about using the mirror was that it stole a little bit of the user's life force every time someone went through it. The ambassador steadied his breathing and spoke the magical phrase that he knew would activate the mirror here and concentrated on the one inside his offices in the capitol city of Kallamar. He watched as its surface shimmered, swirled and changed into what looked like rippling water. Their reflections were replaced instead by what looked like an empty room in another place.

Dalmar looked at the image and remembered how much he hated the magical mirrors, taking another deep breath and thinking about his wife and new baby, he stepped into the large mirror.

An icy sensation scoured across his skin making it feel like he was being stuck by thousand needles and freezing him to the core of his very being. It only lasted for just a moment and Dalmar was stumbling out the mirror's other side. A second later Ferris also tumbled through and fell to his knees. He clutched at his stomach as he fought off the feelings of nausea and chilling cold that accompanied mirror walking.

Dalmar felt a self satisfied smile playing on his lips and allowed it to stay. He had at least managed to keep erect, but then he was more used to the mirrors effects than

Ferris was. They were now in his office where he kept another mirror in Kallamar, the capital city.

Turning to Ferris the ambassador said with a cold look on his face. "You do realize how much I hate to use that mirror don't you? This had better be worth my time because there is nothing in that document releases you from my services and if this is a waste, I will have you scrubbing pots with the kettle girls in the kitchen for the remainder of your time in Castlekeep."

"I really don't know how important this young man is milord, but Lord Cyadine told us that if we ever found him to come here as soon as possible because he was detrimental to the safety of the realm." Ferris said whining miserably. He had thought that the parchment was a way for him to have a little bit of power over the ex Marshall of the military, but now he was beginning to think he made a big mistake, especially where his job was concerned.

Dalmar sniffed contemptuously at the man's whining and said, "Well let's get this over with then." and he strode out of his quarters in Kallamar with the secretary trailing behind him once again. Thinking that it was late in the day and that the Royal Regent wouldn't be in the throne room holding court, he made his way through the palace towards his chambers.

A pair of very formidable looking Krannion knights stood guard in front of the two large oak and ironbound doors that led into Lord Vargas' royal quarters. Each of the knight's wore steel gray armor with a gold ring emblazoned on the front of their breastplates. A picture of a dragon in flight, breathing fire filled the ring. Both carried two very large swords which they unsheathed as the men approached and moved as one in front of the doors effectively blocking entry.

Dalmar recognized the older of the two men as one of the knight trainers who worked here in the palace and who had been here for a very long time. He was a grizzled, seasoned old veteran named Melrick.

"Melrick," the royal ambassador called out in a jovial manner that he wasn't really feeling. "Is he in there?" he didn't bother stating who, knowing that the knight protector and trainer was well aware of who it was that he would want to see.

"Well as I live to breathe, Lord Dalmar!" Melrick said also in a friendly manner. "He's in there ambassador, but he's left orders not to be disturbed unless the palace or the kingdom is being destroyed."

The younger knight next to the knight trainer never moved, he just stood there still as stone, a determinedly serious expression on his face. Something, Dalmar realized looked familiar about him, but he couldn't quite put a finger on it. Dalmar noticed he was keeping both of his dark brown eyes locked on his sneaky little rat faced secretary. "That," the ambassador thought to him self, "said a lot of good things about the young knight's instincts and judgment already." "What about Cyadine? Is he in there also?" Dalmar asked distastefully, he refused to call the royal advisor a Lord.

Melrick shook his head no, "I think that he is in his own chambers."

"Well." Dalmar said still sounding as if he had something foul in his mouth. "According to him," he said throwing a contemptuous glance at Ferris, "the kingdom is about to be. We need to see him and the advisor right away."

Melrick looked taken aback by Dalmar's statement. He wasn't aware of any kind of dire troubles in the realm, other than a little trouble in the realm that was Lord Dalmar's western province. With his position here in the castle guarding the royal regent, he usually knew of such things. "We do?" he asked, his eyebrows rising questioningly, "Have the western Highlords decided to change their revolt into a war or something?"

Dalmar just shook his head no at that and said, "It has nothing to do with that, I'm fairly certain, I really don't know what it is about, but from what I've been able to gather, Cyadine will want to be here for this also, so why don't we send this healthy young knight here," he indicated Melrick's handsome young trainee with the dark eyes. "After him and we will hold the fort down until he returns. We can rehash old times and tell some war stories while we wait."

Seeing the dubious look that flashed momentarily on the younger mans face he added, "Between the two of us, I'm sure we can protect Vargas from any assassins that might come calling during your brief absence."

Melrick laughed at this. The actual chance of any assassins actually making it this far into the castle was slim to none anymore. It wasn't really a laughing matter, though, Dalmar thought to himself, it had actually happened once twenty years ago when the Royal regent's brother, King Dorian his wife Lady Ellanor and their newborn twin children had been killed by a group of Terian invaders who had somehow made their way into the royal chambers during the birthing of the children and was remembered now as the night of sorrows.

Now there was a contingent of Krannion knights in enchanted armor that were stationed inside the castle itself to make sure that the same thing didn't happen twice. Melrick and the other young knight in training here at the door were more for ceremony and show than for real purpose, unlike the old days when the king and queen always had a single knight's champion to stand guard and protect them at all costs known as the Lord of the Winds.

Melrick had also noticed the dubious expression on the younger mans face and he said. "Go ahead Lance," a friendly but commanding tone went into his voice, "I'm sure that myself and Lord Dalmar here who also used to be the marshall of Kallamar's armies can handle this small task for a while."

Dalmar saw the younger mans eyes widen at Melrick's mention of his old title and realized that he hadn't even known who he was, "I am getting old" he thought silently to himself. At one time any soldier who heard his name would have quaked in his boots in fear and rushed as fast as he was ordered.

"Tell him also Lance, just to hurry him along, that I have one of his seekers here with me blathering something about his having found the one. Oh and also that I have one of his parchments," Dalmar added.

The young knight in training stepped forward and brought his arm up and thumped his opposite shoulder in a crisp salute, which Dalmar returned without thinking about, so ingrained was the movement in him. Then the younger man hurried off down the hall after Lord Cyadine.

"Who is he, Melrick and why does he seems so familiar to me?" Dalmar asked the knight trainer once the younger man was out of sight.

Melrick answered his face full of pride, "That is young Liolbane, eager to try and follow in his father's legendary footsteps."

"The protector's son and Lord of the Winds," Dalmar said incredulously staring after the young man, "now I understand why he seemed so reluctant to leave his post, especially after what happened to his father and the royal family."

Melrick's eyes suddenly darkened at this, "His father," the old knight said in a dull, flat voice, "Never did anything except for trying to stop attackers from killing the ones he had sworn to protect and he died while doing so."

Dalmar took a step back from the knight trainer, as he saw the other mans hand tighten noticeably on his sword hilt and held up his own hands defensively saying, "I didn't mean any disrespect Melrick," he had forgotten because it had been so long ago. Melrick had also helped to train the younger knight's father along with his own father too. "I never met him," the ambassador continued, "but any man who slays thirteen men while guarding a door by himself trying to save the royal family is more than worthy in my eyes and entitled to all my respect."

Melrick unclasped his hand from the swords hilt and the angry look faded from his face as fast as it had come and he apologized. "So Dalmar," he asked quickly changing the subject, "How is retirement treating you?" he looked the ambassador up and down saying. "Ambassador status doesn't seem to have put that much weight on you or made you too soft."

Dalmar grinned, saying a favorite phrase that he used in the military. "Eternal vigilance keeps you strong!" he been a soldier for over thirty years and the thought of not maintaining a physical sense of readiness, was a habit he found hard to break and he told Melrick this. Dalmar knew that regardless of whatever post Vargas stuck him in as an ambassador he would first and foremost be a soldier always in his heart.

A tall handsome looking man of about forty five years, who looked extremely fit with hair so blond it almost looked white came striding down the hallway towards the two men in a purposeful manner. He was wearing the red and black robes with gold trim that identified him as the royal advisor and head wizard in Kallamar.

The young knight they had sent after Lord Cyadine trailed along behind him. They all could hear the red and black robes hissing softly across the stone tiles like a snakes scales as he moved closer to them.

The moment that the adviser came into view Ferris bolted from the spot where he had been waiting. Throwing himself at the wizard's feet, he grabbed at the hem of Cyadine's robes saying, "I found him milord, I found him."

Cyadine rather arrogantly kicked out with one foot knocking the fat man away from him, then with a hand he reached out and easily picked the fat secretary up off of the floor and held him up at arm's length with a strong looking hand and arm that looked as if it mighty be better at holding a sword, rather than at working magic. His cold featured face and icy blue eyes studied Ferris' face for a moment before he said in an emotionless voice. "Good then, your mission is complete." then he dropped Ferris, who crumpled to the floor in a heap at Cyadine's feet.

Looking at Dalmar first, his blue ice like eyes narrowed into catlike slits and then at the other two knights, he said to the ambassador in a voice that almost sounded like a serpents hiss. "Who else has he spoken to besides you and them?"

"As far as I know he hasn't talked to anyone including them, he arrived panting and red-faced in my office demanding to be brought here." Dalmar stated eyeing the royal adviser with a cold look of his own. "As soon as possible and when I started to object he brandished this," Dalmar held up the old looking parchment that he had taken from Ferris for Cyadine to see.

"Good then you are finished here." Cyadine told the ex Marshall icily, dismissing him with a casual wave. "Ferris, you come with me," he said to the still cringing secretary lying on the floor at his feet.

"Before you dismiss me so casually, I would like to know what is going on here, I have the right." Dalmar said in a heated voice, eyes flashing dangerously as he reached out a hand and grabbed Cyadine by the shoulder as he started to turn away. "He is my secretary." he fixed a baleful glare on Ferris with those same angry eyes. "And whatever this is, it happened where I am the ambassador. I want to know who this person is and why he is so damned important!"

Cyadine spun quickly dislodging Dalmar's hand from his shoulder by dropping it a little, before answering in a cool tone, a hard edge filled his voice. "It doesn't concern you, Dalmar and if you persist in delaying me, I won't hesitate in putting into actions with you and yours what that document states will be done to those that delay."

Dalmar continued to stare hard at the advisor and saw nothing but his death in those ice blue eyes. Out of fear for his new family he reigned in his anger and dropped his still outstretched hand to his side. The ambassador and the two knights watched as Cyadine turned away again, opened the doors, took his secretary through them and closed the doors behind him. They slammed shut with an air of finality.

"What the hell was that all about?" Melrick demanded, then he pointed a finger at the crushed roll of parchment in Dalmar's clenched and quivering fist. "And what by the gods does that thing say?"

Dalmar handed him the parchment and watched as Melrick read it.

The knight trainer let a long hiss of air escape out through his teeth as his eyes moved down the page. "Is this thing for real?" he asked, as he finished reading the parchment and handed it back to Dalmar who stuck it into one of his pockets.

"It would seem so, Cyadine certainly seemed ready to enforce it quickly enough." Dalmar replied with more force in his voice than he intended. He was still somewhat angered with the royal advisors arrogant manner and tone.

"Whoever this person is that they are looking for, he must be extremely important to warrant such a document as that." Melrick said in a matter of fact manner, indicating Dalmar's pocket with his chin.

"Well it is out of my hands for now at least and I say good riddance!" Dalmar simply answered.

Melrick nodded in agreement.

The two men shared a few more war stories for a while until Dalmar finally made his farewells, saying that he had to return to Castlekeep and before he left he wanted to see his wife and the new baby. Melrick wished him well and as Dalmar turned to leave, he gave a final look at the other knight, the young man with the dark eyes who seemed so familiar, shook his head, then left.

Chapter 7
The Plan

Lord Cyadine Syndell, Kallamars head wizard and royal advisor to the throne and crown led the rat faced secretary through the Royal chambers until they came to a large sunroom where a short handsome older man with a neatly trimmed oiled goatee sat eating a meal with his back to them. He was accompanied by an elegant dark haired woman with finely sculpted beautiful features. The pair were having an animated conversation between bites of food. The dark haired man never turned his head towards Cyadine or the secretary trailing after him as they approached from behind him, but in the manner of one who was used to being obeyed he held up his hand stopping the conversation between himself and the Lady. In a cold and imperious voice he said without turning his head, "I thought I left orders not to be disturbed unless it was the direst of emergencies."

"One of my seekers has returned Sire." Cyadine said in

the same emotionless voice that he had used outside the door.

"Take care of it then Cyadine, I'm sure that you don't need me to hold your hand every time a problem arises do you?" Vargas asked him in an aggravated voice, sounding angry at having been disturbed over what he thought was a trivial matter.

Cyadine eyed the other man coldly for a moment and waited until the Royal Regent had dropped his hand and had taken another bite of the food that he was eating, before he spoke again saying. "Its one of the child seekers returned Sire!"

Vargas coughed and then gagged on his mouthful of food before spitting it back out of his mouth and onto the plate in front of him.

The royal advisor allowed a satisfied smile to cross his lips. Now he was quite certain that he had the Royal Regent's complete and full attention.

Vargas spun in his chair to face him, his features pale as he sputtered in a shocked voice. "Are you certain Cyadine, can you be sure?" the beautiful woman he had been having breakfast with was now completely forgotten.

"I'm as certain as I can be without actually seeing him myself, Sire," Cyadine clamped a strong hand down on the rat-faced secretary's shoulder pulling him forward. "Ferris here was one of our first seekers that I enchanted, I also placed a geas spell on him, which was to compel him to report immediately upon any discovery, as you can see this has happened."

Vargas listened intently to his adviser's words and then spoke to the woman sitting next to him sweetly. "Amora my love, we will have to change our plans to a different day, this is something so important that it cannot wait."

"But Vargas," she said in a sultry sulking tone, "you promised this day to me," she waved a long elegant hand at Cyadine as if she were dismissing him, "tell him that he'll just have to wait," she said haughtily then turned her face back to the royal regent and pouted. She continued to sit at the table until Vargas shouted. "Now!" in a commanding voice that allowed no type of disagreement.

Getting to her feet Amora strolled out across the room towards the door moving her beautiful body in such a manner that she was sure had the attention of both men's eyes as she left.

"Amora," Vargas called after her just as she was about to step through the door, his voice stooping her. "Have a servant find Gunther and tell him that he needs to be here also."

The beautiful woman's face went icy cold, turning she slammed the doors behind her closed without answering.

"So Cyadine," Vargas asked once Amora had left, "Where is he at?"

"Castlekeep, I assume sire," Cyadine answered with an air of disdain in his voice.

Vargas let out a loud groan of despair and dropped his dark head into his hands mumbling, "On top of all of our other problems with Lord Richard Daverge and the other six highlords in the west, why oh why does he have to be in his city of all places?" With his head still in his hands Vargas asked through his fingers. "Why did it have to be now and of all places on Tyrus why did it have to be there, the gods must be working against me?"

Ferris heard these words and felt his blood run cold in his veins, wondering how Lord Vargas would react when he heard that the man that they were seeking was also Lord Richards ward and adopted third son.

Cyadine shrugged his shoulders, not really having an answer for his ruler. He knew already that this was bad news but that there was nothing that he could do to change it at the moment.

"We've had seekers search there before Cyadine, why is it that we've never found him before now? What does he do there, he's got to be twenty years old by now, so he must have a job doing something?" the royal regent asked in a demanding voice.

"I don't know sire, I haven't had a chance to question him yet." Cyadine said, directing a glance over at Ferris, who cringed like a beaten dog when both of their stares fell on him. "Dalmar was the one who brought him in and I thought that you would like to hear his answers first hand and questioning him in front of Dalmar seemed a bit inappropriate."

"Of course you are right Cyadine." Vargas answered as he considered his mages words.

"Dalmar with his bloody sense of honor and decency could bring this whole thing crashing down about our heads especially, if he had found out the true identity of the young man whom our seeker here has found."

Cyadine smiled a contemptuous smile at his lord. "Of course he was right," he thought silently to himself, he just had to take the time to explain it to this idiot who ruled standing in front of him.

The door to the chamber burst open at that moment, the man who entered the royal suites threw back the hood on his cloak revealing a thick mane of long stark white hair. He looked as if he had been outside in the rain. The man would have been considered ruggedly handsome if not for a disfiguring long vicious, jagged scar that ran from the corner of his right eyelid down to his mouth, giving his handsome face a rather hideous evil looking grin. He was tall, powerfully built with wide broad shoulders. Even though he was old, he didn't appear to be old enough to have such unnaturally stark white hair. The large mans metal shod boots rang on the floor as he strode into the room and you couldn't help but notice the silver and gray chain mail armor of a Krannion knight that he was wearing under his wet cloak. Unlike the other two men posted outside the door though the edges of his armor was trimmed in white as well as gold identifying him as a proctor, one of the chosen Lords men who were in charge of units of Krannion knights in the cities. Around his neck he wore a large gold medallion on a gold chain, which also identified his rank as the royal protector.

Vargas and Cyadine also wore identifying medallions that named their position in society's elite upper classes.

The newcomer's name was Gunther Haldron and immediately he began to speak in a gravelly deep voice. "What's going on sire? Amora said that you practically threw her out of here, when she found me practicing in the courtyard with several knights in training."

Vargas almost laughed at Gunther's statement about Amora and then remembering why he had called him here sobered considerably, "One of Cyadine's child seekers has finally returned with information about the child and we were getting ready to question him about his whereabouts when you arrived."

"After all of this time Cyadine, I was beginning to have my doubts," Gunther said with a wry smile and in a derisive manner.

Cyadine sniffed, but said nothing, there was no sense in arguing with the man about something so senseless, the knight had a well-known disdain for most things magical, preferring instead to rely on his prowess with weapons. He knew that he was deadlier than the knight proctor with either one, weapons or spells.

Vargas chose to ignore both of the two men and fixed his attention on the fat secretary with a look that froze him in place. "Now that we're all here," he said in a voice loud enough to get the other two's attention off of each other and onto the matter at hand, "who is he and where does he live in the city?"

Ferris actually cringed again and started to shrink away when he heard the question, then he remembered no matter how bad the information was he had done his job well and had been promised a huge reward for his service, so he spoke telling them all he knew about the young man he had found. He explained the whole story about how he had found him fighting in the pit and about how his quarry having just returned from the academe where he had been trained as a battlemage.

As he said this part about his quarry being a battlemage Cyadine's head jerked as if he had been shocked. The others turned to look at him and he waved them off with a hand, gesturing for the still slightly shaking secretary to continue.

The secretary did so and also told them about him being the adopted son of Lord Richard Daverge, which caused another groan to issue forth from the royal regent. When asked about why he had never found this young man before, Ferris explained that the young battlemage had already left for Westlake before he had been stationed in Castlekeep. Other than asking why he hadn't found him before now all three men sat in silence until the secretary had finished speaking, each letting the news of what he had told them sink in.

Finally it was the royal regent who spoke, breaking the still silence. "He is Lady Alice's cousin and far enough away that he could safely hide the child."

"It would also explain," Cyadine said with a thoughtful expression on his face, "why Lord Richard who for the past twenty years who has been such an active supporter of the throne and the crown is acting the way that he is now and also why the other six western Highlords have fallen in with him. They all have to know who this child is and the claim that he is entitled to since he has been of age for almost two years now."

"It would stand to reason," Gunther added, "that this is also why Lord Richard has orchestrated this rebellion to declare the western states exempt from the new tax laws." He looked at the other two men a moment then continued.

"He can win a lot of people over to his side on just his charisma alone and the legitimacy of this young mans claim is indisputable if he can prove who he is, all will flock to the feet of a king."

"The worst part is," Cyadine said as he tapped at his lips with his long fingers as he always did when thinking or contemplating, "that almost nothing can be done to stop it short of a war for another couple of months until your own son Seth comes of age and can take the crown and throne for himself as the new rightful ruler."

"So where exactly does that leave us?" Vargas asked his dark brown eyes drilling into both of the men who helped serve as his advisors. "I mean couldn't we just dispute Lord Richards claim? We could stretch it out two more months until my son's naming day. I mean how much of a threat could a twenty year old boy pose to me as ruler of this land, that I as its ruler with all of its power couldn't overcome?"

Both Gunther and Cyadine looked at each other in astounded amazement and then they turned their stares to their lord as if they could scarcely believe what they had just heard him say. It was immediately obvious to both men that the Royal Regent didn't quite understand the eminent danger that this boy placed him in, placed all of them in.

"I would worry about it Sire," Gunther said in as direct a manner as he could manage. "I would worry about it very much so if I were you!"

"How so Gunther?" Vargas sneered condescendingly. "We do rule here! I am in control of all of the kingdom and its forces."

"What Gunther is trying to impress upon you, Sire," Cyadine said in a placating voice in an attempt to cool his lord's ire before it boiled over and he did something stupid. "Is that the significance of this boy, if his very existence with his lineage becomes known, would mean that because he is of age to inherit the throne he is in actuality the real crown prince and the rightful ruler of the fourteen kingdoms right now! Unlike you or your own son Seth, who can't and won't inherit the throne and the crown for another two more months and only if there are no direct descendants in line."

Vargas turned a queasy shade of green at hearing his advisors words.

Cyadine continued speaking, "Since this Damien Daverge is of legal age right now, actually you now have no royal power at all. He is really the true ruler here and in charge of all that power you have, which you won't have any more or at least not for much longer anyways if he can prove his claim."

Vargas looked visibly shaken now as Cyadine finished and asked in an uneasy voice, directing the question to both men. "What can we do then to prevent this boy from taking over the throne or at least proving his legitimate birthright?"

This time it was Gunther who answered the royal regent's question. "We have to put a stop to this boy before any of this can happen, remove him before he can lay any claims, draw anyone to him or make it here. He can only be crowned king if he is in Kallamar alive before Seth's naming day."

Cyadine nodded at Gunther's words, even though he didn't like the proctor that much, he did sometimes agree with him.

"Couldn't I just have Dalmar remove Richard Daverge from his office? Have him and his whole family arrested for treason against the throne? Wouldn't that take care of this young man?" asked Vargas, looking at the pair.

"No," said Cyadine quietly and Gunther now shook his head, finding himself agreeing with the royal advisors words.

"That won't do, at least not yet," the Krannion knight

commander stated. "I'm sure that Richard isn't the only person in the west who knows about whom this young man is and he probably has a contingency plan in place just in case something like that ever did happen. More than likely such a plan includes Devlin Bonebreaker, of the dwarves and Lord Gildon Seahorn of Caladar," Gunther cocked an eyebrow and added, "Wouldn't he actually be the young man, this Damien Daverge's uncle?"

"It would," answered Cyadine, then he added with a cynical laugh, "it would also, make him your nephew too, Sire."

The Royal Regent waved this away with his hand, not interested in hearing any of this.

"So what," he asked looking at the two men speculatively, "can we do about this? That we can get away with, that won't incite a revolution amongst all fourteen of the kingdoms? This young man could ruin us and everything that we have done over the past twenty years."

Cyadine struck a thoughtful pose and once again tapped his pursed lips with his long finger, his battlemage trained mind running through every option, then his icy blue eyes lit up. "We'll have Caliban take care of it, quickly and silently. It's time that he proved his worth to the realm," he said referring to his own son who lived with him here in the castle. "He can also take care of any links such as Dalmar after he finishes with this battlemage heir, that way nothing of this can be traced back to us and the young man's claim never gets made. Without an heir, there can't be a revolution, I can go ahead and take care of this link here to us right now," he finished, lowering his strong hand down onto the cringing Ferris' shoulder again and gripped it tightly.

"E...Ex.... Excuse me," stammered the wide-eyed secretary, raising his fearful face to look up into blond haired wizard's cold blue eyes. "What do you mean by taking care of me, I hope it has to do with my reward, I was promised a reward for my services."

"And now you'll receive it," answered the royal advisor and wizard, a small smile playing across his lips. A quick flash of steel glinted in the rooms light and Cyadine's arm struck like a cobra, swift and deadly, plunging a long knife deep into the fat secretary's throat.

Ferris let out a startled gurgle of surprise and the royal wizard quickly stepped off to one side as a fountain of blood sprayed out from the open wound when he removed the blade. The tiled floor at the secretary's feet turned bright red in color.

The fat secretary's legs gave way and the three men watched with no remorse showing on their faces or in their eyes as he collapsed onto the floor, his life's blood spilling out of him in a growing pool.

Cyadine casually dropped the dagger, where it fell next to Ferris' hand, saying as he did so, "I believe, sire, that he tried to assassinate you."

"You might be right Cyadine," Vargas said a slight smile on shrewd face. "Luckily for me you were there to stop him." then all three men laughed at the idea of the fat cowardly secretary ever even trying such a brave act.

Vargas said, "So, we are decided on what we are we going to do about this boy battlemage and," he paused for a moment thoughtfully then added, "the ambassador too."

Cyadine answered, "I'll have Caliban take care of it and link Dalmar in the attempt. Maybe we can even make it also look like a treasonous plot by Richard Daverge so we can legally remove him too."

"Are you sure that your young protégé is up to the task, can he handle such huge task with so much responsibility?" Gunther asked the wizard in a mildly condescending manner.

Cyadine turned to face the proctor for a moment, his icy blue eyes turned cold and dangerous. "I'm sure that he can manage, but if you have any doubts I could have him kill a few of your knights for you if you wish." Cyadine threw a look at the door, "Maybe we could even start with the young man who is stationed outside of this door." referring to Lance Liolbane, Gunther's nephew and adopted son that he had raised as such since birth.

Gunther's eyes flashed angrily and turned dangerous but he quickly got it under control and muttered that, "no that wouldn't be necessary" through tightly clenched teeth.

Vargas had not been listening to the other men's arguing. Instead he was mulling the news he had heard over in his own head when something occurred to him. "If," he asked interrupting the other two men, "the maid who escaped, took the child, why did she go to Castlekeep with it? The queen did drop the other child and we know it fell in the river where it sank, right Gunther?"

The large proctor face tightened noticeably for a moment as he relived his betrayal of his sworn oaths before he nodded his head yes

Vargas continued, "then how are they going to go about proving the legitimacy of this child anyway, how do they know," he asked as the other two men looked at him curiously, "that the young man is the heir? We know through him and the blood magic." Vargas pointed at the dead body of the secretary lying on the floor. "but how do they know? Gunther, you are certain that the other child did indeed drown when the queen dropped it."

"The queen," Gunther said in a matter of fact manner, his voice hard as stone, "had a breast full of arrows. I watched her drop the babe into the rushing water where it sank under. There's no way that any child other than the one that the protector managed to save along with the maid who escaped survived. Everyone else died. The only other person who managed to survive the whole thing was Lady Alice, the mother to the queen and no one exactly knows how she managed to escape."

"None of this matters," stated Cyadine, interrupting the

other two, "we have found the one who still lives and we now know where he is. All we have to do is rid ourselves of him in order to stay in power and that's all we need to worry about doing right now."

"You're right, Cyadine," Vargas agreed, "So get to it then. Have your son take care of it and report back to me when it's done."

Knowing that there was nothing else left to discuss, the other two men turned away from their ruler and made their exit from the royal chambers.

* * *

Cyadine Syndell moved through the palace towards the lower sections that he called his own, thinking to himself. "So the heir to the throne was a new battlemage," The royal advisor kept turning this thought over and over in head. There was a legend amongst his real masters that had to do with a battlemage becoming king. He would have to pass this advice, he decided on to his master, tomorrow after the young heir was already dead.

Once he had himself been through Battlemage School and would have graduated at the top of his class if he hadn't been cast out just days before he was set to receive his black and gold robes. He had been expelled from the order by his own battlemaster who had caught him studying the forbidden types of creational magic with a group of Elvynn mages. The academe did not possess any proof of this, but had acted on the words of his battlemaster alone. This hadn't bothered Cyadine at all. It had in fact released him to study under a new order of wizards and allowed him to have his own type of revenge by teaching the Elvynn Tua-latin all of what he knew of battlemages and of their tactics in warfare. What had bothered him was the fact that his battlemaster had betrayed him for doing exactly as he had taught him.

He had remained in Westlake for several years after being expelled, learning his new craft under the tutelage of the head of the Elvynn wizard conclave Latherias Yematt, but never practicing it there, the danger of being discovered was too great. A lady who he had come to know and lived with for a while had allowed herself to become pregnant against his wishes, he had not wanted the responsibility of a child and had left Westlake. By a stroke of the gods own luck, he had hooked up with a self imposed exiled Krannion knight named Gunther Haldron and the fourth son to the old king of Kallamar named Vargas Salidor and between them with all their disgruntlement, they had hatched a plan to take over the rule of the realm over twenty years ago and they had done just that without any troubles until today.

The royal wizard stepped through the doors to his personal chambers. His chambers were two levels, the first level consisted of several rooms, including a study and training room. The second level was his lab where he worked and practiced his magic.

A young man with hair whiter than even his own blond locks sat kneeling in meditation where he had ordered him to stay until he had returned. The slate blue eyes that burned with an intensive type of inner fire opened as he entered and locked on his own light blue ones.

This was his son, Caliban Syndell, he had left the boy in Westlake when he had gone on to do his masters bidding, to live with his mother the whore, but several years later his master of his order had told him to retrieve the child and train him like he had been trained by the Academe. When his son was only four years old, he had kidnapped him from his mother. Since then, for all of his life, Caliban had trained to be a battlemage and about magic, in both its lesser and superior forms, turning him into a perfectly honed living weapon.

Caliban could feel his father's own cold blue eyes

boring into him hard. He knew then that the time had finally come for his first mission into the realm by the intense look in them. Almost casually he wondered whom the renegade battlemage was, that he was supposed to kill. That was what his father had told him his purpose in the realm was. He had been taught since childhood, that he was to rid the kingdoms of renegade battlemages that were a threat to the throne and the crown. He considered his duty a noble calling.

Dalmar examined his reflection in his regular mirror back in Castlekeep, making sure that all of his clothing, along with his own appearance looked presentable for the ball. He was startled when the door to the inner chamber where he kept the mirror of walking opened and a young man of about twenty years old stepped through into his private quarters wearing a formal outfit of black dress clothes with silver trim. The young mans hair was pale white and he had cold slate blue eyes that seemed totally devoid of any sort of emotion. Dalmar had never met Cyadine's protégé and son, but he recognized this young man instantly. At seeing the black and silver outfit, he had thought for a moment before he had seen the young mans face that the young man with the slightly Elvynn features might have been a member of the Elvynn Tua-latin. The young man didn't speak at first as he entered the room. Instead he eyed the ambassador as if he was taking his measure, for what though Dalmar thought, he wasn't sure.

"My name," the young man said in a cool tone, "is Caliban Syndell, I will be replacing your secretary Ferris for a while and I am also to serve as a body guard for you."

Dalmar drew back a moment startled at the young mans surprising words then he asked. "What happened to Ferris?"

The young man with the white blonde hair let a cold smile that didn't seem to touch his eyes play upon his mouth for a moment before he answered saying. "It seems that he developed a rather sudden and fatal illness and wasn't able to return."

Dalmar returned the young man's stare a moment, refusing to let him know how much the look in his cold dead blue eyes bothered him before he asked. "What do you mean by fatal illness, exactly?" He added for emphasis.

The look in the young mans eyes was one that he had seen in the most dangerous of soldiers eyes. It said that they didn't care whether or not they lived or died, those type of eyes had always unnerved him, just like his did now.

The ambassador already knew the answer to his question though even before the cold faced young man responded. Cyadine must have had his secretary killed for what though he wasn't sure but he had an idea that it had to do with whoever it was that Ferris had found.

"Your secretary," Caliban said in an emotionless voice, "tried to assassinate the royal regent with a poisoned dagger."

"Surely you're joking!" Dalmar blurted out in an incredulous voice as the words hit his ears, then he recovered and said. "Ferris might be a pig and a worm and his character is sorely lacking and sometimes a bit of concern, but the one thing my secretary was and had always been is or was is a coward, I wouldn't think he would have it in him to try and kill anyone much less the royal regent of the realm."

"A hundred gold marks were found inside of Ferris' robes along with a vial containing the same poison that was coating the dagger that he had tried to use on Lord Vargas."

Dalmar shook his head disbelievingly, still not quite believing what it was he was hearing.

"Someone here in Castlekeep sent him," Caliban stated, "and whoever that person is, I am supposed to find out and make sure that they are arrested for treason against the throne."

"Treason!" echoed Dalmar incredulously.

The young man in the black and silver outfit nodded seriously and said, "I am to accompany you tonight to the festival ball at the castle." his slate blue eyes locked on Dalmar's, "to insure that you are well protected and to make sure that whoever failed in this attempt doesn't try to kill you too for your knowledge in this matter also. You are the only link between the throne and whoever sent your secretary to kill the royal regent."

Dalmar heard the distinctive phrase spoken by the young man in front of him when he said, your secretary, he eyed the young man critically and found that even though he was not a soldier, there was definitely something military like about him in his manner and appearance that seemed to suggest that he was indeed quite capable of protecting him.

"Does this," the ambassador asked, "have anything to do with the person who my secretary found today?"

"We believe so," answered Caliban, "they probably found out that he had discovered them and paid him off to try and kill Lord Vargas instead. No one knows for sure yet. Maybe they will try to make an attempt on your life and we can catch them in the act of doing so."

Dalmar considered this, the idea of Ferris actually trying to kill the royal regent, he found it ridiculous, but something was going on here and the only way he was actually going to find out what it was, would be to go along with this story for a while. So he said, "You look suitable for the job then. Let's go. It's time to leave. We have a ball to attend."

Chapter 8
Friendship

Damien entered his chambers, which consisted of a large greeting room, a bedroom off to the right, a library and study off to the left. The first thing he noticed was the large amounts of dust that had accumulated during his long absence. It looked as if everything in all of the rooms had been covered with a thin gray blanket. Not really thinking he stepped through his study and unslinging his traveling pack, tossed it across the room and onto his bed.

A huge cloud of the grey dust leapt up from the bed as the heavy bag landed, filling the air with thousands of dust motes. They glittered like silver fairie dust in the yellow sunlight streaming through the tall windows set in the far wall.

Cursing himself for his own stupidity, Damien said a quick cleaning cantrip, a minor spell that didn't require hardly any effort. A magical broom appeared, sweeping through all of the rooms in his chambers gathering all of the dust into one large pile. Stepping over to the tall windows along one wall, he pulled them open. The west wing of his castle overlooked sheer bleak black walls, tall craggy cliffs and the Eversea Ocean far below. Damien immediately tasted the salt on the air as a slight breeze blew inside. Still using his magic he directed the huge pile of dust through the air between himself and the open window.

As he brought the huge pile of dust closer to the window, he felt a tickle in his nose and knew a sneeze was coming.

Sneezes were by far, the single most dangerous thing that could happen to any magic user, including battlemages and war wizards. A simple sneeze could disrupt any spell, from the simplest to the most powerful in an instant, causing the arcane energies being wielded and gathered to go awry. At best, the spell being cast simply dissipates depending on its strength. Other times though, a sneeze could cause catastrophic results, sometimes even killing the caster or destroying everything around him or her in an explosion of power.

Damien knew that he had to reach the window with the dust before he sneezed and had just cleared the sill when it came, simply dissipating the easy spell. He sighed, grateful that he hadn't had to re clean up the pile of dust, when heard a noise a familiar tapping sound coming from behind him.

The thump of a hard wood staff on the stone floor announced the presence in his doorway, "If you hadn't left that nasty glyph on the door I could have arranged for your chambers to have been properly prepared before you arrived." called a hollow sounding voice from behind him.

"Well said Abraim," answered Damien smiling dryly, he knew who was there without even having to turn around.

It was his father's chamberlain and master of servants, also Damien's tutor in his scholarly studies for many years standing in the doorway. He still carried the same hard wood staff that he had for years used on everyone inside the castle on his staff to keep them in line. It was also the same one that he had used to defeat Travis once when he thought the blademaster had overstepped his bounds. The same one used train him before Tiko.

Damien had heard its tapping on the floor stones as he approached. Any member of the "staff", who didn't act the way they were supposed to, or didn't move fast enough in their duties, would usually answer to the staff. Abraim wielded the long stick like a deadly weapon, swatting hands heads feet or any other part of the body he could connect with if he thought it was needed. Damien could remember himself being on the receiving end of the hard wood staff plenty of times. Not as many as Logan his boyhood friend and companion had, but enough nonetheless. Everyone in the castle loved the fierce old man like an aged uncle. In Lord Richards eyes the old man could make no mistake. His father never ever once had to criticize the old man in his duties and to Abraim that in itself was the highest form of compliment he could ever receive.

Abraim focused his large owl like eyes on Damien and looked him over from head to toe, a disgusted look showed on his gaunt, thin face as he studied the young battlemages dirty and dusty traveling clothes and generally overall scruffy appearance. Arching an aged eyebrow, he stated, "Milord if you will remove those filthy disgusting rags that you are wearing, I will see that they are properly disposed of." he pursed his thin lips together thoughtfully and then added aloud. "By burning again probably."

Damien shook his head from side to side saying, "There will be no burning today, Abraim, they will be washed and returned." As boys, he and Logan had gotten their clothes so dirty and smelly at times that the chamberlain had been left with no other recourse other than burning several of their outfits.

"And, what happened to proper greetings of family members." Damien asked, smiling mischievously. "Where is my embrace?" then he stepped forward, spreading his arms out wide as if he intended to clasp the tall skinny chamberlain to him for a dirty hug.

Abraim's long staff snaked out, as quickly as a viper striking and thumped Damien in the center of his chest with one of its ends, stopping him in his tracks faster than even he could block it.

"I'll not have you come any closer Milord, at least not while you are wearing those filthy things you have on" and he sniffed the air about him distastefully.

Damien smiled a wide smile, holding up his hands in a gesture of surrender and defeat.

The tall skinny old man smiled now for the first time since entering Damien's chambers, "I see that during your time at the academe, the mages didn't find any way to remove your sense of play."

The young battlemage continued smiling, "Never happen Abraim. Life's no fun unless you play," he said stepping over to his wardrobe closet and pulling it open, gesturing to the closet of too small clothes that he knew would be in there from six years earlier. "If you burn my clothes what will I have to wear? I'm sure that none of these will fit anymore."

Abraim looked into the closet then at Damien, sniffed loudly before saying. "I see what you mean. You have grown a little bit since you left haven't you? Well no matter, I'm sure I can find something appropriate for you for the ball. Until then though, take off those filthy rags so that I can have them laundered."

"Not burnt though," Damien added and waited until the chamberlain nodded his assent.

Without even thinking about it, he shed himself of his road stained traveling clothes and handed them over to Abraim, who held them out with one hand at arms length, as far from his body as he could. "You still have time to visit the bathhouse, find something to wear there and go, by the time you return, I'll have found something appropriate for you to wear to the festival."

Damien held up a hand saying flatly and firmly. "Hold for one minute." the pleasant smile sliding from his face and he spoke his next words with a little bit of iron in them. "I will see to my own attire for the banquet and ball, I do not need for you to play dress maid for me any longer Abraim, I have been dressing my own self for a long time now, all I need, is for you to find something for me to wear after the festivities."

Another slow smile now spread across Abraims old face. "You are right Milord and I see that the mages academe also returned you more of a man rather than the mischievous child who left here who never thought ahead. Welcome home, Damien."

It was then Damien realized that Abraim had been both testing him, as well as teasing him to see how he would react about burning his clothes and the whole bit.

Abraim tapped his long chamberlain's staff on the floor bowed his aged white head and headed out of the room saying that he would find some more appropriate clothes for him to wear for after the ball.

Regardless of whatever Abraim found and deemed appropriate for after the ball Damien already knew what clothes he was going to wearing tonight. Before the chamberlain passed out of the door Damien remembered something, actually two somethings he had forgotten about during the exchange and called out. "Abraim, I arranged to have some crates shipped back here from Westlake, have they arrived yet?"

"Yes Milord, they arrived yesterday, if you would like I could have some people bring them up."

"Yes please do immediately, I have some things in those crates that I would like to have and oh." he knew that the next question would irk the old man, so he also knew that he had to ask. "Have you seen Logan anywhere? I figured he would have stopped in by now to see me."

Abraim frowned disapprovingly like he always did at the mention of Logan Longshadow's name. "I'm sure that he's around somewhere and if I know him he will find you when he's ready. He's probably busy stealing something right now or into some kind of trouble somewhere, he always is." The tall skinny chamberlain turned and left, his long staff thumping along as he went.

Damien closed the thick door behind him. Having removed all of his clothes for Abraim, he shivered slightly from a cool breeze that blew in through the open windows and felt goose bumps rise on his exposed flesh. He had to wear something down to the bathhouse, which was right outside the main building of the keep. He couldn't just go down there naked.

The bathhouse was a gift from one the first rulers of Castlekeep, when the keep was first constructed, as a wedding present to his new wife. A natural hot spring ran underneath the city and he had commissioned that a bathhouse using the mineral rich waters from the spring be built.

As Damien had pointed out to Abraim the clothes in his wardrobe closet were indeed too small for him to wear anywhere, attempting to wear any of them would almost be considered obscene. Damien considered this dilemma for a couple of moments, deciding that the side of the building in which he was in, was near one of the exits he could use to get to the bathhouse. If he kept an eye out for guests he should be able to make it without being seen or having any embarrassing moments. Grabbing the blanket off of his bed, he wrapped it about his naked form and peered out around the doorway to his room checking for any guests. Not seeing anyone he quickly headed out towards the baths, the blanket trailed out behind him like a long cloak as he hurried down the hall.

Without any incidences occurring, he made it to the bathhouse and entered quietly, without stepping all the way in to the main part, he quickly peered around the wall separating the entrance from the baths, not seeing anyone, he made his way inside the main room.

The tubs were aligned in neat rows with movable curtains hanging from rings connected to bars on the ceiling to afford privacy to those that desired it. Also there were cubicles set aside for changing, these were filled with thick towels. The floor was a roughhewn flagstone, cut so that it kept you from slipping when entering into or exiting out of the baths. There was also a large pool of the heated water, where you could swim the entire length of the large building. Misty tendrils of thick steam snaked up from the pools, filling the entire room concealing most of the tubs and half of the pool from view.

Damien hung the dusty blanket on a peg that was set in the wall for clothes and stepped over to the huge main pool. The battlemage slowly sank into the hot steaming water and allowed himself to float in the heavy water, thick with minerals from the natural springs flowing underneath.

The heat from the water loosened sore and cramped muscles and as it penetrated his body he felt the day's tensions ease away from him with it. He lay there floating for a while and wondered where in the world Logan was. It wasn't like his boyhood friend not to be around whenever he had arrived. He figured that he should have seen him the moment that he had actually entered the city, but here he had been home for a while now, at least a few hours and had not seen neither hide nor hair of the sandy haired troublemaking young looking thief.

Logan Longshadow was Damien's best friend and had been so since they were both very young boys. Logan was always in trouble and was forever breaking any and all rules. Like himself, Logan was also an orphan, his parents had been traveling traders coming with a load of goods from one of the eastern cities on their way to Castlekeep for the bazaar about thirteen years ago when a band of robbers had attacked them along the highwayman's trail. Both of his parents and his brother had been killed in the robbery but they had also managed to kill all of the bandits attacking them. Logan had been the only survivor of the attack. Without any one left in the world to help take care of him, the resourceful eight year old, had driven his families wagons and goods on to Castlekeep by himself and sold all of the goods at the bazaar. Not having any family though and all by himself with nothing except for the money he had earned, Logan had became a child of the streets. It wasn't long before he was picked up by the cities thieving guild and put to work for them.

    He had learned trading and all sorts of other skills from his parents including several languages fluently, which included Terian, Dwarven and Elvynn. The thieves' headmaster Jediaa Thirel, of whom few knew his true name, realized Logan was the gem that he had in his hands. Quickly Logan was heading one of the childhood gangs that worked the cities streets. That was how they had met.

    Damien remembered that day like it was yesterday while he floated in the steamy hot soothing water. As a child, he hadn't been allowed off of the castle grounds for some unknown reason. One day he decided that enough was enough and had snuck out through one of the servants entrances dressed as one of them in order to see the city. He quickly became lost amongst the cities many streets. Not knowing where he was, he found a small market where he could ask for directions. Then he had spotted a boy about his age, maybe a little older with the sandy blond hair and bright green eyes, stealing a piece of fruit from one of the corner side vendors. Being the ruling lord's son he had marched up to the vendor and in front of the whole crowd informed him of the stealing boy's actions. The vendor, a fat pig faced man, had stepped out from behind his stall and chased the blond haired boy, catching him a mere instant before he could make good his escape. The man drew the young boy up off of his feet and gave him a couple of hard nocks on the head with the knuckles of his hands, accompanied by such a hard shaking that Damien was sure that it had made the boy's teeth rattle before he let him go. They both turned and gave Damien black looks. He hadn't understood why at that time. As the day grew a little longer and his sense of adventure dwindled, he crossed paths again with the sandy blond haired boy where he learned the answer to his question.

It seemed that the other older boy had followed him about the city until he entered a place where no one was around then he had dropped down from an overhead rooftop and cornered Damien in an alley.

Grabbing him by the front of his servant's shirt the sandy haired boy had slammed him backwards into a wall. This time his teeth had rattled in his skull. Holding him in place with one hand wrapped in the front of his shirt and the other clamped up against his throat, the blond haired boy was shouting, "Do you realize what you have done?"

"What did I do? You were stealing!" he had stated, as he had leaned his head back in an effort to draw in air, "and stealing is wrong."

"You ruined one of my best runs in one of the richer parts of the city by drawing attention like that to me and Faren today," the other boy had shouted into his face.

Damien remembered feeling confused as he had asked in a bewildered voice. "What are you talking about? I really don't understand. You were stealing and I turned you in. If you don't change your ways it will probably get worse next time and someday you might even find yourself swinging from a rope in the gallows."

The young man had looked at Damien's face for a long moment before he lowered his eyes and studied his attire.

A King's Quest

"Where do you come from servant boy that you can come off sounding so high and mighty? You act like your some sort of lord's son, where your every need is catered to and you've never had to steal food just to stay alive!"

Damien had let the remark about the castle slide right by as he responded to the second part of the other boys' statement with astonished wonder in his voice. "You have had to steal fruit in order to stay alive here in Castlekeep?" He had never heard of such a thing inside the castle and realized right then that the world outside the castle might be a lot different and more dangerous place than he had suspected. Maybe he should be a little bit more careful.

"Actually," the boy said releasing Damien's neck and shirt, waggling his fingers in front of his eyes. ""Thanks to these, I haven't had to steal fruit for a long time. What you witnessed today was supposed to be a reward for services already rendered."

"What services?" Damien was not entirely sure what the answer would be, but he thought he was beginning to understand the black looks that both the red faced vendor and the boy had thrown his way earlier. They had been stealing from the people in the line and had been splitting the money between them. He had never even heard of such a thing in the castle and had apologized to the other boy, saying how sorry he was and offering to repay any losses he might have incurred.

Logan had stared at him for a long time at this statement until he both broke out into laughter, then they both started laughing.

They had talked away the whole afternoon till early evening about things that boys talk about. Damien learned that while traveling, Logan's parents and his older brother had been killed by raiders. Logan in turn learned that Damien had never known his parents but had instead been adopted as third son of a house, through a promise made from his adopted father to his real father. Logan had explained to Damien about the thieves' guild and how he was in charge of the children's pick pocketing network.

Damien remembered at the time asking Logan what the network was.

Logan had explained to him that network was what the thieves called the guild. He also learned that a man who called himself the nighttasker headed the guild or the network. He was in charge of all illegal and illicit activity in Castlekeep. Jediaa was the night taskers name and nothing went on in his city as Logan called it without him knowing about it.

Damien remembered what Logan had said about running the child thieves and had asked him. "If you run the children then that must mean that you are pretty good at what you do?"

Logan's chest had swelled up with pride as he answered. "The finest pick pocket in the whole city, man, woman or child."

"If you are so good at what you do, how is it that I saw you stealing fruit?" Damien had asked him curiously.

Logan had thought about that for a few moments then shrugged his shoulders. "Anyone can be at the right place at the right time. Most adults tend to overlook me because I am a child. You probably noticed me because you are a child, too." Logan then shook his head repeating from before, "Though, because you did draw attention to me in a public place, I won't be able to work that area for a while. Jediaa won't be too happy about that."

Damien had asked him why and Logan had explained that the section of the city where he had caught him at was one of the richest areas of the city and he made a lot of money there both for himself and the network.

"I'll have to work another area for a while for getting caught and losing money. I don't know how Jediaa will take it, the last thief who lost so much money he had the skin flogged right off of his back with the learning lash."

Damien had stared at the young thief aghast, his mouth hanging wide open, he didn't even have to ask what the learning lash was, until he saw the look of merriment showing in the others bright green eyes and had realized he was joking.

But then he had a thought and blurted out. "If you really think though that you are going to get in trouble, maybe I could have my father talk to this Jediaa so that he won't get too angry. He does have a way of getting people to do what he wants whenever he speaks."

Logan had looked at him incredulously saying. "I don't think Lord Richard himself could put off Jediaa's anger about losing money, much less your adopted father."

Damien had realized then that he hadn't mentioned to his new friend, as he had all of a sudden come to think of the other child, where he lived or whom he was and had said proudly. "Lord Richard is my adopted father and I'm his ward. If I ask him, I'm sure that he would help, I don't ever really ask for much."

Logan's eyes had gone wide when he had heard Damien's words. Then all of a sudden he remembered the manners that he had learnt from his parents and bending his head low, he had quickly knelt down on one knee in front of Damien stammering. "I...I'm sorry milord, I didn't recognize you, I apologize for following you and trying to scare you and for putting my hands on your person."

He had seemed at that moment very scared and very shaken, in fact as long as Damien had known Logan that had been the only time he had ever seen the brash young man scared ever.

He had been awestruck by this display, no one in the castle had ever bent a knee to him and they had all acted as if he was unimportant. Quickly he had grabbed the young sandy blonde thief by the shoulders and had hauled him back up onto his feet. "No need for that, I'm not that important." He looked around to make sure no one else had seen them.

Eyes still wide with awe Logan said, "What do you mean that you're not that important?" he looked at him like he had grown horns right out of his head. "You live in the castle and you are the adopted son of a Highlord of the cities. Your father rules the largest city in the west." he gestured in the castles direction. "You really live in the castle."

Damien had nodded sheepishly, he had seen people act the way that Logan was acting around his father but he had never thought that someone would ever act that way around him. He had thought for a minute about Logan getting in trouble because of him, then he had remembered what the other boy had said about his being an orphan too and an idea had come to him.

"Why don't you come home with me?" he had asked the other boy that day twelve years ago.

At first, Logan had scoffed at the idea, "Me in the castle? I doubt very much that the guards would even let me through the front gates, much less actually inside the castle itself."

"And why not?" Damien asked. Then he realized that he already knew why. He had seen the guards turn away people that they thought were unsavory or didn't belong, just because they could. He thought about this a moment before he answered. He remembered the way that Logan had just reacted by getting down on one knee to show fealty to him. Damien realized then what his position as his father's ward and an adopted son of House Daverge, ruling Highlord carried. He was entitled to a measure of respect. Smiling a half tilted grin he said. "Oh, they will let you in, they'll have to."

"Why?" Logan had asked him curiously.

"Because," Damien had told him still smiling the half grin, "You just knelt to me and taught me a valuable lesson."

A King's Quest

Logan had scratched his head and a perplexed expression had come over his face.

Damien had explained, "My brothers don't treat me with the same respect you did because of my station not because of who I am. That station as Lord Richards ward and adopted son grants me a little bit of power and respect. I didn't realize that until now. The guards have to listen to me, I'm the Highlord's son."

Logan had continued to look perplexed until he heard the last of Damien's words, then a slow almost evil looking smile crept across his boyish face, becoming so wide that it almost reached his ears. Damien also had smiled again and both boys knew then that they had indeed discovered something very valuable in this, for both of them.

The guards had indeed stopped both of them at the gates and weren't going to let either one of them through until Damien had pulled out the Daverge family crest medallion that he had tucked away under his shirt and kept out of sight while he was out so that he wasn't recognized and showed it to them. Even then, the guards were only going to allow him into the castle and seemed intent upon sending Logan away. That was until Damien in much the same way he had seen his father do many times before, reminded them of who he was and told them that the other boy was coming in with him. Or else he would just have to speak with his father about why some simple guardsmen thought that they could tell the highlords son what he could or could not do. Both guards had immediately paled at his words and hurriedly they had offered apologies saying that they were only looking out for his well-being and that they could both pass. Logan had watched the entire scene then he smiled haughtily at the guards as they went through and also bid them a good day, halfway to the castle he passed on to him a gold coin that he had relieved from the guards and pocketed another.

For some reason and to this day he still didn't know

why, both Lord Richard and Balthazar had gone pale as ghosts when he had walked into the great hall announcing that he had been out into the city and had discovered a new friend.

Balthazar had walked over to Logan and without speaking cast a spell over the sandy haired boy, freezing him in place where he had stood. Then he had magically examined him from head to toe. After he was done he had nodded to his father and released the other boy from the spell.

His adopted father became the angriest Damien had ever seen him with the exception of the time when he and Balthazar had argued over whether or not Damien should attend the mages academe.

They both asked him numerous questions about whom he had talked to, whom he had seen and if anyone had gone out of their way to talk to him while he was out. With the exception of the fruit vendor and Logan, he had informed them that he hadn't any contact with anyone in any other sort of way.

They looked visibly relieved at hearing this. Damien had in the manner of all boys though whose curiosity is tweaked by unexpected occurrences asked them why. All they told him was that it was dangerous for a young noble child like himself to be out roaming the streets of a city alone without a proper escort and that he should never do so again without telling them.

Then to change the subject they had asked Damien who his friend was. Much to Logan's chagrin and his not knowing any better, he had blurted out that Logan was the best pickpocket in the city and ran a gang of pickpockets. At this Balthazar had visibly frowned, but his father had seemed pleased and had smiled delightfully. "So you are a pickpocket, huh?" he had asked Logan curiously.

To answer the direct question Logan stood up straight and proudly announced to all that could hear. "I'm not just any pickpocket milord," Logan had bowed deeply and swept his arm out in an elaborate flourish, "I'm the best pickpocket in the entire city and someday I will run the other side of the city you don't command."

Lord Richard had laughed out loud at this statement, pleased at the sandy blonde haired boy's audacity and at the fact that he had shown enough courage to admit the truth in front of him.

Balthazar didn't look too pleased and his deep frown somehow had gotten even deeper on his hawkish face.

Damien's father motioned for Logan to approach his seat. He moved from where he had been standing next to the advisor and wizard forward to stand in front of the Lord of Castlekeeps chair.

Lord Richard gave Logan a meaningful look telling him, "I like you and I think that you would be a good friend for my son to have around. You are near his own age, are not a servant or afraid to speak your mind. I give you permission to come into and go from my castle at any time. But!" He punctuated, making the statement more meaningful, "You may one day run the undercity and the network once Jediaa Thirel is gone."

Logan had taken a step back at hearing this. An amazed look crossed his face, thinking that only the thieves of the city knew the term for it. He wondered how this Lord knew the nighttasker's true name. "I don't ever want to see you stealing from anyone inside of my castle ever again or else. The penalty is that if I do, I will flay you with a whip, salt your wounds and hang you from the tallest turret I can find by your balls for the gulls to pick at."

Logan now looked more visibly shaken, somehow this lord had known the exact punishment that Jediaa exacts from thieves who betray him or lose his trust. Logan had told Damien later that the warning had been two fold in a way.

"Now," Lord Richard said smiling, "Give Balthazar

back his purse and never let me see you do that again."

Balthazar's frown had vanished from his face as his hands had began visibly inspecting his robes and a startled look came onto his face as he had fished around in the pockets of his robe then brought out his open palms, empty handed an amazed expression on his face.

"Saw that huh?" Logan said with a twisted grin, at Lord Richard. "That's twice in one day. I must be getting slow in my old age."

Now everyone in the room laughed including Balthazar who caught his purse out of mid air as Logan had tossed it back to him.

Chapter 9
The Gifts

From that moment on the pair had become inseparable, Damien and Logan became like brothers, Logan began teaching Damien how to study marks and pick out the richest and easiest ones for pick pocketing and Damien did his part by arranging for Logan to school with him and go through both weapons and scholarly training with him.

Kendle and Travis had been a little reluctant at first but when Damien pointed out that he had no one his age or size to train with, they had grudgingly relented. Abraim had completely refused to teach Logan until his father had ordered him to. Logan was the only Castlekeep resident that Damien had seen since he had left for Westlake and the only one who knew about his plans to compete in the tournament. Logan arranged to make a few trips with some jewel merchants, just to visit him from time to time.

About the same time as Damien left for the academe, Simon discovered Logan and learned about his talented background. Immediately, he took Logan under his wing for training in his own ears network.

The slight sound of a boot scraping against stone was the only warning Damien heard, he opened his eyes for a brief instant, only just long enough to see a hand grab his face and forcibly thrust him deep under the water before he could pull any air into his lungs.

Whoever this attacker was, he was certainly trying to kill him. He twisted and fought against the grip that was forcing him under until he had brought his body around under the waters surface and he was facing the wall where he had been floating. The hand on his head did not seem to be letting up any at all, so he grabbed the arm it was attached to with his own hands and using his attacker's wrist for leverage, he lifted his legs up and out of the water thrusting his feet heels first up into his attacker's chest. Using all of the strength that he could put into his legs, he lifted his attacker high up into the air and jackknifed his own body up out of the water, throwing his attacker high into the air and out into the center of the pool with his feet.

His unseen assailant landed in the water with a loud splash and sank under its surface, just as Damien's own head broke out upwards, he sputtered and gagged on the water in his mouth and nose, then gulped a few breaths of sweet air into his lungs before spinning round to face whoever it was who had thrust him under the water.

A dripping wet sandy haired head broke the surface and green eyes glittered with amusement as a soaked handsome faced young man started laughing at the outraged expression on Damien's own face. Logan, Damien realized, had finally made his appearance.

"What was that for you fool? You almost drowned me!" Damien gasped out, sputtering from the water he had inhaled underwater.

"I was just about to let you up, when you kicked me in the ribs. I think that you might have broken a few of them." the other young man laughed as he rubbed at spots that would certainly become bruises on both sides of his chest with his long fingered hands.

The two young men looked at each other across the water, then they broke out into laughter. It had been a little over a year since they had last seen each other but to each of them it felt like only a few moments had passed.

"I was sent by Abraim to tell you that your things are in your chambers and not to spend too much time in here," Logan informed him.

Damien just rolled his eyes and said. "I ought to be late just for old time's sake, but he would probably just blame you for it."

"As always, that is one thing that will never change." Logan answered dryly as Damien climbed up out of the water and made his way towards his blanket hanging on the wall.

Wrapping himself in the blanket after he had toweled himself off, he turned to watch his best friend climb out of the large pool. Logan was just at six feet, with a normal sized build for his size. He wasn't unusual in any way except for his strikingly handsome features, intelligent green eyes and youthful appearance.

Knowing that Logan knew just about everything that went on in and outside of the castle, he asked. "What's going on with father and this rebellion, from what I hear, him and the other six western Highlords are about to plunge us and the rest of the realm into a revolution over taxes?"

The young spythief quickly put a slender finger to his lips in a shushing gesture and whispered, "We don't need to talk about such things here. Who knows who might be lurking around listening to us talk?" then in a high reedy voice that was an exact imitation of Simon's, Logan said. "All the walls in this city have ears and everybody listens through them." Then both young men began to laugh again. Logan had a knack for voices and could copy just about anyone's. This talent had gotten them both into and out of trouble more times than either one of them could count.

After their laughter had faded Logan's face turned serious again, "The whole city is in a bad way with all of these people in it, Damien. Simon even wants me to try to patch things up with Jediaa, so that I can get information from him for both sides."

"You can't do that, Jediaa banished you from all contact with the guild and all of its members when you relinquished your post as his protégé and came to work here in the castle against his wishes."

"I know," answered Logan sadly, "but Simon seems to think that if the right circumstance came up Jediaa might decide to lift my banishment and that I could work both sides gathering information on both."

"Yeah until the night tasker finds out and puts you face first in the Eversea Ocean." offered Damien, "or feeds you to the gulls."

"There is that" agreed the sandy haired young man. "Simon says that I am the best student he has ever trained and a natural talent, but because I am limited in my resources because of my banishment I can't do much good here in the city without being able to have contact with the underside."

Damien nodded, "I agree, you've always had a way with people and places and you know that you can make yourself at home anywhere or in any situation."

"Thank you," Logan said accepting the compliment.

"Is he going to let you come to the ball tonight or does he have you working in the city doing something else?"

"Of course I'm going. In fact before you ruined my clothes, I was going to wear this," and he swept his hands up and down the length of his ruined sopping wet outfit. "I was sent to get you ready and now I'm not ready either."

"Well," Damien returned, "we have about an hour then. Let's go back up to my chambers. If Abraim has delivered the crates that I sent him after, I can manage to find a couple of things in them that might replace those for you, or else I can fix them," and he waggled his fingers at Logan's sopping wet clothes that had formed a puddle of water at his feet.

They hurried back to his chambers with Logan leading the way, keeping a wary eye out for any unexpected guests Damien trailing along in his blanket and soon they were back in his chambers.

"A couple of things is all?" Logan said, glancing around the room at the stacks of wooden crates that covered almost the entire floor in the large greeting room. "I'd say that it looks more like you brought more than half of Westlake home with you." he had expected to hear some kind of remark from Damien but when he didn't, he turned to find that his statement had fallen on deaf ears.

The young battlemage was busy going through several of the crates that had been stacked in his chambers and wasn't paying any attention to him at all. So Logan just stood there silently waiting in sopping wet clothes for his friend to find whatever it was that he was searching for so diligently amongst the multitude of crates scattered all over the floor. He could offer to help but he also recognized the look and knew that whatever it was he was trying to find, he wanted to find it himself.

"Ahaa!" Damien called out excitedly as he finally pulled out a medium sized wooden box that had been buried under the others that was marked with a very large L chalked in black across its top. "This ones for you." he said smiling his half tilted grin, holding out the box towards him.

Logan took it, gave it a vigorous shake and asked, "What is in it."

"Open it and find out for yourself." Damien informed him.

Logan glanced suspiciously now at Damien, then back

at the box as if trying to see if it held any sort of traps for the unwary. He remembered all of their past pranks that they had played on each other throughout their relationship as friends.

"Just open it Logan," Damien said, "I promise it won't bite."

So keeping a wary eye on both the box and on Damien for any sign that he should rid himself of it quickly before it exploded or something, Logan pulled a tool out of the top of his boot and not seeing anything on the lid, began slowly and carefully working at the closed lock. Even though Damien had assured him that the box was okay, he had good reasons for such cautions. Damien had learned from him how to set traps. He had taken what he had learned and refined it to include magic. Two years ago, he had sent him a box that housed a cleverly concealed stinking cloud spell in its lid. Logan hadn't forgotten that one, because for three days, any time he had gotten close to a person they had either held their nose with their fingers or quickly ran away. He had returned the favor last year with a supposed long lost scroll that was written in an ancient language and had asked Damien to use the library at the academe to help translate it for him. The scroll was supposed to tell of a treasure that was hidden somewhere inside the city. Actually it had been a cleverly disguised spell of boils that once deciphered released its hidden spell and inflicted the reader with the malady. Damien had cursed at him in a letter three pages long about the clever spell.

Ten seconds later, there was a soft click and the lock fell open, the large heavy lock slipped out of the clasp and began falling towards the floor. Years of thieving instincts took over. Without thinking Logan's hand shot out, snagged the lock out of the air before it could make any clattering noise with the floor and slipped it into his pocket. Prying the lid upwards only a little bit on one side, the young thief still not entirely trusting Damien's word, pulled another tool out of his boot top, it looked like a long thin metal rod that crooked slightly in the middle and had a small tiny flat mirror on one end and slipped it under the lid of the box. A thieves mirror was what Logan called the small device. He used it for just about everything. As a child he designed the thing and actually made some money, selling it to other thieves around the city. He used the mirror for seeing around corners, under doors and even behind him if he thought he was being followed. Seeing nothing inside, he pried the lid the rest of the way off and slowly removed it. Nothing happened. Taking a deep breath, he moved his head up and over the edge of the box and peered down into it. A delighted cry escaped the spy thief's lips as he saw the contents.

Damien smiled at him from across the room where he had taken a chair to watch Logan open the crate. "Do you like it?" he asked anxiously.

Sitting in the crate was a long black cloak with a hood, as dark as night itself.

"Is this what I think it is?" Logan asked in awe and with trembling hands he pulled the hooded cloak out of the box and let it fall open, the cloak shimmered in the light as it did so. "Night spider silk." he said reverently, caressing the now open cloak with his long fingers.

Night spiders are a very rare breed of spiders that only appear at certain times of the year and only on the blackest of nights with no moon. Their webs are a type of silk that can be woven into material if enough of their webbing can be gathered. Night spiders are another type of creational magical creature brought into being during the early ages of man by the creational wizards when they had the full use of their magic.

Pure creational magic barely exists anymore, having had its use limited by the gods because of the Elvynn's abuse of it until the end of their banishment and exile. Only the Elvynn Tua-latin war wizards and human battlemages are allowed its use anymore. Long in the past, all of the races had been given the gift of this magic but the Elvynn had abused it, enslaving all the other races. At first creational magic had been used for many wondrous things like the creation of beasts and magical items but as power grows so does its corruption and after the age of might and during the wars of power where humans and the other races had rebelled against their Elvynn slave masters, the gods themselves had to step in and save the world from destruction. Night spiders, Kraals, Mar'Cats, Guardian dragons, Bocks, Drakynn and Snap Dragons were only a few of the many beasts formed of creational magic. All of these creatures are unique and slightly different from the similar creatures on which they were based.

Night spider's webbing deflects magic, of almost all types, a cloak of night spider silk is indeed a very powerful magical item and can protect the wearer from almost all sorts of magical spells or attacks. It also makes one nearly invisible when its hood is pulled up.

"You did not buy this did you? Please tell me that you acquired it somehow and that its origins can not be traced back to your father's money." Logan asked him with a direct look.

Damien shook his head no and Logan erupted in an angry outburst obviously not believing him, "How did you come up with the money for this. I won't accept it if you used your father's money to buy this, it's too much, its way too expensive!"

Damien once again shook his head no, "It's gambling money."

Logan blinked in startled surprise at this, "You don't gamble," he informed him.

"You're right, I don't, but Tiko, my battlemaster at the academe does and it seems that he won a lot of money gambling on me fighting in the pits. This and what else is left in the box are but a small part of it. All of this came from my shares of the winnings," and he waved a hand at the room full of crates.

"You must have won a lot of fights then."

Damien eyed him smugly as he said, "Almost every one of them.

"Well you know my motto, gambling gold makes great gifts." Logan said smiling, as he realized what else Damien had said and asked, "Did you say there was more?"

"See for yourself." Damien told him, gesturing back over to the box with his chin.

Lying in the bottom of the crate was actually two more things, a matching pair of white bone hilted Elvynn hunting daggers in silver sheathes with runes carved on each. The daggers themselves were of excellent craftsmanship. Logan saw this, just by the carved bone hilts alone, having not even seen the blades yet. He was struck by something odd then and turned to Damien.

"With those long hilts and short sheathes won't the blades be a little small?"

"Pull them out." Damien said with a touch of sarcasm.

Logan picked up one of the long hilted-sheathed daggers and drew it out. The sheathe was only about six inches long but the blade that came out of it was well over twelve inches in length. Logan gasped in surprised delight as he studied the blades, Elvynn runes were etched along the thin blades length and even though it was long it was surprisingly light in heft and he could tell immediately that it was perfectly balanced and that the steel was very strong.

"Oh these are nice." Logan answered. "How did you come by these?" he asked as he held up both daggers. The sheathes he noticed were fit with leather straps on both the top and bottom and could be tied to the inside of an arm or leg for easy concealment.

"I won those fighting. The Elvynn hunter who lost them was not pleased at all. I actually offered them back to him but he wouldn't accept them. The blades are nice but the silver sheaths are where the magic is at."

Logan turned both of the sheaths over in his hands and looked at the runecrest engraved on them.

"They are magical sheaths of hiding," Damien added. "I don't know exactly what kind of blade you can stick in there or if it has to just be those," he pointed at the daggers, "but I'm assuming they can be used to hold about anything that can fit inside of the sheaths opening."

The young spythief didn't answer. Instead he dropped the sheaths as if they had bitten him on the hands. A scared and horrified look was on his face as he watched them fall to the floor.

"What is it?" Damien asked, now seeing the terrified expression on his friend's face.

Logan continued to stare at the sheaths that were now lying on the floor, rune side up. "I know that symbol," he said in a trembling voice, pointing a shaking finger at the runecrest on the side of the sheath, "I know the family to which they belong."

Damien gaped at his friend incredulously, "What do you mean, you know the family that those belong to, Logan. That's impossible, those are Elvynn hunting daggers, how could you possibly know who owned them?"

"From before." the sandy haired thief said in a hollow sounding low voice and Damien saw a few tears started to well up in his friend's green eyes.

Immediately it became clear to him what Logan was talking about and Damien gasped.

"Your parents and your brother," he said almost reverently, looking over at the young man who was wiping the tears from his eyes with the palms of his hands.

Logan nodded in agreement, as he wiped away a few more tears.

The young spythief didn't like to talk about the times with his parents. The life he had shared with them had been extremely happy and the brutal way in which he had watched them die caused a lot of anguish, inside of Logan years later, even now.

Damien knew the daggers sheaths had touched upon one of those memories that Logan kept hidden even from himself.

Slowly almost haltingly Logan said, "I..I saved the life..." he paused as he tried to remember, "Of one of the Elvynn family members of this runecrest. As a child, he was drowning in the Edgemoor swamps, sinking in quicksand and I saved him."

"What," asked Damien almost fearfully, "were you as a child, doing in the Elvynn swamps of Edgemoor?"

"We had a special trading charter that allowed my father because of who my mother was to trade gems and other goods with the Elvynn and to pass through the Edgemoor swamps and into the lands of Myramoor and the ruined city of Talathandria without any harm coming to us."

Damien had heard of such privileges but never known anyone who had been to their lands or seen the sacred woods of Myamoor where the Elvynn made their homes now, or the destroyed Elvynn capitol city of Talathandria, where once the Elvynn had held all of the other races on this continent as slaves.

Until now, the pair of young men had grown up together and had even arranged visits while Damien was away at the Academe. Never once had Logan mentioned that he had been to the Elvynn lands. He had known that his friend spoke Elvynn but he also spoke five other languages. Damien had never figured out where he'd learnt them.

Logan picked up the sheathes and tied one to the inside of his leg so that it fit in the top of his boot, replacing the dagger he had drawn from there earlier with the new one. The second one, he pulled up his sleeve and tied it in place along his forearm then slid the sleeve back into place concealing the dagger from view.

"Did the Elvynn who had these have auburn hair or sandy hair like mine?" Logan asked looking at Damien.

"Auburn," came Damien's one word answer to the question.

"That would have been Galan then. It looks like he made it to adulthood without Raciss, his brother, managing to kill him."

Damien thought he was going to say something else but instead Logan burst into motion, both Elvynn daggers appeared in his hands as if he hadn't put them away. He spun the blades expertly with his long fingers and they moved with blurring speed. Spinning his body around, he threw first one with his right hand, then the other with his left. Both blades slammed home into Damien's closet door in the other room about thirty feet away side by side with less than an inch between them.

"Oh I like those," Logan said, his eyes lighting up like a child. Gone now was the sadness from his green eyes. As if it had never came, he went over and removed the two blades and slid them back into their sheaths. Damien could tell that he was done speaking about his past, so instead of asking any more questions he kept rummaging around in several of the other crates. He finally found the one that he was looking for, removed the lid and began pulling out clothes. "Do you still want to wear what you have on to the banquet? You know that we will both have to attend."

Logan gestured to his still sopping wet finery that he was wearing that consisted of a green doublet and pants, "As I said earlier, before you ruined it, this was what I was going to wear."

Damien looked at him for a moment then drew on a small bit of energy and said a quick incantation. Logan's outfit began to shed water. It ran in little rivers out of his clothes and onto the floor and after a few moments Logan's clothes were completely dry and unwrinkled.

"Well," said the sandy haired thief in an appreciative tone as he glanced down at his dry clothes, "now that's quite a trick."

"Thank you." replied Damien offhandedly, "we have got to get ready quickly now, you know how my father gets when we are too late for his functions." then Damien stepped into his bedchambers where he was going to change and shut the door behind him. He wanted it to be a surprise what he was wearing. Several minutes later he stepped back out of the bedchamber and both young men inspected each other's appearance.

Like always, Damien thought, Logan looked great, but then the handsome young spythief could wear a burlap bag and somehow he would still look dashing in it, Damien knew this to be different for himself though. He always for some unknown reason looked as if he was half ragged and it was obviously so now, judging by the way Logan was critically eyeing him.

"It's not the clothes this time." Logan informed him, running his eyes up and down his outfit.

Damien kind of figured that. He was wearing his tailored black and gold battlemages uniform and it fit him extremely well. "So what is it then?" he asked Logan curiously, he wanted to look good for his homecoming and he knew that there would be a lot of lovely ladies at the festival who might want to dance with an adopted Highlord's third son and a battlemage.

Logan continued to eye him critically, his green eyes scanning every inch. "Hold on." He turned and went into the washroom, Damien heard him pouring water and searching for something. A few moments later he returned with a basin full of cold water and a gleaming razor in his hands. "It's the hair and beard."

"So what are you going to do with those?" Damien asked hesitatingly, pointing to the razor in one of Logan's hands and water in the other. He had always worn his dark curly hair long and over the last several months he'd been trying to grow a beard.

A dangerous gleam came into Logan's green eyes as he pulled out a chair and ordered Damien to sit.

The young battlemage did so, but asked skeptically. "Are you sure that you know what you are doing."

Using a favorite phrase that Damien had learnt to hate over the years and usually meant more trouble for him, Logan said, "Trust me Damien. When I'm done you'll look more like a king, rather than a shaggy lord's adopted son." then he started cutting.

He was right. Damien thought to himself as he admired his face in the mirror. Gone was his long curly hair and most of the beard, replaced by a soldier's style haircut with short hair on the sides and left a little longer on top. The unruly beard was now a neatly trimmed goatee.

Damien blinked his eyes at his reflection, "I look great Logan, you were right."

Instead of the boyish look of before, he now looked noble, even though he was just an adopted woodsman son. The cutting of the long hair had revealed something in his looks that he had never seen before. He looked neat and clean, rather than the disheveled young man that he always appeared to be.

"Where did you learn to cut hair?" Damien asked as he rubbed his hand over his now considerably shorter hair and continued to study appreciatively his new appearance in the mirror.

"I was sleeping with a lass for a while," Logan said with a smile, "who does this sort of thing for the richer ladies about town for a living. She taught me a few things."

Still looking at his reflection Damien said. "No one will even know who I am any longer and we should get going, as usual we are already a little late."

They checked each other's appearance one last time, nodded agreement and strode out of Damien's chambers.

Chapter 10
The Ball

Damien stepped forward walking past Logan who leaned over in a low mocking bow, deliberately sweeping his arm out in an elaborate flourish saying, "After you sire."

He rolled eyes at his friend's antics and continued on through the open door. A slight thrill of excitement went through his body as he entered the great hall of the castle wearing his battlemages uniform for the first time in public and at home. The black and gold looking uniform drew stares from all in the room as heads turned to glance at him and take notice of his arrival.

Logan stepped up behind him and chuckled softly as he looked out at all of the nobles circling around in their finery, flaunting their jewels and gems about the main chamber and he gave him a devilishly wicked grin. "Look at all the fine jewelry in here!" he exclaimed softly, his green eyes going wide with delight. "One run through this room and I wouldn't have to work again for the rest of my life." then he wriggled his fingers at Damien as if he was picking pockets.

"And my father," Damien said giving him a stern and reproachful look, "would flay you, salt your wounds and hang you from the tallest turret by the balls for the gulls to pick at."

Logan visibly winced, saying as he did so, "He did say that didn't he?" They both remembered Damien's fathers vivid promise as children. "Maybe I'll have to curb my predatory instincts for just one night then."

Turning away from him, Logan began looking about the room as if he was looking for someone in particular and said. "I'll be back, there is somebody here I have to talk to."

Damien offered up a silent prayer to Syreena, the goddess of magic, hoping that Logan didn't get caught stealing off any of the guests here, he knew that his friend was going to do it of course. The young thief could never resist plucking as he called it from a few of the more overly pompous or extremely rude richer guests in the crowd especially those that offended him or his odd sense of honor, he just hoped no one noticed.

Logan looked back once more at his friend, smiled almost evilly at Damien before he melted off again into the crowd of party goers, moving in a confident stride slipping effortlessly in and out of the people as if he was on a crowded busy street.

The audience hall and the main great room were already filled with hundreds of guests, multitudes of courtesans, servants, dukes, earls and various other types of nobles from all over Castlekeep's domain and Gaderia in general. There was also a number of the richer merchants that lived inside the city, all had attended Lord Richard's summons to appear at the festival ball.

Damien saw more than a few eyeing his black and gold

battlemages tunic, so he wasn't surprised when he felt a subtle slight prickling of magical energy on the back of his neck and knew that there were a few magic users here in the crowd as well. He looked around the room trying to see who had just cast the small spell at him. It hadn't been much of a detection spell and he had just barely noticed it, almost like a slow breath across the back of his neck, but it had been there a moment ago.

Something about the touch of the spell also seemed familiar to him, almost as if he would recognize the caster if he saw the person. Spotting a group of men and women all huddled together in a small knot, he knew immediately from which direction the spell had come. Balthazar and several other wizards who were all standing around the advisor were all smiling pleased smiles at him, they must have been testing him a little to see how good his battlemage training really was. Even though he knew the spell had come from this little group he still didn't know any of the faces that he could see besides his old mentors and he would have recognized immediately his father's advisors magical touch at once considering he was the first person to have ever taught him in the arcane arts. "So who was it." he wondered curiously to himself as he peered at the group trying to determine if he knew any of them from before he had left or maybe from Westlake where he had just left. "It had seemed so familiar to him."

He looked around one last time for Logan just to make sure that he wasn't of course causing a disturbance or being detained by the castle guards. The sandy haired spythief had settled himself at a table and was having a conversation with one of the prettiest ladies in the room. Judging from her gestures and smiles Damien could tell that she was enjoying the conversation and the attention that Logan was lavishing on her. He wondered how much she would be enjoying it if she knew that she was actually talking to one of the most talented streetthiefs in the city. Seeing the starry eyed look on her face as she eyed his handsome friend, Damien figured that she probably wouldn't even care. So he took off towards the little group who were motioning him over with friendly waves.

Everyone in the group nodded deferentially to him as he made his approach and Balthazar introduced him. The advisor wore an elaborately scarlet robe with silver trim embroidered with arcane symbols on it. He looked very much the part of a Highlord's wizard and advisor. All magic users can sense how much power another can wield or will someday be able to wield. Damien knew at that moment he was one of the most powerful people in the room and so to did all the others standing around him. He nodded deferentially to each one and offered up a polite greeting, for which, one of the ladies said. "And he's so polite too." in a pleased tone.

There was one other person Balthazar wanted him to meet and asked him to wait a second before going on to his father's table. He stepped past a large wizard and tapped someone behind him on the shoulder. The big man moved to reveal who was hiding on the other side.

Damien caught the flash of shoulder length curly red hair before he saw the face that it belonged to and he knew who had cast the spell at him. His jaw dropped somewhat as he stood there in stunned silence. He felt his heart begin to race in his chest and was certain that everyone around him could hear its pounding. There she was in a floor length dress of black and gold silk that only seemed to enhance her beauty. Her golden brown eyes even seemed to match the color in her dress. She was as beautiful as he remembered her at the academe. He looked at her and their eyes met. Damien felt as if he could hardly breathe.

Cassica Essen, personal battlemage to Lord Gildon Seahorn, ruler of Caladar the second largest city in the west, stood their among the small group of mages gathered around Balthazar smiling at him her golden eyes twinkling, he knew now why he had recognized the touch of the spell caster. She had been two levels ahead of him at the academy. Everyone who had attended the academy within the past four years had been in love with her beautiful and striking good looks.

Damien had a crush on her, just like all of the other young men who had attended the Academe. She always made him really nervous and usually whenever she was around. He became extremely clumsy and uncoordinated. They had actually worked together on several magical projects during his time there. Like him, Cassica was a natural talent. She could see a spell once and know it right away. She was one of the few in the beginning who hadn't given him a hard time about his title or abilities.

"How are you Damien?" she asked with a dazzling smile directed at him that caused him to feel weak in the knees. "I heard you were coming home tonight and would be here."

"I...I am fine Cassica." he stumbled with the words, "H.How are you doing? What are you doing here?" he asked, hating himself inside for not being able to stop himself from stuttering a moment before. His stomach did a nervous roll inside of him and he wondered why he couldn't be more like Logan, always knowing what to do or say to any pretty girl that passed by his way.

She laughed a delightful sound that filled his ears as she said. "I'm good too, I came up from Caladar as a courier for Lord Gildon to bring a message to your father that he felt needed to be delivered by a person rather than a pigeon and to attend the tournament."

"Oh." was all he could manage at that moment, as he realized that she had just said that she was going to fight in the tournament, Cassica, he knew was an extremely skilled battlemage and very competent with both of her short swords that she used in combat. He was saved from having to further embarrass himself by a servants call, announcing that dinner was about to begin.

Thinking he would never have the courage to do something like this again, he stuck his arm out like Logan would have done and asked if he could escort her to her seat.

Cassica looked up at him a rather pleased expression crossed her face, followed by a delighted smile as she placed her arm in his. As a pair they moved to her seat and she commented on his appearance saying that the new hair cut and the trimmed beard really suited him and made him look more like a battlemage.

He gave another embarrassed laugh. Then he thanked her and escorted her to a chair. With parting smiles at each other, Damien went off towards the head of the table where Balthazar had informed him before he left with Cassica on his arm, that his father had a chair waiting for him.

* * *

Lord Richard Daverge had watched the pair of young men enter the hall, marked the time and noticed as always, that both of the young men were fashionably late. He was sitting at his place at the far end of the high table with his fingers steepled in front of him watching everyone around him. He recognized the black and gold colors of Damien's uniform and the green outfit that he had seen Logan in earlier that day, but his eyesight was failing and he couldn't quite make out Damien's face. He watched as Balthazar introduced him to the other mages and was pleased by both the look of respects given to the younger man from the other mages and even more so by the gestures and nods of respect given back to them by his adopted son. Balthazar had informed him that even though he was still young and would become more skilled as time went by, Damien was by far one of the most powerful among them including himself. There was no sense of arrogance or haughtiness

A King's Quest

displayed in his bearing either, even more important the Highlord of Castlekeep noticed was there was no sense of weakness or cowardice in his manner, just a sense of confidence. "This was good" Lord Richard thought solemnly to himself, "Especially, later on when he would need all of those qualities."

As his adopted son escorted the lovely battlemage to her chair, Lord Richard Daverge felt his heart leap into his throat as Damien's face finally came into view. He saw the goatee and the short hair. The resemblance to his true father was so frightening that he quickly looked about the room, hoping that no one else realized the same. Seeing no one paying his son any undue attention and noticing the curious expression on his ward's face, Lord Richard quickly got control of his own facial features and his pounding heart. He motioned him into the chair at his left.

Damien pulled out the chair that had been set aside for Cassica. He smiled down at her as she sat and she returned the smile. With a slow red flush creeping up the back of his neck and towards his ears, he turned and hurried off towards the open chair that his father had indicated for him, before Cassica saw him blushing.

As he approached his father, Damien noticed that the chair to which he had directed him was one of the two chairs that sat to his adopted fathers left. They were usually reserved for his brothers. As he sat down in one of the empty chairs he wondered where the pair was and made a mental note to ask about them later.

Once he was seated his adopted father got up onto his feet and announced in a booming voice that echoed throughout the hall, that the dinner for the harvest festival would now begin.

The guests all moved to their respective seats and began filling their plates from the heaping trays of food that covered every table.

Travis appeared in a moment, opposite from where

Damien sat. "Milord." He said to Lord Richard as he inclined his head in a respectful nod towards him. Lord Richard returned it in kind without saying a word, he was anxious to see his blademasters face when he saw that of his ward.

What happened next was one of the strangest things Damien had ever had happen to him. Travis turned to him and as his dark eyes fell on the young battlemage who was all cleaned up with short hair and a new goatee, looking respectful and presentable. Something about his face caused the blademaster to freeze in place.

Damien watched as all of the color literally drained out the bald blademasters face, leaving it white as a bed sheet and looking as if he had seen a ghost. His eyes took on a haunted expression as he sputtered almost incoherently. "S...s..Sire! H...How did you? W..What are you? I...Everyone thought you were dead," he stammered almost incomprehensively.

"Excuse me." Damien said, eyebrows furrowing and a confused look crossed his face. "I'm very much alive Travis and I think that I'm supposed to be here tonight."

He was so stunned by the expression on Travis face when he saw his new look that he failed to see the alarmed look on his own fathers face at the reaction that Travis had had. Hastily Lord Richard looked around the room again to see if anyone else had heard or seen the exchange, the blademasters reaction wasn't exactly what he had expected. Luckily enough, no one had noticed or paid the least bit of attention to what was going on at the head of the main table.

Hearing Damien's own voice broke whatever it was that had come over the blademaster and now his face and eyes held a look of recognition as he looked at him as if he was truly seeing him for the first time. Damien noticed though that there was still a haunted look in the back of his eyes and his skin was still pale white.

"P..Pardon me Damien." Travis said still stammering his words as he spoke. "I misspoke myself." he pointed a finger at the beard. "Seems that seeing you with that beard reminded me of somebody I once knew a long time ago."

Lord Richard interjected quickly before Damien could respond and ask more questions. "No harm Travis, no harm at all. The sight of that beard on him gave me quite a shock also." He gave the blademaster an unseen fierce look, hoping that it would quiet him. Travis saw the look of warning from Lord Richard and recognized it for what it was. Damien didn't.

"Right milord." answered Travis, hurriedly but when Damien wasn't looking he glared at Lord Richard. Damien couldn't figure what was going on and looked at the pair of them as if they both had gone slightly mad. He did wonder idly for a moment what it was about his new beard and look that had started all of this and also who was it that Travis thought he looked like. Logan had said the same thing before they had left for the dinner and even Cassica had commented on his new look. Maybe, Logan was right and the beard did make him look noble after all Travis had mistakenly called him Sire and that's a title reserved for only Highlords or Royalty, which he was actually far from being. How could an ex-slave turned blademaster know any sort of royalty other than his father or some of the other western Highlords? The blademaster had left Castlekeep only once in the past ten years since his father had freed him from his slave chains. That was to get him from Westlake. Other than that, he had always stayed specifically in the city.

All through the dinner Damien kept his eyes on Travis and noticed that he just picked absently at his food, not really eating any of it. He had both a distracted and distraught look on his face. He kept staring at Damien when he thought that he wasn't looking. His face seemed to have aged ten years since the start of the dinner and now looked very haggard and worn.

Finally giving up and sliding his plate towards the center of the table, the blademaster stood and politely excused his self from the dinner saying that he wasn't feeling very well and that he was going to retire to his chambers for the evening.

"So early Travis?" Damien asked him curiously, stopping him before he could leave the table. "You will miss all of the night's entertainment and dancing."

"I'm not feeling well enough for any festivities tonight Damien." said the blademaster, turning away, but not before he shot another unseen look of cold anger at Lord Richard.

Damien thought that he had seen sheen of tears filling Travis' dark brown eyes as he left. He turned back to the conversation he was having with a lovely young lady that his father had placed there for his benefit. He still wondered whether or not it was the sight of him with his new beard that had brought tears to the blademasters eyes.

Once all of the guests had finished eating, the servants reappeared and removed all of the empty dishes. After they were finished, entertainers paraded into the hall. The same performers that Damien had seen earlier in the day, now launched into dazzling routines and acts. The acrobats flew through the sky and bounced around the great hall. A few bards sang melodies and told tales. One orator wanted to do a tale of the night of sorrows when the old king and queen were killed and Lord Vargas took over as Royal Regent but his father stopped him and asked him to please keep the mood pleasant and cheerful.

Actors performed a play and the troupe's leader, a seasoned old fellow who seemed to know Damien's father fairly well, asked him to come out and join them, which to the delight of all, he did. The actors amazed everyone. All were impressed by Lord Richards' performance in the play including Damien who hadn't ever known that his adopted father could act.

Cassica Essen, Damien decided during the performances, was still a stunningly beautiful young lady. All through the nights entertainment he had hardly been able to keep his eyes off of her, much to the chagrin of the young lady that his father had placed by his side who had caught him several times looking at the beautiful redhead. She was deeply involved in a conversation with a noble of some sort who seemed to be doing a fine job of keeping her attention.

All of the guests now stood up from their places at the table and began making their way towards the ballroom at a signal from his father.

Jabbing Damien in the ribs with his elbow, Logan asked nonchalantly. "So who is she and why do you look like a moonstruck cow?"

"That is Cassica Essen, the one that I told you about several years back," Damien informed him with a wistful smile.

"Ohh," Logan said shaking his head knowingly and smiled, "Your training partner and tutor at the academe. She's definitely a fine one," he added admiringly.

"That she is," Damien agreed, as he stood and also began moving towards the ballroom with the rest of the guests, "that she is."

Not really wanting to dance, Damien stood off to one side and turned his mind toward the question of what it was about his new look that had caused such a reaction at the dinner tonight. Over and over in his mind he turned the event around. But no matter which way he turned it, he couldn't see any reason for it. "Maybe," he thought to himself, "Logan would come up with some sort of answer when he told him about it later, the young thief was very skilled at figuring out puzzles that no one else could seem to find the answers to."

A light tap on his shoulder caused him to turn around.

In front of him was a small pretty young lady with long dark luxurious hair smiling up at him.

"Are you the companion of that man over there?" she asked him, throwing a glance over in the direction of Logan and the same female companion he had been talking to earlier before the dinner.

Damien returned the smile with one of his trademark own lopsided grins and said that yes he was.

"I was sent over here by my sister, who is with your friend to ask if you wanted to join us when we sneaked out of here and got away from all these snobs?"

Damien looked over in Logan's direction and saw that he was grinning at him like a well-fed cat with a bucket full of milk and smiling again at her he said. "I would be delighted to accompany you out of here and away from all of these snobs and take you anywhere that you would like to go."

The pretty young dark haired lady gave him a curious looks, saying. "You misspeak yourself sir, not just with me but with all of us."

"As I said before," Damien said giving her an even stare with a hint of amusement showing in his dark blue eyes, "I would be glad to accompany you out of here." and he put special emphasis on the word you, "and take you anywhere that you would like to go." then he boldly held out his arm as he had before with Cassica and waited for her to take it.

Her face reddened slightly as she blushed, she hesitated a moment and said, "I don't even know your name. I am Asrielle and you are?"

"Damien Daverge," he said simply.

She gave him a more appraising look with her dark brown eyes, then smiling she placed her arm in his. They went over to where Logan and her sister were waiting. If Cassica Essen was interested in him at all, she would be jealous if she saw the beautiful lady gracing his arm now.

* * *

The new secretary to the royal ambassador, Caliban Syndell was leaning against the wall not to far from where the two young couples stood talking. In his hand he sipped on a glass of water preferring not to drink any of the wine that was on all of the tables. He was an assassin mage and needed to keep his wits about him at all times and could not allow them to be tainted or slowed down by the effects of alcohol. All that alcohol could do for him was to slow his reactions and deaden his reflexes and that was unacceptable in his mind. Even more so, his father did not allow it. His body was his temple and he had honed it into a perfect killing machine since almost as far back as he could remember and that was the reason he was here for tonight. Caliban had sworn oaths to protect the crown and throne against rogue or out of control battlemages who might be a danger to the realm and knew that against such a deadly opponent regardless of his level of skill, he couldn't allow any lapses in his concentration. If a battlemage was the epitome of magic and warfare combined into one element, he was the opposite, an anti battlemage of sorts, created and trained specifically in the same manner as they were. But his training was to use their own abilities of cunning and subterfuge against them. In order to kill them, all he had to do was discern this opponent's weaknesses and exploit them.

His slate blue eyes were almost always filled with a cold sort of ruthless determination and he never allowed himself to forget the task at hand. So he couldn't help but notice when his mark and his friend departed from the party with two of the loveliest young ladies there in tow on their arms.

Caliban counted to ten, then he pushed himself up off of the wall and followed after them. The assassin mage trailed along a ways behind the group always keeping someone between himself and them. When the young sandy blond haired man looked behind them, Caliban bent his knees in order to appear shorter than what he actually was. This gave him a better chance of not being recognized by his quarry despite his white blonde hair. Not really sure where it was that they were going, he decided to take a chance and closed the gap between them and himself. As he did so he heard one of the ladies ask the same question he was wondering, where it was exactly that they were going. Caliban smiled as he also heard the reply that the blond man gave to her saying that they were going out through a servants exit in the kitchen, which opened up into the city. Knowing that there was no way that he could follow behind them through the kitchens without raising all sorts of suspicions, Caliban moved off in the direction of the keeps main doors in a deliberately slow almost reeling walk of a drunk. Not possessing an invitation, but looking like a slightly drunken noble leaving the castle would not draw any unwanted attention at all since half the guests were already that way. Once clear of the guards working at the castle's grounds entrance, he dropped the drunken noble act and hurried towards the coach in which he had arrived, grabbed his bag out of it that carried his gear and raced towards eastern end of the castle where he assumed that the small group would make their exit out onto the street.

 Leading the little group Logan held up a hand and told them to wait a moment while he checked to see if the way was clear, Damien furrowed his brow and gave him a questioning look and Logan smiled back conspiratorially and gestured them forward. He whispered into Damien's ear as he passed. "Ladies like things that look dangerous, it makes them feel excited." and he made a show of opening the kitchen door and peering out around it.

 "I was wondering what you were doing?" Damien

whispered back at his friend.

Logan opened the door all the way and motioned the other three young people to follow him into the kitchen. The place was like a mad house. Everyone hurrying about, all of them were doing something. All of the staff had something in hand and yelling they had something else still to do.

He led the way through the mass of people and the cacophony of noise without incident. They finally came to a stout wooden door on the other side of the room and opened it.

A long hallway led down to another door that was guarded by two guards looking very miserable.

"Hail Markus, hail Tomas," Logan said in a jovial tone. "What did the two of you do to get posted here, so far from all of the fun?" Both men shot baleful glares at Logan. Damien wondered if Logan had something to do with their being posted here tonight. "To make it up to you," Logan said pulling out a pouch from somewhere underneath his tunic, "how about you accept this as repayment."

The guard called Markus snatched the pouch out of the air as Logan threw it to him, hearing the heavy clink of coins as it landed in his hands, he smiled for the first time since seeing the spythief.

"Sorry that you two got caught up in that mess the other day, I hope that that," he nodded at the pouch, "will make up for it."

"No problem now," the other guard said pointedly, "But we were beginning to wonder whether or not you would come through with your part."

Damien immediately noticed the change in his best friend's demeanor. A hard edge had crept into his voice as he said coldly, "I always come through, let no man ever say I don't, never forget that." then he smiled a tight grim smile, "so how about the two of you letting us out through that door without anyone being the wiser in our leaving.

The ladies here," he gestured at Asrielle and Meralda, "don't want anyone to know that they are leaving the party with a couple of questionable gentleman like us, they do have a reputation to maintain."

Both guardsmen smiled at this but as the small group stepped forward the guard named Tomas held up a hand saying, "Who is your companion, not some other sneak thief that you have snuck into the castle is he? He's probably up to no good."

"More than likely he has stolen something from our Lord and is attempting to sneak it out of the castle by us." the other guard stated, looking hard eyed in Damien's direction.

Damien stepped forward into the light of the torches where his face and his black and gold uniform was revealed and said in a cold tone. "It doesn't matter who Logan sneaks into the castle or what he does while inside of it. By my father's authority and mine he has and always will have full run of the castle and can do whatever he chooses, whenever he chooses and however he wants to without his having to answer to anyone and anyone who disputes that will find them selves pulling mucking duty in the prison slave ships for a few years of their service, is that understood?" and his dark blue eyes bored into those of the two guards.

The two guards realized immediately then who it was that they were talking to and straightened noticeably, saluting crisply. "Yes milord!" they both said in unison. "No disrespect was intended, we are just simple soldiers trying to protecting the castle."

"Good then stick to that rather than harassing the people inside of it." Damien told them in a manner that sounded almost more like an order than a suggestion.

Now he noticed that both of the women were smiling at him instead of Logan as they exited the door that the guards now politely held open for them, Damien whispered in a low voice loud enough for only Logan to hear. "Ladies also like a man who is confident enough to know when to take charge in a situation." and it was Logan's turn to grin now.

Caliban watched from a side street's dark shadows as the two young men along with their female companions exited out of the kitchen entrance and made their way out into the city streets. His slate blue eyes were cold and hard, though a slow smile slid across his face as he fell in behind them and started the hunt.

A.V. Wedhorn

Chapter 11
The Walk

The cool night air of Castlekeep smelled so strongly of the sea that Damien thought he could taste salt in the air. Music, laughter and multitudes of people filled the nighttime streets celebrating. No one neither noticed nor paid attention to the two couples weaving their way through them until too loud and raucous female voices called out from one of the many overhead balconies that looked out over the street.

"Hey Logan, why don't you and your handsome friend there get rid of those fancy ladies and let a pair of professionals handle those manly needs of yours."

All looked up to see a pair of prostitutes coyly fluttering their eyelashes at them invitingly. Both were scantily clad barely dressed buxom ladies with painted faces, smiling down at them.

"Would if I could ladies," Logan said in a good-natured manner, emphasizing the word ladies. "But I gave my word to these lovely young ladies here with me that I would see them safely home with only their painted lips mussed for the trouble."

Meralda hit him playfully in the shoulder with her small fist. Asrielle on the other hand gave Damien an almost cool appraising look and he wondered what would happen to him if he did indeed try to kiss her.

"Maybe though," Logan said looking about in a conspiratorial manner, as if he was getting ready to tell a secret. "We'll stop back by later and accept your generous offer."

Both of the ladies laughed raucous laughs at this and the one who had spoken a moment earlier said, "Likely story Logan Longshadow and one that we have heard before. Be off with you now and take your ladies home. Don't come back this way or else we might decide to take you up on your offer and not give you any say in the matter."

With a final wave at the ladies, the four young people continued on and were soon out of the brothel section and into the more well to do merchants quarter. They stopped at a rather large, nice two-storied house with an iron wrought fence surrounding it.

Damien and Asrielle turned away and stepped off to one side as Logan and Meralda said goodnight to each other for several very long moments.

Damien wondered what Cassica Essen was doing right now and if she would let him say good night to her the way that Logan was saying to Meralda. Finally Meralda called goodnight out to him also and made her way through the gate and up into the large house.

Asrielle who hadn't spoken now quickly reached up and took him by the chin and kissed him hard on the lips and molded her small body against his for a brief moment saying, "Try to remember me next time, when we are out and not the little red head." Then she turned and ran off after her sister.

How, Damien wondered, had she known whom I had been thinking of? And how did they understand men so well when no man he knew could make heads or tales of them.

Once the door safely closed behind them, Damien turned to Logan and asked. "So now are you going to tell me what is going on between you and her?" he threw his thumb back towards the house behind them.

Logan smiled a roguish smile at him and said. "Her father is one of the richest merchants in the entire city and he cheated me out of a large sum of money."

"What!" Damien said in an incredulous tone, a shocked look on his face. "Somebody actually managed to swindle you out of some money?"

In all the years he had known Logan he had never heard anyone ever getting the better of the sandy haired young man. This was due in Logan's part to his careful planning and manipulations.

"Yes!" Logan said with a rather sheepish grin on his handsome face. "Twice in fact he got me and if you ever mention a word of that to anyone I'll start all kinds of vicious rumors about you all over town."

"Twice." Damien's echoed his friend's words and you could hear a slight bit of humor in his voice. "Are you sure you're not just losing your touch?" he asked Logan smiling and biting back a bit of laughter.

Logan turned to face him and a cocky smile was on his face, "I forgot Simon's first rule, 'Know your enemy.'"

Damien laughed at this thinking to himself how close it was to Tiko's own first rule, 'Never underestimate your enemy.' A thought occurred to him and he asked, "You're not using that girl just so that you can get some information on her house so that you can rob her father are you?"

"Let's just say," Logan answered him with a sly smile, "That girl is a wealth of information about her father, his business and all of his holdings, none of it matters though because she will be my revenge against her father."

"I don't understand," Damien said and then skeptically added. "It didn't look like to me that you were planning anything vengeful towards her at all." Damien flashed his friend his lopsided grin. "In fact it almost looked like to me as if you were enjoying her company, almost as if you were courting her."

"I never said I was going to use her to steal from her father," Logan said eyeing him with a twinkle in his green eyes, "but I do intend on robbing him of one of his most valuable treasures. She's beautiful and she enjoys my company and yes I do have plans for her."

"Well, if you're not intending on using her to steal from her father how are you going to get him back for cheating you?" Damien asked him.

Logan gave him an appraising stare, his green eyes narrowing into thin slits, then he said in an even tone. "This goes no farther than you or me alright, I do have some enemies in this city who could make things bad for me or her if they ever knew or found out what I'm about to say." He waited until Damien actually nodded in agreement before he continued, saying. "I do like her. So much so, that I'm going to get revenge on her father by marrying her some day!"

Damien stopped dead in his tracks at the words he had heard his friend say, they struck him like unseen blows. He felt his jaw go slack for the second time that night. "Are you serious?" he asked, looking at Logan through wide eyes. "Did I just here you say that you were going to marry her?"

"Yes I did." Logan said in a serious sounding voice. "I happen to like her and enjoy her company a lot and she likes mine. At the moment I can think of nothing better than spending than spending the rest of my life with her. Plus it would settle the score between her father and me.

Not right away," he added hastily, "but someday in the future."

Damien still just stood there in the place where he had stopped while taking in the words he had just heard his friend say. Suddenly he stepped forward and clasped Logan about the shoulders with both hands, "I guess," he said happily. "Congratulations are in order."

Logan smiled at him until he asked. "So what does your soon-to-be wife think about your engagement?"

Logan's face reddened slightly before he turned away from Damien mumbling. "Well," he hedged a moment before answering, "She doesn't know about it yet."

Damien looked at him and arched an eyebrow in much the same manner as Abraim did when he was their tutor and they hadn't completed their assignments. "What?" he asked skeptically, "how can you be so certain that after you propose that she'll even accept?"

Logan scoffed derisively saying, "I'm sure that once she finds out how interested in her I am she won't hesitate to throw herself at my feet and beg me to marry her, I am after all the most eligible and handsomest bachelor in town."

Damien looked warily at him out of the corner of his eye as they continued walking again, "And what does that make me then?"

Logan looked at him and grinned evilly, "the ugliest, of course." Damien gave him a sideways glare this time and then they both laughed.

"Uh-huh," Damien said smiling, "more than likely, after she gets to know you like I do, they will probably have to chain her to a greater mondor, to keep her from running away instead!" Damien was referring to one of the giant sized lizards used by the Koraceen nomads in the Sandlands to pull their long caravans. A greater mondor or sand dragon as they are sometimes called, can weigh about fifteen to twenty thousand pounds and can carry or pull just about anything.

* * *

Caliban trailed along behind them following at a safe distance. Using a cloak that he had retrieved from Dalmar's carriage to alter his appearance as he moved. When he was sure of where they would go next, he would go down a parallel street using the buildings around them as cover, alternating his routes, sometimes he would bend his knees to alter his height, other times he would use the cloak as a shawl and wrap it about his head as an old woman would do. Caliban was like a chameleon, even with his oddly white features and almost silver blond hair, he could fit in anywhere. He still wasn't sure whether or not he had been spotted by the sandy haired man. That one, he determined, had very good instincts. Caliban knew that somehow he had sensed his presence by the way that he kept looking around. Or maybe he was just the really precautious type. It really didn't matter to the assassin mage. He knew that he would still make his kill tonight, before it was over.

* * *

Logan and Damien moved along for a while when something in Logan's senses went to work. All of his younger life had been spent on the streets and early on he'd developed a sort of danger sense inside of him and now he was feeling it. He looked about in every direction then he chose a darkened alley with a very little room on either side and moved down it.

Halfway down the alley Damien stepped over something that looked suspiciously like it might have been a dead body. He asked Logan, "What's wrong? Why aren't we going back to the castle?"

Logan stopped and faced him saying, "I don't know

why, but I have been having one of my feelings that says we are been being followed and have been so all night since the moment we hit the streets this evening."

Damien quickly looked about, his trained senses instantly alert as he scanned the alleyway behind and in front of them, taking in everything around them like he had been taught. "Are you sure?"

"No," Logan answered, "It was just a feeling, sort of like trepidation or something."

Damien nodded, deciding to keep his eyes alert for any signs of danger. Long ago he had learnt to never doubt any of Logan's feelings whenever they occurred. He was almost precognitive in his abilities about warnings of danger. That had saved them both a lot of trouble numerous times, so many in fact that he had lost count.

"Have you seen anyone?" Damien asked as he once again scanned the alley. He knew that he could probe outward with his senses like he had done in the woods but here in the city there were way too many people and he wouldn't be able to filter through all of them.

"Not in a while," answered Logan, "But I thought I did once, whoever though it was I think gave up."

"Probably just a foot pad then, out looking for an easy mark." Damien told him and Logan nodded in agreement. "You know," Damien continued, "two drunken Lords out walking about the city."

"I was kind of hoping that whoever it was would have followed us down this alley and showed themselves. But it doesn't look like it's going to happen," Logan said with a regretful sigh and added. "No fun at all."

Damien just grinned and chuckled. "So since our mysterious follower is not coming to our little party, where are we going to go now?" he asked curiously as they stepped on out of the darkened alley and back out into the open streets.

Logan, leading the way out, flashed a quick grin at him

from over his shoulder as he said. "Hold on for a minute and you'll see. It's a surprise." then he continued to lead him deeper into the heart of the city.

Finally they turned down a darkened and deserted street, not much bigger than the alleyway they had been in earlier. Damien sensed that they had reached their destination.

Something about the street was odd and it took him a moment before he could figure out what it was. This street was deserted but everywhere else in the city people were celebrating. He could hear people in the other streets about him and knew that they had to be close to the merchant's market. Curious, Damien wondered where it was that Logan was taking him. For a moment he wondered whether or not it was the thieves guild from which Logan had been banished and he was using his status as Lord Richard's son to gain him access, so that he could talk to Jediaa like Simon wanted, but he realized that the guild was down by the water front. They were nowhere close to there. Besides he thought to himself the matters between Jediaa and Logan were of a personal nature and his friend wouldn't use him in that manner. What was going on between Logan and Jediaa was something that they had to settle between themselves. It would not be settled by anyone else sitting in the middle.

"Are we there yet?" Damien heard himself ask, as his training took over and he once again started scanning the shadows of the dark street for any kind of movement.

Logan didn't answer instead he just waved at Damien to be patient and continued leading him down the dark street until they reached an intersection with another alley like street. Where the two streets met, they formed a T intersection. At the center, a dark building with a shabby looking porch and a battered door stood. Logan stepped up onto the porch and began pounding loudly on the old door with his fist.

Damien noticed a slight flicker of light from under the door.

"Whose there?" called out a muffled reedy sounding voice from the other side of the closed wooden door.

Logan grinned and said. "It's me Moris, who else would it be at your back door this late? Open up!"

"I know lots of its me's," called the voice from behind the door. "It's a very popular name, but I'm not allowed to open my door to any its me's this late at night. My foster son would have my head for doing so."

Damien laughed out loud at hearing this, Logan though, let out an audible groan at this and rolled his eyes in exasperation.

The young battlemage realized then where they were. Logan hadn't always lived on the streets of Castlekeep. He'd been taken in by a man that he'd wanted to remain secret, even from him. This must be where they were now.

Damien knew that Logan had a secret place, but he had never asked where it was. That way he couldn't ever reveal it to any of Logan's enemies even by accident. Sometimes the thieves that Logan associated with could get a bit angry and he needed a place unknown to anyone for him to hide.

He did know Logan lived with a man he had met while trying to steal some jewels from a shop. As a child, Logan got caught with his hands in one of his cases, but instead of punishing him, the old man took him in and taught him a trade. Actually, he helped him learn more of the trade his parents had started teaching him. Logan had always promised to one day introduce him to Moris, his adopted father and tonight finally looked like it was going to be that night.

"After nearly twelve years of living with you Moris." Logan said in a hiss, "I'm sure by now that you recognize my voice."

When there was no response, Logan groaned again then in a much louder voice he said. "It's me Logan, Moris!

Now open this door right now, before people start thinking that I am crazy for standing out here shouting at a closed door and call the watch on me."

"Oh, Logan it's you," came the reply from behind the door, "I thought I recognized your voice."

Logan shook his head again exasperation showing clearly on his features and Damien kept laughing. "Stop laughing!" Logan glared at him. "He does this just to annoy me." Saying that, only made Damien laugh even harder.

"Of course I'll open the door for you Logan," came the muffled voice again. "But before I do, I need to know whom the finely dressed young man is standing next to you. You know you're always warning me to be too careful with all of these refugees and ruffians about on the streets."

Damien knew now that he was also hearing more than a bit of humor in the old man's voice and also he could tell that he knew exactly how to push Logan's buttons. He turned to the door. Not seeing any sort of peephole other than a dirty grimy window through which no light shown. He wondered how the old man had known he was on the porch out there with Logan.

"This is Damien. I told you about him," Logan said really sounding exasperated now. "The one who went to Westlake, to study and become a battlemage."

Several loud clicks sounded from and the battered door was pulled open with a quickness that surprised both Damien and Logan.

A small balding round faced man with bright eyes moved out onto the porch clasping his hands together as he beamed at Damien. "Lord Richards ward?" he asked directing the question at Logan and turning his bright eyes back onto Damien's.

"One and the same!" Logan said in a proud voice as he smiled at the old man.

The old man named Moris gave Damien a wink that was not seen by Logan before rounding on him. "And here

I thought all of those years you were making up those stories about having the Lord's son as a friend just so that you could get out of having to do work."

Logan started to protest but the little old man cut him off with a wave of his hand, "Go get a pot of tea started, while I entertain our important guest, it's not everyday that we have someone of royal blood in our house." Moris snapped. "Somebody would think that I never taught you a bit of manners."

Logan looked at him wide eyed then grumbled a reply of some sort as he headed off into the house. The old man watched him go then happily said to Damien. "Keeping him in check keeps him from getting a swelled head."

The young battlemage laughed and nodded his head, thinking to himself that he already liked this old fellow.

Moris reached out a withered looking old hand and took Damien by the arm steering him towards the door. "Come inside milord, come in and see what kind of fine things I have for sale."

Damien allowed himself to be led in by the old man, listening to him tell him how happy he was to have one of Lord Richards's fine sons here in his humble house.

Logan brought a pot of steaming tea and some cups out of the kitchen. He set it down on one of the cases to cool. Then he began to look through the cases as if he was searching for something particular.

"So milord," Moris said smiling and waving a hand at all of the cases in the room, "How may I be of assistance to you, here you will find some of the finest jewelry in the entire western realm. Could I interest you in one of my finer pieces?" Moris asked as he led Damien once again by the arm to a large display case.

"It's also some of the most stolen jewelry in the entire realm, Damien." Logan said his green eyes twinkling cheerily, "I know. I stole most of it for him."

Moris shot the young thief a baleful look, then reached

into one of the many cases. "Here you go milord, this one looks like it would suit you just fine"

Damien studied the necklace in front of him and started to reach out a hand to touch it when Logan said, "You don't want that one, it's a fake. On top of having some of the best jewelry in the west, Moris also has some of the finest fakes you'll ever see."

Spinning on Logan, Moris gave him another hateful glare. "What are you trying to do? Cause me to become poor in my old age and have to retire to the beggar house?"

"No!" Logan told him and in even tone. "I'm trying to protect my best friend, who also happens by chance to be a lord's son, from a predatory and unscrupulous jewel merchant."

Moris stared at Logan then turned back to Damien with smiling eyes. "No will ever be able to say that I didn't manage to instill a little bit of honor and morals in him." and he pointed a finger in Logan's direction, "Will they?"

Damien smiled at the old man realizing that he had been testing Logan to see his reaction by selling worthless junk to his friend and judging by the smile on Moris' face Damien figured that Logan had passed. The young spythief didn't even notice the look of fatherly pride that Moris gave him at that moment. Damien did and smiled at both of them.

Logan's head was still inside the case and he continued his search until finally he exclaimed. "Here they are!" as he grabbed something up from inside and then stood up holding his hand down at his side.

"Good now that you have finally found what it was you looking for, maybe now you can pour our tea." Moris said snidely.

Logan glanced over at him and rolled his eyes again but he did start pouring the tea.

"So what is it that you retrieved from my case?" Moris asked as he grabbed up the steaming cup.

"Nothing important, really," Logan hedged trying to avoid answering the question.

Moris must have heard something in Logan's voice because he immediately asked the same question again. This time though, there was a little more force in his voice as he asked the second time.

"What difference does it make what it is?" Logan stated. "In this case, it's mine to do with as I choose."

Moris rounded on Damien and asked him. "Its something for that girl isn't it, that merchant's daughter?"

Damien started to voice a reply but Moris cut him off by saying, "You don't have to answer that, I already know the answer." The old jewel merchant took a deep breath as if to steady himself before he turned back to Logan. "I hope that you are not giving her these presents in hopes of hurting her in order to get revenge on her father? Because if you are Logan Longshadow, you won't ever leave this store again with a single item whether it's yours or not! I won't let it happen! I did not raise you to be that sort of man, regardless whatever they taught you in that spying school of yours." Moris shouted defiantly a bit of fire in his voice. The little old man seemed to swell up double in size.

Logan looked at the outraged little old man who was puffed up like a rooster defending his territory and started to laugh, a big laugh that came up from his belly. Damien, who knew Logan's true intentions, found the laughter contagious and he too started to laugh as well.

"What?" Moris still looking puffed up demanded, looking at both of them as if they had gone crazy. "What's going on? Did I miss something?"

Logan gave him a placating smile, "I do intend upon getting revenge on her father, that much is certain but," he held up a hand stopping Moris before he could protest. "Not in the way you think," Logan placed a hand on Moris' shoulder saying as he flashed him a devilish grin, "I intend to marry her."

Moris, who had started to take a sip of his tea, coughed and sprayed the liquid that he had been trying to drink all over the room. "You're what!" the little old man shouted at him staring at Logan in disbelief his eyes boggling.

Damien thought that the old man looked like he was going to have a heart attack. "Did he say what I thought he said?"

Damien and Logan both looked at each other then as if they were one person they said at the same time. "Yes!"

Moris looked around for a moment, found a chair and heavily sat down in it, sighing deeply. "I have always wondered when the day would come." the old man told him and tears began welling up in the corners of his eyes. "And I wondered what I would say to you when it got here and I planned for it but now that it is here I can't think of nothing to say except congratulations and good luck." Moris started to take another sip of tea but stopped and set the cup down, he left the room through the backdoor without saying a word

"Where do you think he is going?" Damien asked Logan who shrugged his shoulders and shook his head. A half minute later Moris reappeared with a bottle of wine and three long stemmed wine glasses. He set these on the counter, opened the bottle and poured the wine into them. "This is a cause for celebration," and he handed each of the young men a glass and took one for himself, "This is Elsberry wine, the finest made, so sip it slowly to enjoy it."

Damien shook his head and said, "I wouldn't be celebrating too much yet, Moris. He hasn't even asked to her yet or even made her aware of his intentions."

Moris took a sip of the wine before he spoke. "If Logan says he's going to marry her, then he's going to marry her. He wouldn't even consider such a thing if he didn't think he has some chance of success. You!" Moris said pointing a finger at Damien, "are his best friend and have you ever known him to take on something that he didn't think he couldn't succeed at?"

Damien didn't even have to consider this and nodded, agreeing with Moris. "Your right."

"Well, there you go. Now he just needs to be getting about it. That way he can make me a grandfather."

A choking, noise came from across the room and this time it was Logan's turn to cough and sputter.

"W..What?" Logan said in between coughs sounding shocked.

"What nothing!" Moris said, leveling a boney finger at him pointing. "Someday you will have children of your own and that means that I will be a grandfather too, at least one boy and girl. But for now let's just celebrate your pending engagement."

And that is just what they did for the next two hours until the small bottle of wine Moris had provided was empty.

The moment that the last glass was drained, Logan announced that they had to get back to the castle.

As they made their way to the back door Damien once again noticed the dirt stained window and was reminded of the question that he had wanted to ask when they had first arrived.

"Moris, with that window being so dirty and grimy, how on Tyrus did you ever know that I was outside with Logan when we first arrived on your doorstep?"

Moris gave him a sly smile, "Not all tricks and magic comes from books or spells you know. Come here and I'll show you a marvelous thing.

He led Damien across the room with a wave of his hand to what appeared to be a hole set in the wall next to the door.

"Logan," the old man said, "Go outside and stand on the step for the benefit of our guest while I show him a little of my own magic."

"Magic!" sniffed Logan disgustedly as he opened the

door and stepped out onto the porch, closing the door behind him.

"Now." Moris said, taking Damien by the arm, "look into this hole here and see what you will see."

Damien looked skeptically at the old man but did as he was bid. He was surprised when he saw the top of Logan's head below him in his field of vision.

Pulling his eye back he asked in a pleasantly surprised voice, "how is that possible, how can we see him like that?"

Moris smiled a delighted little smile at the question, pleased that his little trick had impressed the young battlemage and then said. "Since you are Lord Richards ward and a battlemage I'll let you in on my little secret because you never know when such knowledge may come in handy." Moris told him that through the use of mirrors properly positioned along a tunnel in the wall he could see anyone standing on either porch or coming up the alley.

One never knew when knowing something like that might come in handy and Damien thanked him for sharing the knowledge. He also realized where Logan had gotten the idea for his thieves' mirror. The door reopened and Logan looked back in saying, "We have to get going now."

Chapter 12
The Hunter

Caliban realized that this darkened alleyway must be the final destination of the pair and watched as they entered the backdoor of a building. It was easy enough to spot the doorway through which they had gone, because it was the only bright light shining in the dark abandoned empty street. Once they were inside he continued on down the street at a quick pace, hoping they were going to be there for a while.

When the young assassin mage reached the door to the two-story building they had entered, he saw another street went off to the right directly in line with the door making it a perfect killing zone. A T-intersection formed with the door that his target entered at its head, providing that his quarry left from the same door they entered. He could set himself up at almost any distance in this side street and have an unblocked view of his target. All he had to after that was to sit and wait.

Keeping to the dark shadows so that nobody noticed his passing, the assassin mage moved off about halfway down the alleyway. Caliban picked a spot that was on the other side of a porch and veiled in complete darkness. Squatting next to the wall that he would use as a support, he unslung his bag. He removed a small crossbow slightly larger than a handheld, a bolt and a vial. He left his bag open on the ground at his feet so that he could put the items he was using back in quickly and make a speedy getaway after he was finished.

Picking up the vial, he removed the cap very carefully, being absolutely certain that none of the vial's contents seeped out and came into contact with his own skin. Next he picked up the bolt and holding it with one hand and the vial with another, he poured its contents onto the bolt's tip. A red liquid oozed out slowly and covered the tip, causing it to glow eerily in the darkness. Setting the bolt off to one side, he closed the vial and placed it back into the bag. Caliban picked up the bolt and inspected its tip making sure that it had been completely covered in the insidious glowing red liquid. Satisfied with his work he then loaded the bolt into the crossbow, sat back and wondered how long he would have to wait until his quarry decided to leave the building. He also wondered whether or not he had applied enough glow adder venom to the bolt. Glow adders are extremely rare and extremely poisonous snakes that live in the mountain caves to the south and east of Kallamar. The reason they are called glow adders is that they give off a luminescent type glow that they use in dark caves in order to lure prey to them by the light they emit. Their bites are both paralyzing and deadly. Once a person or creature is bitten, the poison of the glow adder moves into the victim's bloodstream paralyzing them, shutting down the victim's organs one at a time until they died.

Two hours of waiting and finally the backdoor of the building opened, spilling light out into the darkness.

Caliban's waiting blue eyes were immediately drawn to it, but he couldn't see his mark yet, this Damien Daverge who his father and the royal regent wanted dead. He hoped he would be able to get this over with soon.

Picking up the crossbow he sighted down its length at the patch of bright light. The first person out the door was the tall sandy haired blond man who had accompanied his victim into the building. The man stood there a moment then he leaned back inside, said something and stood back up. The next man out the door was a very short one who gave the taller man a hug, then the short man reached out and shook the hand of Caliban's victim as he moved into view. The assassin sighted very carefully now and steadied his breathing as he waited for his victim to turn and face him. Silhouetted in the doorway's light, Damien Daverge made a perfect target. Caliban figured that if for some reason the crossbow bolt didn't kill his target the powerful poison on its tip, certainly would, once it hit his bloodstream. His target turned towards him and Caliban released all of the air out of his lungs to steady the shot then gently squeezed the trigger on the crossbow letting the bolt fly.

* * *

Years of living on the streets had given Logan a survival instinct that he hardly ever neglected to pay attention to, but tonight for some reason, it was different. Logan decided they were ridiculous and he ignored them.

"Anyway," he thought to himself, "who would dare to attack him considering that right now he was in the company of a fully trained battlemage."

"Come on Damien we had better get going," Logan said again. "Before your father starts sending out people to find us."

Damien started to reply as he turned away from Moris

but at that moment the poisoned crossbow bolt struck him dead center in the chest blasting him backwards up off of his feet and his reply came out only as a loud gurgling gasping sound of pain.

Logan spun at the hollow thumping sound of the bolt hitting flesh, just in time to hear the horrific strangled noise that came out of his friend's throat. He saw the bolt impact into his chest accompanied by a spray of blood which filled the air as he was driven over backwards by its force and fell back onto the stone porch.

He just stood rooted in place for a moment as the shock of what he had just seen froze him in place until Moris grabbed him by the arm and yelled at him to help. His foster father had grabbed a handful of rags off of a counter from inside the house and was attempting to use them to staunch the flow of blood that was pouring out of the bolt centered in Damien's chest.

"We have to get him to a priest as quickly as possible!" Moris said hastily, "but we need a way of carrying him with out doing anymore damage to his body, the bolt is lodged close to his heart and could kill him if we move him too much." then he gingerly touched at the wooden shaft where it protruded out of Damien's chest.

Racing quickly back into the house, Logan looked frantically about for something, anything, that he could use. Suddenly he heard Simon's chiding voice in his head saying, 'In every situation there is always a solution. You just have to find it.' He didn't see a thing at first, but his training took over and he analyzed the entire room. He saw what he could use immediately, then cursed himself for not having seen it a moment before.

He grabbed hold of the long heavy drapes that Moris used to cover the windows when he closed up the shop at night and gave them a fierce yank that tore the cloth from its bindings with a ripping sound. Gathering them up in his arms Logan raced back out to the back porch where his foster father was kneeling next to his best friend urging him to hold a wadded mass of rags to his chest in order to stop the bleeding and assuring him that he was going to be okay.

Logan laid out the drapes along side Damien's body, positioning himself at his head and telling Moris to go to his feet.

Together along with a pain filled groan from Damien, they lifted him up and carefully placed him on top the heavy drapes.

With yet another groan as they set him back down. Damien said weakly. "First it was blankets, now it is drapes, what else will I be wrapped in today?"

In spite of the grim situation, Logan smiled down at him as the two men took hold of the drapes and lifted him up into the air.

Moris scolded the young battlemage, saying, "Don't speak milord, you need to save all of your strength and hold those rags in place." With age-spotted hands Moris held onto his side of the makeshift litter. Together Logan and the old man raced back through the house. Logan opened another door that led out onto one of the major streets that encircled the Bazaar.

Masses of people still filled the square despite the late hour. Logan bellowed for them to get out of the way as he and Moris pushed and shoved their way through the crowds screaming at the top of their lungs that they were carrying a dying man.

They were headed to the closest place that had a healer of worth, the castle, but halfway across the plaza Moris collapsed, his old body giving out under the strain and he fell onto his knees. The old shopkeeper was not used to this kind of exertion and now he too was clutching at his chest as he gasped for air.

Concern for Moris clearly etched itself onto Logan's face and he carefully set down his end of the makeshift litter and knelt beside the collapsed old man.

"Forget about me!" wheezed Moris angrily waving him off with a hand, "I'm just too old and out of shape for this, I'm not going to be able to make it, find someone else and don't you dare let it be said that a lords son was killed on my doorstep, I'll never have a bit of business in this town ever again."

Logan scanned the crowd about him that had formed a circle of onlookers when the old man had collapsed. He began screaming for someone, anyone to please help him.

Spotting a young member of the city watch who had came over to see what was happening Logan called out to him, pointing at Damien with an anxious finger. "This is Damien Daverge and he has been badly wounded. I have to get him to a cleric as soon as possible and the closest one would be at the castle."

The young watchman rushed over and started to pick up the opposite end of the litter when two more men stepped out of the crowd offering their assistance. The larger older one saying, "You will make better time with four!"

"C'mon then!" Logan ordered with a sense of urgency clearly in his voice. Then the four men picked up Damien's body and once again hurried on towards the castle.

The guards at the entrance to the castles grounds saw the four men racing towards them carrying what look like a body wrapped in room drapes. The leader held out a mailed hand to stop them and Logan called out loudly. "This is Damien Daverge, he has been badly wounded and is going to die unless we get him inside to a priest quickly."

The leader asked if there was any way that they could help or offer assistance.

Logan told them they could and ordered them to clear a pathway straight to the ballroom. There he hoped to find one of high priests of one of the many orders that filled the city in attendance at the party. Perhaps he would find Ramin who was Lord Richard's own highpriest.

The leader of the guards proceeded to have his men clear a path by yelling at the guests to get out of the way and pushing them bodily when they didn't move fast enough. If the situation hadn't been so serious, Logan would have laughed out loud at the sight of so many a rich pompous nobles being thrown onto their asses, or pushed off the walk into the bushes and hedges by the guardsmen.

The young thief, his three helpers and the group of guards that surrounded them burst into the ballroom. They laid out Damien's body, a bloody crossbow bolt sticking up out of his chest. He was clutching a sodden mass of blood soaked rags to his wound.

Logan immediately began to yell, screaming loudly for a cleric or priest to come and help.

Lord Richard Daverge took one look at the body of his ward, his eyes flashed in disbelief and then they went immediately to shock. Seeing the blood, he began issuing orders in a deep booming authoritative voice that demanded instant obedience from all of those gathered about the room.

Sentinel guards stepped in on his orders and without hesitation, began clearing the entire chamber of all of the night's guests. Using their pole arms, they pushed everyone into an adjoining chamber where the guests could still see what was going on but weren't able to interfere.

Lord Richard was pleased at the speed at which his men worked. The last thing he needed right now was a bunch of curious onlookers. From amongst the guards he dispatched one of them to find Ramin, who was high priest and cleric of the castle and the city's most powerful healer.

"And tell him to be quick about it, my son's life depends on it." he shouted at the man pointing at the body lying on the floor.

Balthazar, his hawkish face looking grave was already at Logan's side kneeling down next to Damien's prostrate form and examining the wound in his chest with gently probing fingers.

Lord Richard now spun on Logan, his steel grey eyes blazing fire. "What happened and how?" he demanded fixing the young spythief in place with an angry stare.

"W...We went out milord." Logan answered with a slight stammer in his voice. He was scared. In all of his years of living and working here in the castle he had never once seen Lord Richard's face look anything like the way it looked right now. "To escort some lady friends of mine home and to visit my foster father whom Damien has never met." he broke down into tears then as he continued. "It was my entire fault milord," Logan said as he met the angry grey eyes of Damien's adopted father with his own green ones, "I felt a sense of danger just before we were ambushed by someone with a crossbow. I dismissed the feeling, thinking that it was nothing. Nobody would dare attack us considering that he is a battlemage and I am fairly well known about the city also."

At seeing the fear-filled look in Logan's green eyes, Lord Richard shook his head to relieve some of the anger he was feeling. He went over and laid a comforting hand on Logan's shoulder telling him that it was all right. Then he turned and yelled in a voice so loud it almost shook the castle itself. "Where in the god's hell is that fat priest?" he thundered scanning the room with his anxious eyes.

"Maybe I can help until he gets here milord?" came a soft-spoken female voice from behind him.

Lord Richard turned to find one of the party's guests separating herself from the others and slipping under the guards pikes and coming forward, he could tell by her dress that she was a cleric, but what he couldn't see was her holy symbol. All he saw was that she had sky blue eyes, short curly strawberry blonde hair and was offering to help in this time of need.

Without even waiting for his answer, she stepped past him and knelt down next to his adopted sons' body and began gently examining the wound with softly probing fingers.

A commotion started in the outer chamber and Ramin shoved himself bodily through the crowd, running. In heaving gasps he said, "I'm here milord!" Taking in the entire situation in one quick glance the fat priest didn't waste any more time on words, instead he ran over and knelt down next to the other cleric bending over Damien's body.

Damien chose that moment to open his eyes and the priest took a second to reassure him that everything was okay while he also quickly and skillfully examined the wound and bolt in his chest.

"You!" Damien said, looking up into the face of the strawberry blonde haired young woman kneeling over him. "I saw you fight today, you fight very well."

"So did you," she answered, then placed a finger over his lips cutting off any other words he was about to say. "Save your strength milord, you are going to need all of it in a few moments I think."

"I don't feel any barbs under the skin holding it into place." Ramin said turning to face the female cleric at his side.

"Neither did I," returned the female cleric seriously, giving him an even and direct look.

Ramin glanced at the symbol that hung almost unseen next to her tunic and felt his eyes grow wide at what he saw there. "If you are a true cleric of Dar then I'm going to assume that you would know."

"I am," she stated, "and I do."

"So when I pull this shaft out then, you immediately need to staunch the bleeding, because if my assumption is right, this thing is blocking an artery and when I pull it out there is going to be a lot more blood than what there already is."

The younger female cleric nodded and removed her

cloak, wadding it into a ball, she placed it next to the wound and waited.

Taking a deep breath Ramin grabbed the shaft in his pudgy fingers and heaved upwards on the bolt, tearing it out of Damien's chest with a great sucking sound and an accompanying fountain of spurting blood.

The wounded battlemage let out a loud cry of pain and his dark blue eyes rolled back into his head as he fell unconscious.

Immediately the young cleric placed her gathered cloak over the wound and applied pressure in an attempt to stop the flow of the blood, which now gushed forth, bright and red.

Ramin carelessly threw the bolt away off to one side, discarding it as if it were a piece of trash, without even glancing at it. Taking one look at the ragged hole before the cloth covered it, the priest looked up into his lord's face and was about to say something but seeing the hard, fierce set of Lord Richards eyes as he looked down on them, decided against it and clamped his jaw shut with an audible click of teeth.

This lasted only a few moments until he changed his mind and felt compelled to tell his lord, how bad his adopted wards injury really was. "Seeing the extent of his injury milord." he said looking up into the cold countenance of Lord Richard's face, "I'll do the best that I can, but I can't promise anything." sweat glistened in little beads on the top of Ramin's bald head from the tension that he felt as he spoke.

"You will save his life Ramin, the welfare of the entire fourteen kingdoms depends on it." Lord Richard told him in a deadly calm voice. "He must not be allowed to die, or else we will all perish in the flames of civil war."

Ramin looked startled and surprised at this but didn't comment on his Lords words. He had more pressing matters to attend to at the moment. Sliding his hands partially under the cloak that the female cleric held to the wound, he felt for Damien's heartbeat. It took a moment but he found its weak and slightly faltering rhythm and softly he began to chant a prayer of healing, asking his goddess Lacina for her assistance in healing the young man whose life was now in his hands. A warm golden yellow glow enveloped his hands as the goddess of life and harvest answered her high priest's urgent prayers. Instantly the flow of blood coming out of the chest wound stopped and the priest felt the torn skin underneath his fingers begin to knit itself back together.

Several long moments passed until finally he removed his hands and the wadded blood soaked cloak. The only sign of the ragged hole that had been in Damien's chest was a vivid red scar over his heart.

The priest expelled a huge gust of air in relief and glanced up once again at his lord saying softly, "He's also been poisoned. I'm not sure how much more of the poison is still left in his system though and he will probably be very weak for several days yet. He is extremely lucky, the bolt struck this as it impacted, which deflected it enough that it didn't kill him outright." He held up an ornately designed amulet with a large gouge cut out of one side that held the battlemages emblem on it, a mailed fist wielding purefire. "A quarter inch to the left," he said to his lord, "and he would have never made it to the castle to be healed at all. It stopped most of the poison from entering his direct bloodstream."

Grasping his own medallion in his hands he said as he kissed it. "It's in my ladies hands now, there is nothing else that neither of us can do." he gestured at both himself and the female cleric next to him.

Richard Daverge's eyes took on a cold calculating expression as he listened to the priest's words. He turned his head about to see if the other guests were in hearing range of the priest's words. Then he looked around at the people gathered around his adopted son. There were the guards whom he motioned over towards the doors with a curt hand gesture. There were the three men who had helped Logan carry the body, standing off to one side far enough away that they wouldn't hear what he was going to say next. Balthazar and Ramin were there but he knew he could trust them to keep their mouths shut and Logan was busy studying the bolt that had been in his sons chest. That only left the female cleric who had helped Ramin and he couldn't just banish her out of the room so he had to hope that she would go along with what happened next. Moving to where he stood over the two kneeling clerics he listened to listened to Ramin's words.

"It's in the gods hands now there is nothing else that I can do." Ramin repeated again weakly, looking up at Lord Richard. Then he sat down on the floor next to the body too exhausted to move.

Lord Richard saw the crowds of guests watching them from the corridors and other rooms. Turning his back to them he said in a voice only loud enough for Ramin and the other cleric to hear. "Regardless what you see or hear next, I am grateful to you both and owe you a debt of gratitude that knows no bounds for saving my sons life."

Both Ramin and the female cleric looked up at the large Lord standing over them, puzzled expressions on their faces.

"Ramin, I'm sorry about this and I don't mean it," Lord Richard said as the grateful look fled his face.

"Sorry about wha.," the priest started to say but was stopped when Lord Richard roared in a thunderous voice, his face now going a vivid shade of crimson. "What!" then he thrust out an arm and in an impressive display of strength lifted the fat priest up and off the ground with only one hand by the neck of his robes. "He had better live! For if he dies priest, so to will you!" Lord Richard bellowed into the surprised priests face, spittle flew from the angry

Highlord's lips as he raged. "No maybes to it and you had better make sure of it, if you value your head sitting atop your shoulders."

"But milord." the shocked priest said, as he started to say something else in protest.

Not wanting his son's killer to know that he still lived, Lord Richard gave the fat priest such a vicious shake that it cut off whatever he was about to say. "If he dies priest then you will die right behind him. I don't want to hear that he's lost too much blood, I just want to hear that you are saving his life." with that said loud enough so that everyone in the adjoining room could hear it he hurled the fat priest back down onto the tiled floor next to Damien's body. Angrily, he spun on the guards and ordered them to escort all of the guests out while closing all of the doors to the castle behind them.

Once the guards had removed all of the guests and the doors were closed to the castle, Richard Daverge turned his attention to the three men who had assisted Logan in helping out his wounded son. Glancing over at Balthazar, he said in a voice just loud enough for only the advisor to hear, "Pretty good show huh, do you think they bought it?"

Despite the grimness of the situation, Balthazar smiled and said, "I almost believed it. I've always said that you missed your calling as an actor sire. That was a brilliant performance. It will be all over the city tomorrow that Damien is dying or dead already."

"Actually I want it said that he is dead," Lord Richard told his advisor, "Have Simon spread the word throughout the cities streets tonight."

Balthazar looked at him and a cunning expression filled the advisors hawk like eyes as he considered this. "Very good sire that is one rumor I'll make sure is spread, it should buy us some time, especially if whoever did this bought your performance like I did and believes that Damien is indeed dead."

A King's Quest

The three men and the female cleric who had assisted Ramin, were all standing off to one side of the room. As Lord Richard moved over closer, the blond haired thief, as he called Logan, was using a bit of cloth to pick up the bolt from where Ramin had tossed it.

"You two," he said and all except Logan turned to face him. Looking directly at the older big man with the dark shaggy hair and his younger companion he said. "If you see my advisor in the morning, I'll make sure that you are suitably rewarded for your assistance in trying to save my sons life."

The older man, a tall thick bodied man with the long coarse shaggy black hair bowed as he answered. "No thanks are necessary milord. We are just grateful to have been there to offer assistance to someone in need. We would have done it whether they were a Highlord's son or the poorest peasant's son."

Richard Daverge nodded his head in agreement with the other mans words. He knew that he too would have tried to do the same. "Well I hope that you will at least accept my thanks and know that I will never forgive the service you tried to offer and I owe you a favor in return and will gladly repay it whenever you need it as long as it is in my power to do so. Both men nodded in acceptance of his words. "Now though I must grieve for the loss of my son and would ask you to leave."

Without speaking a word, the older man and the younger man close behind, walked towards the door that a guard held open for them.

As they reached the entryway Lord Richard called out after a moment's consideration. "Do you have rooms in the city yet?"

"No milord," The older said turning back around. "Not yet, we had only just arrived before all of the excitement."

"Tell the guard then that I said to put you up in you up in the guest's chambers for visiting dignitaries. Stay as long as you like. You will be well cared for."

"Thank you milord, you are a most gracious host." the older man replied bowing to the Highlord of Castlekeep.

Lord Richard dismissed them with a nod and they left the room, then he turned his attention to the member of the cities watch who had also helped. He allowed a kindly smile to show on both his face and in his gray eyes as he looked at the young watchman who seemed to be staring at him in awe and looked as if he was slightly frightened to be standing in his presence.

"Who is your commander, Watchman?" he asked in a calming voice as he tried to put the nervous young man at ease.

"Milord." the young man said in a slightly quavering voice. He swallowed nervously, then visibly straightened and said in a firmer voice, "Watch Commander Thaedrann is my senior, Sir."

His answer didn't surprise Lord Richard, since the watchman had been in the market and he had personally assigned the market to Thaedrann's unit himself, to see how he could handle the pressures of command during the harvest festival.

"Well, tomorrow, I want you and your commander here to meet with me at noon okay?"

"Of course milord, at noon." The young watchman said crisply. "We will be here."

"Good, now get back to your post and thank you for your service watchman-," Lord Richard hesitated, realizing he didn't even know this young watchman's name.

"Watchman Gerund, milord." the young man offered. Lord Richard nodded at this and dismissed him also with a wave. Even though the young man was nervous, Lord Richard noticed he never took his eyes off of his. That said a lot about the young mans character. He had himself been a nervous young man once, surrounded by those he considered his superiors.

Gerund snapped to attention gave a crisp salute, turned and almost sprinted from the room in his haste to get away.

"Now!" The Highlord of Castlekeep thought silently to himself as he made his way over to the two clerics who were still kneeling on the ground next to his adopted son's body. "What do I do about her?" he eyed the young female cleric who had assisted Raman, studying her carefully. Standing next to the pair, he looked down at the young woman mopping at his son's brow with a cool cloth.

Ramin sat on the floor next to her issuing orders in a weak voice. The young woman whose back was to him was nodding her head in response to his commands. Lord Richard could see that his priest was completely spent. All of the energy seemed entirely drained out of the man.

Whatever the poison was used on his son, it must have been a very powerful one. The only other time he had ever seen the priest look so tired was when a plague had boiled up in the city twenty-five years ago and had killed thousands including, he thought with a hint of sadness, his first wife. She had her own beauty destroyed by the disease before it killed her. Ramin had refused to give up in combating the plague and had finally collapsed exhausted on a city street where he was found by the body counters when they accidentally mistook him for one of the many dead ones that littered the streets. One of the men had collapsed from fright when Ramin woke up, apparently coming back to life in their arms while they were carrying him to the wagons laden with corpses. A week later the plague had burnt itself out and the burnt out priest had himself slept for another week, recuperating and regaining strength. He had once explained to his Lord that every disease, poison, or wound that he cured depleted a certain amount of strength from the healer, depending on how bad the injury was. Ramin was the high priest of his goddess, Lacina and completely in her favor had fought the plague in the city for almost two weeks before being burnt out and succumbing to exhaustion, now he looked after having healed his son of this poison exactly as he had then twenty years ago. Someone must have gone through a lot of trouble to have found such a potent poison to try and kill his son with it.

The young cleric moved again. Lord Richard spotted her holy symbol now dangling out in the open and felt his eyes grow wide at the sight of it. The symbol, two hammers crossed with a sword in the center, was made out of mythryll and gleamed in the light. It was the symbol of Dar. Lord Richard realized then who this young woman must be. There couldn't be that many clerics of Dar this far west much less one who was a woman. Kendle had given an accurate description of the fight in the pit earlier and he figured that this must be the woman who had so easily dispatched Uligar Rothe, one of the most powerful fighters in the city. This could change a few things he thought to himself, one never knew where having one of the clerics of justice on your side could come in handy. She could prove very useful in his plans for helping Damien.

Moving over to where she knelt, the Highlord of Castlekeep asked as she looked up at him. "Is there any way that you might be able stay the night here in the castle and help look over him? Ramin is too spent to be of any sort of assistance."

"Of course there is," she said smiling up at him, a crooked little grin "somebody has to."

Lord Richard returned the smile and it struck him as sort of odd and he asked curiously as he looked at her. "Do I know you from somewhere?"

The female cleric of Dar laughed and told him that that was impossible. She only just arrived in the city yesterday from Muldar, the northeastern home of the clerics of Dar and had never been out of the mountains before now.

Lord Richard looked at her oddly and shook his head, not sure why he felt the way he had a moment ago, "It's settled then, I'll have an extra bed brought to my son's quarters for you to sleep in and thank you very much for your assistance. My advisor Balthazar," he gestured at the red robed man with the silver trim on his robes, "will make the arrangements for you."

He turned now to question Logan, hoping to find out what had exactly happened and he discovered to his surprise that the young thief was missing, disappeared from the room.

Unseen by anyone else as they watched the drama that was playing out on the floor of the ballroom, Logan went over and retrieved the bolt, carefully he had picked it up and wrapped it in a cloth sliding it into his tunic. He walked out of the hall soon after he heard Lord Richard scream something about how Damien had better live. Feeling like it was 'his fault,' he went directly to Damien's chambers where he had earlier left some things of his. He retrieved a long black coat that draped the length of his body, which he had over the years sewn numerous pockets and straps into. It held a wide assortment of weapons and tools. The long coat was what he called his fighting coat. He also grabbed the night spider cloak that Damien had given him as a gift and draped it over the coat. To his delight, the pair matched perfectly in length. Going over to bookshelf he pulled out a book and took something out of it. He stuck it into the hidden flap sewn into the top of his boot. He was going out to find this assassin who had tried to kill his best friend, regardless of whatever it took. Vengeance would indeed be his.

A.V. Wedhorn

Chapter 13
The Guild

    Logan slipped in and out of the darkness moving like a wraith through the night. He flew swiftly and silently across the rooftops and alleyways of the city he called home. No one in his old profession who made sounds on the roofs of the city stayed in their job very long.
    Thanks to the ring of spider walking that he possessed, he could stick to any surface with his hands or feet. He had no fear of falling. With the use of the silken night spider cloak from Damien, he was completely undetectable.
    The ring was his most prized possession. Years ago when he had been caught by Moris trying to pilfer his cases it had been that very ring that he had been trying to steal. Instead of calling the city watch, the old man took pity on him and allowed to move in.
    After having lived here almost all of his life Logan knew the large cities rooftops like the back of his own hand, he also knew which houses and buildings were

unlocked, locked, guarded by magical alarms and which ones were to be left alone altogether, to dangerous to mess with at all. These things were last on Logan's mind as he crisscrossed the entire city, hunting for the killer.

He had been to every contact Simon had in the city and had discovered nothing about the assassination attempt on Damien. That was the only thought in his brain right now. Damien had been shot and might not live out the rest of the night. To find his killer was the only thing that mattered to him at this moment. He had run out of all options on finding the killer or a cure for the poison used, except one. The Network, and seeing Jediaa who had banished him. Simon thought that he should try to talk to Jediaa again. Here was his chance to as he arrived at the docks.

Assassinations in Castlekeep were usually a sanctioned event, especially ones against the ruling family in the city and only Jediaa could give that order. Anyone else doing so without the Night tasker's permission would have to answer to him and the penalty was usually death.

Fog shrouded boats standing silent .and still filled the harbor. Each of these boats still housed a guard. Festival night or not, someone was pulling duty in case a few thieves took it upon themselves to relieve a few ships of their cargo. If any of these guards saw him slinking about on the rooftops above the city, some might even sound an alarm. He deliberately kept himself as low as possible as he peered out over the rooftop edge.

Jediaa's guild house was a looming two story, decrepit, looking warehouse that stood by itself away from all of the other buildings in the row. The building's dilapidated appearance with its broken boards and deceiving look was actually a disguise for outsiders. Underneath the rotted boards and ramshackle appearance was a granite fortress, so well defended that it almost rivaled the keep itself.

Logan wasn't sure how he would be received by the people within. But for Damien's sake he had to try. Five years earlier he had opted under Moris' advice to go to work for Lord Richard and the castle rather than taking over for Jediaa when he became old enough and the older man decided to retire. This act of leaving had earned him a banishment from the guild and a share of anger and disappointment in Jediaa's eyes. Until tonight he had stayed completely away from the guild with no contact whatsoever with any of its members as was stated in his exile and banishment.

Jediaa's stronghold was a formidable construct of three-foot granite blocks hidden by the wooden facade. About halfway up the sides of the building you could see holes surrounding the entire structure, these looked to be drainpipes for the rain that came from being so close to the sea. They did serve to remove the rain but they also had another purpose. The drains were attached to a pipe network on the top of the building where hidden guards in alcoves could pour vats of boiling oil onto any unwanted intruders. The rooftop guards were there to serve as both a first warning alarm and to activate the buildings defenses. Logan knew all about the outer defenses and also about what he could expect inside. He knew that he would have to figure out some way of bluffing his way into the interior of the building.

Green eyes twinkling mysteriously, he considered the problem. He loved puzzles and challenges and he knew this one would not be easy. He ran possibility after possibility through his mind for several moments casting out ideas that wouldn't work until he only had one idea left. Damien had been shot and by using this, he might be able to get inside the building. It was ironic because that was really the reason he was here. He would just have to embellish on the story a little.

Dropping a hand down to the top of his boot, he removed what appeared to be a letter from his hiding place. This was the third thing he had taken while in Damien's chambers. Using both hands he held the envelope up into the pale yellow moonlight and examined it carefully. Other than looking a little wrinkled, the letter was still in good shape. Most importantly, was the fact that you could still see Jediaa's full name clearly written in Lord Richard's very identifiable penmanship along with the Daverge family crest embossed on it. It was all he had and it would just have to suffice. He definitely wasn't about to let anyone open it up and read it

Swinging out over the wall Logan dropped about halfway down. He caught himself by the magic empowered ring of spider walking and slowed his momentum. Then he dropped the rest of the way down. Stepping out of the dark alleyway behind the building Logan removed the night spider cloak and revealed himself to the guards stationed all around him. They had been posted there to prevent anyone from doing what he had just done.

Logan saw two of the bums stiffen as he made his unexpected appearance and immediately he flashed them the guild sign with his fingertips. Both saw the familiar signal and noticeably relaxed, motioning him on towards the door.

He knocked the standard three, two, one knock and waited for the door to open. Logan moved through the doorway and into the entranceway, the hairs on the back of his neck stood erect and he knew that the archers hidden in the alcoves off to his left and right were doing their job by keeping him covered with their crossbows.

Logan waved a little gesture of greeting towards them while he waited. A stout burly looking dwarf with a long thick black single braided beard moved out of the dark shadows on the other side of the room and led him deeper into the building where Jediaa was waiting.

Standing at the other end of the hallway he watched Logan carefully and motioned him forward with one hand. The other hand was caressing a well-worn shiny ball that served as a counterweight on a wicked looking large single bladed heavy battle-axe. The axe itself had more than a share of notches in its handle signifying the amount kills or battles to its owner. The dwarf's hand, the one that he had used to motion Logan forward was now in a notch on the wall. He seemed to be holding onto a lever of some sort. Logan was very aware of what this lever was for. It was used to make the floor underneath him collapse and a good way to get rid of unwanted visitors, by way of the hidden spikes located twenty feet below. Fingering his ring of spider walking again, he started across. He wasn't worried about the pit so much because the ring would protect him from falling, but it would not stop the crossbows bolts that would be shot at him or the boiling oil that could be dropped on him from above if he somehow managed to avoid the spikes.

"State your business here, Logan Longshadow." the burly dwarf growled in a deep rough voice. "You know that you have been banned from here and are not welcome inside."

Logan inclined to his head in agreement before the rough looking dwarf. "I know this." and with his head still down respectfully, he continued. "but there is a matter of dire emergency, I have a letter from Lord Richard Daverge himself, addressed to Jediaa."

The burly dwarf named the Golan eyed him a moment before he held out his hand saying, "Here then give it to me and I'll make sure it is delivered."

Logan acted like he was considering this for a moment before he said, "Only I am allowed to deliver it, Lord Richard himself sent it even though he knows about my banishment, he said that only I was supposed to deliver it to Jediaa. It is a matter of a dire importance, a life hangs in the balance."

Golan nodded as he listened, then he turned to the door behind him, slid back a plate on the door and spoke into it, in a voice to low for Logan to hear. Motioning him forward, the dwarf waited until the ex thief was in front of him before he also stepped through the door and shut it behind him closing off the outer entrance.

Stairs were behind the second door and Logan moved down them very carefully, he dragged his hand with the ring of spider walking along the wall beside him in case Golan decided that now would be a good time to drop the stairs out from underneath him. Reaching the bottom Logan breathed a sigh of relief and reached out a hand to open the next door, but it opened in front of him before he could touch it.

This was his final destination and he could hear Golan coming down the stairs behind him as he stepped into Jediaa's inner sanctuary.

The inner sanctuary to Jediaa's stronghold was a huge underground cavern carved out of the very rock beneath the city itself. It was filled with burning braziers, which were placed strategically throughout to give off as much light as possible. It seemed to Logan nothing had changed very much during his long absence, except for a few faces that were turned in his direction.

Another dwarf named Goram, twin of Golan, stepped in next to Logan and all three of them moved out across the chamber.

Dwarven identical twins were a rare happening on Tyrus. Logan had never seen any others here or in the Iron Peak Mountains, which was home to the three-dwarven cities in the north. Kendle had assured him that he had never seen any in Alandria either where the southern hill clan dwarves lived at the feet of the Starcrest Mountains.

Twins like Golan and Goram were cherished and worshipped by other dwarves. The identical pair had been treated like idols for the better part of their younger lives until they had finally grown sick of it. They fled from the mountains to the city to start a new life. Jediaa had rescued the pair off of the streets in much of the same manner in which he had done with him but in their case he had put the formidable pair to work for him serving as bodyguards and protectors.

The twin dwarves have a rather eerie sort of way of communicating during battles. Somehow they always seem to know what the other one is going to be doing at all times and they use this gift to attack opponents simultaneously with rather devastating effects.

A rather large pillow chair could be seen halfway across the back wall of the chamber. This was where Jediaa held court. He could see the small man with his shoulder length dark hair and large dark eyes looking at him. He could see immediately in spite of trying to appear at ease, Jediaa wasn't relaxed at all. His dark eyes never left Logan's own as he came towards escorted by the pair.

Judging by the flat look in Jediaa's eyes, Logan wasn't sure what kind of reception he was going to get and he sighed inwardly at the notion of having to return here. He could also tell by the look in Jediaa's eyes that he hadn't forgiven him yet either.

Years earlier he had hoped to put the Guild life behind him and had severed all ties with his past life. Until now he had never needed the Guild or the network for anything.

Everyone followed his movements, anxious to see what would happen between the ruler of the undercity and his now unnamed prince once marked to follow him into power. Some shouted out greetings to him as he passed by which he returned in kind. The ones whose names he could not remember he acknowledged with simple nods. Even a few of his old team members were present. More than a few of his old associate's shook their heads at him, either dismayed that he had come here to face Jediaa's wrath or just plain shocked by his audacity.

"He misses you a lot lad. Let him have his moment in front of all. He might even forgive you" a furtive whisper came to him from his side as he passed through the crowd.

Logan looked down at an older woman with straight black hair and a black patch over one eye. It was Jas Kajyn, his favorite roof runner. He smiled at her and whispered his thanks back. It was Jas who had taught him how to both throw and use his knives.

Jediaa had never been known for his forgiving nature. He couldn't be, not in his profession. One sign of weakness and his enemies would be all over him, killing him and dividing up the spoils.

The crowds parted and there was the familiar small man, lounging in his chair with his dark eyes still locked on Logan. Jediaa's stare was so intense that it looked as if he were trying to bore holes right through him. Logan was used to the Nighttasker's intensive stares. He had been on the receiving end of them so many times in his younger days that the look didn't faze him.

The powerful, guildmaster was flanked by two other people, who were always close by his side. Jediaa's second in command standing slightly off to his left was Rita Blades, a tall willowy woman with straw-colored hair. Rita was not a beautiful woman but still had an interesting face that made her somewhat attractive. The only weapon that she displayed was her needle sharp rapier on her right side. She was left-handed and that suited her, giving her an advantage in fighting stronger opponents, also the lightning fast rapier was well suited to her nature. Rita was both intelligent, crafty and a really good trader or smuggler depending on what time of the year it was or what her ship was carrying.

The person to Jediaa's right was a man who had been there since Logan had first met the nighttasker. Vidorr Tagnus was Jediaa's own personal hired battlemage. He had given up his third slash black and gold robes. Now he hired out his services to the highest bidder in Castlekeep.

As much as Jediaa had always treated Logan like a

son, his woman, Rita, had always treated him like a pariah, better off left alone. Both she and Jediaa were staring at him, while Vidorr just lounged about lazily as he always appeared to do, his eyes not really focused on anything, but seeing all.

Finally Jediaa dropped his gaze and looked at Logan's appearance, his eyes roaming over his whole body as if he were taking it in for the first time. "You look like you have done rather well for yourself on the outside."

The outside was what all Guild members of the Network called those that were not engaged in illegal living and lived by the law.

"What is this nonsense about a very important letter from Richard? That only I can hear?" Jediaa stated as much as asked. Not Lord Richard as everybody else called him, Logan noticed but just plain Richard. Logan held up the letter with Jediaa's name clearly visible on it and studied it for a moment before he slid it back into his vest pocket. Somehow he knew that without a doubt his ruse would not work on this man and also in fourteen years, he had never ever once lied to Jediaa about anything and was not about to start now. "This." he said tapping his breast pocket. "Is not the real reason I am here, it was just a ploy to get me back inside the door so that I could ask a personal favor from you." The dwarven twins glared at him when they heard that they had been lied to.

Jediaa didn't speak but he did raise an eyebrow and for a moment a bit of color filled his cheeks.

Logan saw that he wasn't going to speak so he continued on. "Damien Daverge was shot tonight by an assassin using a poisoned bolt. The extent of the damage is really bad. It is not certain that the cleric Ramin can save him or if he will even make it through the night. It happened outside of Morris' shop."

Carefully Logan withdrew the poison bolts and held it out at arm's-length for all to see. Logan fixed his green eyes on the Jediaa's dark ones. "I would just like some assistance in finding some quick answers about its owner."

Jediaa held out his hands and Logan very carefully passed the bolt over to him. As he did so he couldn't help but notice Rita's hand tightening on the hilt of her rapier and a spark of white purefire coming up off of one of Vidorr's fingers. It was all the warning that he needed. He knew that if he moved too fast, Rita would skewer him like a pig on a spit for Vidorr to roast him. With his other hand Jediaa reached out and took a hold of his ever present mug of steaming kafee, that he loved so much and brought it back to his lips, sipping carefully on the hot liquid he studied the bolt in his other hand.

Kafee is a bitter dark liquid that is made from beans and supposed to give one energy. Jediaa swears by it and drinks several large cups of it a day. Logan had never found a taste for the bitter brew even when it was sweetened by cream and sugar.

"Answers are what you're seeking, huh?" Jediaa stated, staring hard at Logan through his dark eyes. "Why should I give someone who has left his family to go work for our enemies, any kind of answers to any type of questions, Logan? What is the answer to that question?" Jediaa asked dramatically, raising his hands in an outstretched manner that encompassed everyone in the room. "This is the family that you so callously left behind and who knows how many of us you could have betrayed?" Jediaa laughed sarcastically, "You return here seeking answers to questions!" His sarcastic laughter changed into a loud voice that sounded angry. Like Lord Richard, Jediaa was a consummate actor who had also traveled with a troupe of players once. He had even made a name for himself before being forced to give it up.

Logan's green eyes glittered angrily as he locked eyes with the nighttasker in a hard stare. "I," the steel cold note in his voice caused Rita's hand to clench again on the hilt of her rapier, "never betrayed anyone's trust ever, nor any trust of yours." The coldness of his voice in which he spoke to Jediaa silenced the entire room of onlookers instantly. "My best friend, my life brother, has been shot by an assassin's poison bolt." All eyes were locked on the two men. "Please Jediaa, don't let him die over the fact that you are still angry at me for choosing to take my own road instead of the one that you wanted to choose for me. I remember once that you told me that you too also once chose your own fate, over that which had been decided for you"

Like most of the thieves in the room, Jediaa had a secret past, one that wasn't known by many but some of it was known by Logan. He was the outcast son eldest son of a very prominent noble house in Gaderia, whose father had wanted him to follow in his own footsteps and rule his lands and holdings. Something that Jediaa had no interest in, ironically enough, now he was a ruler of the underground.

Jediaa had always wanted Logan to take over the operation whenever he decided to retire and the fact that Logan had chosen instead to go to work at the castle for Lord Richard and Simon rather than himself had caused him a lot of pain.

The guildmaster always lived by the phrase 'never let your right hand know what your left hand is doing,' unless that hand was Logan. It was how he had survived for all of his years in charge of Castlekeep's illicit and illegal activities. Never had he followed a set pattern or routine. He always changed plans and ever did anything the same way twice. There was only one single thing in his entire existence that he had relied on constantly and that was Logan. Even over his paid mage and his lovely lady.

When Logan left his organization, Jediaa felt betrayed by the one that he considered his son. Because of that betrayal, he had banished him from the guild.

Jediaa heard Logan's words. He also heard him call Damien his life brother and he wondered whether or not he meant it. Life brothers shared a special sort of bond not born of blood. Jediaa considered this. This was how things used to be for them. In spite of thirty years separating their ages, they were closer than brothers at times.

"Life brother huh?" Jediaa muttered softly. Smiling a wide grin he then broke down to a deep loud laugh. "You haven't changed one bit Logan Longshadow since you've been away. You have always had a way of figuring out how to get to my emotions and honor that I didn't know I had." Jediaa shook his head as if he was bewildered. "I don't understand it, who knows? Logan you always possess that damned sense of honor and decency that your dead parents instilled in you." Jediaa threw up his hands in a gesture of disgust. "If only I could have gotten a hold of you before your parents ruined you, what a fine scoundrel and rogue you would have made!"

Logan let his devilish smile show on his lips for a brief moment before he replied. "I am still and always will be a fine scoundrel and rogue Jediaa, regardless of wherever I play the game or which side I play it on. That is one thing that will never change."

Jediaa smirked at the cocky comment then his face sobered abruptly. "You were banned under penalty of returning here," he said now frowning at the blond haired young thief. "You do realize that don't you?" Jediaa asked in a serious voice. Before Logan could answer, he continued. "Sometimes, people act too hasty in their actions and allow their emotions to override their better judgment. Sometimes, the needs of friends or family outweigh the consequences or dangers of our actions. We don't consider the costs." Jediaa then stopped speaking and waited for Logan to answer as if he was judging what kind of response the other man would give.

Logan considered the night tasker's words thoughtfully

for several moments before he responded. "That is the sole reason I have come here tonight Jediaa, regardless of whatever penalty you wish to set on me I will gladly pay it if it helps to save Damien Daverge's life.

Jediaa flashed him a knowing smile, "You should have realize that sooner or later a situation would have occurred in which you would have needed the type of information that only we," he held up his hands again to include everyone in the room. "could provide. Why didn't you just get in touch with some of your old contacts and find out this information without having to involve me at all Logan. I'm sure you could have found a few that would have been more than willing to help you and not told me about it." He threw a look over in the general direction of Jas Kajyn and his old team.

Logan who had lived with Jediaa for years as a child knew this to be a trick question. He knew that his answer had better be correct or else he would not be walking out of here alive. He shrugged and raised his hands in a defeatist's gesture. "I should have known better, but since it was you who banned me, I haven't gone behind your back to get anything and I wasn't about to start now. That is why I'm here, coming before you."

Jediaa's lips pursed for a moment as he considered this situation very carefully, Logan was sure though that the crafty old guild master had already reached a decision and was just looking for the best way to implement it that would best suit him.

Logan now remembered the words of the one eyed female roofrunner, Jas Kajyn, "he misses you."

"You saved my life from those seeking to end it and for that I still owe you." The other man said loud enough for all in the large underground chamber to hear.

He was right of course. Years earlier Logan had stumbled upon a plot to assassinate the nighttasker. Instead of taking gold and keeping his mouth shut he had chosen to take the gold and inform Jediaa about the plot and the plotters, revealing all of their plans to him. Jediaa had set a vicious trap using this information and had caught killers, ending their betrayal.

"Because of this and the fact that I might have acted wrongly towards you when you wanted to go out on your own, I am going to lift your banishment and answer your question, but this," he fixed Logan with a stare, "settles the slate between us. We don't owe each other anything. Agreed?"

Logan was flabbergasted and quickly he shook his head in agreement, this was not at all what he had been expecting coming here.

Everyone present in the hall cheered loudly at this proclamation. Logan had always been a guild favorite, probably because when he was around a lot of the members made a lot of money. A lot of the older members felt that Jediaa had always been wrong in banishing the young man if for no other reason they could have used him as a contact inside the castle.

"If you start coming around here again," Jediaa added, "don't come begging for any more free favors. The next one will cost you, understand?"

Logan nodded his head yes. A pleasant feeling filled his entire body as he realized how much he had missed being here. He was now actually grinning from ear to ear. He was amazed that Jediaa had lifted his banishment. The feelings of pleasure left him though as he remembered why he had came and he turned serious again. "Do you know then who it was that attacked Damien Daverge or what kind of poison was used?"

Jediaa shook his head no in response to the question even before Logan had finished asking and Logan felt his hopes die in his chest.

The guildmaster said in a matter of fact voice. "I would never offer any kind of sanctioned killing against Lord

Richard's ward, you should have realized that first off Logan."

Logan looked at him and said. "I kind of already figured that. I was just hoping."

Jediaa snorted humorously. "There are some foolish things that I have done in my life but attacking or allowing someone from my network to attack Lord Richard's family is something that I would never allow to happen. Now as to the poison used, that is a relatively simple matter."

Logan screwed up his face in confusion. "What do you mean?"

Jediaa gave him a look of disgust. "You are good Logan, probably one of the best street thieves to ever enter this city, but you have been gone from us way too long. The bottle maker is the expert at that sort of thing.

Chapter 14
Poison

Logan could have slapped himself upside the head for being so thick headed. It must have shown on his face because Jediaa started laughing at him. He should have thought of the bottle maker right away. The bottle maker, named Gadas, was a thin weasel like man of average height with dark greasy unkempt hair and shifting nervous eyes that were always darting about. Gadas had been born into a bottle-making household, but early in his life he found out that he liked discovering the insides of the bottles, rather than making them. So he had gone into the identification business and really profited at it. It had been said a lot of times around Castlekeep and other places that if it's stored in a vial, bottle, or flask, Gadas was a walking tome of information on all types of poisons and potions. If there was one person who could identify what it was that had been used on Damien, Gadas was that one.

Logan thanked Jediaa profusely for this information

and apologized for not being able to stay but time was of the essence if he wanted to help save Damien's life.

He had started to turn away in a swirl of cloak and coat when Jediaa stopped him by asking. "What was in that letter with my name on it anyway?" He pointed at the corner of it still sticking up slightly out of Logan's pocket.

Logan laughed before answering, flashing his trademark devilish grin at his old mentor. "It's an official arrest warrant that I stole off of Lord Richards's desk years ago in order to keep him from arresting you."

Jediaa eyed Logan through narrowed eyes for a few moments as he considered this, then he broke out into a howl of deep raucous laughter. After a minute or so he wiped tears away from the corners of his eyes with the back of one hand. "Delivering that." he pointed at the letter again, "to me from you is very funny indeed, since most of the crimes that I was accused of were perpetrated by you!" Jediaa stated in amused voice. "Is it for real?" he asked still chuckling.

Logan nodded yes.

"Well." Jediaa said suddenly turning serious again. "If my information helps in saving his wards life and since some of us know how important Damien really is, I expect some sort of recompense for services rendered." Jediaa eyed Logan hard. "You tell Richard that I will expect a full pardon for past deeds for helping out the throne and crown in times of dire circumstances. Is that understood, make sure you tell him exactly that."

Logan nodded his head again. He didn't understand though he'd deliver the message to Lord Richard exactly how Jediaa told him.

Jediaa could see that he was perplexed about it and said. "Don't worry your head over it Logan. Just deliver my message exactly like I said it okay!"

"Okay." Logan agreed and left.

As he was heading back up the stairs a young boy

A King's Quest

asked the one eyed Jas Kajyn who he was and why Jediaa had been so easy on him.

"That" she said as she handed the young man a dagger and watched him twirl it, "is Logan Longshadow, one of our best. He's so talented, that he can steal the fingers off of your own hands while selling you back your own toes."

An hour later, Logan stood in front of the Crooked Cup, a seedy little tavern far from the docks. It was where he would find Gadas.

Still replaying the last bit of his conversation with Jediaa over in his mind, Logan wondered what it was about Damien's life that could be so important Jediaa thought he could receive a full pardon for past crimes. He knew that it must have had something to do with the assassination attempt on Damien's life. He was certain that Jediaa knew a lot more about what was going on than he was revealing. Logan was also certain that Jediaa hadn't known about the attempt. Considering now where he was he decided to put all of that aside until later. Now only one thing concerned him.

Gadas wasn't much of a threat, but his big bodyguard was another matter altogether. Curin Wassail was a very dangerous and formidable man. He was extremely methodical and very practical in his defense of Gadas, who paid him a lot of money for being such. Curin was expensive because of his skill, but that didn't bother Gadas who was extremely paranoid and willing to pay the high costs of the mercenary's services for his protection. He was the real danger here and the one that Logan knew that he would have to watch out for.

He moved through the open door of the Crooked Cup and weaved across the room, reeling unsteadily, wobbling like a drunk who had been in his cups for way to long. No one glanced twice at him or realized it was only a show.

If he set himself up as an easy mark, maybe he could earn some money after he was through with Gadas. "No."

he reminded himself, "there wasn't time for that tonight." Without anyone noticing he scanned the room with his green eyes. The tavern was poorly lit with hard wood floors and fire smoke stained ceilings. Numerous broken and shabbily repaired tables and chairs filled it. Stepping around the slipshod tables and rag-tag people, Logan made his way over to the bar. Picking out a three-legged stool that didn't look like it would collapse under his weight he sat at the farthest end of the bar and put his back against the wall. This spot allowed him to see every occupant in the room, without allowing any of them to get too close to him. He motioned the bartender over and ordered a mug of ale. Sipping the mug of warm ale that tasted more like warm piss, he waited. A small group of men were in one of the room's corners playing dice for a small pile of silver coins. The holder of the dice was cheating. Not enough to get caught by the drunken men that he was playing with, but enough that he was ever so slowly winnowing away each of his opponent's piles of coins.

Halfway through the mug of warm piss, Gadas made a brief appearance at the top of one of two staircases in the room. Logan hadn't seen any of the other patrons moving towards this staircase so he assumed that this was probably where the bottle maker kept his private office. No one other than the barkeep seemed to really notice Gadas' appearance. Logan thought that this would give him a good chance of making it up the staircase without being noticed.

He noticed that Gadas' eyes hadn't even acknowledged him when he had scanned the room during his brief appearance. It was obvious that Gadas wasn't looking for him but it did appear like he was waiting on someone. There was no profit for Gadas to make by talking to him. Logan wasn't sure whether or not the bottle maker would even speak to him. He might simply refuse to answer his questions altogether. Logan knew Damien might not have much time left and because of that he was going to have to take a chance and use a more direct approach. Hopefully, Curin wouldn't kill him in the process.

Sliding both of the two daggers out of their sheaths of hiding he checked balance on them. He thought about it a moment then decided on a different course of action and put the two daggers back into place. Instead he withdrew what looked like a thimble out of one of the pockets of his fighting coat. Uncapping the thimble item he revealed a needle set in the device that he could slide onto a fingertip. This skin colored object called a needle knife was used mostly by Terian slavers whenever they made raids into the Kallamar kingdoms. The Terians coat the needle with a sleeping potion that works immediately after being stuck into a victim. Then they take them prisoner and make slaves out of them. The needle itself could be coated with anything but Simon liked the idea of using the sleeping potion. A needle knife is so small that it is hardly detectable when in place. Logan was hoping that it would not be noticed when he entered Gadas' office or else Curin might kill him before he could even begin to speak to the bottle maker. Careful so as not to prick himself with his own weapon, Logan acted as if he was interested more in the dice game going on at the side of the staircase than the stairs themselves. Waiting until the bartender was distracted with his attention on someone else, Logan quickly slipped up the stairs.

Grabbing hold of the handle to Gadas' office he yanked the door open and strode boldly into the room with both of his hands held palms up displaying that he held no weapons in either of them.

Both Gadas and Curin jumped in surprise at the young thief's sudden appearance. Curin immediately unsheathed his sword in a whistle of steel and stepped in front of Gadas protectively, blade leveled at his chest, its and keen edges gleaming in the room's light. Logan just looked at them. Then he took charge of the situation, "Sorry for the interruption gentleman but we need to talk." He sat down at the table between himself and the other two men motioning for them to also sit. Both men just stood there staring at him as if he was crazy or something.

Finally Gadas asked nervously, "What do you want? What are you doing here?"

Although Logan smiled his most disarming smile, he could see Curin was not buying it. "Sit please," he said calmly, motioning the other man again towards the chair. "Jediaa sent me here seeking answers to some questions."

At the mentioned of Jediaa's name Gadas' face went pale and Curin's hand tightened on the sword's hilt. Logan wondered what Gadas was up to. He made a mental note to pass the information on later to the nighttasker.

Green eyes narrowing, Logan also wondered if Gadas had anything to do with the assassination and if that was the cause for his nervousness.

"Questions?" Gadas answered in a high-pitched voice that Logan sensed was filled with fear. Curin on the other hand visibly relaxed somewhat.

"What could I possibly know about anything if it doesn't have to do with identifying something in a bottle?" Gadas whined.

Logan's instincts told him Gadas was trying to cover something up. He would have to take care of that at a later time. Right now his only concern was Damien's life. Removing the bloody bolt carefully from his pocket he laid it on the table and slid it halfway across the table towards Gadas. He just looked that it for a moment then he sat down. "This bolt was used in an assassination attempt tonight," Logan told him, "and Jediaa wants to know who bought the poison, what it is and if there's a cure."

Gadas reached out and picked up the bolt by the end with the feathers and examined it. All business now, he turned the bolt over and over again sideways and long ways as he studied it carefully. Out of the corner of his mouth he asked Logan if he could name any of the symptoms that the victim experienced from the poison.

Logan considered this for a few seconds as he thought back to the flight through the markets square. He definitely remembered the stiffness in Damien's body as he carried him. He also remembered Damien had a slight fever and complained about not being able to move his hands and feet.

Gadas listened to him, nodding as he spoke. He pulled out a dagger and shaved a bit of wood off of the tip of the bolt. Then he turned it over a few times examining it closely. To Curin he said. "Fetch me my box please, the one with the holes."

Curin looked skeptically at him and then at Logan. Seeing Curin's look, Gadas said, "He still has yet to receive the answers to his questions. He won't kill me before he has those at least."

Curin bowed slightly and gave Logan a warning look, before going out a door in the back of the room.

"You're Logan Longshadow aren't you?" asked Gadas as he sniffed at the sliver of red stained wood on the daggers tip. "I thought that you were banished from the guild and barred from having any contact with any of its members and us from you too."

Logan knew that he was going to have to answer this question a few times at least until word spread about the city that his banishment had been lifted.

"That's right I'm Logan and yes I was banned from the guild at least until tonight. Jediaa decided that after five years, tonight would be a good time to let me back in."

Gadas' eyebrows shot straight up at this and he said, "Really? I'm surprised. Jediaa is not known for forgiving people he considers traitors."

"I saved his life once and because of this he decided that five years was enough of an exile. I was never a traitor to the guild or did anything against him in any sort of way,"

Logan coldly informed the man sitting in front of him.

Curin came back into the room carrying some sort of paper box with holes in it. The box began to chirp and Logan knew immediately what was in it. Crickets.

Gadas took the box and pulled three thick brownish black insects out, placing them on the table, with the sliver of wood that he had shaved off of the bolt, he pricked each of the insects with it. Logan watched as the three insects seemed to stiffen. First it was their legs then it went up into their bodies until none of them moved at all. Gadas poked the insects with his finger. Then he picked one up and smelled it. Setting the insect back down onto the table he picked up the bolt and looked at it rather intently. He motioned Curin over to the table and asked him cover him with the cloak for a minute. Concealed under the cloak in darkness Gadas continued to examine the bolt and watched in amazement as it began to glow a faint red in the blackness. Pushing the cloak aside he placed the bolt back onto the table and breathed a long deep sigh.

"Well?" Logan asked him in an anxious voice. "Do you know what it is? Is there a cure?"

Gadas' shifty eyes narrowed as he spoke. "I do know what it is and I even know where the poison came from."

Logan's green eyes glittered dangerously as he heard this. Gadas saw his reaction and hastily added, "Not from me, I didn't supply this poison. It is extremely rare and can only be found in certain remote places in the kingdoms. This does, of course, make it easier to identify."

Logan raised his hands as if to say, okay now what?

Gadas coughed somewhat nervously. "I usually charge for the answers to my questions and for my services, not even Jediaa asks my advice without paying for the answers."

"So how much are we talking about, what is this going to cost me?" Logan asked.

Gadas eyed the sandy haired spythief carefully,

considering how badly he needed this information. Judging by the way Logan had reacted when he thought that he had supplied the poison and by how fast he knew this poison to work, he figured that he would be willing to pay whatever the price was.

"One hundred gold marks for this information shouldn't be too much to ask." Gadas stated as he ran his fingers through his greasy looking hair.

Logan's face froze. Steep wasn't the word for the price Gadas set. He knew that he had given away how much he needed the answer to the question. That was why Gadas' price was so high now.

Judging by the way that Curin was looking at him if he wanted his answer, he was going to have to pay the bottle makers fee, for now at least.

Logan reached inside his fighting coat and withdrew a shiny gem that he set on the table and slid across toward Gadas.

Without touching it, Gadas eyed the jewel, his jaw dropping open slightly as he realized what the sandy haired thief had set on the table. Sitting in front of him was a translucent starfire sapphire as big as an eyeball. Extremely rare, starfire sapphires are very valuable. A translucent gem the size of the one that Logan had slid towards him more than covered the cost of the one hundred gold marks and then some again.

"That should more than cover the cost of the information, until I can return with your gold from Jediaa or Lord Richard who also has a part in this."

The glow that had filled Gadas' face a moment ago faded dramatically when he heard what Logan was saying about the precious gem only being a loan.

"You," Logan said in a firm voice, "can keep the gem until the money is paid to you. Don't harbor any kind of ideas about keeping that gem permanently." indicating it with his chin. "Between Jediaa and Lord Richard looking for you, there would be no place to run or hide where they couldn't find you. They both have a lot at stake here and would not take well to you cheating them."

Gadas swallowed noticeably and coughed nervously in an attempt to cover it up, before he replied saying that he understood about the gem and would make sure it is returned personally.

Logan nodded and concealed a smile on his lips by ducking his head. In his greed for the valuable gem Gadas hadn't even bothered to check to see if the jewel was real. It wasn't of course. It was one of Moris' better forgeries and Logan loved using it to get favors. If he lost it in order to save Damien's life, it will be a small price to pay.

Palming the gem, Gadas pocketed it without even giving it a second glance. "The poison," he informed him. "is very rare, it is glow adder poison from the southeastern mountains near the capital city of Kallamar."

Now it was Logan's eyes that widened, he knew about glow adders and their poison. It was both extremely deadly and extremely dangerous to handle. Someone was going to a lot of trouble to kill Damien.

"Is there a cure?" he asked, a worried look showing in his eyes.

"Not really." But then the bottle maker added hastily as he saw the color drain out of Logan's face. "Unless you can get the victim to a cleric quickly enough. It is a slow moving poison. Sometimes they can be saved."

Logan thanked him for the information and leaving he set off back towards the castle. Maybe they had gotten Damien back to the castle in time after he had been shot If not, hopefully having the name of the poison might help in curing him. Saying a quick prayer to Becil, the god of thieves and luck, he took off towards the rooftops.

Chapter 15
Tension

A black oak door bound with iron straps marked the entrance leading into Lord Richard's personal study and chambers. More suits of ancient armor like the ones that stood in the main entrance hall, lined the walls of his study. A log fire burned hotly in the stone fireplace, illuminating the entire room. Richard Daverge stood rooted in place next to it, staring hard into the flames. He contemplated all that occurred in the past two hours, considering what now must be done.

Balthazar also stood in the room, but he was trying to be inconspicuous as he stood off to one side with his hands clasped tightly behind his back. He was worried about his Lord's mindset at the moment. Damien had always been a special precaution of his and with good reason. Ever since his parents had been killed and he had been placed in his lord's care, he had been fiercely protective of the child. Since he had been shot and still wasn't quite past Morid, the god of death's door, he seemed more concerned than was healthy.

The attack on Damien was his sole concern and the only thing that mattered to him at the moment. Whoever had attempted the assassination must have somehow found out who he is. There could be no other reason for it. Richard Daverge was also certain he knew who was behind the attack on his adopted son. There was only one person Damien posed a threat to, who would want him dead. That one person could be extremely dangerous because he was the royal regent and ruler of all fourteen kingdoms, Vargas Salidor, Damien's true uncle. The Highlord of Castlekeep pursed his lips thoughtfully together. Vargas Salidor, his advisor Cyadine Syndell and the head knight proctor Gunther Haldron were all ruthless and relentless men who would not stop pursuing Damien. They would use every method available to try and stop his ward from attaining his rightful and true birthright in hopes that they could stay in power even after Vargas's own son came of age. He hoped his little ruse in the throne room would convince them and their assassin that Damien was dead.

After the night's ordeal, Balthazar noticed that his Lords features looked as if they had aged ten years in the past two hours. Deep lines of worry and concern were etched into the wrinkles of his face, giving it a somewhat worn and tired looking appearance.

The crossbow bolt used in the attack had pierced Damien's left lung. He had survived the removal of it though the poison had left him as weak as a newborn kitten and completely helpless. Kendle had seen personally to the appointment of the sentinel guard force that was posted outside of his chambers. The female cleric of Dar who had helped save Damien's life was in his room with him. If she was half as good a fighter as the dwarf proclaimed that she was, Damien was well protected indeed. He had arranged for his body to be taken to his chambers in the abandoned west wing of the castle. That side of the keep bordered the ocean and unless the assassin could somehow manage to scale the entire outside wall of the castle to reach Damien's chambers, he would have to pass through a whole gauntlet of sentinel guards.

* * *

Alyssa, sat guard in a chair off to one side, in a darkened corner of the chambers of the young man who had fought earlier in the pit that day like herself. She was pretty sure that he had something to do with why she had been sent west by Brother Melvynn and Brother Albin.

Brother Albin the Darian prophet and foreseer had reassured her that her path would be made known to her when she reached it. Now she wondered whether or not if she had indeed done just that.

There was definitely something going on here, of that much she was certain. Alyssa had enough faith in her god to know that such a coincidence as her helping to save the life of a young man who had earlier that day fought a duel in a way to defend her honor was highly unlikely. Her god had set her upon this path and now it was up to her to follow it to wherever it led. It might even help her discover more about herself and her own mysterious past.

Alyssa remembered the Head Fathers last words to her just days before she had left the monastery to embark upon her ministries as a hand of justice.

"Never," Head Father Melvynn Shutton had told her from behind his desk in his office as the man in charge of the monastery called Highhold, "in my entire lifetime as a monk, with all of my devotion to Dar have I ever seen a single cleric with more blessings bestowed upon them than you my dear. Our god, bless him, always grants all of your spells and blessings to their fullest abilities."

Alyssa had of course known this already and her

abilities had become somewhat of a legend about the monastery. She had paid none of this any mind. Instead she just did as she was asked and devoted all of her time and loyalty to her god, her magic, her fighting abilities and her duty. Alyssa felt that maybe she could be a gifted mage if she had so chose, maybe even a battlemage like the young man lying on the bed resting in front of her, but the environment in which she had grown up dictated the ways in which her abilities took shape. She had never been exposed to that type of magic. Dars fortress of Highhold had been the only place she had ever lived and that had been with the all male warrior clerics of his order. She was only the second female ever to have been accepted into the monastery and given the benefit of Dar's powers. The first was the exiled warrior queen Ellanine Salaris, who had been taken in by the monks and who had been granted Dars powers to help regain her stolen throne.

Clerics like priests are considered holy warriors of the gods and not allowed to spill blood with their weapons. They are only allowed to use blunt or spiked weapons, never edged ones while doing their work.

Like Ellanine, Alyssa had been taught in the use of the hammer. This suited her just fine because she didn't really like the blood being spilt that comes with using spiked or edged weapons.

The brothers of the order had considered her special. They drilled her in both fighting and spell casting from the moment she tottered on two wobbling feet and had been able to hold a hammer or say a chant. She was extremely devoted to her chosen religion and her god, she had no one else in her life other than him and the monks. Because of this dedication, Dar had started blessing her with spells at a very early age and continued doing so until she was well beyond the abilities of most normal clerics and headpriests. It had been made apparent to all of the monks at Highhold that Alyssa was uncommonly gifted. By age seven she was casting most minor spells and had by age nine mastered all of them and moved on to the major spells of their order. At age eleven she could wield her hammer better than almost all of the older clerics in the order, much to their chagrin.

None of the other monks held this against her though and considered her a gift from their god to them.

Alyssa had realized early on that she was smaller than all of the men in the order around her and would never be as strong or as powerful as male clerics, but that hadn't stopped her. She also knew that she was a lot more devious than they were.

Using her mind as a weapon as well as her body, she started studying the human anatomy and how it reacts to pain reflexively. Combining that knowledge with her own speed and quickness during fighting lessons, she could be in, out and under the larger of her male opponents before they could react. Along with her lightweight hammer and its iron ball counterweight, she would use her head, knees, elbows and feet to attack her opponent's nervous and body structure, systematically breaking them down joint by joint and nerve by nerve in order to defeat them.

The monks themselves had created their own unique fighting art. She took from it and combined it with several other fighting techniques. Over the course of her time in the monastery she perfected her style so much so that she was undefeatable amongst all of the fighting monks. Several of the monks had even started asking her teach them her skills and techniques.

Alyssa had never known who her parents were or where she had came from. Nor had she ever really cared since she had plenty of love and parental figures amongst the monks. She had overheard that the young man on the bed was also an orphan and so too was his handsome sandy haired friend. The story about how she had been found slightly over twenty years ago at the entranceway to the main gate of the monk's stone fortress called had become a legend.

Whoever had left the infant baby girl at the gate twenty years ago had managed to tear down one of the gold and black banners of Dar hanging twenty feet above the door and had wrapped the little baby in it. As Alyssa had always heard the story told, when the monks had opened the gates on the morning she was found, there she was smiling up at them. The leader of the guard detachment asked, "What's this?" A single beam of sunlight had broken out from the morning's overcast gray sky, shining down solely on the gold and black banner wrapped baby, bathing her in its illuminating golden light. The beam itself only lasted long enough for all of the monks to see it and then it quickly faded away. All people on Tyrus know when a solitary beam of sunlight falls from heaven on a person, it is supposed to be the eyes of the gods smiling down on a chosen one. The fierce warrior clerics felt that this was a true sign from their god and hadn't hesitated one instant in accepting her inside. It was only several minutes later that they discovered that the baby was a little girl.

Until four weeks ago that had been all that she had ever known about her existence and had never been any farther away from the fortress than the small town of Muldar, in which the clerics traded goods. Now here she was hundreds of miles from home and in the largest city in the entire western realm, held as an almost prisoner of the Highlord in charge of the city that was about to be embroiled in a civil war. Judging by what she had seen tonight, she couldn't help but wonder how much of this had to do with the young man sleeping on the bed and if he might be part of the reason why so many battle lines and alliances were being struck here in the west. All she knew for certain was she had ended up right in the middle of it and all of this was threatening to plunge the fourteen kingdoms into a civil war that might tear the entire realm apart.

It had all begun when the head father of the monastery, Brother Melvynn Shutton had called her to his offices for what she thought was to be a discussion about her leaving the monastery, to begin her ministries to spread the word of law about the teachings of Dar and to be an upholder justice. In a unique coincidence, Brother Melvynn happened to be the same young guard who had originally found her and brought her into the monastery. He acted like the father she had never known. At twenty years old, almost all of the young clerics are sent out into the rest of the realm for a period of ten to twenty years. Most of these returned to the monasteries but some preferred to remain in the cities that they had chosen to live in. Others did not return because the world outside of the monastery was a dangerous place. She assumed when she heard about the summons that Brother Melvynn was going to warn her of the perils and dangers of the outer world like he did with all brothers as they left upon their ministries. Instead, she walked in on a meeting already in progress between Brother Melvynn and Brother Albin. A slight sense of unease had crept through her body when she had seen the other man.

Brother Albin was a foreseer or fate seer. He could see or tell something about the destinies of the people he read. Judging by the looks of concern on both of their faces she knew immediately that this meeting was not just about her getting ready to leave the monastery. Since Brother Albin was staring at her with his strange colored gold penetrating eyes, she knew this meeting was about her future.

Almost casually Brother Melvynn had asked her, "Are you prepared to leave?"

"Yes." was all she had said, as she had waited for what was to come next. She hadn't been prepared for the statement that came.

"You are aware and I'm sure that you realize that for unknown reasons you are somehow special to the gods or at least our god and that there is a special purpose for you." Brother Melvynn had stated. She and Brother Albin had nodded their heads in agreement.

"Yes I do," she had said bowing her head modestly for a moment. "Why do you think that that is so? I am nothing but a devout follower of but one god and only one single worshipper out of many."

"That is what we all are my dear but in your case it seems there is something more in store for you." Brother Melvynn had offered, "I was the one that found you, child. I knew the moment I laid eyes on you that you were not there accidentally. You had been brought here for a reason. Dar has accepted no other female in over a thousand years. You are only the second one ever. The first went on to achieve greatness and became a legend known to all in the fourteen kingdoms. Going on this assumption, it would not be stupid to think that there might be a special purpose for you."

Alyssa just shook her head and didn't know whether she agreed with the Headfather's words. She had learned her lessons well and knew a lot about the first and only other woman to have been accepted into Dar's order.

"You know as well as we do that none of us know anything about who you are or where you came from."

Alyssa nodded when he had paused, waiting on her response.

"I took it upon myself," Brother Melvynn had informed her, "since you are getting ready to leave our walls and had Brother Albin here," he had gestured with a calloused hand over at the other cleric, "do a reading on you for me, so that maybe it might help me to decide in which direction to send you on your ministries."

Never before had she ever felt any desires to know the future but right then she wanted to know what it was that the fate seeing cleric had seen that had caused such disturbing looks on the faces of the two men. Here might be a chance now to learn something about her past and herself. Holding up her hands questioningly she said. "Well, tell me, what did the two of you find out?"

Brother Albin gave her a disapproving look then cleared his throat for the first time and spoke. "The future of one's fate is not something to be taken very lightly or ever to be mocked in any sort of way young lady!" And he fixed her with another hard stare from his strange looking golden eyes.

Alyssa knew better though than to show any signs of backing down or Brother Melvin wouldn't even let her leave. She had heard as well as sensed the underlying current of danger in Albin's words and knew that whatever it was that he had found out it must not have been anything good. "Am I going to die or something?" she had asked.

"No child, not anything as dreadful as that." Brother Melvyn cut in. "What Brother Albin is trying to say, is that for some unknown reason after you leave here your future has become clouded by a myriad of threads with no discernable clarity or course."

Now it was Brother Albin who interrupted, "With many dangers and perils showing on all of them. All I can say is your own decisions and actions can predict your future, but those same acts will also reveal your past." The fate seer paused for a moment then added as an afterthought. "It was also revealed to me that all of the answers that you seek and all of the directions that you must travel lie to the west."

As she looked around the walls around her, she thought to herself, here I am in the west, in Castlekeep, locked up as a prisoner.

* * *

The fierce ocean winds of the Eversea scoured the high walls of the massive fortress and threatened to tear the black form clinging to them off and hurl it back towards the sea and the jagged rocks far below.

Logan knew that the ring of spider walking's magic wouldn't let him fall, but trepidation took hold every time an extremely strong burst of wind took hold, pulling at him and his clothes as he scaled the massive castle's outer walls. He just wanted to be able to look in on Damien and see if he was okay. Going this way was dangerous but it also meant that he wouldn't have to answer a million questions every time he turned a corner in the castle about where he had disappeared to or about what had happened earlier. He also wouldn't have to go through an entire gauntlet of guards on his way to his best friend's chambers. Since Damien's quarters were so far from the main castle, he figured that there would be where they would take him in order to keep him safely away from any other attempts on his life.

Crawling to the top of the window, the young spythief peered into the room trying to see Damien. Finally he was able to make out his best friends form sleeping peacefully in his bed. "Maybe," Logan thought to himself, "Ramin had indeed managed to save him without his help."

Scanning the entire room as best he could from his location outside the window, Logan tried to see if there was anyone else in the room with Damien. Not noticing anyone, he carefully pushed the window open and stuck his head inside.

The soft creaking of the window's unoiled hinge alerted Alyssa to someone entering the room from outside. Quickly she moved carefully and silently even more out of sight, stepping deeper into the shadows of her dark corner. Readying a spell, she waited until whoever it was entering was halfway through the window before she said in a calm voice. "There are guards outside of this door and I'm inside of here, one more move and you will be finished."

So intent was Logan on checking on the status of

Damien's condition that somehow he failed to hear the female clerics warning words and continued on climbing through the window.

Alyssa released the spell of holding and the figure halfway through the window was frozen in place, caught by her spell. This only lasted for a brief moment, then almost comically the frozen off balanced figure in the window fell through, crashing heavily face first into the stone floor.

Almost immediately Alyssa recognized the face and sandy hair of the handsome young man who had acted so quickly in attempting to save the life of the other young man lying in the bed.

Logan felt all of the muscles in his body lock into place as the spell caught him and knew at that moment he might have just made a very critical mistake. He hoped that it also was not a deadly one. It was too bad that he hadn't put back on the night spider cloaks hood after leaving Jediaa's. That would have activated the cloak's magic and it might have deflected the spell.

Alyssa stepped out of the darkness of her hiding place. She wondered whether or not she had acted a little too hasty in releasing the spell, but she heard the voice of one of her brothers in the monastery saying, "It's better to be a little safe than a lot sorry." With a dismissive wave of her hand she dispelled the holding spell and waited as the other young man recovered from his fall.

Logan lay there for several moments, then he looked up to see who it was that had caught him acting like a novice. Seeing the prettiest woman he had ever seen in his entire life standing over him with a slightly tilted smile on her face. He felt his face go red with embarrassment. He recognized his attacker as the female cleric of Dar who had helped save Damien's life in the ballroom.

Offering her a sheepish smile of his own, he said nonchalantly. "Sorry about the rude entrance, but I just wanted to see how he was without having to answer a million questions along the way."

"That's okay," Alyssa said simply, "though if I hadn't recognized you, you would probably would be in a lot more trouble at the moment." Then she gave him an almost admonishing look, "Did you truly think that after an assassination attempt that there would not be guards stationed around your friend?"

Logan scrambled back up onto his feet and felt gingerly at the bruise that was beginning to swell on his cheek from where he had crashed face first into the stone floor. "I figured that there would be guards and I thought they might have even stationed one in here so I looked. I just somehow didn't see you."

Alyssa pointed over to the darkened corner out of sight of the window and Logan glanced over and just said, "Oh now I see, a good spot to hide."

Moving across the room he went over and stood over Damien's sleeping form. His best friend had a peaceful expression on his face. As he offered up another prayer to Becil, he asked, "Is he going to live? Is he going to be okay?" He was extremely worried about the poison that Gadas had told him was used on his friend. Even if Damien managed to live out the night, the lasting effects of the poison could still be damaging. Damien couldn't die! More like wouldn't die, at least not yet. When they had first met years ago on the streets as children he had sensed something in the other young man. His gift gave him the ability to sense worth and ability in others. It was why at appearing to be only eight years old he was able to pick one of the best roof crews to have ever worked the cities streets.

The first moment Logan saw Damien, he had felt the inner sense swirl inside of him like nothing he had ever felt, or at least until just a moment ago, the female cleric of Dar in front of him right now, was also stirring up those same senses and only Damien had ever made them swirl the same way they were moving right now. He had always felt a sense of greatness in Damien. Also, Logan had sensed at the same time when they had first met, that his own path was tied to the young man lying on the bed. Their fates were intertwined.

He sensed immediately that this female cleric of Dar also had something to do with that same future of greatness. But what part would she play? Originally Logan's feelings had been the reason that he had offered the token of friendship towards the other man when they were young. All of that had changed over the course of the years that they were together. They had become real friends. Damien was his one true friend and the only person that he had ever trusted completely, Jediaa and Moris included.

Alyssa could see the genuine concern in Logan's face. She realized as she looked at him that he had left the throne room before the priest named Ramin had informed Lord Richard that his son would live.

"I found out what poison was used on him, if that will help in saving his life."

The female cleric of Dar pulled back the cover over Damien's body, revealing a bright red scar on his chest, which showed healing.

"What about the poison and its effects? I was told that the poison used was very powerful and that it kills by destroying the nervous system of its victims."

She met his look and said simply, "On that point, only time will tell, for right now he lives and will continue to live. From what I have been able to gather, that in itself is very important."

* * *

A loud booming sounded on the door to Lord Richards's chambers startling both of the men in the room out of their wandering thoughts. Before the door even swung open Lord Richard knew who it was on the other side.

Travis Longblade, commander of all his soldiers and blademaster to house Daverge burst into the study without even waiting for permission to be given for him to enter.

Gone now was the haunted look from his face that had been on it all through the festival dinner, replaced now by one that flashed between cold rage and absolute concern.

"Is he okay, is he going to live?"

"Yes," Richard answered.

"Why didn't you tell me?" demanded Travis angrily staring at the Highlord of Castlekeep.

"I told you on the day that I bought you from the slave pits, that I would give you a reason one day to live again," answered Lord Richard calmly, "and today as you saw earlier, is that day."

Travis' eyes flashed again angrily and it looked to Balthazar like he was having a hard time controlling his emotions, "You should have told me immediately. I have the right to know, I should have been told years ago and yet you didn't tell me. You kept this from me for what, almost ten years?" the blademaster shouted angrily, accusingly, his normally stoic manner was completely gone.

It took Castlekeep's advisor a few seconds before he realized what the other man was shouting about. Travis somehow knew who Damien was and what he represented. But how was that possible? How could an ex pit fighting slave have any clue as to who or what Damien was? And how had he found out one of the best-kept secrets in the west, when only three people in all of Castlekeep were even aware of it? Another amazing thing Balthazar noticed was the way that the blademaster was acting now. Never had he seen him display any signs of real emotion. The man was a bit surly and dark and he knew that something bad happened to him in his past, so bad that he had sold himself into slavery as punishment. But now, he was here in his

Lords office talking to him like he was an equal. "No," Balthazar corrected himself, "he was talking down to his lord, one of the seven Highlords of the west as if he outranked him, demanding things from him as if he to were a Highlord."

There weren't too many people in the entire realm that outranked the powerful lord of Castlekeep and Balthazar had never seen anyone talk to him the way that Travis was talking to him now.

Lord Richard remained calm as he held up a hand, cutting off any further tirade from the angry man.

"What would have happened if you had been made aware of his existence as a child ten years ago, Travis? He still couldn't have taken over the throne and crown for eight years yet and who," he gave the blademaster a pointed look with his steel grey eyes, "would have served as his protector! Vargas or Cyadine? Which one of them would have kept him safe and alive? They would have made sure that he met with an unfortunate accident and continued to stay in power. This way, he can now take over the throne as a man and needs no one to watch over him. He is also a trained battlemage. You gave up your rights to make any demands of anyone Travis, when you sold yourself into slavery to atone for the deaths that you think that you allowed. Now you are just a simple blademaster who follows my orders and who has," Lord Richard paused to take a breath and put special emphasis on his next words, "sworn himself to me and my commands. Any time you want, I will release you from my service and you can regain your own true birthright and post in the realm, but until you decide to make that decision, anything I do is not subject to your commands. You gave up the rights to make any sort of demands. The only task that you have now Travis is to be the protector of that young man lying in his bed. Keep him alive. Do it under my orders and following my commands, at least until you make a decision about where you want your own life to go! It's time to stop hiding Travis, there is an heir alive to the throne and crown of Kallamar. It is our job to protect him and place him back onto that throne where he rightfully belongs as the true ruler of all fourteen kingdoms. You should know more about that responsibility better than any one else in this room ever could. Maybe," Lord Richard added after another slight pause, "this time we can keep one alive."

Travis let out a short harsh laugh, "I don't need any reminders of my past failures Richard," the blademaster said leaving off the honorific lord title, "I've been living with them for the past twenty years, but you are right. I swore oaths to you and I will keep them."

"There is still an heir alive, Travis, let's do our best to try and keep this one alive this time." Lord Richard finished, repeating again what he had said a moment ago. A somber silence filled the room after Lord Richard finished speaking.

Balthazar watched as a sudden weariness seemed to fill the blademaster's body and his shoulders noticeably sagged.

"I tried to keep them alive," the blademaster said sadly in an almost inaudible voice and tears filled his dark eyes as he spoke, "Gunther killed them all Richard. There was nothing that I could do to save them though I truly tried."

"There is still an heir alive Travis. I promised that I would give you a reason to quit fighting in the pits and live again. Well now it is here, there is still an heir alive and more importantly, you will be needed the most out of all of us in the days to come. You must be strong and steadfast, forget the past Travis and let's concentrate on keeping the future safe." Lord Richard said softly as he reached out and placed a comforting hand on the blademaster's shoulder.

Balthazar noticed the blademaster's face was a firestorm of emotion. More animation showed on his face now than had ever shown there in the previous ten years that the advisor had known him. Bowing to his Lord with barely a perceptible bending of his stiff back, Travis turned and left the room without saying anything else.

Balthazar replayed the conversation he had just witnessed in his minds eye word for word and suddenly he realized why the two men had been talking to each other as equals. The advisor to Castlekeep stared at the closed door, after the departed blademaster, a dumbstruck expression on his face. Then he got a look of awe in his brown eyes. "By the gods, is he who I think he is?" he blurted before he could stop himself, "I never knew," he said in an astonished voice, "I never even had a clue as to who he was, how did he, how is he," Balthazar started to ask but was cut off by a wave of his lords hand.

"You weren't supposed to know Balthazar. Nobody else needs to know either, his business and his past is for him and him alone. He is the one that needs to exorcise those demons and make the decision whether or not he wants it revealed." Lord Richard told him, pausing and waiting till his advisor nodded.

"Why did you think I paid that slaver his asking price of five thousand gold, when I found out he was alive. Did you really think I had lost my mind to pay so much for a simple slave?" Lord Richard asked dubiously then added. "I am not that stupid Balthazar, even though I know you thought I lost my mind at the time, didn't you old friend?"

Balthazar didn't answer at first, still in a dazed sort of shock, then he muttered, "I always said that you were one of the most devious men I've ever met milord," he paused for a moment and said in a thoughtful voice, "Wouldn't you be able to have the boy placed back on the throne on his word alone?"

"If I had found him immediately after the old king and queen had been murdered, it might have been possible, but Vargas has been the ruler and regent of the realm for twenty years. It would probably be a little difficult to do that now just on his word alone and in case, you hadn't noticed he's not a boy any longer, Balthazar."

The advisor realized that his Lords words were correct Balthazar finally broke the still silence of the room again, "Would you like for me to contact the other six Highlords about what happened here tonight, Milord?"

Lord Richard took several more long moments before he finally answered his advisors question. "Yes, tell them all of it and include Devlin in the news too," referring to the dwarven Iron king. "Inform them dire circumstances have occurred. We must act right away and their presence is required here immediately. By first mornings light if possible, inform them that the heir is still alive but we are going to make it appear as if Damien is dead and are mourning his loss."

Balthazar heard all of this and shook his head in agreement, "They won't like having to use the mirrors again and this will be the third time this month." Repeated use of the mirrors which zaps the user's life force was beginning to take its toll on the other western Highlords.

"I realize this," Lord Richard stated, "but tell them that Vargas and Cyadine have already made a move against us. Now is not the time to worry about such things, we all have to act now as one or the rest of the realm will be destroyed by civil war."

"Very good then Milord." answered Balthazar and the advisor bowed his head respectfully, leaving the ruler of Castlekeep alone in his chambers. He hoped that his lord didn't spend the rest of the night mulling over the problems of tonight without getting any rest. The lack of sleep might begin to show just when he was needed the most.

Chapter 16
Revealing the Truth

Damien woke early the next morning after the attack on him and looked up to find his room occupied by two other people, one he knew. It took him a brief moment before he placed the strawberry blond haired woman asleep in the other chair. He remembered then that he'd been shot in the chest. He felt around at the place where the assassin's bolt had struck him. Feeling nothing but scar tissue, he lifted the cover and glanced at his injury. The jagged hole from the night before showed as a red scar but the wound itself was gone. Now he remembered being carried into the castle, Ramin kneeling over him, attempting to heal him along with the female cleric of Dar who had fallen asleep in his chair. They must have succeeded he thought thankfully, as he pushed his body upright in the bed because it seemed to him that he was still alive.

The sound of the bed moving caused the other two

occupants in the room to bolt awake. Seeing that he was sitting up, the female cleric of Dar came over to his bed and immediately began to examine him. She made him open his mouth, stick out his tongue, roll his eyes and grip her hands as tight as he could. When she winced from his tight grip, he quickly released her. She was pleased. "The poison," she said turning to Logan who was staring anxiously as the both of them, "doesn't seem to have affected any of his motor skills." Then she turned to Damien and asked. "How do you feel? Is there any stiffness or tingling in any of your extremities?"

Damien seemed a little taken back by her more than direct manner. She was issuing orders, but he responded, "I feel fine, in fact I feel great." then he pushed himself up off the bed and did a few stretches, just to make sure that there wasn't any pain. He gave a satisfied smile at finding none and said, "What are the two of you doing here?"

Logan looked at him sharply and turned to the female cleric asking her, "Are you sure, that the poison in his body didn't affect his brain any, cause he seems to have forgotten that someone tried to kill him last night using a poisoned crossbow bolt?" then he turned back to Damien, "She's," he threw a look in the direction of the cleric, "actually the guard, appointed by your own father to look out for you, I'm just the intruder that she caught sneaking in through the window in the middle of the night."

Damien raised an eyebrow at this and asked rather skeptically, "You were caught sneaking in through a window? I don't believe it."

"Not one of my better moments," offered Logan with a sheepish grin and a shrug of his shoulders, "but I blame it all on my concern over you."

"That still doesn't explain the need for guards!" asked Damien curiously. "Why are they out there? Why are you," he threw a quick glance over to the female cleric, "in here? I'm not that special that I should warrant such attention."

A King's Quest

"Someone tried to kill you last night." Logan said reproachfully. "You're a lord's son. Why else do you think there are guards in here and out in the hallway, to protect that pretty hair of yours that you don't even have any longer?"

Damien sniffed at this comment from his friend and ran his fingers through his now much shorter hair. Ever since he had burnt all of the hair off of his head as a child, he had always been a little self conscious about it. Not even bothering to answer his best friend because he knew that he was right and that Logan would only tease him more so about that point, Damien turned instead to the female cleric and said, "I'm sorry I don't even know your name, even though we have already met twice in a round about sort of way and I think that you helped in saving my life."

Alyssa offered him a half tilted smile that Damien noticed mimicked his own in a funny sort of way but on the opposite side of her face. "Alyssa of Muldar," she said not offering any more than that.

"Alyssa, huh? Is there a second part to that name or is that all that you are going to reveal?" Damien asked, he was aware that some people from the mountains where Alyssa was obviously from wouldn't give up their last names for odd reasons, like they thought that people could gain control over them through their names.

"Alyssa," Logan stated before she could answer, "is parentless, just like us Damien."

"Really?" asked Damien, throwing a curious look in her direction. "Are you an orphan like us whose parents died but were known, or one of the abandoned?" Damien figured out before she even answered that she must be one of the abandoned, which was why she hadn't offered up a second name to him. She confirmed this by nodding and saying that she was of the latter. She told him that she had been left on the doorsteps of Highhold, the fortress of Dar. She had never known who she was or who her parents were. Unlike most of the abandoned children in the realm she didn't feel like them because she had a large family. The monks who always turned away female children took her in and taught her their ways and skills.

Most abandoned children lived their entire lives, never really knowing who they were or who they are. It's a sad life if there isn't anyone who ever accepts them.

"So can anyone tell me then what is going on?" asked Damien eyeing the both of them, "Or at least why someone is trying to or tried to kill me?" as he also rubbed absently at the new scar on his chest with the fingers of one hand.

Logan and Alyssa shook their heads no. The female cleric added, "I'm not allowed to leave your chambers either."

Damien and Logan looked at her at the same time but it was Logan who spoke first. "Really and how is it that you know that?"

"Last night while you two were both sleeping," She said, her sky blue eyes flashing angrily, "I desired something more to eat and was going to go down to the kitchens for a moment. When I was informed that under the command of your father that I was not allowed to leave your chambers. I was told that if I needed anything, it would be brought to me, until he gave further word. I told them that they were being preposterous and when I tried to step further out of the room they all drew their swords on me and didn't resheath them until I was back inside here."

Logan listened intently then threw back his head at this and blew out a long deep breath, when he brought his head back forward, a cunning expression was on his face as he looked at both Damien and Alyssa.

Damien recognized this look very well. It was the same one that crossed his friend's face whenever he found a problem important but perplexing. "Why don't I walk out there and see what they have to say about my leaving, I don't even think that they know that I am in here yet." he told them, as he stepped across the room. A few seconds later, he stepped back in, holding his hands up in the air defensively.

After the guards closed the door, Logan turned back to Damien and demanded in an almost furious voice, "What is it that you have done since your return that has earned you such unwarranted attention and protection? They almost skewered me with their swords when they realized that I wasn't you or her!" He pointed a long finger at Alyssa.

Alyssa cut in adding, "You might want to put a why as well as a what into that question."

Damien shook his head helplessly at the both of them, "I have no idea what the reason is or why, the only thing that I've done since my return home other than being shot, was to fight Thaedrann in the pit." He stopped as an idea came into his head and he asked, "You don't think that Thaedrann tried to kill me last night over the incident in the pit do you?"

Logan shook his head no, "That's an interesting idea but no. I'm positively certain whoever did this wasn't Thaedrann. According to my sources he couldn't have purchased the poison that was used on you in this city. Whoever tried to kill you, brought it from somewhere else."

"Do you think if Thaedrann couldn't have done it," Damien asked, conceding the point, "that it still could have something to do with the cities tournament and somebody from outside of Castlekeep did this because they didn't want me to compete? There is a lot of honor and gold at stake with winning the tournament of cities."

Logan looked at Damien. He hadn't even considered this angle in his mind.

"No." stated Alyssa firmly looking at the pair of them. "It has nothing to do with the tournament either. I am absolutely certain of that. Your own father told Ramin that you couldn't be allowed to die! That keeping you alive was necessary to ensure that the rest of the fourteen kingdoms didn't fall into chaos."

Damien felt his eyes grow wide. He was just a first level battlemage and only an adopted third son. "Why would his father say something like that. It was in a Highlords house, but still he wasn't really important to anyone much less the entire realm."

"You also have to consider the show he put on by picking up Ramin one handed and then hurling him back down onto the floor," Logan said.

"Especially," added Alyssa, "when he already knew that you were okay."

Damien looked at her oddly, not quite understanding what it was that they were talking about.

Seeing the confused look on the young battlemages face, the female cleric clarified by saying. "Your father went through a very convincing act of discrediting Ramin in front of the everyone in the castle to make sure that they believed that you weren't going to live until morning. There definitely is a lot more than what we know going on around here."

"He certainly had me convinced," offered Logan, "I believed him so much that I even went to see Jediaa in order to find your killer myself."

"You did what?" Damien asked incredulously, his eyes gaping wide now. He knew all about Logan's banishment from the guild in order to work for the castle.

Logan grinned a pleased smile, "And he reinstated me back in the guild. He also seemed very concerned about your recovery. He put me on the correct path to find out what kind of poison was used on you."

"Really!" said Damien, not quite believing what it was that he was hearing.

"Yes, but there was something funny in his manner when he heard you were injured and he gave me a cryptic message to tell your father." Logan paused there dramatically, always the storyteller.

Alyssa listening intently demanded. "Yes, what is it?"

Logan smirked, pleased that he had gotten exactly the reaction he had wanted. "He said and I quote," his voice dropped into a low rich sounding baritone, that Damien assumed even though he had never met the man was a perfect imitation of the Nighttasker's voice. "Tell Richard, not Lord Richard," Logan added, "that if my information helps any at all in saving that boys life, I want a full pardon for any and all past crimes."

Damien considered this for several moments before he finally said with a bewildered expression on his face. "Another mystery and another question about why all of a sudden my life and well being are so important to everyone. And now we are all being kept prisoners here in the castle. I guess you're both right. There is definitely something going on here that we don't know about, but wouldn't it be a lot easier to explain if it was just one of my opponents trying to keep me from the tournament or Thaedrann trying to kill me to get revenge?"

A loud rapping that sounded like wood on wood sounded at the door, startling all of them. Both Damien and Logan recognized the familiar sound, having heard it for years as children and Logan rolled his eyes in mock exasperation as he stood up and went to answer the door.

Alyssa said with a touch of defiance still in her eyes, "Maybe this is someone bringing us some answers! I have no intention upon staying here as a prisoner for very much longer. It is against the law for any lord, Highlord or not, to imprison a cleric of Dar without proof of just cause. We are the upholders of The Law of the Kingdoms."

Abraim's tall, stooped figure stepped past Logan as he entered into the room, giving him a distasteful sniff as he did so. He faced Damien and announced in his hollow sounding voice, "Your father would like to see you now master Damien. Please make your way to his chambers with me immediately."

As the other two young people started to move towards the door, Abraim held out a hand saying coolly. "Only Damien is to go to this meeting. The rest of you will be dealt with later it seems." The chamberlain turned, giving Logan another displeased look. He then departed out to the hall and waited for Damien to accompany him.

Alyssa let out a loud and frustrated sigh as she sank back down onto the chair that she had been sitting all night. Logan just returned the old mans dirty look, not bothering for once to say anything at all.

A short while later Damien stood in front of his father's large desk. Lord Richard eyed his adopted ward for several long moments through his steel grey eyes, carefully studying him. He had received word from the guards that Damien was fine. If there had been something wrong he was sure that female cleric of Dar would have let him know. Finally he said as he continued to study his sons face, "You really are your father's son, aren't you."

Damien, not sure that he had heard correctly looked at him curiously and said, "Excuse me? What was that about my father?"

His adopted father did not reply. Instead he stood up and opened the door to his private council room. Gesturing for Damien to enter and followed him inside.

Lord Richard's private council chambers were where all of his really important decisions were made effecting Castlekeep. It was where he sometimes met with the minor lords of Gaderia when passing certain types of laws. Balthazar had magically enspelled the room years ago, insuring conversations spoken in it could not be overheard by outsiders. The glyphs and wards of countermagic that he had woven into the stone walls themselves would prove rather nasty to any who truly tried.

This time seated around the table was a very different sort of group of lords. Seeing who was all gathered in the room, Dmien felt his stomach tighten up into a ball of nerves.

Including his father, all seven of the western Highlords were present. Each was seated about the large polished wooden table. Also standing about the room was Kendle, Balthazar, Travis and the dwarven Iron king, Devlin Bonebreaker. He was a stout older looking dwarf with a full black beard that hung down well past the center of his chest, it was shot through with salt and pepper streaks of grey that he had braided five places, two up front and three in back. Five braids in dwarven culture signified royalty. Only members of the iron king's household could wear their hair this way. He threw Damien a gruff smile, which he wanly returned. Kendle hardly ever braided his own hair with the five braids, but he could have if he wished to. Lord Gildon Seahorn, a roughish looking man with a pointed nose and shaggy honey brown hair was ruler of Caladar, the second largest city on the western coast. He was seated at the table next to his father on his right. On his father's left was Lord Michal Monro ruler of Kirksey, an inland city that traded along the rivers that flowed east. He was a portly man with a round face, cunning manipulative eyes and devious nature to match. His eyes were locked on Damien's own. As they met he threw the younger man a derogatory look filled with disdain. To his left sat Lady Tyler Linsdale, the ruler of Toomsa, another one of the seaport cities to the far south. She was the only female Highlord in the fourteen kingdoms. The expression on her face and the look in her eyes mimicked the Lord of Kirksey's. Lord Baxx Blackspear, ruler of Talandra, Lord Jarvis Whiteknife of Mycar, Randon Nandoo who ruled over Tallamoor, the canal city and Rialdo Stringcutter, who wasn't actually a Highlord but was still the ruler of the southern and slightly eastern halfling nations of Silverwood and Asher Downs. He was the diminutive child-faced halfling who was also sitting at the table. These nine rulers were the most powerful people in the western realm. All of them had banded together against the rule of the royal regent Lord Vargas in opposing his new tax laws.

"What," he silently asked himself, as he looked at all of the faces that were turned in his direction, "does any of this have to do with me?"

"He looks fine to me," Lady Linsdale said disgustedly, as she shook her raven black haired head back and forth. Her haughty featured cold face and eyes were locked on Damiens, studying him closely.

"He's fine now but that doesn't take away what happened last night. An assassin's crossbow bolt almost cost him his life." Richard stated.

"Richard here," said Gildon Seahorn, to the Lady of Toomsa with an almost fatherly expression on his face, "is sometimes overly obsessed in his concern for the boy at times, but I think that he is justified in this meeting here today and in its purpose."

Lady Tyler gave a disdainful arrogant sniff and turned away from Damien as if he was nothing more than a servant that she was dismissing.

"Regardless of how he is now, or how he was last night." came a gravelly voice from across the room, "We all know this was the royal regent's actions last night. The time to act is now and it is time to begin what we all swore to do in this same room twenty years ago when he came into our care," said Devlin Bonebreaker, somewhat gruffly and in a curt manner.

Damien saw the pale-faced, redhead, Randon Nandoo nod in agreement with the dwarven Iron king's words.

"What is going on here?" Damien interrupted, "Why are you all here? What is it that I have done?"

Lord Richard took a very deep breath. He eyed the others around the table momentarily. Fixating his eyes on Damien, he spoke, "You, my son have done nothing, but there has been a crime committed. We in this room intend to see justice come to pass to those who committed it and that justice includes you."

Damien realized at that moment that maybe he should listen rather than being upset and he might get a few more questions answered. With a nod to his father he indicated that he should continue.

"Twenty two years ago King Dorian Salidor married Lady Ellanor Seahorn of Caladar, his sister." Lord Richard gestured with a large hand in the direction of the shaggy haired Highlord of Caladar who nodded in acknowledgement. "They were married for almost a year and a half and during that time the Lady Ellanor became pregnant, with twins."

Damien recognized this as the story about the night of sorrow. The same sad story about the deaths of the old king and queen that his father last night had forbid the orator from telling at the ball. But he wasn't sure what it had to do with him.

"King Dorian announced the day of the birthing of the two babies to the entire realm and invited all of the fourteen Highlords to Kallamar to celebrate the joyous occasion, not ever had twins rulers been born into the realm.

People from all over went to witness the birthing including Dorian's only surviving brother, his fourth brother, Lord Vargas Salidor, his advisor and wizard Cyadine Syndell and a group of unknown Krannion knights led by Gunther Haldron.

Damien gave his adopted father a strange stare. This was not quite the same sad tale of the night of sorrows that he had always heard. The version told by the story tellers and orators didn't include any Krannion knights but one, the Royal Protector and Kings Champion, Bertravis Liolbane, who single handedly fought off a hoard of Terian raiders by himself while trying to save the royal family until he was finally defeated and the Terians killed him. The King and Queen and their newborn twin children that his father was talking about were also killed while they were trying to escape out of the royal palace.

"The knight renegade Gunther Haldron, led the unknown Krannion knights into the castle unseen by anyone. He probably did so with the help of Lord Cyadine's magic and took them straight to some of the chambers near the royal quarters. Once there, Gunther had them all change into Terian raider outfits and waited for the signal to attack from Cyadine."

Damien chose this moment to interrupt asking, "Father, are you saying that the now royal proctor of the Krannion knights and cousin to the kings own champion who took over his duties after his death led and staged an attack on the old king and queen and killed the entire royal family in order to remove them from power?"

His father nodded, yes.

"Why?" Damien's voice trailed off for a moment, "What would make a man do such a despicable thing as that? He swore vows and oaths to the throne and the crown. Is there any proof of his treachery and what does any of this have to do with the royal regent?"

This time it wasn't any of the Highlords that answered instead it was Travis. "Love and greed!" he growled in a bitter sounding voice. The tone in his voice was so upsetting that it caused all of the other heads to turn in his direction. The stoic baldheaded man ignored their looks and turned away deliberately. He stared out of the window without giving any other reply.

"Vargas," his father continued after taking a sip of the wine and after it was apparent that the blademaster wasn't going to elaborate, "his wizard and Gunther staged the whole thing, according to Lady Alice the queen's mother, who escaped with one of the children bundled up in her arms hidden in bloody birthing rags. Afterwards Vargas, Cyadine and Gunther killed all the witnesses to the crimes of treachery tht they had committed. Their news made it out that they were the heroes who had fought through the Terians, trying to save the king, queen and their two newborn twin babies but not in time."

Damien felt his mind racing and a sudden question popped into his head. With bated breath he asked. "What happened to the children?"

Lord Richard looked at all of the other lords at the table again for a moment and then back to him and said slowly, "You are one of the children, the one that Lady Alice, your grandmother, escaped with. Only she and you survived the night of sorrows. You, Damien, are the rightful heir to the throne and crown of Kallamar and the true ruler of the entire kingdom."

He stared blankly at his father and then at the rest of the group for several long moments. A disbelieving expression came over his face. He had been struck dumb by the impact of his father's words.

He recovered a little bit and suddenly licked his dry lips. Finding it hard to speak, Damien cast about for a moment before he asked in a frightened voice, "What happened to the second child, what happened to my twin?"

This time it was Lord Gildon, Damien's new found uncle, who spoke, "No one really knows for certain what became of the second baby, we think that it was with your mother and was killed by the same arrows that Gunther's disguised knights used to kill her. All that we know for certain is that only one maid and Lady Alice survived the trap that Gunther laid in the escape route under the castle, two burned out rafts were found, one carried the dead body of your mother," the shaggy haired lords voice cracked a little. Damien could tell that he still ached over the loss of his sister, "which was filled with arrows from Gunther's archers and the second one, that had her lady in waiting in it was found empty. Gunther claimed that when he reached the landing and tried to save your mother, he had arrived too late but that he saw her drop one of the children into the rushing waters of the underground river as she fell backwards into the raft. We have," Lord Gildon waved a hand at himself and the other Highlords, "searched everywhere for any sign of the second child but nothing has ever been found, other than some bloody rags in the second maids burnt out raft. We never heard of any children being put to the sword by unknown killers, so we assumed that neither had Vargas nor his accomplices never found one either."

"Or at least until yesterday," cut in the Highlord from Kirksey, eyeing Damien with his piggish eyes.

"So you are telling me," Damien responded slowly in an incredulous voice, "that I'm the heir to the throne and crown of Kallamar and that I might have a twin out there somewhere in the realm possibly?"

"We don't know for certain but it might be possible," stated Lord Gildon eyeing him with his light brown eyes.

Damien felt his mind race, as it occurred suddenly to him that maybe he wasn't alone in the world. He had a twin somewhere out there. The pieces just sort of fell into place in his mind as if he had always known all his life that it was so. He had another question he wanted to ask but right now he still wanted to hear the rest of the story.

"How was it that I and Lady Alice survived and ended up here?" he asked instead, turning his attention from the round lord, back to the man who he now figured to be his uncle. Damien noticed but didn't pay it any mind that even Travis, who had been staring purposely out of the window until now, turned back around at this part of the tale and started paying attention to what it was that Lord Gildon was saying.

The Highlord of Caladar flashed a proud smile and said, "My mother, your grandmother in fact, Lady Alice, had grabbed you when the attack began and had hidden with you under the bed while your father, your mother, their protector and her ladies in waiting fled the birthing rooms with their attackers right behind them to the tunnels under the palace. After they had all passed she simply crawled out from under the bed, wrapped you in the bloody birthing rags that were lying on top of the bed, effectively hiding you from view and then strode out of the room."

Damien, listened intently to the story about his newly discovered grandmother, amazed at her audacity and at what he was hearing, "Didn't anyone even bother to question or stop her while she was leaving?" he asked incredulously, now completely caught up in the Highlord's tale.

"Oh she got stopped alright," Lord Gildon said, flashing him a crafty smile. "By Lord Cyadine, now royal advisor and wizard himself, whom we all suspect of having hatched this plan in the first place." Again, he gestured to the lords around the table before he continued, "When he asked her what it was that she was doing, she thrust the bloody birthing rags wrapped around you up into his face. He quickly motioned her on, thinking that she was nothing more than a simple midwife. After that she hurriedly made her way out of Kallamar and back to Caladar. We brought you here and hid you with Lord Richard in Castlekeep, thinking that it would be better to hide you until you came of age than to put you in the palace where you might have met with an unfortunate accident like your parents.

"How did the royal regent, his advisor and Gunther manage to get away with this crime, if my life was saved then?" Damien asked curiously.

This time it wasn't Lord Gildon who spoke but his adopted father, who took over again and continued on with the story, Damien just listened.

"Vargas, Cyadine and Gunther very deftly and very proficiently shifted the blame to the Terians cause of the dead disguised knights immediately. As the last member of the royal line due to the horrendous deaths of your parents and their protector Vargas quickly proclaimed himself royal regent, so that something could be done about the Terian assassins. Vargas controlled the entire investigation. Gunther and Cyadine had killed all of the knights who had helped them in their treachery. No one dared come forth and speak. There wasn't any proof that they were involved."

"What about me and Lady Alice?" Damien asked, looking around at all of the people in the room, "You say that I'm the heir to the throne and that she saved me. Couldn't you have just have told her story to the rest of the Highlords and revealed me telling everyone that one of the heirs had survived?"

"How would we have proven it?" answered his father with a shrug of his shoulders, "Who would have believed us at the time? The king's own brother and the second in command of the Krannion knights said that all had died. Without any direct evidence to the contrary, we couldn't make anyone believe us. So instead we hid you. Again, we did it for your safety. As a member of the royal house and fourth son, Vargas would have still been in charge and ruler until you came of age."

A high-pitched male voice cut in, "And how easy my young king, would you think it would have been for the three who arranged to kill the entire royal family, to kill off a newborn baby or arrange a mysterious childhood accident that would leave Vargas and his own minions still in power until he had a son of his own?"

The way that this was said, so coldly and deceitfully, Damien knew without looking that the speaker was the Lord of Kirksey. The fat Lord was famous for his schemes and plotting and had never been known not to always have at least one plan showing and three more plots up his sleeve in progress.

"You," His father said, "were vulnerable as a child and even though you are now a trained battle mage you are still vulnerable. More so even now with Vargas aware of your existence. I am sure that he will pull out all stops to keep you from assuming your true birth rite, removing him from power or at least maintaining that power until his own son Seth takes over."

Damien turned his head towards Balthazar in the corner, then swung back around towards his father, "That's why the two of you got so scared that time and acted the way you did when I escaped out of the castle as a child and why you two argued so much over my leaving to go to the academe to study, isn't it?"

Both Balthazar and his father nodded and Damien felt a feeling of satisfaction sweep through him at solving this little mystery that had always haunted him for years.

"No one," his father continued after the interruption, "figured that Vargas would ever have a child of his own, I don't really think that even he planned on it, at least not for several years, that way he could remain in power as regent for a very long time. When Seth came along, it put a time limit onto how long his own reign would be, unless he killed his own son. That limit is only two months away now and Seth will be named king unless we manage to restore your true birthright to you and place you back on the throne where you rightfully belong before that. You are the true heir to the throne of Kallamar Damien, the stopper of chaos and the rightful ruler of the fourteen kingdoms, I and the lords and rulers that stand here in this room with me now are going to do everything in our power to place you back on the throne. Only one person deserves to rule the Fourteen Kingdoms by right of birth and bloodline and that one person is you, not Vargas, nor his son serving his father's lackey!" Lord Richard said, his gray eyes shining fiercely.

"What if it's not me?" Damien asked aloud, voicing the question that he was examining in his own mind that he had thought of earlier.

The others at the table frowned and perplexed

expressions crossed their faces as they all looked at him uncertainly, not really sure what he meant.

Seeing the looks, Damien realized that he had spoken aloud his thoughts. He looked at each of them in turn as he spoke the next words again carefully. "What if it's not me? What if I'm not the true heir but the second born instead and not the rightful heir to the throne? What if my twin is the firstborn?"

Everyone in the room looked at each other in disbelief and astonishment. It seemed that nobody in the council room had even conceived of this possibility.

Finally it was King Devlin of the Iron dwarves who spoke. "It doesn't really matter at this point Damien. You are our only chance we have to avoid an outright civil war between the east and the west that could destroy the all of the kingdoms if we keep opposing Vargas' new laws."

Everyone in the room nodded their assent including Damien.

"With Vargas' reign," stated Lord Richard firmly, looking into the eyes of everyone present in the room. "There comes a great evil, upon all of the lands and its peoples."

Damien looked around the table at the Lords gathered round it, then over to the wall where Balthazar, Kendle, Travis and King Devlin were, then went back to the table again, meeting the eyes of each with his own dark blue ones, including the scornful looks of Lady Tyler and Lord Michal, before he asked his next question.

"What people would side with me against the ruler of Kallamar? He holds all of the power. Is the rule of Vargas Salidor so bad that I should plunge all of Kallamar into a possible civil war, just so that I can be ordained king?"

Lord Richards steel gray eyes and face went grim as he said. "You should already know the answer to that question. Take a look outside at all the people fleeing west. More and more, cruel and unjust laws are being passed everyday. Innocents are being punished while murderers prosper. The realm has a balance and control that is being torn apart by the will of a murderer. A murderer who killed your own parents. As to the answer of your first question about who would follow you, when the attempt was made on your life last night, I called an immediate council with the other six western Highlords. As you can see, every one of them is here." He stopped speaking and as he did so every one of the Highlords, King Devlin of the iron dwarves, Kendle and Rialdo Stringcutter who looked uncomfortable, rose ceremoniously and stepped out away from their chairs. His father faced him, surrounded by the other standing Highlords, the two dwarves and the halfling, a fierce light shining in all of their eyes. Speaking as one voice, they all stated, "We are all gathered here today to pledge our allegiance and fealty to you Damien Daverge, our lives our lands, our honor and our duty all belong to you the son of King Dorian and Queen Ellanor and true ruler of the fourteen lands and the realm of Kallamar."

Then again as one, all of the western rulers knelt, bowing their heads, while lowering their eyes before him in fealty. Damien stood there shocked for a moment as he looked down upon the bowed heads and he realized that he had to accept their oaths or else they would all be shamed. Nervously, best as he could, he bowed deferentially to all. Then he went to each one, touched them on the shoulder lifting each one back up onto their feet as he accepted their pledges of fealty to him a simple adopted lords third son who wasn't really sure what he was doing.

"So?" he asked looking at them after they all had retaken their seats. "What are we going to do then about ousting Vargas, his wizard and his knight, from their seats of power? How are we going to go about proving I'm who you say I am and restore me to the throne?"

Chapter 17
Proper Places and Plans

Now it was Balthazar who spoke for the first time since Damien had entered the council room, "We will need something that can prove your own birthright to all that can not be denied by any. Something, that can not be brushed aside by the royal regent like our mere words," he motioned to the lords sitting at the table. Damien saw Baxx Blackspear and King Devlin bristle slightly at the mention of their own words being just 'mere'.

"A talisman," the Castlekeep advisor continued, undaunted by the dark looks that the pair was throwing in his direction. "One that can not be disputed by any and only one that can be worn by the true ruler or his legitimate heirs."

Damien looked at his father's advisor doubtfully, "and where," he asked, "would we find such an item," Then he stopped. "The Dragon rings," he muttered apprehensively casting a fearful look towards the other wizard who just simply nodded at him.

The Dragon rings were powerful talismans of ancient Elvynn creational magic. They were created for the lesser races by a group of rebellious Elvynn high mages who had opted to help the lesser races in their fight against their oppressors with their governing during the wars of power after the age of might. Anyone other than a legitimate ruler or direct descendant of the first family's bloodline who tries to wear the rings is bitten by the actual rings themselves and dies a slow horrible death. Legend says that the rings also somehow allow a magical ruler to contact the guardian dragons that protects them in cases of dire danger.

"Of course the Dragon rings!" came a snide female voice from the other side of the table, "What else dolt, did you think he was talking about?" A condescending and derisive tone in her voice filled the words that she spoke. Both Damien's adopted father and his uncle rounded angrily on the Lady of Toomsa. Calmly, Damien spoke first, before either one, silencing them with his next words, "My Lady," he began softly, turning his full attention on her. Damien remembered now how it had been Logan who had bowed to him but had taught him a long time ago then who and what it was that he was. Now it was time, he decided, for a little lesson about respect, bearing in mind who he was now, considering the looks that she and Lord Michal had been throwing in his direction.

"I believe that you are forgetting your place here in these surroundings," He said icily, the chill in his voice cooling the room by several degrees.

"My place!" said Lady Tyler as her eyes widened in disbelief, then repeated the same phrase again this time more shrilly as she threw a dagger filled glare at him, "and what could you kindly please tell me exactly is my place here then." she finished just as coldly as he had.

Damien returned her look with one of his own, his dark

blue eyes boring into her in much the same manner as Tiko had used on him on occasion when he too had also forgotten his place. "The correct phrase," he said in a cold toneless voice as his eyes hardened into chips of dark blue ice, "is could you kindly tell me exactly what my place is here then, Sire?" he put special emphasis on the last word he spoke.

Lady Tyler drew back as if she had been slapped by his words and for a moment her face looked like she had swallowed a frog or something and her eyes bulged outward before Damien continued speaking, "You and all of these other Lords and rulers have just sworn fealty to me as king and named me the ruler over you and yours and your lands, I would kindly advise you to remember that before you speak so to me again such a manner or else I will order my new guards here in this Castle that now belongs to me, to arrest you and throw you into the deepest dungeon that they can find here until you can remember your place."

Now all of the Highlord's heads in the room jerked in surprise at his words. All except Kendle's and his uncle, they were both trying to hide the laughter that threatened to spill out of their mouths from behind their hands. Travis also met his eye and gave him a barely noticeable nod of silent approval.

The reaction that came next from the rebuked female Highlord was completely unexpected. Instead of standing up and stalking out as he thought she would, Lady Tyler Linsdale of Toomsa broke out into a fit of laughter. "I was wondering how long it would take for him to get enough of me and Michal here," she poked the round lord from Kirksey next to her with a long nail, "and show a little backbone, not really long at all was it Michal?"

"And I was just getting ready to start on him myself," said the round Highlord, "but I think that if I do, he might put me in those same dungeons that he is very quietly threatening you with Tyler."

The two Highlords beamed at him and Lady Tyler offered their apologies for their actions and words, "We just wanted so see what you were made out of a little bit and find out whether or not you had the backbone in you that your father was known for. Cause the tasks ahead of you will be both difficult and hard since Vargas found out that you are still alive. I'm sure that they will be perilous as well. We still swore to you and would have followed you anyway, but we wanted to know a little more about you. Sorry for the test Damien."

Damien felt a sudden surge of anger rise inside of him. Everybody had been testing him since the moment he had came home, but he quickly squashed it, knowing that if he was to regain his birthright if he was the true heir, more than likely he would be tested several more times along the way and would need to show patience rather than anger.

Turning to Balthazar, he asked. "How do we go about recovering the rings? And what will we do with them to prove that I am the true king afterwards?"

"The rings should have been placed along with the bodies of your mother and father in Illsador, the Godshall and hopefully it is there where we will recover them." answered the wizardly advisor.

Damien felt a prickle of fear go through him at the mention of Illsador, the Godshall as it was more commonly called. It sat high above the Annulith Mountains to the east and north on the highland rim, a flat barrenless rocky plain that marked the boundary with the nearly impassable Terians Mountains. It was in this place where the gods of the realm lived and walked when they were here on Tyrus. It was also the place where all of the rulers of Kallamar had been buried since Doral Markennan, the first free human king and bloodline ruler of the fourteen kingdoms.

The journey was perilous indeed, through treacherous mountain passes and across wide chasms. With it being the end of the harvest season Damien knew that snows would soon begin to fall in the high mountain ranges and northern lands, but that wasn't what filled him with fear. Neither was it the gods, who had little to do with men themselves and rarely made their presence known. It was the creature that protected the Godshall that bothered him most and the reason he stared incredulously at his father's advisor and at the rest of the Highlords shaking their heads in agreement with him.

All knew the Godshall or Illsador was guarded by one of the largest of the creational magic creatures that the Tua-Latin had created and that it had been there for a long time, keeping out any that did not belong in the hall, save the royal bloodline. The ancient Elvynn creational wizards only created a few of these large creatures, however all of them were alive even after two thousand years had passed. The ancient wizards had taken a little of the essences from of all of the races of dragons and created several Guardian Dragon who could protect them from the gods own wrath if ever needed and gave them a dragons intelligence. Guardian dragons are the largest and most powerful creatures on the entire planet now and created out of magic. A guardian dragon can become chameleon like and clone its surrounding so well using its magic that it becomes invisible unless it wants to reveal itself. They can absorb and cast back all types of magic used against them and are impervious to almost all types of weapons. They can also use all of the powers from the ancient races of dead dragons, all of the essences of dragon's breath weapons, fire to lightening, cold, gas and acid once per day each. They were created this way for the same reason as their name to guard things. The gods had taken one, the largest and smartest of all of its kind and put it in place to guard their home. Damien knew that if he wasn't the true heir and that if somehow this were all a lie or a mistake, the dragon would never let him leave the Godshall with the rings that they were supposed to be linked to it or at least not alive.

Damien asked apprehensively, "What is our plan? You do have a plan besides just getting the ring back?"

Now all of the Lords looked at him and grinned, slow wide smiles that showed that they definitely had a plan in mind.

"We will have a funeral, because you are dead! Killed by an assassin's bolt," his father answered with a cunning expression on his face.

"This," said Baxx Blackspear, speaking for the very first time, "should buy us some time for you to make it to the Godshall without anyone other than us knowing you are still alive."

"After you recover the rings," piped in the cheery sounding voice of Rialdo Stringcutter, "You and the small group traveling with you will go to the citadel to get the knights to swear allegiance to you by showing them the rings in your possession, during their knight's council and promotion tourney ceremony."

"We," said Lord Michal, speaking for the first time without the scornful tones in his voice, "will go to Kallamar for the yearly Highlords Council and announce that you have been found and are at the Citadel with the knights and we will demand that Vargas relinquish the throne and crown to you, to whom it rightfully belongs."

"What happens," Damien asked, "if the knights refuse to follow me even though I have the rings? And there is Vargas, what if he refuses to give up his throne to me?"

"The knights have to follow you, if you wear the rings," came Travis' voice again from over by the window, "its part of their sworn oaths of valor and duty. Only the rings creator, the rightful ruler or a legitimate heir can wear the Dragon rings, anyone else trying to put them on dies a slow and painful death from their dragon heads poison, that's why Vargas can't wear them himself or use them, because he's not a true heir or a legitimate ruler. His son can but only after he is proclaimed and that's why this needs to be done fast. With the knight's council and the Highlords Council only a few weeks away, it will be cutting it close to the time of Seth's actual naming day."

All in the room looked in stunned shock at the blademaster, Travis just turned away and looked back out of the window once again ignoring their probing stares.

Kendle's uncle Devlin spoke next in a gruff curt manner, "and if Vargas refuses to abdicate that which is rightfully yours, we will cross that bridge when it comes. We need to assign someone to accompany you to recover the Dragon rings in Illsador."

"That is where we stand now." offered Lord Richard and Damien looked at him curiously, "Part of the group has already been chosen in a way. We need to keep this secret, so hopefully the cleric of Dar will accompany you. Her presence as an upholder of laws for the kingdoms will also help establish our credibility when you recover the ring and present it them to both the knights and the other seven Highlords. If she does not want to go, she will be kept somewhere in the castle until the ring are recovered and you have made yourself known to the knights and the rest of the realm. The same goes for Logan. We can't afford to be discovered before you at least make it to Illsador."

Devlin spoke again saying, "Kendle will be going too, there isn't another dwarf in the entire realm who knows the mountains and their passes better than him except for maybe my brother Edrynn, his father."

Damien cast a quick sideways glance over to the other dwarf leaning against the wall, who returned it accompanied by a quick wink and an encouraging smile."

"Travis," his father said, "will also accompany you, he will serve as your protector and blademaster. That gives you a person in a position of authority in case you need it."

"Braden Ravenclaw, my master at arms and

blademaster will also accompany you. He is an accomplished ranger who knows well the perils and dangers of traveling through the wilds and he is the most accurate man with a bow that I have ever seen." said Lord Gildon.

"That's all we need then," interrupted Damien, "any more and we will be too noticeable."

Travis nodded his head in agreement and spoke again, "Who is going to lead this little expedition, into and beyond the mountains?"

Lord Richard, smiled at him and said, "You are Travis. Your presence will be needed," and he gave the blademaster a direct look that seemed to convey more meaning than just what his words said, "with Damien as your second in charge."

"What about this man Braden?" interrupted Damien, indicating his uncle with his chin, "or Kendle?" he pointed at the dwarf.

"You are the king! Who else should be put in charge over you? You have been trained for this sort of thing for the past six years, so put away your doubts." answered Lord Richard.

All of the other Lords at the table nodded at this and at him. There was an angry mutter from over by the window as Travis spoke again. "I don't approve of this!" the blademaster said in a voice that made his thoughts on the subject well known. "It's dangerous for him to go with us. What if we lose him?" the blademaster pointed at Damien, "then we lose everything, with no other to take his place!"

"I know," Lord Richard said irritably, "You have made your point several times now." He fixed Travis with a hard stare through his steel grey eyes. It was obvious to all that they had already had this same conversation earlier before he had arrived. "But!" he said in a commanding manner, his voice carrying a hard edge. "That is how it is going to be! Only he can recover the rings! And the dragon won't let anyone else leave with them. If you have any doubts about that, ask Kendle, he knows."

All heads in the room turned towards the dwarf, who immediately started paying intent attention to something on the head of his axehammer and was obviously not going to look up or respond. Through his dark reddish beard, Damien thought though that he saw a flush of red color the dwarf's normally ruddy cheeks as he deliberately avoided all of their gazes.

Eager to stave off what looked like what was going to be another argument between the two men, Damien quickly interrupted the pair with a few questions of his own. "What is our plan then and how soon do we leave?"

A relieved expression showed in his father's grey eyes at not having to argue with Travis again. He knew without having to be told, that this wasn't the first fight they had about this since last night.

"First we have to stage your funeral," Lord Richard stated, "I say we do that the day after tomorrow. I will have the criers make the announcements this morning and throughout the rest of the day, to make sure that everyone believes that you are indeed dead. All of us will attend. Then I will announce that I am going to get married and name Thaedrann as my third heir. It will give him the birthright that he so rightly deserves, as long as he swears to follow you, that is. If not he can spend time along with his mother in the deepest dungeon I can find. After the funeral and the wedding, everyone will either be sleeping off the remains of the night before or leaving for somewhere, so you should be able to slip out unnoticed. Why don't you go back now to your chambers, while we prepare for your funeral and Damien, keep out of sight!" his father ended.

Realizing that he had a lot to think about concerning his own destiny, Damien nodded to all one more time and made his way out of the council room, using the least used corridors as he returned back to his chambers.

His mind was in a haze as he entered the final corridor that led to his chambers. He had remembered to use the corridors that Abraim had pointed out to him. Those he had promised would be clear of any other people.

"Yesterday, he had only been a simple battlemage returning to see family and have a happy homecoming. Today, he was unofficially the ruler of Kallamar and the Fourteen Kingdoms with his uncle, Vargas Salidor, Regent Ruler of the realm, trying to kill him. It was all too much, he decided after a moment. Until he was named king or had the Dragon rings on his fingers, he would still consider himself the adopted third son of house Daverge. Now he did have a mission, to seek vengeance for his parents and his twins' untimely deaths. He had never wanted the mantle of leadership and the only thing he had ever dreamed of commanding was a unit of battlemages someday. With his two adopted brothers ahead of him in line for succession in Castlekeep, Damien never even considered a position of ruling as a lord or Highlord to be his and certainly not the position as the rightful heir to the throne and the crown. He considered both his adopted father and Balthazar's actions during his childhood. Without being aware of it, he had also been groomed and trained by them. They had ensured that he was extremely well versed in all manners of court activity as if he were royalty himself. He hadn't understood the need for such nonsense as a child but now he knew why they had insisted that he learn. According to Travis, he had a duty and a responsibility to both the kingdom and its people, to see Vargas the usurper ousted from the throne. It was his throne and crown to reclaim as the proper and rightful ruler.

"I just got home to Castlekeep. In three days I have to leave again," he silently said to himself. He had never been anywhere but Castlekeep and Westlake and now he was being asked to leave again. A strange feeling of uncertainty went through his body but he squashed it instantly. He had made his decision and he knew that it was the right one. His life was truly changed he hoped with the royal regent and his accomplices trying to kill him, not for the worse.

The guards stationed in his hallway stepped aside and let him pass by without saying a word. When he entered the door to his chambers Alyssa and Logan both jumped to their feet and demanded to know what was going on. They both stopped when they saw the almost distressed look that was clearly on his face.

"What is it?" asked Logan

"Remember," Damien said looking at his best friend as he went over to a chair and sat down heavily, "when you said that the haircut you gave me last night, made me look nobler and that I reminded you of somebody?"

"Yes. Why is that important in some way now? Does it explain why we are locked up in here like prisoners?"

Damien ignored the questions as he said, "I also told you about how Travis acted at dinner. How Travis fits in yet I'm not quite certain, but it seems that I do indeed resemble somebody."

Both Logan and Alyssa gave him anxious looks as they waited for him to elaborate, but didn't interrupt.

"Where I just went was to a meeting with all seven of the western Highlords, King Devlin and Rialdo Stringcutter," Damien started to tell the pair.

Logan interrupted at that moment to say incredulously, "All seven Highlords of the western realm here? In Castlekeep?"

"Yes, Damien said nodding, "In fact they all came to see me."

"What!" said Logan an utterly bewildered expression on his face, "why would they have all come to see you, Damien? I mean I understand that you were shot and all, but why would all seven of the Highlords come to check on the welfare of the third adopted son of a Highlord of Castlekeep?"

"I'm not just a third adopted son, that's why." Damien stated and blew out a long breath, "It seems that the person who you thought I looked like was my own real father."

"How could that be Damien?" retorted Logan, "I never even met your father, remember? He died saving your adopted father's life, long before we ever met. I wouldn't have any idea if you resembled him or not now would I?"

"Not that father, he was just an unlucky front for who I really am, who happened to die at the right time and in the right place." answered Damien,

Logan felt his inner feelings begin to swirl, like it had earlier when he had looked at the female cleric and knew that something important was about to be said here.

"Who is your father then Damien if not the one they told you?" Logan demanded with a straight-eyed stare.

Damien drew a deep breath and said with a slight tremor in his voice. "It seems that I am the surviving son of a set of twins born to the old King and Queen who were killed during the night of sorrows. I am now the sole heir to the throne and crown of Kallamar and the next king of the fourteen kingdoms, the reason that you thought I looked familiar is because I look like my father, King Dorian Salidor."

A loud gasp came from across the room where Alyssa stood and she covered her mouth with her hand. "The true king's son?" she said through her fingers.

"Excuse me," said Logan a disbelieving expression on his face, "did you just say that you are the king of the realm and the old kings surviving son?"

Damien didn't answer. Instead he nodded and leaned forward in his chair, placing his elbows on his knees, looking at the both of them as they absorbed what he had just told them.

It was Alyssa who finally spoke first, saying. "The fate

seer at the monastery told me that I would find something in the west that would be important. I think that I just did. So you are the heir to the throne, huh? That explains a lot about the guards and your father's comments last night."

"It also explains Jediaa's statements to me," Logan stated more to himself more to himself than to the other two, but how did he know who you are? I wouldn't think that your father would be the type to spread around such information"

Damien just shrugged his shoulders at this not having any sort of answer to Logan's question.

Alyssa gave them a meaningful look as she focused on him, "What exactly did they say? I think we should hear the whole story since what you have just told us might also include us. We are the ones locked up in here in this room with you as well."

Using his memory gift, Damien repeated almost word for word what happened since he left their chambers.

Alyssa again spoke, "So we are to either go with you to recover these rings or else we become prisoners here in the castle?" Her eyes flashed dangerously for a moment as she said this. Damien remembered that she was a cleric of Dar and that made her a very dangerous person.

"I'll go then. This journey will help me find out who that I am. Somehow I sense that this is what it was that the seer meant, so you can definitely count me in," Alyssa informed them.

Logan had one of the biggest smiles that Damien had ever seen on the thief's face. A slightly evil looking leer filled his eyes, "So now you are the king. I'm the best friend to the king. Imagine that! I would love to see the look on Thaedrann's face when your father tells him that he has to kneel to you or be thrown in the dungeons." Alyssa threw him a reproachful look and Logan mistaking it on purpose added. "Ohh I'm in, you know that I'm going along."

"We aren't allowed to leave here though until the time that my father says that we are to leave." Damien finished telling them.

"That's not exactly true either," said Logan throwing a glace over to the weapons rack that stood along one of the rooms' walls, "We can always leave," he gestured at himself and the female cleric, "It's you that has to stay put so that nobody discovers that you are still alive and blows the whistle on everyone's little deception." Behind the rack was a hidden secret door that led to another room farther down the hall and around the corner from the posted guards.

* * *

After Damien's exit from the council chamber, Balthazar made arrangements for the other Highlords to have quarters in the castle. It had been a long night for all and every one of them was extremely tired.

Lord Richard himself wanted to get some sleep also but he knew that he still had one more matter to attend to today and went back into his study to wait until noon and the appointment that he had scheduled for that time.

The Highlord of Castlekeep snapped awake at the intruding knock which permeated his sleep filled brain. Its intrusive sound was coming behind his closed door. Shaking his head to clear the cobwebs of sleep and to regain his senses once again he realized that he must have dozed off while sitting in his study chair. Focusing both his eyes and his concentration on the door he remembered what was going on. Richard Daverge decided at that moment that his visitors could wait outside the door for a brief moment and he yawned, a loud sound that seemed to wake him a little more. Crossing his fingers in front in a sort of steeple he took on a serious expression and barked out a command to enter.

In through the door walked Thaedrann Rynall, his true third son, accompanied by the young watchman named Gerund who had helped save his other son's life last night.

Thaedrann appeared tall and proud like usual, as he stepped across the study to stand in front of his father's desk. But Richard Daverge noticed some of the brashness and arrogance that usually accompanied his son's manner seemed removed today. Thaedrann's face moved into the light and for a brief moment Lord Richards' eyes widened at the sight. He had heard the story about the fight last night and also Kendle's version numerous times, but he hadn't realized the extent of the beating that Damien had given his other son.

Both of Thaedrann's eyes were blackened from his broken nose and both of his lips were bruised and split. You could barely see where he was missing his front tooth. He also appeared to be limping slightly. His attitude seemed to be somewhat more humbled as he reported to Richard. He had never seen Thaedrann exert such control of his emotions. "Good," he thought silently. "Maybe this attitude change will last and Thaedrann would grow up some."

Having been beaten so by Damien would either make it very difficult for him to take any kind of orders from him and make him a liability and dangerous to their quest, or else he will be a better follower in accepting Damien's leadership and rule. This was the real purpose of this meeting, if Thaedrann passed he would be rewarded but if he failed to pass his fathers judgment, for the sake of the throne or at least until Damien was put upon it he would rot in his dungeon, there was a lot more at stake here than one man's wounded pride.

He lay the report down in front of him that he had been picked up to use as a distraction. Barely even looking up, he spoke. "Gerund, could you please wait outside for a moment?"

After the watchman had left, Lord Richard said, "I understand that you and Damien had a dispute the other day while at the pits."

"Milord, I can explain," Thaedrann began, but Lord Richard cut him off, stopping his words with a silent shake of his head from side to side.

"Is the matter for which the fight was fought over ended? Are all of the grievances settled between the two of you?"

Thaedrann humbly dropped his gaze and shook his head. "Yes, milord. All grievances and disputes are settled between us. There is no ill will or bad intentions on my conscious towards him."

"Well enough said then," returned Lord Richard, carefully studying his youngest son with his gray eyes, seeing nothing that showed deception on the other mans part, no fidgeting or shifting of his gaze. "Sit down Thaedrann," he gestured to one of the large chairs that was in front of his desk, "and I will tell you a story."

Thaedrann hastily sat down. He had originally thought he was to be rebuked for his action in the pit with Damien. At worst to be demoted from his post as Captain but he saw the weighing expression in which his father was looking at him. He realized that there was something else going on here and whatever it was, it was a lot more important than his dispute with Damien. He had heard along with at least half the city that someone had tried to kill him last night. He hoped that he wasn't getting the blame for it.

Lord Richard began telling him the whole story or at least what he knew of it about who Damien really was, telling him that he was alive and how his parents had been killed and also how he was to be the next ruler of the kingdoms. He told him that he was sorry that he had not been able to claim him as his son and that he was going to rectify that situation as soon as possible and that included finally marrying his mother. He finished by saying,

"Tomorrow I will announce that Damien is dead and we will hold a funeral for him, then there will be a marriage. Damien is the heir and we, including you my son, must pledge loyalty to him is that understood!"

Thaedrann's heart leapt excitedly in his chest when he heard the word son come out of his father's mouth for the first time and smiling he said that it was understood, then he asked. "Does my mother know? I mean about the marriage that is?"

"No! She doesn't, so don't tell her about it either. Also don't tell her about Damien being the heir either. The lads life is in a lot of danger, he will avoid some of it for as long as the rest of the realm thinks that he is dead. Your mother would talk to her handmaidens, then half the realm would know of the deception within two days."

Thaedrann nodded in agreement. He knew how much his mother liked to talk. Then he asked a question he always wanted to ask, "Does this mean that I can finally call you father?"

The joyful smile on his sons bruised and battered face was contagious and Lord Richard found himself also smiling. "It does son, or whatever else you want to, but not quite yet." and both smiling men stood up and Thaedrann hugged his father for the first time.

After they were finished his father said to him. "Inform Commander Bayle and Watchman Gerund out there that you are to be removed from your duties on the city watch. I want Gerund promoted to lieutenant, with the prospect of taking over your post whenever Bayle thinks that he is ready. Now I'm going to get some much needed sleep for a while before I pass out again on my desk."

Thaedrann knew that he was being dismissed and with a proud smile he turned and left his fathers chambers.

Chapter 18
Infiltration

Caliban was sitting in his new office going through Ferris's things, smiling coldly as he heard the news that the Lord's third son, the man he had been tasked to kill as a renegade battlemage had passed away during the night as a result of poison from an assassin's crossbow bolt. He had accomplished his first mission for his father and the throne and crown. It had been a success that would make him proud, hopefully. What he heard next killed the slight thrill he was feeling and caused a stir of suspicion to crawl through his brain like a worm through an apple as the messenger said that all nine of the western rulers would be present for the funeral and that the ambassador should also attend. The ambassador's invitation though, wasn't what caused the assassin mages brow to crease in a worried frown. It was the part about the six western Highlords and the two other rulers also being in attendance at the funeral.

"Why would the eight of the most important people in

the western part of the realm, feel obliged to attend the funeral of a third son of House Daverge and an adopted one at that? There was no reason for it other than a meeting between the rulers, but they had already met two other times this month. His father had told him that when they had discussed his purpose for coming here to Castlekeep. There was no logical reason for them to be here again now unless something wasn't right.

Another thing his father told him about was the importance of this mission. So much so Caliban decided that he had to get into the castle and see the dead body for himself. Caliban ran scenarios through his head about how and what he would do to get into the castle. As he watched the blazing ball of the red setting sun sink into the Eversea Ocean, he realized that his time had arrived.

The sentinel guards that patrolled the parapets would be the most difficult obstacle, but he had decided earlier that there was an easier way. He knew that he could use his own magic, but the other way minimized the risk and he chose it instead. He rifled through the ambassador's desk, looking for papers to be delivered to Lord Richard. He would return them after he was through, but for right now they would serve his purpose. Since there were times that the royal secretary did act as messenger for the ambassador, he could use them to act like he was delivering them now. They would easily get him onto the grounds and inside of the castle itself. If he was questioned about why he was there at night he could as a young man newly appointed to his job appear to be slightly overzealous in the pursuit of his duties. Everybody knew how punctual and perfect Dalmar was with his military background and those reasons would make his own case for him.

Caliban chose a baggy outfit of black which fit nicely over his specially designed and expertly crafted Elvynn leather armor. It molded perfectly against him and fit like a second skin, so well that it could hardly be seen underneath his clothes. He didn't think that he would actually need the armor since this was just a reconnaissance mission for information purposes only, but he heard his fathers voice in his head, 'It was better to be prepared than to be caught completely unaware.' The armor was a powerful talisman artifact created from before the banishment of the Elvynn. It would give him all sorts of spell abilities and protections. He would also out of precaution bring his Elvynn fighting knives with him. One should never be caught in a fighting situation completely unarmed. The Elvynn called the knives quieelin. The fighting knives were handheld double bladed knives that ran along the outside edges of both of his hands like giant cats claws with a crosspiece that went across both the top of his hand and the palm, when slid into place. The blades could be used for cutting, stabbing or slicing. A metal fore piece protected his fingers and served as a shield against cutting or hacking attacks. The armor had sheathes built right into the sides about mid thigh where the blades were carried. Enchanted runes of sharpness and strength had been carved into the sides of the blades themselves. They could slice or cut through just about anything.

Moonlight illuminated the streets as he moved through the early night. It was only the second night of the festival and revelers still filled the streets with noise. Caliban showed the official seal of the royal ambassador to the guards at the castle entrance and they let him pass without any questions whatsoever. He thought that this was a little odd at first until he remembered all seven of the Highlords were also at the castle by now and they probably had entire retinues of servants going in and out of the grounds attending to their bidding and every need. He thought this ought to make his own little mission here even easier.

The trick was to find out why the other six of the Highlords or the other two rulers were actually here and whether or not his victim was truly dead.

Caliban moved into the same hall where the injured battlemage had been brought last night. He glanced around the room for any sign of the blood from the body and saw that there was none, but what he did see over beside the fireplace that was cold stone at the moment surprised him.

Somebody had somehow missed the battlemages amulet that the priest had removed last night and had set by the stone. Caliban glanced quickly around the room to make sure that nobody was paying any attention to him. Seeing that no one was looking, he stopped and propped his boot up onto the hearth as if he was adjusting it. Quickly he bent over and recovered the scarred battlemage amulet that belonged to his mark. As he stood back up he fingered the grooved cut in its side where he figured his bolt had struck, before he slipped the amulet under his leather breastplate. Then he continued on through the hall. He would save the medallion. One never knew where such an item might prove useful later on.

A few quick turns and he was out of the main corridors of the large castle. He scanned the area around him. Seeing nobody, he said the words to a spell that he had prepared for this occasion. As he continued on down the corridor, his body faded from view, vanishing from sight as the invisibility spell took hold.

Servants moved through the hallways, entering and leaving rooms, going this way and that. He listened to snatches and pieces of conversations and soon was certain that indeed that all of the eight other rulers were already here in the castle and had been to an important meeting held earlier in the day in Lord Richards' personal council chambers. This still didn't answer his question though of whether or not his mark was still alive.

One of the conversations he did overhear though seemed a little odd as he came across the Highlord from Caladar talking to his blademaster about a trip to Illsador he would be making in three days. "Why would anyone," the white haired assassin mage wondered, "be going to the Godshall at this time of the year when winter was about to come into the mountains and the lands of the Highland Rim?" He filed this away for later consideration and continued down corridor after corridor for a long time, searching.

He found the quarters of all seven Highlords, King Devlin and the halfling inside of the castle and was about to end his search when he rounded an empty corner of hallway and found it filled with guards. All of them looked like seasoned veterans. All were armed with swords and looked ready for anything. Sensing that maybe he had finally found something that might be worthwhile or yield some answers to his questions, Caliban moved slowly up the corridor with barely any sound at all. His every sense alert for anything that might give away his presence to the guards, even though they couldn't see him, there was nothing that prevented them from hearing him unless he cast a whisper walk spell. He decided though that he was going to save that spell in case he needed it to get by the guards, right now he was content enough to listen to their conversation.

Soon he was close enough to hear it. They were, he realized, talking about the almost unheard of female cleric of Dar who had helped in saving their Lords son and about how beautiful she was. Especially when she was angry like she had been earlier.

There it was and he listened in on the guard's careless carefree statement, "the Lord's son that she had helped save." Caliban quickly turned and moved down the hall. This news, he knew would not please his father at all. He ended up paying a painful price for failure or mistakes whenever his father was displeased

* * *

Balthazar, now fully rested from his own afternoon nap, had decided to pay a nighttime visit to Damien's quarters. He figured that neither his ex apprentice nor the other two young people in the room with him would be asleep, not with the news that they had received earlier today, he was also curious about how Logan had actually gotten into the room too. He had just turned one of the corridors corners before he reached the one with the guards in it and he felt it somewhere in the hall ahead of him, like a shimmer across his skin. Magic was being used. He wasn't sure where but he knew it was close by.

Caliban's thoughts had drifted for a moment, worrying about his father's reaction to the distressing news that he had failed and he didn't notice the red robed advisor turn the corner at the far end of the hall. Even though he didn't know the advisor personally, he did know about him, from both word of mouth and through his own fathers mouth, who had said that Balthazar was not a man for him to be dealing with. Although he was not battlemage trained like himself, his father or his mark, he still was a very powerful and competent mage and Caliban figured that any man who his own very powerful father was wary of, he would do well to steer away from. His eye caught the sudden jerk of movement as the others frame stiffened in momentary surprise and Caliban knew that during his momentary lapse, he had been detected.

The red robed man began casting immediately and Caliban figured that he would be casting either a dispel or detect magic spell, either one would reveal him to the other man. Rather than trying to stand toe to toe with the other mage and work a spell of his own, he had prepared several before coming on this mission, he quickly cast about instead looking for a place to hide instead.

There was an open door diagonally across from him and as Balthazar finished the incantation, moving like quicksilver, Caliban threw himself through the air and in the direction of the opening. He hoped that the other mage was too far away to hear any noises that he made. He cleared the doorway at the same time as a flash of magic energy exploded through the corridor. Instead of a simple dispelling spell, Balthazar had cast a disruption spell, the most powerful version of removal magic. Caliban curled up his body and rolled into a ball to help absorb the impact of his diving leap. If he had been caught in the disruption spell, it might have with his lack of concentration at that moment, tore all of the spells he had memorized from his own memory and left him temporarily magic less and unprotected. Knowing now that his own magic was what had alerted the other man to his presence, he released all of his own protection spells. He figured that he had only had a few moments before the other powerful advisor found the open door and the cracking sound of the disrupting spell drew the guards from other hall.

His slate blue eyes searched everywhere for a place to hide. Seeing nothing he started to prepare for a fight that he wasn't sure he could win, unless he could gain a measure of surprise over the powerful advisor when he spotted the window along the far wall. Another idea occurred to him, a much safer one and one that he would probably live through. He grabbed hold of the windows latches and attempted to yank it open, they didn't move. He frantically pulled again and still they stayed shut. The room appeared to have been deserted and over the years and Caliban correctly assumed that through the course of disuse and time, the wood in the windows frame must have swelled from the salty air and water, causing it to wedge the windows in place effectively sealing them against opening probably better than any type of lock ever could. Knowing that he was quickly running out of time, Caliban grabbed a chair, lifted it and hurled it out through the glass panes. If the other men in the corridor outside of the room weren't aware of his position here before the sound of the breaking glass, they were certainly informed of it now.

Balthazar thought for a moment that maybe he had over reacted after he released the powerful spell and found that there was nothing at all in the hallway. From his own place in the hall he couldn't see the open door farther down. He assumed it was probably just a case of nerves. Everyone who knew that Damien was still alive was probably a bundle of raw edged nerves. The guards in the other hall came running around the corner at the other end, swords already drawn and held at the ready. Seeing only the Castlekeep advisor at the other end of the hall, waving at them with a dismissive sheepish gesture and a rather embarrassed expression on his face, they figured that there was nothing wrong. Balthazar was silently cursing himself for his incompetence when he heard the sound of something going through a window down the corridor in an adjoining room. The departing guards swung back around at the sound of noise and all of them headed towards that direction.

Caliban looked out over the expanse of sharp jagged rocks that stuck up out of the dark water hundreds of feet below the towering castle wall, if his next spell failed he knew that he would be killed when he crashed into them, so just in case he used a little bit of inner magic to augment his leap out from the window, hopefully it would carry him out far enough, just in case.

The red-robed advisor ran into the room as he stood up on the ledge. Quickly Caliban finished the incantation and leapt far out into the black darkness.

Balthazar knew at the sight of the man in black throwing himself out the window that whatever this man had been here in the castle for he might have already found it and the only thing of importance was Damien's still being alive.

Caliban felt the wind blowing into his face and tearing at his long almost white hair as he fell, he released the flying spell he had been holding and he instantly felt his body grow lighter and after a brief moment his falling stopped altogether. Flying usually requires intense concentration by the caster, but to Caliban who loved to do it and who had spent hours after hours and day after day doing it so much that it came to him almost naturally he could almost relax. He hovered momentarily in the air, suspended by his magic in order to get his bearings and risked a quick glance back up towards the window that he had jumped out of.

Balthazar knew that if he allowed the figure in black to disappear all of their plans might be placed in jeopardy. As quick as he could cast, he sent several silver lightening bolts streaking out the window after the fleeing figure.

Just in time it seemed to the young man in black that he looked back. With only a second to react as the first silver bolt came straight at him, Caliban tucked himself into a tight ball to make himself as little a target as possible and rolled through the air. He just barely avoided being hit by the first and largest of the sizzling bolts. So close was its path to his that it set his baggy clothes on fire. He smelled some of his hair also catch on fire but the two remaining bolts sailed harmlessly on by him.

Quickly he ripped the flaming clothes off of his body, hurling them towards the water and then he dove towards the dark water after them. He hoped that the advisor would think that he had at least wounded or injured him with the bolt. He flailed his arms and legs in the air as if he was completely out of control. At the last moment he pulled out of the dive and skimmed only inches above the water's shiny black surface. He slapped it hard with his palms, making a loud splashing sound.

Flying along the tops of the white capping waves, he headed towards the docks. It was the farthest place he could think of from the castle and the other powerful wizard.

Balthazar cursed silently under his breath as he saw the

flames ignite the escaping mans clothes. Then he watched the black figure of the fleeing man plummeting towards the waters surface in what looked like a desperate attempt to regain his control of his magic. The water was too black for him to actually tell whether or not the man crashed into its dark surface but he thought he might have heard the sound of a splash. Deciding that he must have struck close enough to the escaping figure with the bolts to disrupt his or her concentration because of the flailing arms and legs and the burning clothes, the advisor turned away from the broken window. Sighing in frustration he looked into the concerned eyes of the Captain of the guard in charge of protecting the heir's safety.

"Did he manage to get by you, or to find out anything about your charge in the other room?" the short hawkish advisor demanded curtly, his eyes locking on the guard force commander.

The Captain met the advisors piercing look and said in what he hoped was a reassuring manner, "No one has been into or out of that room since Lord Richards' son returned several hours ago other than to bring them food. I knew the servant that did so personally. Of that I am absolutely certain, I have been at the door myself all afternoon."

Balthazar snorted through his large, hooked nose, doubtfully. He knew that the man in black must have found out something. He hadn't attempted to hide and wait until he was clear. Instead he had thrown himself out of a window in order to escape. That was answer enough to him that he had found what it was that he had been seeking. "But what," thought the hawkish looking advisor, "could he have discovered, if the captain was telling the truth? How would he have found out anything without actually seeing Damien's body with his own eyes?" A sudden idea occurred to Balthazar and he asked the captain, "What was it that you and your men were talking about before I arrived in the hall and found the intruder leaving?"

The captain heard this last part and visibly winced at the derogatory tone in the advisor's cold voice, then considered this question for several moments before his face froze and he gasped in a sharp intake of breath.

Balthazar knew even before the words were spoken that something was said amongst them that shouldn't have been.

"One of my men was commenting on how beautiful the female cleric of Dar was, the one who saved Damien's life." The words were barely out of the Captains mouth before Balthazar ordered them back to their post and set off in the direction of the city watch's commanders quarters. Hopefully, he had indeed managed to down the flying man with his bolts of lightening and he was floating dead in the ocean. But if he hadn't he would inform Bayle Jensen who would alert the city watch to keep an eye out for any signs of a partially burnt wet man moving throughout the cities streets, maybe even with no clothes on at all. With all the people moving about in the city, he seriously doubted that they would find anybody matching his description and with it being festival time there were probably more than a few naked men roaming the streets, but he had to try just in case.

Caliban felt his body begin to grow heavy as he came to the docks. The spell was completely used up. He wished he had thrown a smirk at the Castlekeep advisor. It had been the first time he had really been able to test his own skills against another qualified opponent other than his own father and he had almost not been able to resist. Balthazar would be hurrying to alert the city watch about him. He knew he probably had about twenty minutes before a possible description of him was magically posted through out the city. Normally he could just go through the city and might even make it back to the ambassador's estates wearing armor, especially here with all of the tournaments going on. But even black Elvynn leather armor on a dark night like this was sure to be noticed by someone due to the crowds. If somebody recognized it as ancient talisman armor, it would draw unwanted attention to him. The first guard that noticed his slightly burnt and frazzled hair would indeed mark his appearance.

The docks were almost completely empty as the crews of the ships were in the bazaar shopping, selling and swapping their wares. An abandoned broken three-wheeled wagon with a torn canvas cover had been pushed off to one side of the street and as Caliban's slate blue eyes fell on it he knew that he had found his way across the city.

Quickly he went over to the wagon and slipping one of his hands down into one of the leg sheaths, he pulled out one of the long double bladed glittering fighting knives and began to cut a large piece out of the wagons canvas tarp top. He wrapped the large brown piece of canvas about him like a giant cloak, then he bent over and began smearing some of the wagon wheel grease on his hands and he ran them through his pale white hair and onto the skin of his face. When he was done, his hair was black and the griminess of his appearance was enough that nobody would think him of any importance other than a dirty street person. Thirty minutes later he easily scaled the wall to the ambassador's estates. Using his magic, he was back in his quarters without anyone being the wiser. Caliban knew that he had to use the mirror of walking to contact his father and tell him about what he had discovered and didn't relish the act.

* * *

Lord Cyadine Syndell was practicing his battlemage forms that he had learned in the academe of mages over twenty years ago from his old Battlemaster Trakiko Matsuri, the elderly Esian exile. His tall muscular body flowed from one pattern into another with perfect grace and fluidity. So completely focused was his mind on his daily exercises that he failed to notice the swirling in the mirror behind him that announced his son's reflection in it.

Caliban watched his father move, each angle and movement never wavering or shaking, honed over the course of a lifetime into perfection. It was several moments before finally he interrupted with a slight cough.

The royal advisor and wizard to the throne of Kallamar froze in mid movement, standing on one leg, with the other held high in the air at head level sideways, his heel cocked outward.

Maintaining perfect balance, Cyadine turned and faced the mirror of walking, without lowering his long leg and asked. "What is it my son, I can see that something is wrong, it shows in your eyes?"

"He's not dead father, I failed. I don't know how but somehow Damien Daverge is still alive."

Cyadine lowered the outstretched leg and with one eyebrow arched critically asked. "How?"

"It seems that somehow Lords Richard's high priest and a female cleric of Dar," both of the advisor's eyebrows shot upwards at the mention of a female cleric of Dar, "managed to save his life, I even used glow adder poison to insure that he would die in case the bolt missed his heart and the only reason it missed was because of this."

Caliban reached in under his armor and fished out the golden medallion of a battlemage with its mailed fist clenching fire and the large gouge cut into one of its edges from his own crossbow bolt.

Cyadine listened without speaking as he eyed the medallion, taking in all that his son was saying about the rightful heir to the throne and crown still being alive.

"Tell me everything, including how you found out he was still alive. There must be something more going on here. Richard is obviously planning to buy time."

So, Caliban in the manner he had been taught by his

father recalled everything that had occurred since he had left Kallamar in exact detail.

Again Cyadine listened, his ice blue eyes intently staring at his son. Soon, a calculating expression crossed his cold-featured face. "You were there. Did you hear anything else that you might have overlooked or considered unimportant at any time?"

Caliban reran the events over again in his minds eye again and then again, just as he was about to tell his father that there was nothing else, he remembered the conversation between Lord Gildon and his blademaster Braden Ravenclaw about Illsador.

Cyadine saw the expression in his son's eyes and he knew before he had spoken that the young man had indeed remembered something.

"I did overhear something strange, Lord Gildon Seahorn was talking to his blademaster about taking a trip to the highland rim, I thought it odd that they would be going so far north this late in the year."

Cyadine quickly put the pieces together, "That is Richards plan," he answered, looking at his son. "What do you mean father?" asked the white haired young man.

"Richard is trying to buy time by making us think that the heir is dead, while he sends Damien after the Dragon rings. After all, only he can do so, the dragon nor the rings themselves won't let anyone else take or wear them unless they are the rightful heir or of the creator of the rings blood."

"What are you talking about father, who is this young man and what does he really matter? What is he the heir of? I thought that you said that he was just a renegade battlemage disloyal to the throne and the crown."

Cyadine realized that he had made a mistake by voicing aloud his thoughts. Now, he had to tell his son more than he had wanted to before. "The western Highlords are trying to say that he is the son of the old king and queen and if he comes into power somehow then we will all lose our places here. His survival puts all of our lives in jeopardy, he must be removed before he can claim rights to the crown and throne."

"Are you saying that the man I tried to kill last night could possibly be the rightful true heir to the throne and the crown father?" Caliban asked, giving his father a direct look.

When Cyadine saw the look in his son's slate blue eyes, he wondered whether he should have held this information back. Caliban had a fault, a misguided loyalty to Seth Salidor, their ruler's son. He thought that Seth was going to be king one day. It was he to whom his obedience and skills belonged. He had trained his son to obey his every word and command without question. This was the first time he had ever questioned him about anything he had told or asked him to do. He had also, instilled a sense of duty to the ruler of the land and had had him swear fealty to the throne and the crown. Vargas and Gunther would be in charge of the realm in some manner of speaking until at least his masters return. He would now have to try and distract his son's mind away from thinking that his mark could be the rightful heir.

"Yes and you are going to do it again!" Cyadine told him. "This time you will succeed rather than fail. You need to figure out a way to either join with them on their quest for the rings in Illsador, or devise a way to follow them and kill him after he gains them. It's too dangerous to try to kill him again in the city. We're not really even certain that he is an heir," His father lied. "But if he makes a claim, it could stop Seth from achieving his own birthright."

"How should I go about such a thing? What would you suggest, father?" Caliban asked.

A cunning expression filled Cyadine's cold blue eyes. "I'm sure that you will find a way. Don't try to kill him again, at least not until after he recovers the rings." Then the advisor told his son the second part of his plan.

After he was finished Caliban gave a slight forward bow to his father. He stepped back away from the mirrors surface. With a wave of his hand Caliban dismissed his father's presence from the mirror and went back to his own quarters.

Cyadine frowned after his departed son. He had not expected Caliban to fail. He was nearly infallible in the carrying out of his duties. It seemed to Cyadine that maybe this heir had been a little lucky. The tall wizard didn't usually believe in luck. He had been carefully trained by his battlemaster to plan meticulously. That way there was little room for errors or mistakes. He had passed those same skills and traits onto his own son like the man he had at one time considered as a father had passed them onto him. Until that man had betrayed him.

"Now," Cyadine thought to himself as he toweled the sweat from his muscular body. His plans had changed. He would have to make Vargas aware that the true heir was still alive. The change though would also serve to remove Richard Daverge and Dalmar Ariaas from the equation as well."

He realized they couldn't go on with another outright assassination attempt now. Caliban's failure, the fact all of the western Highlords were now aware of Damien's rightful place as heir to the throne and Vargas himself had drawn too much attention to them by his new tax laws worked against it. If the rest of the Fourteen Highlords learned about a second attempt, they might all band together to take away Vargas' regency and remove them all from power

If his next plans went well, he wouldn't have to worry about the heir much longer anyway. The whole realm would be after him with blood in their eyes. All would consider the act that they were about to commit despicable. That mattered little to the royal advisor. He had carried out many despicable acts in Vargas' name as advisor and wizard to the throne and the crown. His lord only cared about results and not how he got them. Cyadine knew that he would do whatever it took in order to accomplish whatever needed to be done. His own Elvynn master had instilled the importance of this in him. For doing only what he had been taught to do in keeping a creative and open mind he had been not allowed to gain his own coveted black and gold robes and had been asked to leave for using forbidden types creational magic. His Elvynn masters had found him and had taken him in along with his anger at this affront and had used it to get him to join with them. Promising him revenge against the battlemages who had cast him. Now he was the power behind the throne of all of Kallamar.

He would have to wait now until this Damien Daverge had recovered the rings. Once he removed them from the tomb itself, Cyadine had a plan already devised and waiting for him.

Chapter 19
Preparations

The next two days for Damien passed by uneventfully. He was buried yesterday and wasn't even allowed to attend his own funeral. Both Alyssa and Logan were allowed to go and informed him of all of the details, including the fake tears shed by the Lady Ianna, who claimed to all that would listen to her, that she had loved him like her own son.

This statement had caused Damien to choke on the cup of tea he had been drinking. Alyssa gave him a scolding. Logan informed him that he and Kendle had been put in charge of purchasing all of their supplies for the journey north. Logan also told him about the wedding planned for tomorrow. Afterward, the three discussed plans for the day after the wedding celebration, which was also the last day of the festival. All of them would be leaving on that day. This conversation continued until Kendle arrived and announced that it was time for him and Logan to go do some shopping around the city. As Damien watched them depart, he wished that he could have gone with. Between Kendle being the trade ambassador for both races of dwarves and Logan being the shrewdest dealer in the city, he was certain that the merchants in the square wouldn't know which way was up by the end of the day. He and Alyssa spent the rest of that day together discussing and debating the differences in their selective abilities and training. There wouldn't be much time for wasted words once they were on the trail.

Caliban was given the task by his father to keep an eye on the castle for the next couple of days to see if he could learn any more about the heir's plans. If he didn't find out anything useful, he was going to leave Castlekeep and head towards the Highland rim in hopes of scouting them after they left the confines and safety of the city.

There were only a few routes that they could take to Illsador. With Seth's naming day not to far away, his father figured his mark would take the most direct route possible. Caliban was on point outside of the Castle searching for information on Damien's movements or any of the people closest to him in the castle. That was how he spotted the sandy blonde haired young man from the other night and Kendle Stonebreaker, who was another of his marks companions leaving the castle.

The young assassin mage was more prepared for following the skilled sandy haired man today than he had been the first night. This time he had learned and rehearsed several druidic alterself-spells and could stay with the pair for more than a few hours before the magic wore him out without either of them ever knowing he was there. Caliban hoped to learn when they were leaving and more. As the young man and the dwarf stepped past towards the market, he quickly ducked off into a side street and said the words to the alterself-spell.

The somewhat smaller and more delicate featured woman that stepped back out of the side street coinciding with the departure of the almost white haired and white skinned tall muscular young man looked nothing like him. The only thing that even tied the pair together were the searching slate blue eyes.

The disguise worked like a charm. Immediately, he heard the dwarf tell one of the merchants that they couldn't wait that long. They were leaving the day after tomorrow in the morning for a mining expedition into the mountains and would need the packs delivered to the guards' tower at the main city gate by tomorrow evening at the latest. As the pair continued their shopping, Caliban trailed along, he managed to get close again another time when he changed from the beautiful woman into a gnarly old begging hag who was rather repulsive looking with misshapen gnarled hands and a humped back. This time he managed to drop two enchanted stones, one into one of the dwarf's pouches and another into the young blond man's coat as they haggled. If neither discovered the stones, Caliban would know their location for the next three days thanks to another enchanted stone in his own pocket that would grow warmer or cooler depending on how far it was from the other two. He stayed with them for a short time more until he finally grew bored by their constant haggling over prices and drifted away.

Caliban knew when and where they would be leaving from and now all he had to do was find a way to join their party. He would have to leave the city quickly and travel fast north. He managed to convince the keeper of the stalls back at the ambassador's estates that he was on a dire mission for the ambassador and had commissioned one of the royal flying griffons to fly him north to a location in the wilds. He hoped that he would be able to enlist a little more help in helping him to join the small group going to Illsador.

Three hours into the flight and Caliban pulled the straps on the griffon's halter causing the large well-trained intelligent animal to circle the woods below. A shabby ramshackle collection of huts and wooden buildings filled the clearing far below him. The young assassin mage knew that he had reached his destination. A rabble warren called thieves hollow.

Directing the fierce creature to another clearing about a mile from the camp Caliban landed and ordered the griffon to stay out of sight. Checking to make sure that he had the whistle to summon it out of hiding when he was finished, he disappeared into the woods in the direction of the camp.

Thieves hollow was just that, a hollow in the woods that housed a motley crew of cutpurses, cutthroats, criminals and murderers who had all fled from societies laws, restrictions and justice.

Caliban hadn't even been sure that he could have found the secret location in the woods below the Annulith Mountains even with his father's directions. But he had and now as he approached the camp he kept a wary eye out for sentries or guards. Moving like an extension of the early evening shadows in the forest, he slipped into the camps perimeter. Only one man stood guard on the path that led into the camp and at seeing no one else around, Caliban slipped in behind the man, silently unsheathing one of his slip on fighting blades. With the speed of someone who has been training for this sort of thing all of his life, the young mage assassin slipped his arm without the weapon under the guards right arm and jabbed his stiffened fingers up under the mans chin into the nerve cluster there, not hard enough to knock the unsuspecting man unconscious, but enough to cause his head to jerk backwards away from the sharp stabbing pain and for his back to arch as he did so. Caliban's other arm and hand repeated the same maneuver, this one though was the one with the blades on it.

As the man opened his mouth to shout a warning and sound an alarm, Caliban easily slid one of the long talon like blades into the man's open mouth effectively silencing him.

"Do you feel death?" he whispered in a deadly tone, into the now shaking mans ear as he stood on his tip toes trying to avoid the deadly blade in his mouth, a single drop of blood slid out of the man's mouth and onto the back of Caliban's hand. Realizing that the razor sharp blade had cleanly sliced the man's lip open, Caliban lifted the edge of the blade slightly so that it didn't cut any deeper. He wanted the other man to be able to answer his questions. If he accidentally sliced his tongue off on the magically enhanced blade, he wouldn't be able to. The frightened man mumbled something unintelligible from around the sharp blade in his mouth, as his eyes tried to look behind him and meet those of the white haired killer who held him pinned. The sharp tip of the slender blade barely scraped across the roof of his mouth and the guard knew that if he moved again he would be dead in an instant.

"Is Micak Foss still in command around here?" Caliban whispered into the man's ear, "just blink once for yes or twice for no and if you try to move your head again or talk you just might remove your tongue."

The still shaking man blinked his eyes only once.

"Good, now I'm going to remove my blade from your mouth, but don't try to yell out a warning," Caliban stuck the second of the claw blade into the man's back just under his ribcage, "Or I will gut you like a pig for roasting, am I understood?"

Once again the other man blinked once and Caliban slowly slid the sharp blade out of the man's mouth.

"Now take me to his location and if you try to speak, it better not be louder than a whisper," Caliban hissed, "or else I will still gut you and then both of my blades will be bloody instead of just this one." He held up the one set of blades in front of the man's eyes, showing him the drops of blood that ran down the full length of the blades, just to make sure that he understood.

The entire camp was extremely quiet and for a moment Caliban wondered as they moved through the dead silence, whether there would be enough people here for his plan to work. As they made their way to its far end, he began to hear numerous voices shouting, arguing and laughing.

A large open-air tent had been erected and about thirty men and women were gathered around a couple of wagons. One man was inside handing out items to another who held them up for all to see. It became obvious to the young white haired man that this was a celebration of a raid on some unlucky merchant or trader gone well and now the men were dividing up the spoils between them.

None of the bandits noticed the pair approaching until they were on top of the little group, then a large bear like man called for silence and all did as he instructed. Caliban recognized the large man from his father's description immediately as Micak Foss.

He was a large bear of a man who was almost as wide as he was tall. His head was huge with wide beady bear like eyes and he was covered by so much black hair that Caliban wondered whether or not he might be some sort of were creature of the sort he resembled.

As the white haired young man stepped out a little from behind the guard that he had been leading and using as a partial shield, he saw the thieves hollow leaders eyes go wide in startled recognition.

"Is this some sort of wizards trick, Cyadine, or have you finally become Elvynn enough to manage to stay young."

"This is not any sort of wizards trick," Caliban coolly answered, "and nor am I the man that you mistake me for."

Now the man's bear like yellow eyes narrowed into suspicious wary slits. "Then who the hell are you? You had better answer correctly and quickly or else it might be the last thing you say." As the leader of the hollow finished speaking, Caliban felt the cold touch of a very sharp point prick the back of his ear. Turning his head a little he saw a tall lanky woman with dirty black hair that had so many twigs in it that they almost seemed to be growing right out of her head. She held a miniature crossbow in one hand with a knocked hunting bolt in its slide, it was the tip of this that had pricked his ear and had gotten his attention.

Barely acknowledging her presence, the white haired white skinned man answered the question. "I'm Caliban Syndell, Cyadine's son and student."

"Really?" answered the man named Micak giving him an appraising stare, "Prove it, for I never heard of my friend Cyadine having any son. Though, I must say that the resemblance is rather startling." The bear like man who ruled in Thieves hollow wiggled his fingers at the girl behind him with the crossbow.

Caliban turned just in time to see her holster the crossbow with one hand and draw out a large hunting knife with the other which she thrust in a lightening fast stab in the direction of his face. Without barely a moment to react, the assassin mage did the only thing he could do and threw his head backwards along with the rest of his body so that he bent over backwards before he went down to the ground onto the flat of his back. The thrusting knife missed his eyeball by a hairs breath, it passed so close to his face that the ladies fingers around its hilt caressed his cheek as he fell. Kicking upwards from the flat of his back with his foot, he drove his heel upwards into her groin. A whoosh of air escaped from the woman's mouth and she dropped the knife from her hand instantly and as she bent forward in obvious pain. The long bladed knife fell to the ground where it landed tip first in the earth next to Caliban's body, without pausing he grabbed the hilt in his hand, rolled sideways from the spot where he had been a moment before and at the same time he flipped the knife over in his hand so that he was holding the blade in his fingers, coming up onto his knees facing Micak. As their eyes locked, he smiled a small smile at the thieves hollow's leader as he threw the knife and uttered an incantation.

The spinning hunting knife split in the air as it flew into two knives of equal size, then those split into four and so on until a little over thirty of the long bladed hunting knives streaked though the air and slammed into one of the wooden kegs. It shattered into a thousand wooden splinters, sending its frothy ale contents exploding into the air. Thus completely drenching everyone around it.

"Bravo," called out the big man as he clapped his hairy large hands together, "that was truly impressive! So how is your esteemed father and what is it that I can do for him?"

The pair talked long into the night and by the time Caliban whistled for the griffon, another part of his father's plan had been formed. One more thing was left to do, but that would have to wait until the night after the wedding when the group was set to leave the castle.

* * *

On the day of the wedding, much to Damien's surprise Alyssa asked Logan if he would escort her. Logan had readily agreed. The pair looked splendid in their outfits for the occasion. Logan wore a forest green doublet and matching trousers that were almost the exact same color as his eyes.

Having nothing to wear to the wedding, Alyssa had to rely on Abraim's judgment to come up with something for her. A green embroidered dress that he found somewhere looked resplendent on her. The chamberlain left her short curly strawberry blonde hair alone but he did find a black and white sea pearl necklace for her to wear. At first, the female cleric of Dar balked at wearing the fine clothes and what they required, complaining that she didn't know the first thing about how to act in such things. For the first time ever Damien heard the chamberlain compliment Logan by saying if she listened to him and followed his lead she'd be fine. His manners were impeccable in these types of situations.

Even Logan had thrown an incredulous look in the direction of the owlish eyed chamberlain who returned it with a raised white eyebrow, indicating the beautiful young lady in front of him. Quickly Logan hurried to agree.

Like the funeral of earlier, Damien stayed in his room by his self, once again alone. He stared out the darkened window of his bedchamber smelling the salt filled air, contemplating all that had occurred in the short time that he had been home. He had just arrived back in Castlekeep a few days back as the adopted third son to a Highlord's house. All of a sudden now he was the heir to the throne and crown of Kallamar and getting ready to leave his home on a quest to make him a king.

It was definitely enough to stir the brain, causing more than a few thoughts to swirl around in his head. He hadn't foreseen any of the changes that were coming into his life. He realized that Vargas, regardless of how he came into power, wouldn't give it up easily after all this time. Especially not if he was the type of man that Travis and Kendle described him as. His father said earlier Vargas was in power for all the wrong reasons. As he had been taught at the academy, Damien knew that he had a duty to the people of the realm whether it was as a battlemage or as a ruler. To present oneself as a champion of justice, as Tiko had taught him. The young battlemage tried hard not to dwell on the odds that were stacked against him and the group. He didn't expect anyone back for a while with all of the celebrating going on in the halls below for the wedding reception and the last night of the festival. Logan had mentioned to him earlier something that had caused him to smile right before he turned away from the window and headed of to bed. The young spy thief mentioned that a certain pretty, red-haired female battlemage from Caladar had won the championships at the tournament in both hand-to-hand and weapons combat.

As Damien drifted off to sleep he wondered idly how he would have handled himself if he had ended up fighting Cassica Essen in the championships and whether or not he could have brought himself to actually defeat her. If she smiled at him in just the right way he knew without a doubt that he couldn't have beaten her.

* * *

Almost all of the people in the mansion at the ambassador's estates were asleep, including Dalmar. Caliban was completely packed and ready to leave but he still had two things left to do. He opened the doors to the ambassador's bedchambers and slid into the room, moving as silently as a ghost. He put his back against one of the walls and stared down at the sleeping figure lying on the bed, illuminated by a sliver of moonlight shining through one of the room's high windows.

The ex Marshall of Kallamar's armies slept peacefully under a thin white sheet. Caliban unslung the weapon that was strapped to his back and loaded the same crossbow he had used on whom his father told him was an imposter to the throne this Damien Daverge other night, with a bolt that he had stolen off one of the Castlekeep soldiers while he was invisible inside of the keep. He had made a mistake the first time when he had tried to assassinate his first mark with a heart shot and wouldn't make that same mistake twice, this time he would go for a head kill.

Dalmar had spent almost all of his life as soldier, so when he subconsciously heard the click of the crossbows quarrel locking into place, his trained soldier's instincts woke him up. Instantly awake in the manner that only a soldier can manage, he rolled over in the bed, sitting up and looked for the source of the intruding sound that had stabbed so deeply into his subconscious. He spotted the dark form of his new secretary standing off to one side of the room, his white hair glowing eerily silver in the room's dim light.

Not seeing the crossbow in the other man's hands the ambassador asked. "What is it? What's wrong? What are you doing in here?" he demanded at the end of his questioning when it looked like the other man wasn't going to answer.

Caliban didn't answer for several long moments. Instead, he continued to stare silently down at Dalmar lying in his bed. Finally he responded in a voice that was devoid of emotion, "I've found the plotters and now I'm almost done here."

Dalmar's face paled slightly when he realized what the dead eyed young man meant. He saw a loaded crossbow leveled at his head, held in an unwavering hand.

"This is the end then?" the royal ambassador asked his would be assassin, refusing to flinch in front of the younger man. Dalmar knew that he was only seconds from dying. "Why?" was the only question that he could think to ask as he saw his death coming.

"Power." was the one word answer that he heard an instant before the trigger was pulled.

The bolt caught the ambassador dead center in the forehead, killing him instantly. The assassin mage walked over to the bed and stared down at the dead ex marshal of armies. He wondered for a brief moment as he studied the dead man lying there with a slight trickle of blood flowing out from around the bolt in the center of his forehead, whether or not he was in fact doing the right thing for the throne and the crown to which he was sworn to obey. This man lying in front of him had also sworn those same types of oaths. Now he had been killed by both his father's and Vargas' orders. Caliban decided then that when he returned to the capital city he would have to have a long discussion with Seth about these events and find out his thoughts.

Knowing that right now wasn't the time or place to be contemplating such matters, Caliban quickly reached under his shirt and removed the second of the two items that he had taken from the castle. Eyeing the scarred item in his hand almost wistfully for a moment as if he wished he could keep it, he dropped the battlemages golden medallion belonging to Damien Daverge onto the floor at the foot of the bed. Quickly he said the words and drew upon the arcane energy around him and the magical ability in his armor to cast a soul banishing cleric's spell. Normally he couldn't cast such a powerful spell but wearing the Elvynn armor he could cast any type of magic. The soul banishing would prevent any cleric from reviving or reanimating the now dead ambassador corpse. The creational armor encasing Caliban that granted him this power grew warm to the touch as it used clerical magic to do this. When it was done, there would be no finding out from this corpse who had done this to him.

All that he had left to do was gather up his things out of the secretaries office and discover the body in the morning, discover the evidence, sound the alarm, plant the seeds of deception and report what happened to the capital city of Kallamar, then his father and the royal regent would step in and take over. As exactly his father had planned.

Chapter 20
Tunnel Rats

Travis had set up for everyone to meet in Damien's chambers the morning after the wedding. But Kendle was nowhere to be found.

The entire group waited for about a half hour and Logan was about to suggest that someone needed to go find him when the dwarf stumbled into Damien's room. He was red nosed and bleary-eyed. His beard and hair was a tangled mess of knots and snares. Immediately he began to grumble and curse about the out of the way location of Damien's chambers and how far he had too walk to get there with his throbbing head.

"A hard night with too much ale Kendle?" Damien asked him teasingly.

"No," softly muttered the obviously hung over dwarf, as he rubbed at his temples with his thick fingers. "A fine night of drinking with my uncle."

Logan caught Damien's eye mischievously and

shouted into the dwarf's ear, "Looks like it might have been a little too much of a good thing."

Kendle winced at the loud voice in his ear and Alyssa concealed a smile behind one hand as she looked over at the now cringing dwarf.

"Now that everyone is present," said Travis looking at each one in turn, "it's past time that we get leaving." He turned his scarred baldhead in Logan's direction and asked. "Is everything ready? From here until we get out of the city everything depends upon you."

Logan simply replied that all was arranged and he was ready whenever they were.

Yesterday before the wedding, Logan had been tasked with arranging for their way out of both the castle and city and for a way for them to meet with their gear that he had sent out ahead of them. He had told Damien part of his plan was using Simon's network to arrange getting their gear outside of the castles walls, how they would wear pilgrim's robes and how they would all leave with several groups of refugees. Logan deliberately left out what route they would be taking out of the castle. Damien suspected what route it was and knew that it could be extremely dangerous path.

Everyone in the group had a dagger with them, but that was the only weapon Logan allowed them to carry. He said they had to look and act the part of pilgrims, otherwise there was no way that they could exit the city. Damien was sure that all of the groups members carried more than just one single dagger on their person though, including Logan who was wearing as always, his own long black fighting cloak that he knew contained a walking arsenal of weapons and tools sewn into its lining, hidden pockets and sleeves.

Logan had numerous ways that he could get the group out of the city unnoticed, that was the easy part. According to Braden, the ranger and blademaster from Caladar, getting them out of the castle without anyone seeing them or finding out that Damien was still alive was the hard part. The battlemage put every option to the test in his mind until he was left with only one that seemed feasible. Damien had questioned the spythief on how and he had been deliberately vague in his answer, not wanting to reveal too much right away. It was this plan and location he settled on as they all exited Damien's chambers, following the sandy haired thief. Logan led the small group out of Damien's chambers and deeper into the abandoned part of the ancient castle. Damien realized immediately where it was that they were heading and he groaned audibly.

Alyssa heard the groan and for a moment thought he was in pain and shot him an unseen look of alarm, which he quickly waved off with a hand, as he stepped up closer to the cleric, "I'm alright," he reassured her, "I just realized where it is that we are going."

The path that Logan was leading the group on was one that was well etched into both of the young men's minds. Both had used this way of exiting and entering the castle on a regular basis as young boys. Logan had discovered it through some ancient maps found in an abandoned library in Damien's part of the castle, until an unexpected occurrence had stopped the boys from using it. They had, through the plans that Logan had found numerous other hidden passageways and rooms throughout the entire castle that were unknown and they had explored every bit of all of them.

Some of the passageways were known to the staff of the castle and were used a lot of times so that they could move quickly through the large castle unnoticed while attending to their duties. That was in the main part of the keep. The passageway that the sandy haired spythief was leading them to now was one that Damien was sure that no one other than him or Logan knew anything about.

There were a few other ways out of the castle that could be used, but all of them required a disguise or magic and since there was a chance that the royal regent had a few spies in the city watching the keep itself, no one wanted to try any of those routes. This escape route was guaranteed. Using it had always required the boys to either bring a change of clothes with them or Damien had to learn a cleaning spell for the occasion. The few times the spell had failed caused Abraim to have to burn their clothes because of the smell.

A storage room was located off the abandoned library where Logan had found the ancient plans to the castle and it was to there that he was leading the group.

After they were all in the storeroom, Logan and Damien grabbed hold of several stone floor tiles and began to pry them up from the floor using their daggers. The concealing tiles closely resembled the rest of the floor and would have gone unnoticed by anyone except for maybe Kendle who immediately recognized them and laughed.

"Dwarvish concealing stones," commented the dwarf, "I haven't seen any of those in years." the redness of the dwarfs face and the remnants of the hangover were quickly fading away. Not much could harm a dwarf and if it did, it didn't take one long to recover.

"Oh you're about to see more dwarven pieces of workmanship, the deeper we go Kendle," Logan told him with a smile.

"Is there any other kind of better workmanship?" responded the dwarf.

No one answered, because all of them knew that when it came to building castles, fortresses, keeps and strongholds, there was no one better than dwarven builders except for maybe dwelven and no one spoke of them. Even the Elvynn during the times when they had ruled over the other races, had used dwarven builders to build their cities or at least until they created the dark dwarves.

Once the concealing stones were removed, a large door hidden under the floor revealed itself. An ancient dark stone staircase was behind the door and it descended deep into the bowels of the castle.

Logan motioned for Damien to lead the way. Damien said a quick word of magic and a glowing ball of light flared up out of his hand. The ball soared upwards and hovered at a spot above his head where it lit up the darkness that filled the descending staircase. Logan reached into one of the pockets of his coat and removed what looked like a large ruby and gold earring and stuck it through a hole in his left ear. The earring was standard guild issue to any thief that achieved roof runner leader status and allowed its wearer to see in the blackest of darkness as if they were in broad daylight. It was the only thing that the young ex thief had kept from the guild during his banishment.

Slowly all six members of the group descended down the cool dark staircase. Thirty minutes later they entered a corridor that was so narrow that the only way that they could get down it was in a single file line. Damien heard Kendle murmur something about a dwarven backdoor and realized that this was exactly what he and Logan must have found when they were younger. In every dwarven structure that the dwarves built, they always incorporated a secret back door that was only known to the builder that designed the castle.

Just as it looked as if they couldn't go any farther down the ever tightening dark tunnel, it opened up into a large corridor ending in a stone slab wall.

After they were all out of the tight tunnel and into the wider corridor, Logan gestured to a torch stand and asked Braden and Travis to put a torch into each of the holders that were set into the rock wall. Damien ordered, "Put both in at the same time."

"That's right," returned Logan. "I almost forgot about that."

"You did forget about that part," Damien told him with

a tilted half smile.

An audible click sounded and a grating noise filled the larger corridor as one of the large rocks in the wall spun and turned sideways. Beyond the wall a small opening and a second stonewall into which there was set a large thick iron ring. Before moving to the ring the young spythief reached into one of his pockets and withdrew a large brown-stopper vial.

"At least," he said looking over at Damien, "I didn't forget this."

"What is that?" asked Kendle eyeing the bottle warily as Logan opened the vial and a pungent odor filled the small passageway.

Logan dipped a finger into the bottle, a sticky yellow looking substance appeared on the end of his finger and he spread it under, around and in his nostrils before he handed it to Damien who did the same.

"Don't worry about what it is." he told the dwarf. "Just be grateful for what it does."

Damien finished and passed the vial onto another member of the party and each of them smeared the yellow looking substance around their noses. Once that was done Logan moved into the small opening and gestured for Damien to help him. Together they turned the large iron ring counter clockwise until another click sounded. The stonewall turned sideways just like the rock wall had done earlier.

A foul stench oozed out through the now open slot in the door. Everyone in the small party knew that without the vial that Logan had passed around to them, they would all be gagging uncontrollably from the strong stench of feces, sewage, slime and filth that filled the corridor.

"Where exactly are you taking us?" asked Alyssa wrinkling her nose. Neither Logan nor Damien bothered to answer. Instead they just beckoned for the others to follow and stepped through the narrow opening. Logan did instruct them though to watch their step, "It's about to get very slippery and you definitely don't want to fall into the water."

A large underground channel about fifteen feet across opened up before them and a river of brownish black water about calf high flowed sluggishly about their legs as they all stepped into it.

Everyone realized where they were but it was Braden who vocalized it. "A sewer!" he exclaimed more than he asked.

"It's the only real way to get out of the castle completely unnoticed," Damien told the group and Logan nodded in agreement. Then they set off, with Logan taking the lead.

The sandy haired thief looked back over his shoulder and said softly, "Keep as quiet as possible please."

"Why?" demanded Travis instantly on alert, both of his hands going towards the hilts of both of his weapons.

"Nothing!" hissed both young men in unison.

"We just don't want to disturb anything or alert anything to our presence." Logan told the blademaster, but it was obvious they were hiding something.

"Is he going to be in any danger?" the tall thin ranger with the short brown hair and prominent cheekbones asked, directing a pointed glance in Damien's direction, "The future of the throne and the sake of the realm is at stake here and if he dies, then this is all for nothing."

Logan's usual humor filled demeanor changed instantly, gone was the mischievous smile and his green eyes hardened noticeably as they locked onto Braden's.

"If I thought there was any kind of danger that would hurt or kill us as long as we careful, I wouldn't have brought us this way. There is a chance that we could have a little trouble, but as long as we keep somewhat silent and we keep moving we should be able to make it through here without any problems."

The tall ranger started to say something else but Travis cut him off with a wave of his hand and Braden bit the rest of his reply and fell silent.

Travis decided not to press the issue. He figured that if it was really dangerous Damien would've let him know, regardless of Logan's own recklessness at times. Damien knew the importance of this mission and what was at stake.

In spite of his statement, Logan still scanned every corner with his green eyes and seemed constantly on alert as they continued onward. Every once in a while something in the slimy brown water would brush up against one of their legs and the first time it was Alyssa, she gave a loud startled shriek that seemed to echo off of the tunnels around them. Both Damien and Logan immediately put their fingers to their mouths and angrily made shushing sounds.

Embarrassed, the female cleric sheepishly smiled and nodded at them.

Logan heard a scraping sound echo off of the rocks and he looked back over his shoulder anxiously casting his green eyes all about in the darkness.

"What do you think?" Damien asked looking over at his friend and sensing his nervousness. "Think they are still here after all of this time?"

"I'm not sure." Logan answered then he added, "But I suggest we make a little more haste. I don't want to be caught in these tunnels if they are. Especially since none of us have any weapons other than a few daggers."

"If what are still here?" demanded Travis again. He couldn't let this go on any longer, his dark eyes settling on the two younger men as the scraping sound faded off into the distance.

"Let's move!" Logan ordered in a hissing voice not bothering to answering the blademaster's question. "We'll tell you on the way to the exit, but now we need to make haste."

"When we were younger," Damien began keeping his

voice low as they started to run. "We used this shaft numerous times to get out of the castle unnoticed."

"That was until the rats found it." Logan continued.

"Rats?" asked Alyssa a fearful look filled her eyes and she also began casting her eyes about behind them, scanning the tunnel, for any signs of movement.

"Well how dangerous can they be if rats are all it is?" Kendle said loudly, a relieved look on his face as his voice echoed off of the water and carried on down the tunnel.

Damien again quickly brought up a finger to his lips and silenced the loud dwarf in mid sentence with a sharp shush.

"These are really large and dangerous rats and they track by sound," he informed the group.

A keening whistle like sound pierced the silence of the tunnel faintly far off in the distance behind them.

"These are a pack, a massively large pack, of giant rats that moved into the tunnels scouring for food, Logan finished.

More whistles answered the first far off, then slowly they began to sound everywhere.

"Forget silence now." Damien ordered as he broke out into a full run followed by the rest of the group. "Those whistles mean that they know we are here and they will be coming soon."

"Just how large is this pack and these rats?" Travis asked as he ran.

At that moment Alyssa tripped over something in the brown murky water and a glistening pile of white human bones appeared for all to see, glowing eerily in the light from Damien's spell.

"That big," Logan said pointing at the bones as they all raced past and Kendle grabbed the clerics arm and helped her back to her feet.

The scratching sound they had heard returned in a loud rush and much louder than before. Now it sounded like the skittering of claws on cement was all about them, followed by squeaks and squealing noises.

The entire group was now all racing as fast as the could through the tunnels splashing and sloshing water everywhere. All pretense of a silent exit from the tunnels was forgotten.

The high-pitched scream of the rats filled the air of the passageway and echoed in everyone's ears now. The group could now see large shadows moving on the walls behind them.

Damien risked a quick look back and could just see the hoard rounding a corner behind them, thousands of red eyes glowing fiercely in the darkness.

"How much farther do we have to go?" asked Travis panting from the run through water.

"Not much more hopefully," Logan returned and he too risked a look back behind him.

The large rats were closing quickly though and both him and Damien knew that they were not going to make it. Knowing he had to do something to slow the rats down in order to buy them enough time to reach the exit, the young battlemage gathered his magic about him and quickly cast two spells.

Two bright balls of light filled his hands. The first one pulsed and throbbed with radiant light, the second was a fiery orange globe that almost appeared to be on fire in his hand.

Damien lobbed the first ball of white light behind them and yelled not to look backwards. A blinding flash of white-hot light exploded in the tunnel behind him as the strobe spell went off. The magical explosion of light tore into the first wave of rats behind them, burning their red eyes and causing them to go blind and stumble in a searing explosion of white light. This halted the wave of bodies for a few moments.

Cocking his throwing arm back as far as he could

Damien threw the fiery globe in his other hand as far as he could behind them, then he started to count to ten as the timed fireball landed amongst the pack that had started to circle around the pile of blinded rats.

"Run faster!" he screamed out loudly to the others. "Things are about to get really messy in about ten seconds."

As they saw the light at the end of the tunnel, a loud booming sound filled the tunnel in a deafening roar. Flames erupted just as the group reached the tunnels exit.

The group quickly scrambled around to both sides of the exit way and hugged the rocky wall. The tunnel ended abruptly at a cliff's edge which ran under the castle and dropped off about a hundred feet down to jagged points of sharp rocks that jutted up out of the breaking surf far below, large waves crashed into the cliff wall at the bottom.

The stream of giant rats chasing after them were not able to stop their momentum and poured out of the end of the tunnel in a river of bodies, they kept going right out over the cliffs edge, crashing down onto the rocks, far beneath Damien and the others feet.

An explosive fire blast of flames and heat blew out right behind the rats like a blast of dragon's breath and illuminated the early morning cliffs in a bright orange glow. All of the small group felt its fierce heat and a shower of burning blackened bodies accompanied the blast filling the air with dead burning rats.

"By Becil's tools that was close," breathed Logan graciously, offering up a small prayer to the gods of thieves.

Kendle let out a relieved chuckle. "I don't think that you'll ever have to worry about that pack of rats any more ever again."

Everyone hugging the cliffs edge laughed nervously in the early morning light.

Braden turned to Travis, his angular face smiling.

"You never told me that things were so interesting around here."

The blademaster looked at both Damien and Logan, "They usually aren't unless those two are involved."

Logan smiled a wry smile at the blademaster's words and Damien just shrugged his shoulders helplessly.

A cold wind blew and Alyssa shivered slightly. Her face was unusually pale, "How long," she asked with a shaking voice, "are we planning on staying here on this ledge, I have a slight problem with narrow places," she told them as she shivered again and Damien knew that it was not just from the cold wind.

"She's right we can't stay here long," Logan answered as he stepped up to the front of the group.

"Stay close to the side, away from the edge, be careful it's slippery and don't fall, it's a long way down with a sharp hard landing at the bottom."

Kendle groaned at the young mans attempt at humor and the others just shook their heads.

The wind lashed at them in fury as they walked along the narrow ledge.

Soon they made their way to another small opening in the rock and Logan led them through it and up another set of stony steps. An oak door stood at the top of the steps. Logan stepped up close to the door, placing an ear against the door and motioned the others around him to silence. After a few moments of silence Logan grabbed hold of the handle and opened the door.

The door opened up into what appeared to be an abandoned stable house's tack room. After the group filed into the room, Logan went over to another door and once again put his ear to it. Hearing nothing he opened the door slightly, withdrew his thieves mirror out of the top of his boot and slid it out through the narrow opening. Seeing nothing reflected in its surface, he opened the door a little farther, peered out and then opened it the rest of the way.

The smell of horses now became prominent as they moved into the stables, not as much as compared to the smell from the sewer. Logan handed the pilgrim's cloaks to the other five. "Put these on," he ordered.

Once they were all dressed, he opened up the door. Sticking his head out, he looked all around the outside of the building for any body watching them. The young thief led them out into the city streets and to the closest of the cities gates. Everyone that they came in contact with along the way quickly moved away from the foul smelling group.

A dense morning fog had rolled in off of the stormy ocean, its gray twisting tendrils wove their way throughout the city and even though the streets were still full of people, Logan managed to find a few that were not so crowded and soon they were out the cities gates. Unseen, Simon, who had been told by Logan the way that they would exit, watched as they left the city, then quickly he turned and made his way back to the castle to report to Lord Richard that they were gone.

Travis took over command once they were beyond the cities walls. They continued walking on foot for several miles until they came upon a small troupe of castle guards patrolling the edge of royal forest.

The soldiers were mounted upon several horses and several more in tow carrying supplies. They dismounted and handed the reins over to Travis along with the several packhorses. Damien noticed through the cowl of his hood pulled low over his face, that the soldiers upon recognizing the blademaster all sat up straighter and more upright in their saddles.

"Are these our mounts?" Travis asked the senior soldier.

"Yes sir!" said a grizzled veteran who also gave the blademaster a curt nod.

Everyone in the small group took a set of reins from a soldier. The horses were not like regular Gaderian stock.

Instead they were mountain horses, with stocky bodies and shorter legs, used to navigating treacherous mountain passes and known for their sure footedness. Both Travis and Braden immediately started inspecting the animals, checking their hooves and legs, making sure that all of the beasts were of sound body. After they were finished, everyone, including Kendle who absolutely hated horses, chose their own mounts. Once they were all mounted on their horses, Travis spoke a few words to the soldiers and they were on their way again.

Soon they moved off of the main road and into the royal hunting grounds. A vast section of woods that belong to Lord Richard and where Damien had always believed until a few days ago was also where his father had lost his life to boar's tusks.

The woods were mottled with the early morning sunlight rays that filtered down through their leaves. The land was well forested and all types of game could be found here.

Damien knew that a few rangers patrolled certain locations ensuring that no one was poaching on the protected lands. He wasn't sure whether or not they would run into any of them, but he was sure that his father must have put out the word that they would be passing through. Somehow the rangers always seemed to know whenever anyone was entering what they considered their forest.

The forests ran northward until they connected with the Iron Peak Mountains. Travis planned to lead them through the forests staying away from any civilized roads until they reached the mountains then they were to skirt around the edges of the Dwarven Kingdom and its three cities before they swung northeast on into the Annulith mountains and across Wolfchase pass rather than through the haunted chasm called the Bryn Maw which was a shorter but much more dangerous route to the highland rim where Illsador, the Gods hall was located.

A.V. Wedhorn

Lord Richard, Balthazar, King Devlin, Rialdo and the other six western Highlords all stared out the windows of the tallest turret of the castle and watched the little group move out of the safety of the city and into the wilderness of beyond, knowing that all of the realms hope's lay in this endeavor and its success.

Caliban stretched in his chambers then he got up and got dressed, as he did so he placed his hand in his pocket. A slow smile spread across his face as he found the cold stone there and knew then that the group had left the city.

Chapter 21
Assassinations and Deceptions

Stepping out of his chambers Caliban moved in behind the estates chamberlain as he carried the tray that he always took to the ambassador in his quarters every morning. He traveled way behind the manservant so as not to be too noticeable but also close enough that he would be the second person on the scene, that way, no suspicion could be passed on to him.

The clatter and crashing of the tray, pot and cups breaking on the stone floor and the sharp gasp that followed told the young white haired man posing as Dalmar's secretary, all that he needed to know.

The dowdy faced chamberlain came running out of the bedchambers screaming that the ambassador was dead and that someone had killed him in the night with a crossbow.

Caliban immediately called for the guards or a captain and when an officer came into view, he stepped in beside him, introduced himself and taking him in tow they went into the ambassador's bedroom together.

Dalmar lay sprawled out on the bed, an almost surprised expression was on the ambassadors face as if he wasn't expecting company, the look was marred though by the crossbow bolt's fletchings protruding out from the center of his forehead.

"Somebody needs to alert the city watch," the short squat guard captain said, directing one of his men towards the door. One of the men who had accompanied him raced off down the hall.

"Have them bring a priest to, maybe there might be a way to reanimate the ambassadors spirit to find out who did this." the captain called out after the departing soldier, then the squat man turned towards Caliban and asked. "Who are you again, what are you doing here and was it you who found the body?"

Caliban explained to the guard captain who he was a second time and how he had just arrived as a special envoy from Kallamar to serve as Dalmar's personal secretary and to investigate an assassination attempt and plot against the royal regent by someone here in Castlekeep.

The captain just grunted a response at this news as he stepped across the room and over to the ambassadors body. "Since you are the one who is here from the capitol, I will let you be the one who informs the royal regent of what it is that has occurred here."

Caliban slowly nodded as he looked down at the floor attempting to conceal the smile that almost came to his lips, everything was going exactly like the way his father had planned. He was also glad now that he had taken the chance and cast the soul banishing spell earlier this morning upon the body lying dead in the bed like his father had ordered him to.

A stray beam of sunlight shone in through the window and caught the gold medallion in its light where it was spread out across the floor.

Squatting down onto his knees Caliban pointed at the reflective object on the floor next to edge of the bed and asked. "What is that?"

"What is what?" asked the captain, turning away from the ambassador's body and back to him.

Caliban again pointed at the object lying at the foot of the bed shining in the morning sun.

The captain stepped back from the body and went over to the spot where the other man was pointing. Carefully he fished the object out from underneath the edge of the bed and pulling it up by the chain he held the spinning battlemages amulet up into the light. Prevalent on one side of the medallion was a large gouge missing out of it.

"I've seen that medallion before," responded Caliban as he looked at it, feigning a perplexed expression.

"Well out with it young man," ordered the squat captain, "It might help us catch his killer more quickly, before he gets too far away."

"That's just it," answered Caliban still maintaining the act and the expression. "The owner of that necklace is dead."

"What?" asked the captain loudly, "what do you mean by dead?"

"I mean just what I said, the owner of that medallion," stated Caliban, facing the captain, "is Damien Daverge, Lord Richard's dead ward. I saw it removed from his body the other night at the castle when the highpriest Ramin was trying to save him from the bolt of an assassin who killed him too."

"Go!" ordered the captain, "and report what we have found here to the royal regent since he sent you here, I will send word on to the highlords castle informing Lord Richard about what has occurred here."

Caliban turned and headed of toward Dalmar's study and the mirror, seeing no one else in the hall, he didn't even bother this time trying to hide his smirking smile of success.

Cyadine was waiting this time for the mirror to start swirling and the moment his sons face appeared in its liquid like surface, he immediately asked. "Has it been done, is Dalmar dead?"

Caliban smiled a mirthless smile as he answered, "Yes father, it is done, the evidence has been planted and the heir has left the city with his group. A guardsman has been sent to inform Lord Richard of the death and he should know within the hour."

"Are you ready to leave then and join them, are our other plans already in place."

"Yes," answered Caliban, "my bags are packed and Micak Foss has men ready to attack me."

"Good, then go and get started, I will be there soon enough and take over things in Castlekeep. You need to be long gone by the time we break the bad news to Richard."

Caliban didn't answer, he just nodded and turned away from the mirror heading off towards his chambers to retrieve his traveling gear and the interesting forging items that he had found in the ex secretary's desk.

Ferris it seemed had been a bit of a forger and had seals and stamps from all fourteen of the kingdoms Highlords houses and enough documents with each of the Highlords writings and signatures on them to fake just about anything they could write. When Caliban had told his father about this little discovery it had changed their plans some and instead of being a merchant robbed in the woods to the north of Castlekeep, he would instead be a messenger, being attacked by robbers, from Damien's own father who would be out of power by the end of the day and couldn't dispute the letter. Shouldering his pack he went off to the griffon stables. He had another long flight north to make.

* * *

Cyadine turned away from the mirror, his red and black advisors robes with the gold trim swirling as he strode purposefully out of his quarters towards the palace throne room.

The palace throne room in Kallamar was a remarkable achievement of dwarven craftsmanship. Tall decorated alabaster pillars held up the high vaulted cathedral ceilings. Beams of golden sunlight streamed through the large overhead windows illuminating the sunstone throne that was along one wall. The dais for the throne was set on a single massive slab of crystal marble that glowed with a golden light from the illuminated throne. The crystal almost looked like it pulsed inside with a life of its own. Next to the ornately carved and designed throne were two slightly smaller chairs on the dais that were for the royal family.

Vargas was the only person sitting atop the golden chair in the palace throne room. He was, Cyadine noticed looking rather bored as he watched it fill with people and their petitions. When he saw his cold-faced advisor enter the room with a smile on his usually emotionless face, the royal regent knew that all had gone well. He was well aware of the advisors plans, so it came as no surprise to him when Cyadine whispered into his ear that Dalmar was dead, killed in his sleep by an assassins crossbow bolt. The pair had rehearsed this news so that he could pull off the act that he had planned with out any problems.

"What!" Vargas shouted loudly into the throne room so loud that his voice echoed off of the surrounding stonewalls and all of the heads in the room turned in the direction of the royal regent's startled sounding voice.

A credible look of distress was showing on both the advisor and the royal regent's face.

"What do you mean he's dead?" Again the royal regent spoke in a voice loud enough to be heard by all in the large palace throne room.

Cyadine bent low and again whispered into Vargas' ear.

"Assassinated," the royal regent said in a shocked voice, not quite as loud as the others. A hushed whisper of voices raced through the throne room like flames across dry twigs as everyone waited to hear who it was that they were talking about.

Gunther Haldron appeared in the throne room wearing his proctor's armor and rank medallion as if drawn by the appearance of bad news, this too was part of the act being put forth by Cyadine for the benefit of the onlookers.

Vargas pushed himself up off of the sunstone throne and with a distraught expression on his handsome face announced to the entire court in a voice that cracked with emotion that a great tragedy had occurred in Castlekeep during the night while they were sleeping.

Continuing the royal regent announced above the murmurs that now buzzed through the air like muted bees, that Dalmar Ariaas, a hero of the realm had been killed during the night before in Castlekeep by an assassins crossbow bolt and that a hunt will be put in place to identify and bring to justice the ex marshalls killer immediately. Then he announced that this day's activities were to be postponed until he could find out more about what had occurred in the far western city.

Word of the assassination spread through the Palace like wildfire and Vargas wondered how long it would be before Dalmar's young and fiery new wife Becka Ariass made an appearance.

To Gunther, Vargas announced that he wanted a contingent of Krannion knights, about thirty, ready to leave within the hour and two third ranked battlemages also. He would be leaving for Castlekeep immediately to find out some answers personally.

A King's Quest

* * *

Lord Richard and the western rulers were discussing their future plans over breakfast when Balthazar stepped into the private council room, his face looking grave.

"It appears that I have some rather bad and horrible news," he informed the group of lords and all of their heads turned to him, some of their faces blanching in fear. Realizing the way what he had just said was being taken by the faces in the room, Balthazar hastily added, "Damien's alright, but there has been another killing. Somebody assassinated Dalmar Ariaas last night, while he was asleep in his bed inside the ambassadors mansion. Wait." the hawk faced advisor said, holding up a hand as the others in the room all started to speak. "There's more, it seems that whoever killed him also used a bolt from our own castle guard and Damien's own battlemages medallion was found at the foot of Dalmar's bed."

Stunned, incredulous expressions now replaced the other looks on the faces of all in the room as they listened to the last of the advisor's words.

Finally it was King Devlin who spoke. "I think now we are seeing the results of our late night intruder the other day."

"How could this have happened?" asked Lord Richard to no one particular as his steel grey eyes scanned the room. "And where or should I also ask how in the gods hells did someone get a hold of Damien's battlemage medallion?"

No one answered that question either and all still looked at each other for several moments until Jarvis Whiteknife said in a quiet voice.

"You do all realize what this means don't you?" asked the white haired, bushy-browed Highlord from Mycar.

Everyone in the room turned to face him and he continued. "Somehow Vargas or someone in his employ knows for sure that Damien is still alive and is now acting upon that knowledge in order to gain something. Whatever that is, we need to find out and quick, to try and avoid whatever it is that is coming next. You can be sure that Vargas is acting upon it."

"I suggest then that we all take a trip over to Lord Dalmar's estates to see the events happening there first hand," stated Lord Richard and the seven western highlords, the dwarf king and the halfling ruler quickly filed out of the room heading towards the ambassadors estates.

* * *

Drekar Thirel and Becka Ariaas were hard at work in the battlemage garrisons post training grounds. Working and training with a contingent of first slash battlemages practicing double and triple spell castings and countering spells. Xen Stonehart, the High commander of the battlemage garrison in the capitol city and fourth slash battlemage stepped out onto the field in a crisply cut, severe black and gold uniform that fit his lean frame very well but did nothing to hide the distressed look on his face.

Drekar, seeing the older high commander with his thin wispy hair and sea water green eyes coming towards them, called out in an amplified voice across the field for all of the battlemages training to cease casting immediately.

Xen approached his highest third level commanders who helped run the garrison, with a somber expression on his face and a sadness filling his eyes. He motioned for the other two to walk with him out of earshot of the other training battlemages, then, he called out in a commanding voice for the other battlemages to change to weapons, form into fighting ranks and to continue practicing.

A wave of energy filled the area as the first slashes cast steelskin spells on their bodies to protect themselves from each other's weapons and started attacking one another.

The High commander felt a knot of apprehension fill his throat as he thought about telling the pair of the bad news he had just received from a Krannion knight that had burst into his office a few minutes ago.

Xen never liked the telling of loved ones that a member of their family had died and he knew that if the day ever came to him that it didn't bother him anymore, he would retire his black and gold battlemages uniform.

Definitely, the emotional and highly volatile red headed Becka Ariaas was not someone he relished bringing this dire news to, especially with a newborn baby having just arrived a month earlier.

Trying to stay as far away from the subject of his visit as he could for a few moments, he asked, "How goes their training? Are any of them ready to be elevated to second level?"

Becka motioned to a black skinned man with a short wide handsome face. He was attacking his opponent with short fighting sticks in each of his hands in rapid multiple succession. His body rippled with well-toned muscle and his long multi-braided hair thrashed about while Becka stated, "Eboe Zailann is more than ready, he already commands all of the others here and they follow his lead without any questions."

Drekar nodded his head in agreement with his associate's words, but sensed he somehow that this was not the reason for the high commander's visit to the training grounds and asked, "What is it, sir? You look rather distraught!"

Becka too now sensed that something was wrong. When the high commander's seawater-green eyes met hers, she saw the distressed look in them. She felt her heart freeze in her chest and her knees turn weak with dread.

"Dalmar," she whispered without even waiting for her commander to speak to speak his name, "something has happened to my husband hasn't it sir?"

Not able to think of a gentler way to tell her, Xen Stonehart just nodded. Knowing that she would want the blunt of it, he told her all that he knew from the information that had been given to him by the knight.

For a moment the red haired woman said nothing, then she collapsed forward, down onto the earth, landing on her knees, a loud sobbing wail escaping out of her small chest. She had known when she woke up this morning that something was wrong and immediately had raced to check on her newly born baby girl, ensuring that she was okay. Never had Becka considered that something had happened to her newly wed husband whom she had just seen a few days before when he came to deliver news to the royal regent and his advisor. Sure he was older than her, but his days in the military where he had been in the front of danger were long past him and he had appeared to be in perfect health.

Becka continued to cry and sob for several minutes until finally the tears stopped coming to her eyes and she raised her tear stained face up to meet Xen's own face staring down at her.

Anger blazed now in her dark green eyes and her face was twisted in fury as she hissed out her next words. "How did Cyadine manage to do it? How did he manage to kill my husband!" She shouted this last part with such force that both Drekar and Xen took a step back from the woman whose clenched fist had become a sparkling, writhing ball of white hot, arcane energy called purefire. It is the closest form of pure creational magic that a battlemage was allowed to wield and only if fighting Elvynn magic users. Only at third level are battlemages are allowed to learn it. It was this same type of fire that was clenched in the fist on the battlemages symbol medallion.

All of the third level and above battlemages in Kallamar knew of the royal advisor and how the powerful wizard and masterful fighter had been cast out of the academe just days before gaining his black and gold uniform for the practicing the forbidden parts of creational magic before it was allowed. It had been whispered for years that if he had managed to stay in the academe or in the black and gold ranks that he might have been one of the fastest climbing mages who had ever worn the robes and might have actually commanded them all someday and still was definitely one of the most dangerous mages to ever have been taught at the academe. Losing his black robes hadn't taken away any of Cyadine's abilities or training.

Cyadine Syndell was a specialist battlemage, taught in the forms of special combat and warfare by the academe. Only a very few special students have ever been taught this way by the old Esian battlemaster named Trakiko Matsuri, who had once commanded all of the armies in Esia. The only lands or people never to be ruled over at any time by the Elvynn. It had recently been rumored that Trakiko had just finished training another student in the specialized combat and warfare, which was only the fourth one that he had ever trained in such tactics. Only two other student's names had ever been released before this third one, no one was even sure who the fourth one, who was actually the first, was.

Dalmar had told her about the document that he had received from his secretary and about the threats that had been whispered against him and his family by Cyadine. She was absolutely certain that the cold blooded arrogant advisor had something to do with her husbands death and whatever had occurred when he had came to Kallamar. She knew also that it must involve the royal regent and whoever the man that her husbands secretary had found in Castlekeep.

Both of the other battlemages continued taking steps back away from the furious woman's temper, helpless looks on their faces because neither one had any answers to her questions, also fearful that she might lash out at them with the almost pure energy that she was holding angrily in her fist.

Only a few very powerful battlemages were so gifted to be able hold what she was holding now in her hands. Neither Drekar nor Xen could conjure up such a large ball of the purefire to which most other types of spells were rendered useless or torn apart by the pureness of its arcane energy.

Becka knew that neither man held the answer to her question and could probably only tell her how he died, she could care less about that, she only wanted to know the answer to why he had died.

Visibly, with an almost tremendous effort, she gained control of herself and released the energized ball, then said another quickly spoken incantation. A soft pop filled the open air of the training grounds and the distraught red haired female battlemage was gone, teleported away and was nowhere to be seen.

"She's gone to the castle to confront Cyadine, of that you can be certain." informed Drekar.

"I know," answered Xen, "and we had better get there and somehow stop her before she either destroys the entire palace or gets herself accidentally on purpose killed by Cyadine."

The two began to cast their own teleportation spells when Xen held up a hand for a moment and called out in a booming voice that filled the entire training grounds.

"Attention," all of the heads in the area turned in the direction of the high commander's voice. "As of now, Eboe Zailann, you are, effective immediately, promoted to the rank of battlemage second slash. Take charge of this group until we return and train them as you see fit and when you think they are finished release them to their own."

The handsome wide faced muscular black man smiled a pleased smile and clasped his two hands in front of himself, fist into palm and bowed in a battlemages salute as

A King's Quest

he faced the two higher ranked men who rather quickly returned it, then he turned back to the group, stepped out of the fighting ranks and immediately began correcting and showing the others their mistakes.

The high commander and the other battlemage finished their own spell casting and teleported to the castle, expecting the worst.

A special area had been designated for battlemages who teleported into the palace. It was into this spot that Becka Ariaas appeared in a bright flash of light, she knew that the other two men would be following right behind her. Quickly she crossed the palace floor and trapped a Krannion knight on duty there demanding to know where the royal regent and his advisor were. Two soft pops behind her announced the other two battlemages arrivals. Not bothering to wait for them since she had her destination, the red haired battlemage departed the throne room. Becka now had a marginal control of her emotions but still she could feel everything roiling inside of her like a tidal wave just under the surface threatening to spill over. Her husband's handsome face just kept filling her mind's eye.

Hurrying footsteps closed in on her and she knew that the high commander and Drekar Thirel had caught up with her.

None of them spoke as they continued on towards the palace knights quarters that the royal regent and his advisor had gone to with the proctor in order to retrieve enough men to accompany them to Castlekeep, in order to find out what had happened to the royal ambassador.

The palace guardians section of the Krannion knights, were all lords or nobility in some manner or another. All had sworn both oaths to the throne and crown, to defend the palace regardless of the cost to them. 'Till death do we serve' was their motto. In swearing so, they all had acquired special enchanted armor that helped in that duty.

Palace knights could wear either chain mail or plate mail in the course of the duties. Both sets of armor were enchanted with repelling and shield spells that were supposed to deflect magical energy directed against it, in order to help the knights during combat against Elvynn war wizards or any other enemies of the realm that might be attacking the palace using magic. All battlemages know this about the armor and they also know about its weaknesses.

A brash young knight with an arrogant face and haughty attitude, wearing the enchanted chain mail stepped in front of the advancing female battlemage and demanded that she stop. Becka wasn't wearing the official black and gold robes of her station as the other two men behind her were. She had opted instead during the training session to change into a plain brown training outfit so as not to soil her own clothes and in such an outfit she looked sort of like a miscreant being chased by the other two battlemages behind her through the palace. Despite with the fierce expression that dominated her tear stained face.

The young man, seeing that she wasn't going to stop, held up a bare unarmored hand in front of her and attempted to physically stop her. Becka, never slowed she just smiled and reached out a hand to touch the other mans exposed flesh.

The magical armor was designed to protect the wearer from things attacking it, but it didn't actually give any sort of protection to the person inside of it if you touched them.

The moment that their flesh touched, the young man with the arrogant expression on his face jerked as if shocked then he froze in place, going completely still as the holding spell Becka cast upon contact froze him in place.

"Becka!" came the admonishing sharp crack of her name in a voice that halted her.

"He's only held, Xen, you know I wouldn't hurt him, not for just being arrogant and pretentious fool."

The second guard drew back and in as courteous

manner as he could manage and held open the door for the small redheaded battlemage saying, "Ma'am."

Neither, Becka or Xen said anything to him as they passed into the knights quarters but as Drekar passed by the second knight he whispered with a smile on his face, "he will be fine in a few minutes, but warn him that unless he fancies dying fast, never attempt to stop any woman ever who looks that determined again, especially not a red head." The young knight smiled at him and said that he would.

The royal regent, his advisor and about thirty knights were standing in the room looking expectantly at the door when it opened and the fiery red headed battlemage came striding into the room. Cyadine had felt the angry flare of magic from outside of the door and had told the royal regent.

Vargas stepped out from the group and moved in front of the female battlemage saying immediately. "I'm sorry Becka, I'm sure you heard the news, this is the group that I'm taking to Castlekeep with me right now while I personally investigate what happened there, nobody kills a hero of the realm without the murder being investigated. I asked for two third level battlemages to accompany me and I would be delighted if you yourself would be one of those that goes along."

Becka stopped, startled by the regents placating words and determined manner, unable to gather her scattered thoughts she just nodded and looked over at her commander to see if it was okay with him.

Xen nodded his approval and also added that Drekar would too be going with them as the second. To this the royal regent just nodded his approval and asked that if they were all ready then. Not giving time for the female mage to confront Cyadine about her husband's death. He ordered him that a doorway to Castlekeep be created.

Cyadine smiled inwardly a pleased smile, everything

including handling the emotional female battlemage had gone exactly as he and Vargas had planned. Now all he had to do was convince her that it was indeed this Damien Daverge who had killed her husband and regardless whether or not he was the heir, she would probably kill him for them and save him the trouble later on if everyone else failed. Drawing on all of the arcane energy inside the palace, Cyadine wove the intricate spell that took several long moments and then cast it.

A spark filled the air in front of him then as if burning a hole in paper, it expanded, its flames burning a hole into the very air itself as the fire spread outward from the center, it formed a large fiery burning circle.

The ambassador's chambers in Castlekeep were revealed on the other side of the circle. Once it had burned a hole big enough for all to pass through, Cyadine gestured them all onwards.

A few of the Krannion knights looked warily at the burning magical doorway that had opened up before them, but on a sharp command from Gunther Haldron, they hurried through to the other side.

Vargas and his entourage went through next and as Xen Stonehart watched the fiery doorway collapse back in upon itself behind them, the high commander of Kallamars battlemages wondered exactly how powerful the royal regent's advisor and wizard had become. He didn't think even Becka who was his most powerful battlemage here in Kallamar could open one of the fiery doorways or portals as they were sometimes called past Westlake, much less across the length of almost all fourteen kingdoms to Castlekeep. Knowing the amount of power that such a spell required he thought that maybe he should report this display to Siraethiel Shanasar, back in Westlake, just in case.

Chapter 22
The Removal

All three of the parties arrived at the now dead ambassadors palatial estates at almost the exact same time. The first to arrive was Bayle Jensyn who is the head officer in charge of the city watch. Accompanying him was a mousy looking cleric of Lacina. As the city watch commander and the cleric stepped into the house and began talking to the squat captain in charge of the ambassador's security force, the door to Dalmar's study opened and a force of thirty or so Krannion knights, all wearing plate mail armor with swords drawn, moved out into the hall and cordoned it off by forming a large protective circle of steel. Into this walked the dark haired royal regent himself, Lord Vargas Salidor, appointed ruler of the realm. He was followed next by the commanding proctor of the capitol cities division of Krannion knights, Gunther Haldron, who was immediately recognizable by his straight thick thatch of pure white hair, large size and ragged scar that disfigured his face, Cyadine Syndell, head wizard and advisor to the throne and crown in his red, black and gold robes and two unknowns, one a black haired man with an almost cruel looking face that was offset by his gentle looking soft brown eyes wearing a battlemages black and gold uniform and last was a small redheaded female who also looked like a battlemage but wasn't wearing her colors.

Bayle Jensyn wondered who she was exactly when she pushed past him, the cleric and the squat captain before they could stop her and charged into the dead ambassador's chambers without waiting on the others. He got his answer a moment later when he heard a plaintive wail erupt from the diminutive red headed lady in the other room followed by cries of no and sudden pain filled sobbing.

Lord Richard and his party chose that moment to also enter the hall farther down and were immediately stopped by the Krannion knights with the already drawn blades.

Gunther Haldron told the knights to stand down and allowed them to enter, saying that for the moment this was the commanding Highlord of the city.

This statement caused an alarmed look to flash momentarily on Balthazar's face and quickly he looked around to the other eight rulers with him and his lord to see if they to had heard the statement. Judging by the disapproving stares on all of their faces he was sure that they had.

All in the hall fell in line behind the royal regent as he led the procession out of the hallway and into the dead ambassador's bedchambers.

Becka Ariaas was collapsed over the body of her dead husband in a heap, sobbing and moaning incoherently as she clutched at him.

As everyone entered the bedroom, her head turned upwards from where she was cradling her husbands face to her chest. As her dark forest green eyes fell on Cyadine a look of madness filled them, she leapt up off of the bed and threw herself at him screaming in pure anguish. Gone was every instinct of her battlemage training as she tried to claw out his eyes with her fingernails, screaming loudly. "How could you, you bastard! How could you!"

Everyone in the room was caught by surprise by the unexpected attack, including Cyadine, who, before he could even react had a set of red slashes gouged into the skin of his face by the irate female battlemages nails. Quickly the advisor grabbed a hold of her thrashing and kicking body as best as he could and attempted to wrest her from him.

As she continued to scream and attack the advisor with flailing feet and hands a loud voice called out in such a commanding manner that it froze the female battlemage in mid movement.

"Enough Becka Ariaas, contain yourself, this will not bring Dalmar back to you!"

Everyone in the room turned to regard the honey brown haired Highlord with the long nose as he crossed towards the frozen red headed battlemage being held at bay by the other man.

Lord Gildon Seahorn took Becka out of Cyadine's hands and into his own arms where she collapsed against him without saying a word. Then as he stroked her red head with one of his hands, she started to sob again into his chest but this time a lot more softly than she had earlier.

"This is the cleric that I brought along to see if we could find out who exactly was the one that killed the ambassador." Bayle Jensyn said as the Highlord from Caladar stepped away from the others with the red headed battlemage and he stepped forward.

"Then lets get to it immediately." said the Royal regent as he gestured the cleric forward, "The faster we find out who did this, the faster we can apprehend Lord Dalmar's killer and put Lady Ariaas' mind to rest that he will be put to justice."

The mousy haired cleric knelt down over the body of the ambassador and began to slowly chant in prayer as he moved his hands the entire length of Lord Dalmar's body, he finished his prayers and opened his eyes. As he looked up to what he expected to find, a startled expression jumped into his eyes. Quickly he bent back down to the body and began praying over it a second time. This time as his hands went the length of the ambassador's body and white vapor like tendrils drifted out of from his fingers and floated down over it until it was completely covered in a smoky haze. Again the cleric opened his eyes and once again a startled look of surprise filled them, it was followed right away by one of shock and disbelief. In an almost muted voice the man muttered something that couldn't be understood by anyone else in the room.

"Speak up man louder so that you can be heard," the Highlord from the canal city, Randon Nandoo ordered.

"I said that he can't be raised, not now and not ever, somebody has cast a soul banishing spell over him, he is gone beyond recovery."

Even Becka who had almost stopped sobbing pulled her head off of Lord Gildon's chest to stare at the cleric.

"How is that possible," came a cold voice from the other side of the room, as Cyadine pushed his way past the others and stepped over to stand next to the body, looking down on the cleric, "are you sure, absolutely certain?"

"Y..Yes" the other man said stuttering his reply as he looked up into the royal advisor's cold imperious pale face and ice blue eyes. "I cast two spells on him and his spirit is gone, completely gone."

Cyadine spun back around and looked to the face of the Highlord from Castlekeep with his piercingly light blue eyes demanding. "Who here in this city has the ability to cast such a spell, there can't be that many who can work such powerful magic, even in a city of this size?"

Everyone in the dead ambassador's room knew that

A King's Quest

only higher level priestclerics can cast soul banishing spells, with only one exception to that rule, clerics of Dar can also cast them in removing the vilest of criminals from society in the pursuit of justice.

Lord Richard realized as did Balthazar at this question from the advisor that there was more going on here than what they knew and both sensed that Cyadine was up to something and looked askance at each other before the Highlord of Castlekeep responded.

"Only two high priests live in the city that can cast such a spell and one of them is my own highpriest of Lacina, Ramin Teas, the second is Gianna Blackthorn, the high druid of Gaderia and she is away in her forests on her yearly sabbatical and has been so for the past month.

"Are there any clerics of Dar in the city then, who might be able to cast such a spell?"

Both Balthazar and Lord Richard threw suspicious stares at the royal advisor, as this question was asked, each wondered how loaded it would be to answer or how much really Cyadine might know.

Choosing his words very carefully Lord Richard answered by saying that there had been a female cleric of Dar in the city but that he had no idea exactly where the cleric was now or why it mattered." Balthazar hadn't given him any sign that the royal advisor was using any magic to detect whether or not he was lying, but one could never be too certain in matters where the cunning royal advisor was involved.

"We need to find this cleric then, I want you to dispatch your entire city watch, send them out into the streets and scour every house and every building until you find out where she is." Ordered the royal regent, stepping up to the front of everyone and addressing the city watch commander directly. Gunther would you please also accompany the commander on his mission, that way there is a presence of royal command.

The white haired man did nothing but nod as he stepped forward in his proctor's uniform to join the commander, the uniform was a ploy by Cyadine to let his watchers know when they about asking their questions.

So fast that it was almost unnoticeable, Bayle threw a glance in the direction of the Castlekeep Highlord but at seeing no trace of any objections on his or any of the others faces, all were completely unreadable, he saluted the royal regent, turned crisply and strode purposely out of the bedroom with the Krannion knight proctor following closely by his side.

Cyadine smiled slightly, he already had some people in place waiting to tell anyone who questioned them that they had seen the female cleric leaving the city in early morning today, with a small group of people all dressed as pilgrims headed north towards the mountains.

"How is it, Richard Daverge?" Lord Vargas asked now turning his attention towards the tall blonde haired Highlord as he held up the gouged battlemages medallion that glittered in the morning sunlight that had been given to him by the houses captain of the guard, "that a battlemages medallion ended up in here at the foot of Lord Dalmar's bed and do you have any idea whose it might be, or should I recall the watch commander and tell him to search for a battlemage also?"

"No sire." answered Lord Richard unemotionally and formally, his face though looked as if he was tasting something vile. "I already know to whom that particular medallion belongs to."

When he said nothing further for a moment, the dark haired handsome regent pulled at his oiled goatee with one hand and arched a questioning eyebrow in the Highlords direction.

After another moments hesitation Lord Richard answered unhesitatingly, "It belongs to my own adopted ward and son whose funeral we had three days ago. I'm not really sure how it would have gotten here."

"Well maybe that should be the answer to our next question then, after we find out about where this female cleric of Dar is. I would say after we get out of here and on to your castle"

* * *

Caliban once again was circling the hidden refuge known as thieves hollow from up high on a griffon. He was pretty sure that this was the same one that had brought him here before because of the way that it seemed to know exactly where it was that he wanted to go, once they had set off in the same general direction that he had taken last time. The blond haired assassin mage did alter a little at first as he veered towards the other two-locator stones and felt them grow warmer to his touch as he passed near to his quarry. He deliberately kept the griffon high in the clouds and completely out of sight as he did so, in order to avoid being detected. This part of the mission couldn't handle any types of suspicion, it would already be a delicate enough manner to be taken in by the company traveling to Illsador without having even more suspicions being cast on him by an unexplained watcher.

Micak Foss personally met him on the ground as he dismounted from the large creature. The large griffon took one whiff of the large bearish man and immediately its eagle like head screamed a fierce sound, then it snapped its beak like a large steel trap in his direction.

The large man never flinched or showed any outward sign that he had even noticed the large beak, but he did after a few moments slowly take two steps sideways and backwards away from the other creature almost unnoticed by all but Caliban who smiled. Micak caught the slight gesture and returned it as he thought of how only his friend Cyadine would have also been the only other man to have noticed the move.

Seeing the way that the fierce beast reacted to the large bear like man made Caliban wonder again whether or not Micak Foss was a bear were creature. Griffons and bears were legendary enemies of each other.

"And good day to you master of the hollow," Caliban said as he pushed the griffon aside and told it to stay in the forest until he called for it tomorrow. The great creature bowed its noble head to him, gave Micak a baleful glare, then spread its massive wings and took off into the sky above.

"And to you son of a friend." came the response from the man once the griffon had departed the clearing.

"There has been a change of plans Micak, I need to know whether or not you have a good forger."

"What good would a thieves hideout be without someone who can do proper documentation for the authorities when they require it, come with me lad."

Micak led him through the cluster of ramshackle huts and makeshift buildings until they came to one that actually had a full roof and walls. Inside was an almost cozy room that was almost entirely filled with a large table and reams of parchment, quills and inks, of all types and sizes. A halfling with reading glasses perched on his nose was standing on a footstool hovering over a piece of parchment eyeing it critically. Both of his hands were stained with ink and Caliban assumed that this had to be Mick's forger.

"Let me introduce you to Guin Scrollwriter, he can copy or make just about anything, just tell him what you need and we will see what he can come up with."

The round-faced Guin nodded in Caliban's direction and he returned it as he moved over to the table opened up the sack of things that he had found inside of the old ambassadors secretary's desk and upturned it onto the table. The seals of all fourteen Highlords houses and about fifty rolled scrolls fell out and rolled everywhere.

Guin started to shoot him an angry look as the bags contents rolled onto the document he had been working on until he saw what it was that the bag contained and a look of pure pleasure and delight filled his round wizened face, his aggravation of a moment before completely forgotten. With almost shaking hands the halfling took the seals into his hands and examined each very thoroughly, occasionally grunting and sighing as he set one aside.

"These are the real things, true seals of all fourteen Highlords," he said in wide eyed astonishment, finally after he was done with his examination, "where on Tyrus did you get these?"

"That master forger," Caliban said in a flat voice to the halfling, "doesn't concern you, all that matters is can you forge me a true looking document using these ones from Richard Daverge."

"Using these," came the reply from the forger, as he now looked at the scrolls, I can forge just about anything!"

Hearing this Caliban nodded and explained his plan saying that time was of the essence and that this had to be done by tomorrow morning, for that was when he would be due to meet up with and join Damien Daverge's party.

"Just tell me what you need and we will get to work immediately." came Guin's reply as he eagerly fingered the kingdom seals in anticipation.

* * *

All seven of the western highlords, the dwarven iron king, the halfling ruler, the royal regent, the royal wizard and advisor to the throne, thirty Krannion knights, two battlemages of third rank and Balthazar Tolarus, advisor to Castlekeep filed into the main throne room.

Without waiting for anyone's leave other that his own as was his right, Vargas went directly over and sat in Lord Richard's seat of power, this was another thing that had been planned out by Cyadine. It immediately put the royal regent in a place of authority above all others in the room, as he did so a heavy silence filled the air of the western Castle.

The first thing that Balthazar noticed was the way that the sentinel guards and the Krannion knights started eyeing each other warily as they studied how each was armed and armored. Both forces of soldiers were intently aware of the friction between the Capitol city and the western realm and several hands on both sides went slowly towards the hilts of their weapons.

The man left in charge of the knights also must have also noticed the looks and the hand movements and with a sharp bark of command he ordered the knights to lower their visors and assume positions of attention. That way Balthazar assumed they would not be giving anything away in their expressions or movement of their intent here.

Lord Gildon dispatched one of the servants who hurried out of the room on some unknown mission and Balthazar ordered that drinks and refreshments be brought immediately.

At about the same time as the drinks arrived so did another small diminutive red haired battlemage. At seeing the other woman across the room she raced to the newly widowed Lady Ariaas and enveloped her in a hug.

Judging by their similar appearances everyone realized that they had to be sisters.

Cassica Essen, the female champion of the tournament of cities, cradled her older sister's head against her shoulder and whispered unheard reassuring words into her ear as the other woman began to sob again.

No one else spoke in the audience room and it was almost an hour before Bayle Jensyn reappeared with Gunther Haldron right behind him, stating that he had news on the location of the female cleric of Dar.

"Several people had seen her the night before at Lord

Richards' wedding celebration in the company of a blond haired man who was the known best friend of his adopted dead ward and whose medallion was found at the ambassador's house. No one that was questioned," Bayle Jensyn informed the gathered assemblage, "had any idea of her location after that until some men were questioned at the main cities gates who reported seeing her, the blond haired best friend, Travis Longblade, my lords blademaster, Kendle Stonebreaker and two other people that they didn't recognize leaving the city early this morning disguised as pilgrims headed north." A distressed look was on the Captains face as he finished this last part, he knew that something was going on here and that it smelled suspiciously like a setup.

"The men at the gate also reported" Gunther Haldron added in his gravelly voice after giving the captain a reproachful look that was seen by all, "that they appeared to be fleeing the city on foot early this morning, because they had no packs or gear with them and carried no sort of weapons on their persons. Running away was how one said it appeared to him"

An icy cold feeling filled the pit of Lord Richard's stomach as he heard the royal proctor's condemning words. Gunther Haldron had never been to Castlekeep and the Highlord was glad that Travis was far from the city at this moment. He knew now by the mans words, without any doubts that the royal regent was behind the failed assassination attempt on his son and the more successful one on his friend the royal ambassador and they had done all of this to set plans in motion to rid themselves of Damien. "Even now, here it was that the group who was accompanying Damien was getting accused." the large Highlord thought to himself angrily.

Lord Vargas Salidor eyed Lord Richard accusingly from his own personal ruling chair and said in a cold voice. "Could you please take a moment to explain what is going on here and tell me why your personal blademaster and commander of arms is fleeing the city with a woman that might be involved with the death of my personal royal ambassador here. I would also," the royal regent said before Lord Richard could answer, "like to hear your explanation too dwarven king." his eyes drilled into both of them.

Lord Richards face went wooden as he stared at the ruler of the fourteen kingdoms and through clenched teeth after he carefully considered his words said. "I absolutely have no idea."

The other six highlords, also sensing what was happening here all exchanged worried looks with one another.

Vargas turned his accusing stare in the direction of Devlin Bonebreaker and asked. "Do you then have any idea of what is going on here or what your own nephew might be up to, or are you too suddenly ignorant?" he added this last at the end contemptuously.

The dwarven iron king stood as still as mountain stone as he faced the royal regent. In a cold indifferent voice he growled simply, "I am not my nephew's keeper."

In the exact manner in which they had rehearsed this, Vargas let a red flush of anger suffuse his features and in a quivering angry voice said as he rounded back on Lord Richard. "First you take the initiative to declare your lands tax exempt from my own royal decrees, in part laying the grounds for a civil war against the throne and the crown. Then my own people here in the west inform me that you have gotten the rest of these Highlords here," the royal regent pointed a finger accusingly at the other six nobles gathered around the chair, "to follow your own lead and leadership against your own sworn oaths of fealty and loyalty to the throne and the crown. Now my own ambassador here, a hero of the realm and ex commander of the military has been murdered by a crossbow bolt from one of your own castle guard and maybe by someone who was seen in your castle last night as a guest celebrating your own wedding who was also seen fleeing the city in the early morning by witnesses and," the royal regents voice boomed throughout the hall now, echoing off of the stone as it rose louder and louder as he accentuated each statement with a stabbing finger, "you have the nerve to tell me that you have no idea is going on here!"

A feeling of dread crept through Balthazar's insides as he spotted the superior looking expression and small smile that was creeping across the royal regent's advisor's usually cold featured face, he almost looked like the dog who had escaped from the cooks kitchen with the largest meat bone.

Lord Richard steel grey eyes never wavered in his continual stare at Lord Vargas and he still said nothing, knowing that at this moment there wasn't anything that he could say that would vindicate him. The royal regent it seemed was holding all of the cards and was playing only the ones that favored him.

Seeing that the large blond haired Lord was not going to respond, the royal regent drew a deep breath as if trying to calm himself, then spoke in a more subdued manner. "Lady Ariaas," he called out softly to the red headed battlemage, who lifted her head and tear streaked face up off of her sister's shoulder to look at him through red eyes filled with pain and sorrow.

"I promised you swift justice and retribution in the handling of your husband's killer and as of that moment it seems that until we can recapture this fleeing cleric of Dar and her companions or accomplices who seemed to have fled with her, I can not deliver that."

Becka Ariaas, not really sure what to make of the royal regents statements, scrutinized the dark haired man along with everyone else in the room who seemed to be holding their breath.

"What I can do at this moment," the royal regent said to her in a reassuring tone, "is to take some steps now, to insure proper justice will be done in the future."

Turning to Richard Daverge the royal regent and ruler of all fourteen lands of Kallamar, said in a very distinctive and clear voice. "There is almost enough evidence here to accuse you of treason against the throne and crown Highlord Richard Daverge and possibly implicate you as well in the murder of Lord Dalmar Ariass."

A few loud gasps and even more shouts of outrage filled the room at the mention of the word treason.

The royal regent ignored these and continued on speaking, "At the least, I think that there is a reasonable suspicion that something is going on here and that somehow your own people might be involved in the death of a royal ambassador to the throne and the crown. There is also the fact that you have been conspiring against the laws of the land in declaring your self exempt from them. You might even in some way be guilty of killing your own adopted third son" he added at the end. Vargas paused then a moment to take a breath and glanced about the room, when his eyes fell on Drekar Thirel, the other battlemage who had accompanied him a pleased look filled his eyes before he continued on, "So until this matter involving the assassination of a royal employee and a hero of the realm here in your own city possibly involving some of your own people can be resolved and the perpetrators are captured and you are exonerated or until the meeting of the Highlords council in Kallamar, I am removing you from your place as ruler of Gaderia and Castlekeep on the grounds of inciting treason against the throne and the crown and possible murder of a royal subject."

By now the main audience hall of the castle was completely filled with onlookers and again numerous shouts of outrage and cries of dismay sounded everywhere. So many were now heard throughout the large hall that the

Krannion knights guarding the royal regent once again placed their gauntleted hands unconsciously upon their sword hilts in fear of retribution or revolt. This time no words were spoken to stop them. It was their sworn duty to protect him

The royal regent continued to meet the steely grey-eyed stare of the larger Highlord with his own dark brown eyes as if daring him to disagree.

"I do not know," Lord Vargas then shifted his gaze to all of the western highlords as if he was disgusted with each one of them, "how deep the plots of treason run here in the west so my verdict will also include your own sons too in it." then changing the subject he said loudly, "Battlemage Drekar Thirel please come forward."

The tall black haired battlemage with the kind eyes and cruel face looked startled at hearing his name but hurried over to stand at attention near the foot of the chair in which the royal regent sat.

"Sire," he said bowing to the ruler who he would have sworn was eyeing him now with a grim look of satisfaction in his dark brown eyes.

"Aren't you the eldest son of a Gaderian noble house." the royal regent asked him.

"Not quite sire I have a disowned older brother who hasn't been seen in years, but," he started to say while looking between both the Highlord and the royal regent as they exchanged stony eyed stares, neither ones eyes wavering or shifting from the others.

"But nothing," interrupted Lord Vargas," as of right now though you are an heir to a prominent noble house in Gaderian here and you are also a high level commander in the royal chapter of Kallamar's battlemages and until the highlords council meeting or until this cleric of Dar can be captured and questioned about this murder, I hereby appoint you the temporary ruler of Castlekeep on grounds of rank."

Drekar Thirel seemed frozen in place unable to move as he heard the royal regent's declaration. Grounds of rank made him less than at ease. Unless his older brother stepped forward, that would make him the ruling Highlord of Castlekeep.

Lord Vargas continued on, "You may of course rely upon the use of Lord Richard's advisor in leadership matters in ruling the city itself. I want you and Lady Ariaas to arrange for a party to track down this assassin and capture her and all with her. In matters regarding commanding decisions I expect you to report directly to me or my advisor, is that understood? Nothing occurs here without our explicit approval at least until the highlords court or until the post becomes permanent. I will have no more innocents put to death or assassinated by any people in this court." almost accusingly he leveled his gaze again at Lord Richard and then back to Drekar.

"Sire," Drekar said protesting, "I can't be put in charge, its against the," but whatever he was going to say was cut off by a silencing gesture of Vargas' hand.

"It will be as I have said and that is all!" hissed the royal regent in an angry tone and he waited until the battlemage nodded before he finished by saying to all in the hall. "I am also placing a thousand gold piece reward for the capture or information that leads to the capture of this outlaw female cleric of Dar or any others in her group of assassins. I want the word to be spread throughout every village and every hovel in every corner of the entire fourteen lands by nightfall, is that understood!" he stood there eyeing the rest of the highlords until they too nodded in agreement with him. "Now you are all dismissed and Lord Richard, until this assassin is captured or the highlords council is called you are not allowed to leave the grounds of your abode. That goes for you too wizard." said the royal regent eyeing Balthazar, then he turned his dark eyed gaze again to Drekar. "If either one of them is caught

A King's Quest

leaving the castle I want them beheaded and I will leave these knights here," the royal regent indicated the thirty Krannion knights that had accompanied him, "to help you enforce my edicts, Battlemage Thirel. Commander Braddock," Vargas said addressing the knight who had earlier ordered the other knights to lower their visors, "you are in charge of the knights and second in command enforcing my orders. See that they are obeyed."

The knight commander snapped to rigid attention and crisply saluted, right fist thumping his left shoulder, acknowledging the orders. Drekar, his pale face worried did the same, clasping his fist in his other hand in front of him in a battlemages salute.

Motioning for both Cyadine and Gunther to join him the royal regent said that they would be going back to the capitol city by way of the ambassador's estates.

Turning to everyone else gathered in the hall the Royal regent and ruler of the land said, "Unless you have business with Battlemage Thirel or Commander Braddoc you are all dismissed."

A.V. Wedhorn

Chapter 23
The Rescue

The entire morning and most of the day was spent riding down trail and paths. To Damien it seemed that they must have backtracked and retraced the same paths a few dozen times or more. Travis was ensuring by doing this that no one would possibly be able to trace their path unless they were a master hunter and woodsman.

Braden Ravenclaw, acting on Travis' orders, scouted both ahead and behind them looking for any signs of pursuit or of anything else that seemed odd or out of place and might be a cause for concern. He also went about laying several false trails to throw off any pursuers.

Finally towards the end of the day they came to the edge of a small clearing in the woods that had a small stone cottage with a thatched roof standing in the center of it.

With a gesture from Travis, Braden took off again, circling the edges of the clearing, looking for any signs of life. Not seeing anything other than a plume of wood

A King's Quest

smoke that drifted upwards out of the small cottages stone chimney that they all could see, the ranger came back and reported nothing found.

Travis accepted this and asked if the ranger could imitate a blue jaybirds call. The ranger nodded and put his fingers to his lips and blew out a shrill blast of air that sounded exactly like the loud birds raucous cry.

He started to blow a second time, but the blademaster stopped him by saying, "Only once, twice means that we are in trouble or are being followed."

After seeing that there was not going to be a second blast, a large muscular figure stepped out from the woods edge at its darkest point, a gloomy sort of mist had started to cover everything and nobody had seen the muscular young man with the long peasants bow, drawn and held at the ready, hiding only thirty feet from them.

Alyssa immediately jumped sideways and at the same time she snapped out her hammer. In almost the same movement Logan's long bladed Elvynn hunting daggers appeared in his hands so fast that it looked as if they had materialized out of the air about him.

Both Travis and Kendle exchanged pleased grins, "At least a few someone's in this group are prepared for an attack when it comes unexpectedly," replied Kendle, looking at both Logan and Alyssa, who were crouched with their weapons held at the ready. Then they both frowned and looked rather skeptically over at Damien who hadn't moved.

The young battlemage glanced around and found that Braden who had been right next to him had also disappeared. He then realized that the only person who appeared unready for an attack and hadn't moved when the man had stepped out of the woods with the bow drawn was him.

A good battlemage is taught by their battlemaster to always be ready for anything and to be able to adapt to any situation. He was taught by the academes best battlemaster and also taught in the ways of special warfare and tactics. He already judged by the way that Travis and Kendle had not reacted to the man stepping out of the woods, that he wasn't any sort of danger to him.

Rolling his eyes at the still skeptical expressions on the other two's faces, Damien released one of the spells that he had prepared earlier in the day in case something occurred and shouted loudly the spells command word. "Net!"

A golden glowing writhing orb shot out of his hand and flew across the short distance separating them from the man with the drawn bow. As the writhing orb moved across the clearing, it expanded into a large glowing thick roped magical net.

Fear showed momentarily in the muscular young mans eyes as he tried to move aside but the magical creational was on him too quickly. The glowing magical net expanded so fast that it made escape impossible, then it was on him, ensnaring him in its threads. Quickly as if it was alive the magical net wrapped and wove itself all about the man's body. Its glowing ropes captured and held him motionless in barely the time it took to draw a quick breath.

Everyone looked at Damien, shocked somewhat by the quickness of the spell including the captured man who still held his bow half drawn, but now was unable to release his notched arrow.

Damien smiled smugly and crossed his arms, fixing both the blademaster and the dwarf with an amused look as he said simply. "I am a battle mage."

Logan placed his daggers back into their hidden sheathes, looped an arm about his shoulders, smiling a wide smile saying. "That you are my friend," he looked over to the other man still held fast in the glowing net, "and I'm glad you are on our side."

Braden rematerialized out of the woods again as if he had never been gone, his woodsman's bow hung loosely in his hand.

After Damien released the other man from the magical net, which also dispelled it, it faded away as if it was never there.

Travis made introductions all around, the large young man with the bow in hand was named Mathis Woodshorn and he looked even bigger when they got closer to him and Kendle told him so as he eyed their new companion up and down from head to toe. Next to where the man was standing was an unusual item that didn't seem out of place in the woods, but once it occurred Damien that this was actually the young muscular mans second weapon, he felt his eyes grow a little wider, both in appreciation and in awe. He had never thought of using such a thing as a weapon but for the large young man in front of him such a weapon indeed made sense.

The item that the other man retrieved from where it had been leaning against a tree was a huge woodman's maul, used for splitting logs and stumps. With its sharpened giant triangular head and wrist thick wooden shaft, the weapon seemed more than appropriate in the large young mans hands.

Mathis led them to the small cottage where he had already fixed dinner in anticipation of their arrival and after everyone had removed their gear, they all sat around the table to eat.

Seven large wooden bowls filled with savory stew and plates laden with thick loaves of bread and cheese were already in place waiting on them.

Travis explained that Mathis was actually Allyn Woodshorn's, the man who had saved Lord Richard's life from the boar twenty years ago, true son and that he had been training for knighthood for the past ten years and hoped to become a Krannion knight and also a Lord as per the promise made by Lord Richard at his fathers death bed for saving his life. The blademaster also informed the group that Mathis would be accompanying them on their journey to Illsador and then on to the Citadel to become a knight.

Damien leaned his staff alongside the fireplace and was surprised to see a rather motley assortment of weapons already gathered there. Kendle's and Alyssa's war hammer and axehammer were there, along with Travis' mace and long sword. Braden's longbow and sword along with a huge quiver filled with an assortment of different types of arrows and his own battle staff. The most unusual of all though was still the gigantic thick handled maul. The only weapons not in the pile were the ones belonging to Logan who kept all of his concealed on his person either inside his fighting coat or in his boots and belt.

"Woe to anyone who decided to interrupt their dinner." Damien thought silently to himself. His trained battle mage's mind noticed that there was more than just Logan's hidden weapons missing, he was sure that amongst all of them the assortment of weapons in front of him was nothing compared to the assortment of hidden weapons that wasn't in the pile. With one exception, Mathis, who in his plain homespun jerkin had nowhere to hide anything at.

Another thing Damien noticed about Mathis was that he seemed to be on eggshells around Travis. Damien knew that Logan had also noticed this from the looks they had exchanged. Mathis was constantly circling the room and the blademaster, in order to make sure everything was perfect just like how Damien and Logan used to do as children whenever Travis was training them.

Damien could tell that he was trying hard to get the stern blademaster's nods of acceptance and approval. For what though, he wondered, then he realized that Travis must be the one who was training him for the knighthood. Damien wasn't sure how this could be possible because Travis wasn't a knight himself, he was though a champion arena pit slave who had survived there for almost ten years without ever being defeated. So he was definitely qualified in that respect to teach anyone and the muscular young man was certainly acting like he was his squire or student.

As far as he knew he had never seen this large young man before, not here in the woods where he had came to sometimes as a child, or in Castlekeep at the castle. Putting those thoughts aside though as the smell from the stew stirred the inside of his stomach he moved into the chair that had been set at the table for him.

The dinner was a delicious stew served with seasoned potatoes and spicy beef that all found delightful and tasty.

After dinner Mathis cleared the table of its dishes and brought out a steaming pot of hot kafee and offered the bitter brew to anyone who wanted any. Travis, Braden and Logan all took cups. Both Damien and Alyssa turned down the bitter brew and then smiled at one another as if they shared some sort of secret. Damien wasn't exactly sure why Logan took a cup either, he knew that Logan didn't favor the stuff all that well either, which was made evident by the copious amounts of sugar and cream that he put into his cup. Damien figured that he must be up to something but wasn't sure what. More than likely he was just looking for a way to overhear more of Travis and Braden's conversation.

Kendle pulled a small flask out of his pocket and filled a cup with whatever it was in the flask. He offered Damien some but the young battlemage refused, he had tasted the dwarf's liquor before and knew better. The brew was so strong that it could probably scorch off the eyebrows of someone who was just trying to smell it much less drink it.

Alyssa spoke for the first time since entering the small cabin. "So now that we are out of the castle hopefully unnoticed and undetected. What is our plan?"

"Yes Travis." Logan asked curiously looking at the blademaster across from him. "Do we have a course to follow?"

All eyes turned in the blademaster's direction.

Travis pointedly looked at Damien and said. "Sire, what course would you suggest that we choose since ultimately you are the one in charge of the entire expedition?"

Now all the eyes looked to Damien including Logan who smirked at him noticeably.

Damien was used to being put on the spot by Tiko for years though while he was at the Academe and didn't miss a beat.

Speaking clearly and loudly in a firm voice he returned the blademaster's look and said. "Nothing has changed yet in our plans, so I would think that we would go with what was decided back in the castle until something occurs that might make us change our course of action."

Kendle groaned noticeably in a miserable sounding manner. "Isn't there any other way we can do this without having to go up there to that God's forsaken and forlorn place." complained the dwarf.

"No!" said Travis curtly. "And since you are only one of us who has ever been through the Annulith Mountains or to the highland rim where the Gods Hall is, you Kendle will be the one who leads us there."

Kendle groaned again and turned back to his cup of dwarven spirits and took two large long swallows.

* * *

Caliban had tracked the group to the small cabin in the woods by using the locator stone. Hoping that nobody had cast any spells against scrying, the assassin mage cast an ears spell and directed it towards the cabin. Caliban listened from the darkness that had fallen over the woods, to the entire plan and smiled a smirking smile. Everything was exactly the way that he had figured it would be. Leaving, he jogged back the few miles to where he had left the group of men who had accompanied him and the paper that he had had forged yesterday.

No one in the group he was following would know of what had occurred in Castlekeep today. His father had told him the entire plan and he was going to reveal enough of it in the scroll and from his own mouth to make the lies he was going to tell believable. The best told deceptions are those hidden in veils of truth, echoed one of his father's lessons in his head. Now that he was sure of their destination he had a perfect location in place for his ambush by the bandit party.

Damien woke with the first rays of sunlight, seeing that there wasn't quite enough room in the cramped cabin for him to do his morning stretches, he went out side and started to circle round the cabin where he could have some privacy. He stopped when he heard the low murmur of prayer coming from around the cottages side, turning the corner he found Alyssa kneeling on the dewy grass with her head down.

A makeshift altar that consisted of her silver mythryll amulet of Dar hung over her hammer was stuck in the earth in front of her while she consulted with her god, asking for his blessings in the gifts of spells.

Damien silently moved off a little farther away so as not to disturb her and started his own daily morning ritual.

A short while later the rest of the party awoke and soon Travis had all of them heading out once again in the direction of the Annulith Mountains. They would skirt the edge of the dwarven iron peaks before turning northward again.

Braden quickly went on ahead of the rest of the group, disappearing like a ghost into the early morning forests mists without a sound. Everyone else rode out in a single file line, following behind the blademaster with Kendle bringing up the rear.

The air of the forest smelled of pine and wood, animals

fled at the sound of their approach and nothing seemed out of place until they topped a small ridge that overlooked a small wooded valley.

Braden had dropped back and as they all approached he held a finger to his lips motioning for silence.

As they all squatted next to the ranger who had dropped to a crouch, Travis asked him in a low whisper, "What is going on?"

Something is coming," he told them, "and it seems to be running." They all could hear voices in the distance chasing whatever it was through the trees.

The small party watched as a harried looking pale skinned young man with hair so light it almost looked silver white, burst out of a wooden thicket wearing some sort of uniform and carrying just a crossbow. The harried looking young man paused momentarily to lean on a tree and breathe heavily as he tried to catch his breath. The rest was extremely short lived though as a guttural voice called out loud enough for the small group hiding out on the ridge to hear, that he went this way. The man leaning on the tree also heard this and began run again across the wooded valley, weaving between the trees in a zig zagging motion, his long white hair trailing out behind him.

"What is this?" asked Kendle reaching for his axehammer, strapped to his belt.

"I don't know," answered Travis frowning as he observed what was going on below them, "but he's wearing the uniform of a Kallamarian diplomat." He pointed out the running mans outfit with a finger.

A large group of about ten men burst out of the woods chasing after the fleeing man brandishing an assortment of drawn weapons. One of the men chasing the fleeing man was carrying a bow. He dropped down to one knee as he came into the little clearing and drew an arrow back to his ear. Taking careful aim the man let the arrow fly just as the whitish blond haired man ran out from behind a tree in a straight line.

The arrow caught him in the back of one leg and the white haired young man dropped like a shot deer stumbling over itself. Clutching at the wound with one hand and dragging the crossbow he carried behind him in the other, the white haired man pulled himself back behind the tree he had just left.

Arrows sprouted like little branches from the trees trunk that the wounded man was hiding behind as several other men with bows opened up, firing on him.

"Who the hell is that?" Alyssa hissed as they all watched the drama begin to unfold as the fleeing man fired a crossbow bolt back and caught one of the men attacking him in the head with a well placed shot that sent the rest of his attackers scurrying for cover behind a few trees of their own.

"More than likely it appears that they might be bandits out of thief's hollow," returned Kendle gesturing at the men hiding behind the trees, "and we stumbled upon a botched robbery attempt."

"This close to the city and Lord Richards lands?" returned Logan curiously, glancing over at the dwarf, "That's very odd, most highwaymen don't come this close to where the patrols go. It's way too dangerous."

"It appears," said Travis, glancing over at the young thief who had moved up next to them without even a sound. For someone who had grown up all of his life on the Castlekeep's streets, the blademaster thought, Logan was almost as quiet as an Elvynn in the woods, "that these ones are either desperate, stupid or trying to have a little fun then at this other man's expense. I wonder what he is doing here this far from the city? He seems a little under equipped for a journey this far into the forests."

Always thinking about possibilities and probabilities, Logan asked. "Could their being so close and so far from thieves hollow, or this man they are chasing have anything to do with Damien and or our mission? Maybe they are a lure to draw us out."

Travis looked over at the young thief approvingly and considered this for a moment and then said, "I'm not sure but that is a good question."

"Are we going to do anything to help this man?" asked Braden as he unslung his bow from his back and stepped around Travis sliding up towards another closer hiding place.

Quickly the ranger's keen sight spotted the ten men and the one that they were chasing hiding behind their respective trees and had marked their location to the others.

Travis told the others to keep low as possible as they all crawled forward a little closer to take a look at the bandits that were staked out in the clearing below and firing arrows in the direction of the almost silver haired young man who was just barely keeping them at bay with a few more of his own well placed crossbow bolts.

Damien noticed that all of the bandit's attentions were focused on the one single man opposing them and that none of them had even glanced upwards in the general area of the small party that was watching them from above and he told the others this.

At hearing his words, Kendle said, "I could take the half giant here," he indicated bald headed Mathis with a tilt of his head, "with me and we could take a long way around and maybe come up behind them."

"No," said Travis, "Lets see what happens here for a moment, I don't want to get into a fight if it isn't necessary. Accidents happen and if one happens to Damien, there isn't any reason for us to even be out here."

Damien looked at the blademaster who he thought was being a trifle over protective and said, "I can protect myself well enough Travis with out anyone having to die because of me."

It seemed that Alyssa also agreed with Damien and

was shaking her head in total disagreement with the blademaster's words.

At that moment another well-placed arrow shot caught the hiding man in the shoulder, with a cry of pain he dropped the crossbow and collapsed to the earth.

Alyssa unslung her hammer now as the man fell and said with a face full of indignation and fire. "Heir or not! I can not let anybody be massacred in front of me without at least trying to do something about it blademaster, I am an agent of the god of justice and morality sworn to uphold the law, it is my duty to protect this man!"

She was definitely a cleric of Dar, Damien thought to himself as he heard the outrage in her whispered words. She was not about to let a crime take place without doing anything about it or making the criminals pay a punishment for committing it.

Travis never got a chance to reply as Mathis also stepped forward to join her. His dark eyes showed that he agreed with her wholeheartedly and the two began to make their way silently down the small ridge towards the attacking force of bandits hiding behind the trees firing arrows at the fallen man who was attempting to crawl back again behind some cover.

"Hold on a minute you two," said Braden with a hiss, he was drawing back the string on his large bow, "at least let me soften up the way some before you go." With that said the brown haired ranger released an arrow and drew another. All watched as the shaft of wood struck the tree beside which one of the bandits were hiding behind.

In startled surprise the man drew back and his head appeared, face looking in the direction from which the unexpected arrow had come. The second of the ranger's arrows caught the man dead center in the forehead sending him toppling over backwards with the same startled expression on his face.

"Catch them by surprise and they almost always look."

came the rangers reply as he smiled at the pair who started again down the ridge. "Lets go Travis, we can't let the children have all of the fun," the ranger called back over his shoulder as he set off down the hill in an attempt to save the life of the wounded man with the crossbow and almost silver white hair.

Kendle and Logan both, Damien noticed had already disappeared into the forest and the young battlemage wondered whether or not they had left before or after Alyssa and Mathis had started down the hill. Both the dwarf's and Logan's sense of right and wrong could at times rival any cleric of Dars.

"Use those protection spells of yours Damien and try to avoid the arrows," Travis grumbled as he too unsheathed his weapons and descended.

Damien smiled a crooked smile as he fell in behind the blademaster and they too went down to join the fray that was about to erupt below.

The companion of the man who had been shot by Braden's arrow was the first to notice the group coming down the hill and called out a loud warning shout to the rest of his companions. Seeing the strawberry blonde female in the lead and thinking that he could easily dispatch her with little or no effort, he almost casually took his time as he set down his bow and started to draw out a short sword.

Alyssa saw the contemptuous sneer on the mans face and charged him, as she did so she whispered a quick prayer for strength and the thief watched as her body seemed to grow noticeably in size and proportion, her hammer was already cocked in mid swing. Her opponents eyes widened in fear as he realized that she was going to reach him before he could fully draw his own weapon and he tried to avoid her swing by sidestepping the attack.

The cleric of Dars hammers head, with the help enhanced by the strengthening spell that she had cast on herself, caught the hilt of the weapon being drawn out and

A King's Quest

the impact of the strength enhanced strike sent it flying off into the woods somewhere behind the bandit.

Now weaponless, the man did the only thing he could do and came at Alyssa with outstretched hands. Quicker still though the female fighting cleric reversed the swing of her hammer and drove its shaft upwards just as the mans hands grabbed her shoulders, the metal shod end went between his arms and caught him on his chin with an audible crack of bone, that sent her attacker reeling over backwards, out cold.

Two more of the bandits turned away from their intended target and charged at the group moving down the face of the ridge. As the bandits moved forward to engage, one of the smarter ones stayed hidden in a clump of brush until Travis passed by, then he jumped up and out with his sword held high up over his head in two hands.

Damien had been circling around towards the wounded man, saw the hiding man spring up behind the blademaster and cried out his name in alarm.

Travis didn't bother to turn to see what was happening. Instead he just dropped and rolled sideways out of the path of the downward swinging sword.

Spinning around low as he regained his feet the blademaster barely managed to jump backwards out of the attacking mans swords backslash swing. As the sword swept by Travis was ready now and brought his own mace down in his own vicious sideways swing.

The heavy spiked ball of the mace tore through the bandit's hand, ripping the skin and shattering the bone underneath.

The bandit wailed in pain, but the blademaster not really caring continued forward and thrust the tip of his razor sharp long sword held in his other hand deep into the mans throat, the keen blade went straight through almost to the hilt. Giving the blade an almost savage like twist, the blademaster nearly decapitated the man as he yanked the sword sideways out of the bandit's neck. Watching as the other man crumpled to the forest floor Travis spat in an almost disgusted sounding voice as he shook his head from side to side saying only one word. "Amateur!"

Damien caught by surprise at hearing such a comment come out of the normally stoic mans mouth cast a startled sideways glance over at Travis who saw the look and returned it with a wicked grin of his own which made Damien grin too. For a moment Damien almost thought that the blademaster was being flippant.

This sound of metal crushing metal followed by a loud crash caused both Damien and Travis to turn back towards Alyssa and Mathis.

Mathis using the giant maul like a battering ram slammed the massive triangular shaped iron head into the armored breastplate of another bandit, sending him flying through the air into the forest. As the young man's baldhead swung around and his eyes met those of the other bandit, he took one look at the woodsman's large muscles and turned running off after his flying companion.

Logan and Kendle had silently slipped off while Alyssa and Mathis had argued their case in front of the blademaster. Now they were directly behind two of the hiding bandits, one of who was the one who had fired the arrow into the fleeing mans leg. Kendle, who was a lot better suited for making his way through mountain passageways and tunnels rather than wooded forests, never saw the leaf covering dry twig that was under his boot. It snapped audibly when he put his weight on it, alerting the other two men to their presence.

Knowing that he had ruined their surprise attack on the two, the dwarf did what he always did. White striped beard flying over his shoulder, he charged headfirst at the closest man.

The man with the bow dove sideways avoiding the oncoming dwarf's charge but in doing so he also dropped the bow that seemed to be his only weapon of defense, knowing that he had to do something though to protect himself, he turned to the dwarf and threw a punch directly at Kendle's face. An almost evil like grin flashed on the dwarfs features as he saw the punch coming and dropped his head just enough so that it struck him in his rock hard forehead rather than on the nose where it was intended.

The mans hand connected with a meaty sounding thud which was followed by a scream of agony as he fell backwards clutching at his now broken hand in apparent pain.

"The hardest part of a human's body is his skull," Kendle said grinning at the injured man who was now clutching his shattered hand to his chest with tears of pain in his eyes. "And as a dwarf, my skull is twice as thick and hard as any humans."

Logan let out a loud laugh as he called out. "You got that right, I just never thought that I would ever here you admit it."

Kendle shot the sandy haired thief a dark look before he stepped forward to finish off his opponent. He tucked his long braided reddish brown and white striped beard into his belt and almost casually thumbed the snap loose on the sheath of his axehammer and shook it free. The wounded man turned around and he too fled into woods.

Logan was not having as easy a time with his opponent as Kendle had, instead he seemed to be in a fight with a rather skilled bandit. Both men were thrusting and parrying each other's attacks without either one of them seeming to have any impact on the other.

Every time that Logan would come in with only one of his new long bladed Elvynn fighting daggers he was using his opponent was ready and would take a small step backward quickly raising either his buckler on his arm or the sword in his hand to deflect the blow harmlessly away, the same thing occurred whenever he attacked Logan also who either turned his blade aside or used the long bladed dagger to keep him at a distance.

The two men circled each other probing at one another's defenses, each intent upon finding a weakness in the other one. The fight had gone from being merely just that and turned into more of a deadly duel. Logan finally found the first weakness and as he turned his body slightly away from his opponent he dropped a third blade concealed in his sleeve down into his hand. Stumbling slightly with his next attack he laid the flat of his long bladed dagger on his opponents buckler a bit too long. The other man sensing that is opponent was off-balance with his weapon set for breaking couldn't resist and chopped downward with his own sword as hard as he could. Seeing his opponent's weight shifting with his attack, Logan let the blade go as soon as the other sword struck it.

The bandit's short lived delight turned to dismay as his own momentum not meeting any resistance from the dropped dagger carried him forward off balance exposing the whole right side of his body to the sandy haired spythief. Logan thrust the third dagger deep that now filled his empty hand into the man's ribs, driving its needle sharp tip up into the man's heart and lungs.

All of the other bandits had melted back into the woods at the sight of the other group except for the one that Logan had been fighting and the rest of the group with him had gathered around to watch the duel between them.

"What gave him away?" called out Travis to the young thief after the fight was over.

"Overconfidence," Logan remarked recalling his facial smirk when they had started to fight. "You know, any one of you could have jumped in to lend a hand though I wouldn't have minded at any time."

"He wouldn't let us," responded Damien, throwing a glance in the blademaster's direction as he gestured to himself and Alyssa."

Logan fixed the blademaster with a dark glare.

The tall blademaster shrugged. "Call it a test, none of us had ever seen you defend yourself and I wanted to know whether you could or not."

"Well I hoped I performed well enough for your benefit," Logan said angrily and then bent down to retrieve his dropped dagger, which he slipped back into its sheath of hiding.

"Maybe," offered Alyssa, in an attempt to prevent further bickering between the young thief and the older blademaster. "We should check on the life of the man we just saved."

Everyone realized that during the heat of the short duel between Logan and the now dead bandit, they had forgotten about the wounded man. Now they all hurried through the trees towards him in order to check on his condition.

Alyssa knelt down next to the white-haired young man prostrate body. It seemed that the energy that had filled him during the chase and the battle had finally faded as his wounds had overtaken him, leaving him weak and barely conscious.

Probing at the wounds gently with her fingers, Alyssa checked the damage, seeing that neither arrow was touching anything vital, she motioned for Kendle to grab hold of his arms and for Braden to grab his legs. Then the female cleric of Dar placed her hands on one of the arrow shafts and gestured for Travis, who appeared to her to have seen his share of battlefield injuries, to take the other arrow in his hands. Nodding as he did so she held up three fingers and began to count. At three, they both simultaneously yanked out their arrows.

The light skinned young man went completely white with pain and gasped audibly. Once the arrows were free, Alyssa began the prayer that Damien knew now by its sound, was a healing spell.

The young man wearing the Kallamarian diplomat's

uniforms eyelids fluttered open after she was finished, the slate blue eyes cast about for a moment before they locked on Travis' own.

Pushing himself upright and leaning against a tree for support, the now healed young man pulled a scroll out of his pouch. With a deadly serious look on his face he asked the blademaster whether or not he was Travis Longblade.

Travis looked around at all of the other, then reluctantly he nodded yes. As he answered, the other man turned over the scroll case revealing the silver falcon of House Daverge and held it up toward him.

The others watched as the blademaster opened the case, withdrew the curled parchment from inside and began to read. His face turned to granite like stone and his dark eyes glazed over with anger. Without saying a word he passed the scroll over to Damien, who said aloud for the others benefit what it read.

To Travis Longblade,

Lord Dalmar Ariaas has been killed by an assassin and the blame has been passed on to a certain female cleric of Dar of your acquaintance. You and the rest of your party have also been implicated in this assassination as conspirators in a plot against the throne and the crown by the royal regent himself. A thousand gold piece bounty has been placed on each of your heads and word is going out to every city and every village in the realm for you to be captured as I write this. I have personally been removed from my post as Highlord here in Castlekeep by the royal regent until the council meeting of Highlords where I might also be tried for treason against the throne. I can offer no help to you at this moment except for the messenger who delivers this. His name is Caliban and he was Lord Dalmar's personal assistant and protector. He as a member of the

Kallamarian court and might be able aid you in the coming trials. The gods grant you luck and keep all safe.

 Richard Daverge
 Ruling Lord of Castlekeep

Alyssa stood stock still as she heard what the letter read, a stunned expression on her face. Finally she said in a weak voice, "Did I hear that I killed a royal ambassador of Kallamar?" as she pointed at the parchment with a quavering finger.

"And that there is a thousand gold piece reward for your capture," said Logan in a manner that suggested he might try and turn her in. Both Mathis and Braden shot the young spythief dark looks.

"Lord Richard told me that Lord Vargas said that the reward was for any of you who are found with her also." said the white blond haired man as he scrambled upwards onto his feet and checked at his healed injuries with gently probing long fingers.

"Well it seems that the other side now has made some moves to try and stop us from obtaining our goal." growled Kendle, "or at least laid some obstacles in our path in an attempt to slow us down some.

"What exactly does this mean?" asked Alyssa, her mind still in turmoil at the news that she was the one accused of killing a royal ambassador and a man named a hero to the realm.

"What it means," answered Travis in a matter of fact voice. "Is that we are now outcasts and outlaws wanted everywhere throughout the entire realm. The usurper of the throne and the crown has named us dangerous criminals and murderers."

"It's a brilliant tactic to capture or delay us. " said Damien to all, not really sounding surprised, they had discussed at dinner the night before what Vargas and his little group of traitors might attempt to do in order to stop them from succeeding since their first attempt had failed. But this thought Damien, was a tactic worthy of a well-trained and seasoned battlemage. Travis had figured that Vargas and his advisor Cyadine would use soldiers in an attempt to stop them and his lineage from being made known to the public. The idea of casting Alyssa, though as a murderer and criminal was brilliant in its simplicity. "If successful he might even be able to delay us until the day of Seth's naming day. Which would make this adventure pointless." Damien finished. "If Seth takes the throne ahead of me, I have no claim any longer."

Instead of having to keep the search for them silent and secret, using only the military, Vargas and Cyadine had made it a matter of the people, be a hero and catch the murderer who killed a hero and every soul in the entire realm would be on the lookout for them especially with a thousand gold marks at stake for each of them to sweeten the pot. He would have to sit down with Travis and discuss this. To Damien it seemed that they had forgotten rule number one and they had seriously underestimated the enemy and their desire to stay in power and they would have to rethink their strategy because obviously he thought to himself, someone on the royal regent's side was very good tactically.

"Why me, what does he have me doing that was so horrendous that he isn't guilty of ten times over and done ten times worse if everything that's been said is true?" Alyssa angrily asked as her face flushed red. "I am a pillar of justice and my job is to uphold the laws of the land and enforce them, not to kill people and break them or to murder them in their sleep." she finished in righteous indignation.

"Aren't you dead?" asked the white-haired young man as he stared incredulously at Damien with wide eyes. "I mean I went to your funeral at the castle."

Everyone in the group froze at the unexpected question

and looked at Damien then they all as one turned their eyes to Travis questioningly. All of them were wondering the same thing and Kendle even began the finger the shaft of his axe hammer as they considered the other mans words and what they meant.

"How," asked the blademaster, looking at the now healed man direly, "do you know who he is?"

"I was for the past several weeks until this morning when I was asked to flee with this message by Lord Richard to find you, the ambassador's new personal bodyguard and assistant. It's my job to know who's who in the city where I'm stationed and I would be surely lacking in my duties if I didn't know the ruling highlords sons on sight or members of their family, or staff" stated the young man propped up against the tree, meeting the blademaster's look.

Nobody could find anything wrong with this argument so finally Travis asked. "How did you find us?"

"I didn't find you, I actually found them," the young man said pointing over at a few of the dead bodies lying on the forest floor with a grimace. "They must have thought that I was some type of soldier or authority figure, cause the moment I landed when I saw them, they immediately attacked me and chased off my griffon. I thought that I was a dead man until you two," he paused and looked over at Alyssa and Mathis, "started coming down off of that ridge." he had actually counted on the nature of the female cleric of Dar to come to his rescue. All over town was the story about how she had healed the man that she had fought in the pit because of the unfairness of the fight and he figured she would try to save him also.

"Since you do know who he is," responded Travis satisfied with young man's answer, "and since you also know now that he is alive, we can't let you just leave here." He eyed the young man in front of him thoughtfully for several long moments. "Since Richard trusted you enough to take the chance to have you bring us this message," the blademaster held up the document, "you'll just have to join with us for a while until we can figure out what to do with you. Did your griffon fly off with all of your gear and equipment?"

"Excuse me," said Caliban anxiously, "I cannot stay with you, I have to find my lords true killer," he turned his face towards Alyssa's, "I don't think that you or any of you had anything to do with his death. His secretary also turned up missing this morning also and when I searched his quarters it appeared that he left in somewhat of a hurry."

"That will have to wait for a while," said Travis interrupting him, buying Caliban's anxious act, "we cannot let you leave here with the knowledge that he is alive." The blademaster glanced over at Damien, "The sake of the realm is at stake, if you try to leave we will all be forced to stop you."

The sound of steel sliding out of sheathes and snaps being unfastened sounded all about him. Every one of the faces in the group around him turned grim.

Inwardly Caliban smiled, outwardly he let a nervous expression show on his face as he said in a slightly shaking voice, "I will call back the griffon, I'm sure that I can," said the young man, as he pulled a golden whistle out from underneath his uniforms tunic.

As Caliban started to place the whistle to his lips, he felt the sharpened edge of a sword blade touch the side of his neck and the tall brown haired man with the angular face that he assumed was Braden Ravenclaw said warningly. "It had better be only one griffon that your whistle calls, if any more than one shows up you will be the first to die."

Caliban nodded and blew the whistle. No sound issued from it, but after several minutes a giant shadow passed over them. Caliban blew once more and the mighty beast flew down between the trees and landed at his feet.

Gathering his traveling pack, his armor and his weapons, from where he had tied them in place and laying them down on the ground, he then ordered the griffon back to Castlekeep. As he turned back to the group the assassin mage reintroduced himself again as Caliban and asked them what was going on and where was it that they were going.

A.V. Wedhorn

Chapter 24
Disciple

Acting on Vargas' orders once they had returned to the capitol city, Cyadine called a meeting of all of the royal ambassadors and was having them all come in from their various postings throughout the realm. Every one of them would be present or else they would lose their posts and quite possibly their lives if they did not.

The royal regent's summons had been very clear in its directness. One of their numbers was dead and he wanted to make sure that it didn't happen to any of the rest of them. This last part was a little touch added by Cyadine to keep the blame away from them. He had a description of the murderess and of each member in her party that she was traveling with, it also told the story of who it was that she had killed. He knew that it wouldn't take long for the word of the ambassadors or the words of the Krannion proctors who were in a similar meeting with Gunther to be spread out into almost every populated corner of the realm especially with the almost outrageous sum of gold that the royal regent had put up for their capture. The fact that almost the entire realm would do the searching for them caused Cyadine an almost indescribable amount of cynical pleasure.

The advisor and wizard had along with his son, concluded that the group with the heir would stay away from most villages on their way to the Godshall, just because of its remote location and unavailability. After they had recovered the rings and if they defeated his trap, then they would become fair game. He would release Caliban or Gunther upon them to do what needed to be done. Until then Caliban was under explicit orders to remove any members of the group that he could, but only by making it look like a completely unavoidable accident which couldn't be traced back to him in any way that could jeopardize his situation. If all had gone well today, Caliban should have properly inserted himself into the group and would be traveling with them to Illsador. If not, his son would be lying dead somewhere in the northwestern forests and had failed in his mission.

It would sadden Cyadine much if this possibility came to pass, especially with all of the time and training that had been put forth into his son. To lose such a valuable instrument in this game of powers would be a true loss.

A loud chime sounded in the outer chamber of his quarters. The magical glyph that he had placed on the mirror of walking to let him know if it was being used or activated seemed to be working properly.

"Maybe," Cyadine thought to himself as he was gathering up all of the scrolls that he would pass out to the other ambassadors at the royal regent's summons, "it was Caliban reporting his success at joining the group."

A tall thin old man with long silver steel grey hair, draped in long deep black robes with silver trim that were etched with runes of power and radiated magic stood as cold and emotionless as a stone statue in the mirrors surface. It was immediately apparent from the distinctive angular and sharp features on his almost grey face that he was of pure Elvynn blood. His intent piercing eyes dominated the mirrors surface and as Cyadine saw the figure, he dropped the scrolls and hurried over to stand before him. Quickly he knelt, practically throwing himself down upon his knees, with his head bent down, his forehead almost touching the tiled floor, saying simply in a subdued voice one word. "Master."

A voice that sounded that was soft and low like a snake's sibilant hiss, but seemed to be filled with power, asked. "What is the news about this discovered heir who is a battlemage, my disciple?"

"Master," Cyadine said again deferentially to the other, "he travels out of Castlekeep to Illsador to recover the dragon ring's, my own son should be accompanying him in this quest."

Latherias Yematt, the Elvynn High mage who ruled over the conclave of Elvynn creational war wizards called the Tua-Latin eyed the kneeling, prostrate man on the stone floor before him, his pale yellow eyes glowing with inner fire. "Is there any word or sign of the child that was born with him? If they came together and one of them is a battlemage, it could finally signify the end of the banishment and the beginning of the retrieval as was foretold and promised by our god Olanntian."

"No master," said Cyadine, still prostrate upon the floor in front of the mirror. "Only the one child is known to exist at this time and until something happens to change that or if he recovers the rings, there is nothing else to report."

"Well enough," said the ancient Highmage after it seemed that he had weighed and measured each of the royal advisors words as if determining their merit. "As to the status of causing distrust and a revolution amongst the populace of the realm, where do your actions stand there?"

At this question the royal wizard and advisor face changed from reverence to one of sly cunning with a bit of confidence on it. "A lot has occurred in the past three days since last we spoke, Master. The most prominent and best member of the humans military was killed last night and the Highlord of Castlekeep, one of the largest cities defending the western side of the continent from where you would be arriving has been removed from power due to evidence that might link him to the other mans murder. He was also the chief protagonist against the tax laws that I had the simpleton Vargas pass to incite revolt among the masses. When the council of lords is called, the other six highlords who sided with him will be called to task for their own actions too and will be removed from power also. This should, if this heir signifies the beginning of the retrieval, throw the rest of the realm and its kingdoms into complete turmoil and utter chaos allowing for all of your well laid plans to easily succeed."

At hearing these words of his most prized of students, the expression on the Elvynn high mages aged face turned to one of cruel pleasure and slowly a thin-lipped smile made its way across his cold face.

How, like so many other times over the past twenty-five years, he wished that this quarter Elvynn servant were truly one of the pure born. So far could he have taken this disciple of his, born of such natural abilities and magical power with so Elvynn like a mind. If it wasn't for his tainted blood, Latherias knew that he would have immediately named Cyadine Syndell his second in the Tualatin conclave, so much pure power was there in him for a mere human that sometimes he wondered whether or not if the human lived long enough, if he would someday even pass him in his power levels and ability. He would make a much better second than the twisted and scarred Morgrynn Phyrus, who plotted as much against him as she did with him.

The small group of wizards that he had sent over here to the human lands years ago to find a way to disrupt their leadership and cause chaos in their realm by finding disgruntled wizards in their fabled city of mages had stumbled across a pure cut diamond, when they had found the hatred filled disgraced young man who had just been ousted out of their battlemage order for practicing forbidden magic and who had also been trained by their best battlemaster and who somehow was a companion of the kings younger fourth brother. Latherias was convinced that this powerful human with traces of Elvynn blood was a gift from the Elvynn god of power, Olanntian himself and maybe a sign that signified the banishment was near its end.

Through a small group of wizards and himself, they had personally trained this half human to be a powerful creational wizard, battlemages could cast creational magic and were allowed to progress more and more into it, the longer they stayed in the ranks, nobody in the human lands though could even hope to ever achieve the level of one trained by the Tua-Latin who had hundreds of years to learn their craft and spells, none thought Latherias Yematt except for maybe this one single half human who was kneeling in front of him or maybe his son or the Elvynn rulers sons traitorous half breed who commanded the human mages, Sirathiel Shanasar.

Several hours later after the meeting with the ambassadors was over, Cyadine received the news he wanted to hear as his sons face finally appeared in the mirror and told him that he had successfully infiltrated the party of Damien Daverge and would be accompanying them on their trip to Illsador thanks to the help of Ferris the dead secretary.

Cyadine consulted the map of the kingdom in his chambers and plotted a route that would avoid most cities and would take the group from Illsador if they even managed to recover the rings to the citadel where they would probably go next in order to attain the knights help in regaining the throne for this Damien Daverge, maybe now he decided it would be a good time to learn a little more about this young man and who it was who had trained him at the academe, with this knowledge it might help the advisor in being able to figure out what actions he might take against him due to the training he had received.

If he was anticipating correctly the route that he thought that they might take, once they had recovered the rings and if they somehow managed to escape his golath, the royal wizard could have Gunther lie in wait somewhere close to the Elvynn swamps of Edgemoor near the city of Embry and capture and kill them before the ever reached the Citadel.

The Elvynn Highmage, who had trained him for the past twenty years, had his own agenda and that involved creating chaos amongst the fourteen lands that comprised the entire realm. Cyadine was doing all that he could to help them accomplish this. If this battlemage born heir signified the end of the Elvynn banishment, he had been promised a quarter section of the entire realm for himself that he could rule as his own, if this heir did not signify the end of the banishment and was killed before he could regain the throne, Cyadine would still be a major force behind the throne even when Vargas relinquished power to his son, but if this heir succeeded then he would be put to death along with all of the others who had plotted against and murdered the heirs father and true king. As always the advisor found himself nestled in a complex web of plots and schemes.

* * *

Krannion knight third commander Braddoc Ceran had

already organized a party that would go off after the fleeing murderers. He had wanted to go on this little hunting expedition himself but knew that he couldn't thanks to the royal regent's command stating that he was to stay and help maintain order here in Castlekeep. He would stay and insure that the battlemage talking to the ex ruler of this city also did as he was told to do. Battlemages were a product of the west that they used here rather than knights such as him and even though he had worked closely with several for years he still didn't entirely trust them. So instead of going himself, he chose the best man in his group of knights to go in his place.

Jados Lodry, was a deeply tanned knight with light brown hair, a rugged face and a square chin, who never failed at anything and who could, thanks to his hunting lord father in the southeastern Starcrest mountains, track just about anything on legs. Jados would lead a party of ten knights heading north after the fleeing criminals and either capture or kill them, he didn't really care which.

"No one should get away," Braddoc thought to himself as he checked the men's equipment insuring that all was in order "with killing any man in his bed and bed clothes while he was sleeping, such an act was considered despicable in his eyes and especially a man as noble and honorable as the ex marshall of armies."

After they were finished, Drekar Thirel, Lord Gildon Seahorn, Lady Ariaas and the other red haired woman who was wearing a brown cloak with two slender short swords strapped to her waist and traveling pack slung across her shoulders came over to them.

Drekar addressed the other man that had been left in charge of the city with him by stating that Lord Gildon had a small request.

Commander Braddoc bowed slightly and motioned for the Highlord to speak.

Lord Gildon said in his rich sounding voice. "As you

are already aware of Lady Ariaas' husband was killed, I would like to ask if it were possible that you might be able to allow Lady Cassica here," the honey colored haired lord directed a look at the diminutive pretty red haired lady with the traveling pack and the two short swords at her belt. "Her sister, to accompany your men on their mission, I'm sure that she could prove most useful and offer some valuable assistance."

Jados Lodry looked skeptically first from the small read headed lady, then to his commander and back to Lord Gildon, before he said. "I think that myself and the knights accompanying me on this mission will be more than enough to see that is done."

"Lady Essen, sub commander Jados," Lord Gildon stated, using the mans formal rank, "won the harvest festival tournament of cities fighting championships a few days ago in both weapons and hand to hand combat and as of right now she is the most skilled fighter in the entire western realm and also a second slash battlemage too. Do you have anyone in your party sir knight, who might be able to counter the powerful clerical spells that a well trained cleric of Dar could be able to bring against you?" It was apparent from the way that Lord Gildon said this and from the tone in his voice that he already knew the answer that he was going to receive from the commander.

At hearing the statement about her winning the tournament of champions, more than just a few of the knights standing about in the room gave Cassica appreciative nods of recognition and congratulations. These were all skilled fighting men and could appreciate anyone with so much ability in their ranks whether or not it was a man or a woman and even more so since she was a battlemage and could lend assistance magically.

Jados Lodry looked about helplessly for a moment at his men but he already knew that they had no arguments and neither did he that could counter the highlords statement and finally said reluctantly he was right and that she should join them.

"Good then," said the Highlord clasping a large hand onto the Krannion knights shoulder, "she should be a welcome addition to your party."

Cassica up until this moment hadn't made a move, but at this final statement she stepped forward and as she eyed the sub commander and his senior commander she threw back her cloak slightly to reveal the black and gold uniform underneath it and said coolly, "Technically, I outrank you sub commander Jados, but for the course of this expedition or unless I see a reason to change things, I will place myself under your command for the time being."

Jados drew back a little at this bold statement coming from so small a woman but then he saw the determined look in her dark brown eyes and nodded saying that, that was fine with him.

"So when then do we leave," asked the small pretty redheaded lady smiling now that her point was made, "I promised my sister that I would find out the truth in this matter as quickly as possible."

Commander Braddoc answered her question before his subordinate could speak, "Tomorrow, I am to contact Lord Cyadine later this evening, he is using his magic to try and possibly locate any sign of the path that these criminals might have taken, having this knowledge would prove invaluable in leading to their capture and would I think be a lot more prudent than heading off north in the direction that they might have taken."

Lord Gildon at hearing these words and knowing that they might indeed buy Damien and his group a little more time hurried wholeheartedly to agree with the knight's commander's wise statement.

"Tomorrow at first light then it is then." answered Jados, "I expect everyone here going with me to get a good nights sleep, for tomorrow we ride hard after these criminals who would kill a hero of the realm."

Commander Braddoc actually waited till the next morning to report back to the capitol city of Kallamar and the royal regent himself personally took his report and that of Drekar Thirel's also.

The royal wizard informed them that he had it on good information that the party that they were seeking had gone north, towards the Annulith mountains, possibly towards the Bryn Maw and it was there that they should start their hunt.

Commander Braddoc informed Jados Lodry of this and the group of Krannion knights along with the female battlemage set out after the fugitives.

* * *

Travis pushed the group hard for three entire days and by mid morning of the fourth day they moved out of the forests and began their ascent into the mountains. He had pushed them so hard because he planned on taking an extra day and travel around the Bryn Maw rather than take his chances with the ghosts of dead gods and live ones too.

During the wars of power where the lesser races, humans and anything else other than an Elvynn had fought to escape the tyranny of their enslavement, a massive battle had taken place in the large mountain pass. Thousands of beings of all races had fallen during the three day battle called the Endwar. The amount of blood that had been spilt there had stained all of the rocks in the Maw a deep red that served to this day as a reminder of the deadly battle. The gods themselves had also fought during those three days, each with their respective races and religions. One had even fallen, killed by the hand of the first free king, Doral Markennan, wielding the ancient talisman sword Spellbreaker, the only weapon on Tyrus that could create purefire.

It was the Elvynn warrior goddess Ishmyra, consort to the Elvynn god of war and power, Olanntian.

She was killed by the talisman vorpyll sword, which was one of the few things that could hurt a god. When the avatar form of Olanntian found his love, dead on the battlefield after the war was over, such was his grief and anger over his loss of his love that he cursed the entire area. So powerful was the curse that every night for the past two thousand years, the dead in the valley arise, take up their weapons and replay the battle that took place there. Anyone caught in the haunted valley when night falls has to fight their way through or risk getting killed by the battling ghosts, if they are killed, they fall under Olanntian's powerful curse and have to spend the rest of eternity fighting in the endless battle.

Even during the daytime the sounds of battle can be heard as echoes on the wind and the presence of the ghosts there can be felt as whispers on the skin.

Sometimes it's been said that you can even find the god Olanntian himself in the valley at night hoping to see a sign of his beloved fighting there or in the daytime weeping over her death.

The valley is also treasure trove of weapons and glorious items, if you can get in and back out again without getting killed and becoming part of the curse itself.

Kendle, Damien knew had once traversed the Bryn Maw at night and it was there that he had acquired his mighty axehammer that swung at his hip but it was also where he had gained the white stripe that ran the length of his beard. It's been said too that the Bryn Maw was the same place where the royal proctor of Kallamar had gotten his pure white hair from also but no one seemed to know from where he had acquired the disfiguring jagged scar that ran the length of his face.

Travis had stated in a matter of fact manner that they had no intention of going through the haunted pass themselves, but had said that he wanted their trail to look like they had indeed gone through it, in case there was pursuit behind them which with the news he had received yesterday from the newcomer Caliban, he knew there would be.

Braden and Mathis would lay a false trail to the valley with their horses then set them free to go on their own. Originally they were going to ride the beasts all the way to the Highland Rim, but now with the news about the reward and with possibly half of the realm chasing after them in order to receive it, Travis had figured that if it looked like they had entered the haunted valley it would deter most of their pursuers from following. They would circle around instead and go across the Wolfchase pass, a still dangerous and treacherous route to take but also one with no ghosts, haunted memories or dead gods to deal with either. There was no really easy way over the mountains. Once long ago there had been a way through the mountains when the legendary dwarven city of Malfarra had existed but that was no more either and no one lived who knew the paths to it except for maybe Kendle.

About mid morning of the next day Braden and Mathis returned on foot, announcing that their deed had been done.

Caliban listened to this and knew that there was no way that he could alert his father to this change, so that he could warn the following group of the danger they might be in.

As everyone in the group started up into the mountains Damien unpacked and unwrapped his battlestaff, he intended to use it to help him navigate the climb upwards.

Turning to face the others with the weapon in hand, the silver emblem of Tiko's family crest gleamed brightly in the sun momentarily, just enough to catch the eye of Caliban, who gasped audibly as he recognized the symbol that was also on his fathers study and training room wall.

Everyone in the group's heads turned in the direction

of the white blonde haired young man, who quickly, as his mind raced to cover up what he had seen, asked as he changed his startled expression to one of awe, "Is that an Esian ironwood staff?"

Damien smiled at the other mans question and answered that it was indeed and a gift given to him from his battlemaster at the academe.

Caliban nodded and almost reverently asked if he could see it.

Damien passed the fighting staff over to him and he slowly almost lovingly caressed the black shaft and ran his fingers over the roaring tiger crest, his father always talked about the weapon in reverence and now his former battlemaster and teacher had passed it on to this young man whom he had been sent here to kill. For a moment as Caliban spun the staff in his fingers end over end and he debated whether or not he should turn one of the fighting grips to the right and release one of the hidden blades, a right handed twist of the grip would send the blade accidentally shooting into whoever the end was pointed at. With an almost sad smile he let the opportunity pass. He needed this so called heir to try and recover the rings first and more than likely the powerful female cleric of Dar could save the life of whoever he shot if the he wasn't perfect in his attempt. The same teacher who had trained his father had also trained this man that the rest of the people in this group was calling the heir to the throne and crown. He almost smiled at the irony of the situation.

Caliban was positive that his father hadn't known about this little piece of information or else he might have himself come to kill this dark haired young man instead of sending him. His father had sworn an oath to never allow any other of Trakkiko Matsuri's or Tiko, as his father sometimes called his former teacher, students to live, since he had been so disgraced by the battlemaster.

"This would also," Caliban realized, "mean that he

would have to be very careful if or when he engaged in any type of combat, since he had been trained by his father who had been trained by the same man who had trained the other battlemage in front of him." He was certain as he handed the staff back to its owner now, that there would be some distinct similarities in their styles and abilities. His father's old teacher must have found him extremely worthy of the weapon to pass it down from father to son. As they all started up the pass, Caliban wondered whether or not he should tell his father. The news of another student would consume him and fill him with rage, maybe he would wait a little before he did so, at least until they had recovered the rings, maybe even after Seth was crowned King. He could present him with the rings that should belong to him rather than this imposter who was trying to start a revolution.

A.V. Wedhorn

Chapter 25
Blizzard

    Travis taught and lectured Damien on the rules of the Kallamarian court and about what he could expect at the Citadel from the knights after they had recovered the rings. He also went over the history of the fourteen kingdoms and its rulers. These lessons helped to pass the time as they made their way higher and higher into the mountains passes. Damien was amazed at the vast amount of knowledge that the ex pit fighting slave had about the royal court, the fourteen kingdoms and the realm itself. This in fact reminded him once again of his theory that there was a lot more to the surly blademaster than what he and everyone else had been told about him.
    Every once in a while Damien would glance about behind them and stare in wonder as the lands they left behind and below unfurled out beneath them. It resembled a living patchwork quilt the higher they climbed. At first all you saw were the lush green foothills, then the forests in

autumn golds, brilliant oranges and fiery reds. Followed by multicolored fields and clearings filled with fall wildflowers blooming, the higher they ascended the larger the land tapestry below them grew.

The colorful scenery and forests that they were leaving behind them, Damien thought to himself, was nothing compared to what was in front of them as they climbed into the breathtaking beauty of the mountains before them.

Alyssa seemed to love where they were in the mountains as she pointed out numerous things to Logan. She told them all that they reminded her of her home in the cleric's fortress in Muldar.

A well-laid path snaked and winded its way up into the towering mountains ahead of them. Splendid formations of stone and spires of rocks loomed all about them. At times the group made their way across thousand foot gorges that fell away to both sides of the paths they took. Kendle led the way the entire time, going up, never once wavering in his path, he too seemed as much at home here as Alyssa did. Once they had to go a little out of their way as they had skirted the remains of a leftover landslide that had closed off part of the narrow path they were on, but other than that there was very little difficulty in their passage.

The higher they climbed, the harder the air about them became to breathe as it thinned out around them soon even the littlest action seemed to Damien to be an exertion. Once far away he had spotted what he first thought to be a large eagle winging way through the mountain air possibly hunting for food, until he realized that it was much too big for its surroundings, the large flying bird was a kraal, another creational magic creature.

Kraals are extremely large, intelligent eagle like birds that come in all shapes and sizes, which are bred by the Terian northmen for all sorts of duties in their mountain top cities.

Damien squinted his eyes as he studied the massive

bird, even though this bird was rider less, he immediately noted its black color. Black Kraals, the young battlemage had learnt at the academe, were specially trained war birds, cause they were the largest and most intelligent of their kind, they were trained and bred in much the same manner as were Krannion knights warhorses, specifically for fighting. The steel shod talons of a war Kraal can either rake and claw a man to pieces and its massive beak can crush or tear just about anything and its black color serves as camouflage for nighttime raids. A war kraal can easily carry three unarmored people on its back or two heavily armored ones.

Kendle and Travis, Damien noticed, had also seen the large bird but were paying it no mind. Instead as they all rested the pair seemed to be studying the sky and whispering to one another in tones to low to be overheard.

Nothing else happened the rest of that day but as they settled down for the night in the high mountain passes, Damien noticed that unlike the other nights, there was an extremely cold bite to the wind.

He awoke the next morning to a slight crackling sound all about him as he sat up. A thin sheen of silver ice and icicles covered everything around him. Travis had made him cast a warning alarm glyph last night around the camp far enough out that they all would have had plenty of time to prepare if anything had wandered in during the night but it hadn't warned him about the ice.

Every one of them had slept the night away peacefully and he recognized all by their huddled ice covered forms, each was still sleeping but himself and now Alyssa who started into wakefulness just a few seconds after he himself had and had also sat up almost as if somehow she had known that he was awake. As they both had, for almost the entire week, they flashed smiles at each other as if they knew what the other was thinking. Damien started to stretch as Alyssa slipped off a little to say her morning prayers.

As Kendle awoke and looked about first at the frost, then at the sky above, then he went over and woke Travis saying something about his being right the day before.

Dark and heavy clouds filled the sky overhead, their steel grey color looked like an ugly dull blanket had been stretched across the whole horizon making everything seem bleary and drab, muting all of the bright vivid colors of yesterday.

Quickly Travis raised the rest of the camp and made everyone of them hurry in their preparations for leaving. In less than half an hour, they were back on the path and going as fast as the trail ahead of them allowed.

Alyssa whispered to him later as he tried to ask the blademaster what was going on but had been ignored, that it looked to her like a blizzard might be moving into the mountains about them and they might possibly be caught in the middle of it.

As the day progressed the overhead sky turned from dull grey to an ominous black in color. The air about them grew colder and colder.

Damien noticed that the breath coming out of his mouth was forming grey clouds around his head.

Once the sun started towards the edge of the horizon, an icy wind began to fiercely blow through the mountain pass as the light started to fade. It lashed and tore at their exposed skin like a flaying whip that brought tears to their eyes. Everyone in the group huddled lower in their cloaks, pulling them tighter against their bodies as they tried to protect themselves against the freezing cold.

Damien was grateful to Kendle for his foresight in purchasing the fur lined cloaks that he had made each of them pack in their equipment as they helped now to protect and save their bodies heat, without them he was certain that they would all already be human icicles.

At first, the snowfall that began was light but soon

more and more began to fall until so many flakes were falling that they obscured everyone's vision making it hard to see one another. A full-blown blizzard had begun to howl across the mountaintops like a screaming banshee.

In a voice that could be barely heard over the howling wind, Travis called a halt to the group under a rocky outcropping that acted like a somewhat shelter, protecting them momentarily from the stinging wind but not the freezing cold. The blademaster did a quick head count, making sure that everyone was still there, as he did this, Braden cried out over the wind that they were going to have to find some kind of indoor shelter soon or else they were all going to freeze to death out here.

"Aren't there any caves here in these mountains?" Alyssa asked Kendle, through chattering teeth, her normally red lips had turned blue from the cold.

Travis began to dig around in one of the packs and Damien asked. "What are you looking for? Can I help?"

Travis pulled out a long length of rope and held it up saying, "Everyone, feed this through your belt loops, it will help to keep any of us from getting lost in this." he said as he waved a hand at the snow, even as close as they were, all of them could barely see the gesture.

"Good idea, Travis." called out Logan, "I definitely wouldn't want to fall off of one of these ledges."

"Kendle," the blademaster said, "You take the lead, you have the most knowledge about these mountains and will be the best one of to see anything that might help or serve as shelter."

The dwarf nodded and moved back once again to the front of the line.

"Damien," the blademaster ordered, "you fall in behind Kendle and keep one of those spells of yours ready, preferably an incapacitating one."

Damien raised his eyebrows in puzzlement and asked before he could stop himself, "Why?" curious despite the cold about the order of the line.

It wasn't Travis who answered his question. Instead it was Caliban who spoke. "Why," he said as he said as he blew into his freezing hands trying to warm them, "well if we find a cave in this blizzard, it will probably be occupied by something else that is also hiding from the storm and might not like us taking away its shelter. If it's a bock or something like that we might even have a nasty fight on our hands."

Bocks like Kraals were another version of a creational magic creature. They were gigantic bears twice the size of a regular bear with an almost human like intelligence and vicious demeanor, which multiplied tenfold when one was woken up out of its sleep or disturbed, they too were sometimes made into pets by the Terian northmen.

"Oh!" said Damien rather sheepishly, "I see."

"Logan," Travis said, "You follow Damien."

"So I can be eaten third." Logan stated jokingly, which earned him a dark look from the blademaster and a barely stifled laugh from Alyssa and an outright one from Kendle. Mathis, Caliban and Braden said nothing at all. They just stayed huddled under their cloaks preserving their energy against the freezing cold and biting wind.

As they moved back out of the brief shelter of the rocky out cropping, the icy cold winds tore at them once again.

An hour later and Kendle still hadn't found them any sort of shelter, the blowing snow made finding any sort of landmarks difficult, but the dwarf was certain that there was a cave around here somewhere and if the group wanted any chance of surviving the night he knew that he had to find it.

He had once spent a summer up here in this exact location mining gems years ago, all he had to do now was find that same shafts entrance. He froze in place, stopping as the blowing snow parted briefly, but in that instant he saw something he recognized. Squinting hard into the wind, his reddish brown eyes searched the walls of rock.

Giving the rope a sharp tug, he set off in the direction where he thought he had seen something familiar. Five more feet further and he would have missed it altogether and they might have all perished in the freezing cold, but blessed be Garn's powers, he had found the shafts entrance in that brief moment of clearness in the blinding blowing snow.

It appeared to be no more than a large split in the cliff face itself but Kendle knew that this split was an entrance to a whole network of ancient dwarven shafts and mines that ran under the entire Annulith mountain range. He also knew that at one time long ago they had once led to Malfarra itself, the original home of the dwarves after the split from their Elvynn masters.

Behind the split in the mountains face was a cave, large enough for all of them all to fit in comfortably. Kendle thanked Garn once again for having showed him this spot, then he led the rest of the group inside of the mountain.

The cave that they had found appeared to be completely empty and not occupied by any thing else living other than them, which was a relief to them all for the cold had slowed them all down to the point where they might not have been able to fight off an attacker right now.

Kendle asked for some light and instantly two glowing balls flared into being as both Dámien and Alyssa cast simultaneous spells. The cave was also completely empty of the blinding snow and screaming wind too that was blowing outside of its entrance, but it still was bitterly cold.

The dwarf went about the cave for a moment searching then he let out a whoop of delight as he discovered a pile of ancient looking logs stacked in the corner.

"Damien," he called out, "lets use a little bit more of that magic of yours and get a fire going to dry us out and

A King's Quest

chase this chill from our bones and don't set yourself on fire while you are doing it." the dwarf added at the end with a chuckle that caused Logan to laugh and caused Alyssa, Braden, Mathis and even Caliban to look at the young battlemage curiously.

Damien threw a humorless sour glare at the dwarf then ignoring the others looks, hurried to comply. Soon a roaring fire lit the cave in an orange glow and filled it with warmth.

"What exactly is this place, Kendle?" asked Logan once his teeth had stopped chattering. He had been exploring the cave and had discovered a second entrance that looked like it had been cut into the side of the mountain by tools and went down deeper into blackness.

As they all moved over and huddled around the fire, taking in its warmth and heat, Kendle explained to them that it was an ancient dwarven waystation, put here when the dwarves ruled this entire range of mountains for this exact purpose.

He had found it on his mining quest years ago as a younger dwarf. All dwarven men when they reach the age that they are about to be considered adults are sent on a mining and treasure quest, where they go into the mountains to prove that they can indeed survive and to acquire any gems, jewels, or treasures that they can mine or find.

Damien knew a little about Kendle's quest, he had instead of mining the mountains, tried to raid the haunted Bryn Maw and Illsador, the Godshall, their final destination, of their treasures rather than spending months mining in the mountains searching for little or nothing. He had succeeded at one and failed at the other. This was how Damien knew that he had been expelled from Illsador by the guardian dragon protecting it personally. The Bryn Maw expedition was where he had acquired both his powerful magical Axehammer and the snow white slightly off center stripe in his beard. Every once in a while he would talk about his excursion into Illsador and of his encounter with the guardian dragon. But as to the Bryn Maw and about what happened to him there he always keeps a closed mouthed and stays tightlipped.

Knowing about this place told Damien that the dwarf must have actually done a little bit of some mining here in the mountains.

"In order for me to tell you about this place Logan," Kendle said gesturing at the mountains about them, "I have to tell you a little about some of my own history."

As Travis opened up their supply packs and started handing out dried beef and vegetables to all of them, Kendle Stonebreaker began his tale.

The thick-bodied dwarf motioned for them all to sit then explained to them that himself and his brother Beldrin were unique among dwarves and as far as he knew, they were the only ones of their kind in the entire realm.

What made the fierce dwarf so unique wasn't his reddish brown beard with its odd white stripe, or even his status as trade ambassador, which was a rare thing with dwarves, nor was it the fact that he was King Devlin's nephew. These things made him and his brother different but they didn't make them unique.

What made Kendle and his brother so unique was that they were dwarven crossbreeds, the only known two in existence in the entire realm.

A crossbreed is a dwarf that has both mountain dwarf and hill dwarf parents.

"What makes us so rare is that both races," Kendle explained to the group, "deliberately separated themselves from the other a little over a thousand years ago."

All were listening intently and it was Mathis who asked the obvious question, when the storytelling dwarf deliberately paused. "Why did the dwarves split?"

Kendle held up three thick fingers and counted them

off as he answered. "The first was distance, one race being in the far western edge of the realm and the other being in the southern most southeastern part. The second part was their ideas on lifestyles which were and still are distinctly different and third and most important was that they had a long time ago preferred it that way on both sides and wanted to separate.

The two races hadn't had anything to do with each other for four generations until my own father, Edrynn Stonebreaker, decided along with his brother Devlin, who is the Iron king of the mountain dwarves that it had been far to long since the dwarven nations had been separated without any contact and since my father had done such a good job at establishing trade routes with the Terian northmen who lived on the northern side of the Annulith mountains and with running things in Castlekeep, that he would be a logical choice to travel to the southern hills and reestablish contact and maybe some trade with their hill dwarf cousins in southern Alandria.

"My father," Kendle told them, "traveled to the south to the Starcrest Mountains and Hammer hill, the hill dwarves center of government where he was met with great affection by his southern cousins and decided to live with them for a while to better understand their culture. Edrynn, had never really liked the close confines of the mountain life and that had been what had prompted him in the first place to travel into the Terian Mountains and also into Castlekeep so much. He liked the southern dwarves lifestyle so much so that he moved in with the ruling family, accepted their name crest of Stonebreaker and worked at their forge. He fell in love with the head clan leader's daughter Heldra and married her, that union between mountain dwarf and hill dwarf produced me and my older brother Beldrin."

Kendle paused for a moment and noticed that all of them were staring at him as he told the story. Quickly he took a swig from his flask that he had fished out of his pocket and continued on, "The reason my father liked the southern dwarves so well is part of the reason there is this cave here.

Iron mountain dwarves or just mountain dwarves as they preferred to call themselves are a strict society like the ones that the ancient dwarves that lived here followed, where one follows the path laid out for him by his own birth. If your father's father's grandfather was a smith then more than likely you to would be a smith. Iron mountain dwarves unlike their southern cousins prefer mostly their own company, staying mainly in their mountain kingdom except to trade. They did do some trading with Castlekeep located south of their mountain kingdom and had been doing so for several hundred years with much success, my father opened relations with the Terians. Originally when the dwarves of the Iron Mountains had settled amongst the peaks, there had been only one dwarven city but over time the dwarves under the iron peaks flourished so much so that they had expanded their kingdom to make two smaller cities. Undergrounds rivers connected the three dwarven cities. All three of them used the same rivers to move goods out of the mountains and into the cities on both sides of the mountain for trade.

Both races of dwarves are actually the same race, all dwarves having been forged on the anvil of Garn, our god and creator according to them. Before the split in their race and after they had been freed from the Elvynn, all of the dwarves had once lived together under the Annulith mountains in the ancient and lost city of Malfarra, which means Silver City in the ancient dwarven tongue.

Now nearly two thousand years later and ten generations removed, Malfarra's meaning has changed to mean the dark city and it is a word used by both dwarven mothers and grandmothers to frighten misbehaving children. Dwarves don't speak of why we had to abandon and leave the silver city. All of original ancient dwarves had foresworn talking about why they had left their ancient home and had forbidden discussion about it to others. All though had fled the ancient home and had gone south to the southern most part of the realm, to the foothills of Alandria next to the Starcrest mountains.

The ancient dwarves had fled their mountain home in the middle of winter and only about half of their number survived the brutal winter and the journey south. Only a third survived the rest of the difficult winter. The ancient silver city dwarves gave up their mountain stronghold lifestyle of being one massive group and instead formed into many family clans each taking one of the many southern hills for their own. Like the ancient dwarven race they still maintained one ruling family, but also like the humans they also chose a council of the heads of each family to assist that ruler in making difficult decisions.

The biggest hill in the foothills was set aside for the ruling family and also served as the meeting place for the dwarves and festival hall. Each family clan maintained their family lifestyle and heritage. Next to the main hill was where the forging was done for trade purposes and they named this hill Hammer Hill, because at almost any time of the day on any day of the year you can always here the sound of hammers banging on steel. These hills saved the dwarves from extinction and gave them a place where they could begin anew, but after about five hundred years some of the dwarves became restless and longed once again for their homeland, they longed to feel as the old dwarven saying goes, the weight of the mountain on their shoulders. Also the Alandrian foothills where the dwarves now lived did not possess the ancient metal of mythryll that all dwarves prized. Mythryll was and still is the magical silver metal that the ancient dwarves had used to forge many a magical and powerful item or weapon like my Axehammer. Instead the foothills were rich with ores of iron and gems.

Sometimes a rare vein of mythryll could be found but these were nothing compared to the riches that could be had from the metals located under the ancient mountains. A group of the younger hill dwarves petitioned the council for permission to travel back to their ancient homeland and see what if any of their ancient city was still there, or to look for another suitable place in another mountain range.

These dwarves wanted to leave the hills and go back to the mountains and the old lifestyles. The council elected instead to send out three parties, two to search out a new mountain home if possible and one to search out their ancient home in the Annulith Mountains. The two search parties that went to search out suitable locations for a new dwarven settlement in the mountains returned saying that they had found a location in the far west in the Iron Peak mountains where my uncle is now king. Of the third search party that had gone to Malfarra nothing was ever heard from them again. The place where we are now is one of the remains of that ancient dwarven homeland."

"So you're saying that the end of this tunnel might lead to the ancient dwarven treasure city of Malfarra?" asked Logan, his green eyes going bright with excitement.

"No," answered Kendle curtly in a serious sounding voice, "I know where this tunnel leads, the ones that go to Malfarra only lead to death." he said this last part with such foreboding in his voice that you could actually see the light die in Logan's eyes.

It didn't take very long for the companions to fall asleep after the dwarf finished with his tale. They were all exhausted, both physically and mentally from the day's journey through the mountains and the snow.

In the morning Damien was the first to be roused by Travis. "It's time to move, we must leave here," the blademaster said before he moved on to wake up another of their sleeping companions.

Still feeling like he was asleep or hadn't even slept at

all, Damien gathered his belongings and stood up in the darkness of the cave.

Mathis went over to the entrance they came though the night before, only to find it completely iced over from top to bottom. Turning back to the others he announced that they were snowed in.

Everyone went over and examined the icy wall, it gleamed silver and red with the fires light.

Travis turned to Kendle and asked, "Do you think that you could break a hole through it?"

Kendle glanced over at Travis and said as he shrugged his powerful shoulders, "Won't know till I try." then he motioned for all of them to step back away from the frozen ice wall and pulled out his axehammer. Lightly almost reverently he ran his fingers over the rune of Garn inscribed on the top of the silver mythryll weapon. A light blue glow began to emanate from the head then it spread out over the whole weapon until it was completely covered and pulsed with the glowing light. Kendle wrapped his hands into the weapons leather straps, gripping it tightly with his strong hands, he drew back his arms as far as he could and swung the mighty weapon at the icy wall. A ringing bell like sound filled the domed chamber and echoed off of the stone around them as the weapon struck, nothing else happened at first, then slowly a massive crack split down the center of the ice wall, spreading out in myriad spider web like cracks.

Quickly the dwarf jumped back as the frozen wall collapsed inward, large chunks of shattered ice rolled out across the floor as a wave of snow poured into the dome like cave. After the snow stopped there was a small speck of light shining in through a narrow little opening high up at the top.

"I got rid of the wall but it would appear that we are still snowed in." growled the dwarf irritably as he looked upwards to the small splinter of light coming in through the hole.

"I could melt us a way out," offered Damien, looking between the dwarf and the blademaster and creating a spark of fire on his fingertips. "and I won't set myself or anyone else on fire either."

"It wouldn't do us any good," returned Kendle grinning, "if there is this much snow in here, I'm sure the rest of the mountain is covered with just as much on all of its trails."

"So what options does that leave us?" asked Alyssa.

"Not many," returned Kendle, "We can either stay here and hope that the snow melts before we starve to death or we can take our chances going through the mountains insides."

"Didn't you say that the dwarven city of death from which no explores or glory seekers have ever returned, lies within this mountain." stated Caliban as he looked skeptically at the dwarf through his slate blue eyes then back to the dark forbidding hole.

Kendle returned the look with a foreboding nod, but as he did so he also withdrew a dagger and knelt. Using the daggers tip, the dwarf drew a ragged circle in the earth in front of him explaining that this was the mountain range that they were in. He made a dot on the northern edge of the circle saying that here was about where they were, then he drew two more precise circles on the inside of the first, in the exact center of the roughly drawn outer circles he drew another smaller one. Then he connected the two outer circles to the smaller circle in the center with spokes like a wagon wheel.

"Actually as long as we stick to this," Kendle stabbed at the outer circle with the dagger, "we should be fairly safe. My ancestors set up these mountain way stations in such a manner that you could go around or through the entire mountain range. I have passed through the outer loop. With the exception of one particularly nasty spot where an underground river flows through the mountain, which makes the passage a bit narrow, there is no danger. It's either through there," Kendle pointed a thick finger at the back entrance to the cave, "where we could possibly make it to the Illsador exit in a day and not freeze to death, or out there," he indicated with his other hand, "where it could take three or four more days and we might freeze to death in the meantime."

Travis looked first over to Braden then on to Damien, who responded by saying, "You told me at the beginning of this journey that time was of the essence, if we were to be in Kallamar before Seth's eighteenth naming day."

He said this in such a serious manner that it caused Caliban to turn and look at him oddly. For a moment, the imposter had almost sounded and looked like the royal regent in a way and had spoken this statement like he really was a true heir to the throne.

Logan, who had always seemed to have a fascination with maps, was bent down low over the one that Kendle had drawn in the dirt and was studying it. "Is this in the center," he asked looking up at Kendle, "Is that Malfarra?"

"Yes," came Kendle's one word answer. It was as plain as the bulbous nose on his face that he did not want to discuss the long dead dwarven city anymore.

Logan though wasn't actually interested in the dead city, instead he asked the dwarf, if he could tell him the locations of the other way stations that exited out of the mountains.

Kendle knelt back down next to Logan and began pointing out the locations to him that opened up next to Illsador, the Elvynn swamps of Edgemoor near Embry and the southern exits that led to Westlake, Kallamar and the Citadel.

Damien, somehow felt a bit of tension around him and turned to find Alyssa standing near the entrance into the mountain, staring at it apprehensively.

A.V. Wedhorn

Remembering the way that she had acted on the ledge above water and what she had said about not liking narrow places, he gave her a reassuring smile and placed a comforting hand on her shoulder as he said. "We will all be in the same place together."

Chapter 26
Ghosts

Both Cassica Essen and Jados Lodry studied the looming mountain range on the other side of the Bryn Maw. A massive amount of heavy grey snow clouds had moved over the top of the Annulith Mountains, obliterating them from sight. Cassica knew from the looks of those clouds that a blizzard had to be tearing its way through the passes filling them with snow.

She silently hoped that Damien and the companions with him were okay. Lord Gildon had informed her and only her who he truly was and where it was that they were heading. She had been thrilled and pleased to hear this. During their time at the academe she had worked very closely with the other slightly younger battlemage and unbeknownst to him, she was actually quite fond of him, with his amazing memory and gentle self-assurance and confident manner.

The first time she had met him was when he had had

two black eyes and a swollen mouth from a beating he had received somehow. He had refused to tell her or anyone else about it including the academes headmasters when they questioned him. The beating though hadn't killed any of the fire that burned inside of him and somehow she had known then in that first instant that Damien Daverge was someone special.

Lord Gildon had confirmed those same thoughts when he revealed his true lineage to her.

There had been nothing yesterday that she could have done to slow the knight's passage into the mountain ranges. She hoped that the snow didn't slow down the others enough to allow the knights and her to catch them. She knew where it was that they were heading but she wasn't going to reveal that information to the rest of the pursuing knights in her party. Her orders from Lord Gildon, was to stop the knights if they got too close, somehow. She had no desire to hurt or harm any of these men with her who thought that they were just doing their honorable duty by trying to capture a murderess that had killed a hero of the realm.

Jados Lodry once set on the correct trail by the Royal Regents advisor, Lord Cyadine, who had told them that he had received a report saying that a group that matched the description of the one that they were chasing was headed towards the Bryn Maw and the Annulith mountains, had set off like a hunting hound on a scent.

That was how they now found themselves standing in the early morning light at the edge of the red stained rocks that marked the entrance to the day long pass and haunted battlefield of the Bryn Maw, listening to the sounds of the past nights battle fade away with the coming of the early morning dawn.

There was little sign of the bloody battle that had been fought here slightly over two thousand years ago called the Endwar, at least during the daylight hours, other than the dark red blood stained rocks that filled the pass, but as Cassica passed over the unseen boundary that marked its entrance, she felt her skin begin to crawl as if something unseen was barely touching her. It also felt to her like she could almost the hear voices of the undead soldiers shouting out indistinct orders in her ears like a low buzzing of unseen bees and the muted clash of weapons seemed to fill the air at times about her. Glancing about at the knights that were alongside her, she saw that they too had looks of unease on their features and were hearing and feeling the same things.

Neither could she see anything of the weapons of power that were rumored to fill the pass as she scanned the ground with her golden brown eyes, but she also knew from her lessons at the academe, most weren't revealed until after nightfall when the indistinct voices and screams that she was hearing as whispers on the wind would become real again as the forces that died here began fighting again their same never ending nightly battle.

Halfway through the day they reached the midway point of the Maw, the red rocks all about them had changed slowly to a deeper stained dark black, this was she knew, where the most blood had been spilt. It was here where the bloodstained rocks were almost black that the group of knights and Cassica heard the sounds of someone moaning and crying ahead of them.

This sound was clear in quality, instead of muted and indistinct and you could actually here the anguish and sorrow in its tone as the sobs filled the canyon and echoed off the walls.

The color drained out of the read headed battlemages face at the sound, Cassica had learnt her lessons well at the academe and knew the legends and rumors that were associated with this deadly and haunted place. According to her masters in Westlake there were only two reasons that true sound could be heard in the Maw and night had yet to fall for it to be the sounds of battle.

"By the Gods," breathed Jados next to her, his eyes filling with fear and uncertainty, "what or who is making that horrible sounding noise?"

"Are you sure that you really want to find out?" asked Cassica warily, as she looked ahead to the turn in pass from where the unseen figure or thing making the sounds was coming from.

Krannion knights had little to do with things that didn't pertain to honor, weapons, or warfare, things supernatural in nature either magical or unexplainable caused them to feel unease, they relied heavily on battlemages or clerics of Dar to handle such things for them.

Now here in the Bryn Maw, surrounded by the unseen ghosts of the undead and the muted sounds of an ancient battle that had spilt more blood than all wars ever combined, they all looked to her for any sign of reassurance.

"Sometimes," she thought to herself as she felt a shiver of fear run through her and she tried not to show it, "men can be such babies."

All of the knights watched with trepidation in their eyes as Cassica said the words to both a whiperwalk spell and a cloaking spell that prevented others from seeing or hearing them and cast both about herself and the rest of the party. Everyone slid their weapons silently out of their sheathes as they slowly advanced around the turn.

A powerfully built large man with copper colored hair tied in a long braid sat on one of the blackest rocks in the Maw, his body was sagging forward and his head was clasped in his hands as he sobbed into them. Another body lay on the ground at his feet. This one was a very beautiful woman with pale blonde hair and cold features still in deaths embrace. Cassica saw that a slash of a talisman sword had ripped her armor open at the chest, delivering the deadly blow to the heart a thousand years earlier.

The grieving man's sobbing and wailing stopped the instant that the party's eyes fell on him and he raised his head up out of his hands, looking at them through copper colored eyes that matched the color of his hair, despite the two spells that Cassica had cast.

"Humans," said the voice that came out of the man's mouth. It cracked with power and caused them all to cringe fearfully, some of the knights even stepped backwards away from the force in the voice that seemed to fill the air about them and echoed almost violently off of the stone.

It was immediately obvious as the figure rose to his feet and the stone cracked and shattered underneath his boots, that this was no ordinary man in front of them.

He was taller than any of the tallest knights around her and his features were handsome, but there was a look of cruelty to them also, he looked sort of Elvynn in a way. The deep set copper eyes burned like hot coals set into his face as he regarded them angrily.

"What do you want humans?" he demanded harshly, "Come to gloat over a god in the pangs of his sorrows over the injustice of his beloveds death?" undisguised malevolence sounded in his voice and the force of the words hurt their ears.

The Krannion knights all about Cassica, now too realized who this figure mourning in the maw was and all but sub commander Lodry shrunk back a few more steps, fearfully away from the tall figure. Jados despite the being that faced them stood firm beside the female battlemage as the met the stare of the grieving god of war and power Olanntian, mourning over his lost love, the long dead goddess of beauty, Ishmyra.

Here was the god himself in avatar form walking on Tyrus.

Slowly Cassica sheathed her swords then with her hands held up showing that she held no other weapons or meant no harm, like she could really hurt a god anyway she thought to herself, she stepped forward. Jados did the same but unlike her, he kept his hand clenched tightly on the leather wrapped hilt of his sword.

Softly in an almost pleading voice the young red headed female battlemage knelt and apologized to the god of war and power for disturbing him in his time of mourning, saying that she was sorry for interrupting.

The face of the god who had fathered the Elvynn race as the first race of Tyrus, turned to granite like stone and he asked again what it was that they wanted and why were they here.

Now his manner was neither friendly nor hostile and this more than his anger caused a sense of fear to rise up inside of Cassica, she looked over to the Krannion knight standing boldly beside her swallowed and answered.

"My Lord, we are tracking a murdering cleric of Dar and a group of possible assassins who might be with her."

A displeased look showed on the gods face at the mention of his kinsman's name, whom he also blamed for the loss of his love lying on the cold stone earth at his feet, then his expression changed from one of sorrow to one of almost pure pleasure and delight.

"Did you just say that one of Dar's children is responsible for a murder, a female one?" the gods eyes were ablaze now with a fire of a different sort as he focused them intently on the female battlemage.

Before she could blink or any of the knights could react in her defense, the Elvynn god of war and power was beside her, grabbing her arm in his power filled grasp. Cassica cried out in pain and tried desperately to pull away from his touch, which caused a feeling like liquid fire to wash through her whole being, her insides writhed and twisted in searing agony.

"Yes!" she gasped as she kept squirming in his grasp, trying to shrink away from his painful touch.

Jados Lodry had seen enough and charged the god with

his sword drawn and sent its keen edge sweeping straight at his head.

Almost casually, Olanntian raised his other hand and froze him in mid swing with a word of power, not even deigning to recognize the attack for what it was. Then he turned back to Cassica and spoke.

"You're a battlemage aren't you?" the god asked. "One of Syreena's warriors trained to defeat my prized Tua-Latin war wizards in combat."

Cassica knew that she could not lie to this god being, so she simply said "yes!"

"Good, good," said the god as he smiled almost wickedly, "you show a lot of strength and I think you will need it soon. What you have told me about this female cleric of Dar is very good news indeed. There has not been one since Ellanine, the battle queen. Maybe," the god said almost to low to be heard even by Cassica who was right next him, "this marks the end. Or the beginning again"

Focusing his attention back on her he told her to stop struggling against what she was feeling as the burning that began again in her this time even worse than the first. "You are being given a gift female battlemage, this news that you have revealed to me is the best thing that I have heard in two eons. For you and you only," the god of war and power told her, "I am lifting the curse that is over this place whether it is day or night, you may as long as you live and don't interfere with anything that occurs here, pass through the Bryn Maw, completely unmolested and unharmed. If you elect to interact with any of the accursed souls in the valley, you forfeit your invulnerability to the curse until the next morning and have to battle the spirits of the dead the same as any other mortal caught in here after dark." The god pointed a finger at her warningly and said, "Remember this though, you will still be able to see the tragedies and horrors that occurred here," as he said this his eyes fell back to the body lying on the cold blood stained stone of the valley floor. "Those memories," he continued, "might still leave you scarred for life like myself, but no weapon or no spirit in here will be able to cause you any harm unless you allow it to happen from here on."

The copper haired god then released both Cassica from his grip and Jados from his power and they both crashed heavily down onto the rocky blood stained earth.

Olanntian turned and pointed a finger at the far horizon, opposite from where they had entered and said almost casually to Jados, "You had all better hurry, for only the battlemage has been given my gift, the rest of you will still suffer your own fate if you are caught here after the sun fades."

Jados, Cassica and the rest of the knights turned their heads to follow the gods pointing finger. All of them were alarmed to discover that the sun that had only been barely midway across the sky when they had came upon the mourning god, was now three quarters of the way across it and would soon touch the other horizons edge.

As they all turned back as one to glare at the God who had delayed them for what had seemed like only a few moments, but what must have been several hours, they saw that he was gone from the blood stained valley, but his mirthless laugh filled the air about them.

Cassica realized then that the hate filled god had deliberately delayed them. Olanntian harbored a well known hatred for the Krannion knights order that bordered on the edge of insanity. Doral Markennan the first free king was who had killed the goddess Ishmyra, the stunningly beautiful lady, Cassica assumed was who was lying on the ground at their feet, with a vorpyll talisman creational sword. He had also founded the Krannion knights to help in protecting the people of the realm. The God of war and power, might have given her the gift of free passage through the valley, but unless they all hurried towards the other end, he had doomed the rest of the knights with her to a night filled with battle and possibly sentenced them to eternal death in the valley.

Knowing that they didn't possess much time, the group of knights and the female battlemage rode their mounts as swiftly through the valley as the mountainous terrain allowed them to.

The setting sun now seemed to be racing against them towards the horizon and the tall mountains shadows that loomed on both sides of the valley started to stretch towards them like long dark groping fingers trying to catch them and pull them into the night.

The darker it got, the more distinct the voices, screams and shouts of the long dead ghosts that filled the valley became in their ears, no longer sounding like the droning of buzzing bees.

Misty figures and shadowy wraiths began to coalesce in the air about the group, a ghostly sword not yet fully formed cut at one of the knights and he gasped as the blade passed through both his enchanted armor and his body, the knight himself was unharmed but his face had turned white with fear and his eyes looked panicked.

Jados rode his mount up alongside of Cassica and over the ringing of their iron-shod hooves on the bloodstained rocks called out to her.

"Is there anything that you can do before the darkness fully sets, magically to get us out of this or here before we all possibly die?" He knew as well as she did that, thanks to the treacherous god they definitely weren't going to make it to the end of the valley before darkness set. If not for their run in with Olanntian, they would have made it out with plenty of time to spare and the concern for his men's lives under him was etched on Jados' facial features.

Cassica's mind raced through all of her options, she wasn't able yet to open a doorway or portal, the fiery means of traveling distances was still a ways beyond her abilities, if she did even try, there was more of a chance that the fire that burned the hole in fabric of space, would more than likely consume her instead. It was possible though for her to teleport herself three times and that might get her to the edge of the Bryn Maw and to safety, but she could only manage herself and two others, that would still leave the other nine knights in the valley having to fight their way out. She told all of this to the knight's commander, who shook his head disheartedly.

"I can," Cassica offered, "cast several defensive spells that might aid you after the sun sets."

"No!" Jados said adamantly shaking his head at her side to side, "save your spells, you might need them before this night is over, our magically protected armor will serve to protect us all the same. In fact I'm ordering you not to interfere with us at all," as Cassica started to protest, he cut her off by adding. "You are the only one who is allowed to go through here unharmed and if we should all fall in the battle to come, somebody needs to continue our mission and also inform our families of our passing."

Cassica knew that the knight was right but she found it hard to accept his foreboding words, they went against both her training and her nature, but grudgingly she finally relented and agreed.

The figures that had started out as misty wraiths and ghostly forms began to solidify as the sun dropped behind the mountains and shrouded the land in darkness.

The first of the solid undead that truly materialized was a cadre of ancient Elvynn cavalry carrying a banner pole with a silver swan on a black background hanging from it. The moment that the fully formed undead Elvynn soldiers saw the human knights, they dropped their steel headed war lances into fighting positions and charged.

Krannion knights have been training on how to defeat Elvynn fighting forces for almost two thousand years, in much the same manner as battlemages trained to defeat the Tua-latin creational war wizards and it showed now as the

Elvynn cadre of twenty cavalry charged straight ahead in a wedge formation at the knights.

Jados Lodry held his knights in a tight formation until almost the last moment then when it was too late for the Elvynn soldiers to break out of their charge. The sub commander barked out an order and the knights around him swept out into a v formation on both sides of the charging cavalry with swords drawn. Sweeping back in with their swords swinging before the Elvynn cavalry could alter their attack and mount a proper defense, they hacked the unprepared Elvynn cavalry soldiers to pieces.

Out of instinct and training, Cassica started to work on casting a spell to help the knights. A gauntleted fist smashed hard into the side of her head, disrupting her casting and almost throwing her from the saddle. Before she even managed to reseat herself, she had both of her short swords drawn and in her hands as she rounded on her unseen attacker accompanied by the whistling of her blades in the air.

Jados Lodry pulled sharply back on the reigns of his horse and watched as the two short swords sliced through the space in the air where his head had been the moment before. Then he shook his head at her and reminded her of what he had said earlier about someone having to live to go after the ambassador's murderer and tell their families if they fell here tonight. With a more subdued reaction Cassica resheathed her swords.

As the knights finished off the cadre of Elvynn cavalry, more battle filled screams erupted all about them, as one the group turned to find themselves almost in the middle of another battle. Thousands of arrows filled the sky over their heads and screams of pain filled the air on both sides of the party as the wooden missiles began a rain of deadly death.

Cassica watched in helpless horror as one of the Krannion knights fell to the earth dead, as an arrow from overhead found the slit in his visor. She could have very easily cast a shield spell large enough to protect them all from the deadly barrage but both the gods warning and the plea and pain in her head from Jados' fist kept her from doing so.

Jados Lodry ordered everyone else to form around him and then he led them closer to the valleys walls, hoping that most of the fighting would stay out on the valley floor itself where there was a lot more room to maneuver troops.

Cassica looked all around her and could see battle lines and formations being drawn and formed on both sides of the small group.

A horns shrill blast tore through the air and rolling waves of undead men, halflings and dwarves surged forward to meet the undead Elvynn forces. The two armies crashed together in a spectacular display of weapons and bodies and in mere moments it was nothing but a tangled bloody mass hacking at one another. Horses could be heard screaming over the clang of metal on metal as the smell of the blood assaulted and filled the beast's nostrils and filled them with fear. Every once in a while Cassica thought she also heard a Mar cat's mighty roar also tear the air with its fierce sound.

A group of Elvynn men and woman all dressed in black robes trimmed in silver stepped forward out of the enemy ranks and Cassica felt the urge to help out again as the Tua-Latin creational war wizards started to do their spellcasting. Fireballs and lightening bolts flew upwards out of the wizard's hands and soared into the ranks of men, exploding in loud destructive booms of heat and fire. The lines of free men wavered under the Tua-Latin's magical barrage but did not break and they continued to press on press on forward.

Behind her Cassica heard the sound of metal on metal and she turned to find her own knights engaged in another battle with some Elvynn soldiers trying to outflank the human forces. Not able to do a thing to help she watched in horror as two more of her companions fell to the earth dead and lifeless.

Cassica had never witnessed the type of carnage that she was seeing now. Even though she had trained for this sort of thing in the battlemages dome in Westlake and had thought herself properly prepared, nothing was like what she saw here now with the charred blackened bodies fused with melted armor lying in scattered piles everywhere that the fireballs and lightening bolts had struck. The smell of burnt flesh and dead bodies almost overwhelmed her senses and the screams of the wounded and dying filled her ears. She knew from her studies at the academe that soon would come waves of gas and waves of lightening rather than bolts from the Elvynn wizards. She wondered where were the humans own mages or the Elvynn ones who had opted to side with the humans, like Aldine Fallbrook or Toriass Shanasar, who had came to the besieged humans aid and had killed almost all of the creational war wizards fighting here in the Endwar, then she remembered that they had survived the battle at Bryn Maw and only the dead who had died here fought tonight.

Jados had ordered everyone including herself to abandon their horses, claiming that they drew attention to them and if they wanted to make it out of the valley alive, the less attention their way the better. All of the knights had positioned themselves along the mountainside walls with their swords facing outwards and were actually making good time until Cassica heard a low rumbling roar over their heads followed by several sharp hisses.

A group of Elvynn Marcat riders had positioned themselves on the wall and were now launching themselves out over the knights and dropping down amongst them. Marcats were gigantic cats that weighed well over a thousand pounds and were as big as a large horse and can easily carry a man or two on their backs. They are extremely dangerous due to their lightening like speed and agility, razor sharp claws and needle like long fangs. Like all types of cats there are no places that a Marcat can't climb or jump to and right now these were jumping off of the cliff sides above and landing on the knights below them.

Jados screamed for Cassica to keep moving as the large cats tore into the knights on the ground. On foot without their horses, the sub commander knew that him and his men were doomed against the speed of the cats.

One of the giant beasts landed directly on top of one of the knights. As he collapsed under its weight, the giant cats razor like claws tore and raked at the mans enchanted armor, leaving gouges and furrows on shiny steel surface of the armor, though it seemed unable to pierce its protections. The battle trained cat changed tactics and its jaws and fangs locked on the man's neck and head instead. The giant cat shook the knight like a mouse, snapping his neck instantly. The other knights kept trying to mount an effective attack against the Marcat riders, but being on foot rather than on horseback put them at a serious disadvantage against the far faster and more nimble creatures.

Every time one of the knights would thrust a sword at one of the armored cats, it would either bounce sideways out of the way, or leap high into the air over the knight's head and rake at him with its sharp knife size claws. Two more knights fell from this type of attack while Cassica watched before Jados screamed at her again to leave. He knew that they were outmatched. More would fall the longer that the fight progressed. Against the faster beasts, escape would be impossible if they tried to run away.

With hot tears of rage over the unwanted deaths of the knights in her eyes, she cursed the reason that they were here and the ones who had sent them to their deaths, she did not blame Damien or his companions for the knights falling about her, because she knew the truth. She blamed instead the royal regent for his lies and subterfuge that had led them here and she would if she survived this make sure that the knight's families knew the real truth.

The six remaining knight's were pinned up against the stone wall with their swords pointed outward again trying their best to hold the Marcat riders at bay.

Cassica swore loudly and regardless of her safety, she started to return and offer assistance when her eyes met those of the sub commander's staring past the riders directly into her own. There was a pleading, begging look in them as he motioned for her to go on. He knew that they would die here tonight and in that one look he communicated to Cassica that it didn't matter to him or the other knight's, they had trained all of their lives to die in combat, but they didn't want to be responsible for her dying also.

Giving the square jawed determined looking Jados Lodry a final look of understanding and with a heavy heart, Cassica Essen turned away from the fighting knights and fled, running as fast as her feet would carry her towards the end of the valley.

It took her longer than she expected and as she reached the end of the valley the first rays of the morning sun started back over the edge of the mountains sending the dark shadows away and the cursed ghosts back into the past, with she was certain, bearing the souls of the knights that had been with her. Cassica felt completely drained of all her strength as she stumbled out of the blood stained rocks in her own blood stained clothes, alone now and all by herself in the wilderness of the Annulith mountain range, she collapsed onto the plain brown stone on her knees and sobbed uncontrollably into her hands over the loss of the knights as the morning sun rose.

A.V. Wedhorn

Chapter 27
Death and Dragons

    The farther under and into the mountain that the group went, the more and more the darkness around them got blacker. Even the light from the spells that that Damien and Alyssa had cast seemed to be dimmed somewhat by the almost impenetrable blackness of the deep mountain. The temperature though changed in a way, gone was the freezing icy cold that was on the outside of the mountain, replaced instead by a dark sort of cold that felt different but went along with the blackness that almost seemed to creep into ones soul.
    Alyssa hated these narrow confined spaces like this, they scared her and she longed for the open sky, she was determined though not to let the others know of her fears, she knew that they were irrational but that did little to lessen them. Clerics of Dar were supposed to be brave in the face of all dangers and never to look weak. She prayed a small comforting prayer to her god and immediately felt a

A King's Quest

sense of peace sweep through her, strengthening her resolve and hardening her determination. With the help of her god and the strength he gave her, Alyssa knew then that she would make it.

Kendle seemed to feel nothing of the despair that filled the others and led them on with no occurrences for several hours through the mountain, following the ancient tunnels that the old dwarves had laid out on his map to get to the way stations the group made good time. They had to detour though and go deeper into the mountain, farther than what Kendle had wanted to, all the way to the second inner loop on the wheel map that he had drawn in the rocky soil up above, due to a tunnel collapse. A slight buzzing sound began to emanate from the tunnel along with a slight vibration moving along the rock when they reached a certain section of the deeper tunnel. The farther they went, the louder the noise became until it was a reverberating roar and the rocks now seemed to be constantly vibrating with the sound.

"What's going on," shouted Logan over the roar that was filling the tunnel, "what in the world is making all of that noise?"

"Hold on a minute more and you will see." returned Kendle back over his shoulder.

The group had reformed their order when they had set out from above and rather than being near the front, Logan and Caliban, their newcomer was pulling up the rear, Kendle was leading followed by Damien, then Travis, Braden Mathis and Alyssa.

The dwarf rounded a bend in the tunnel and informed Damien and Alyssa in a loud voice that they could extinguish their lights. Logan, Damien noticed as he dispelled the light ball that had been following them was wearing his earring still that allowed him to see in the blackest of night clearly.

The moment that the light was extinguished a glow

began to illuminate from the stone about them, they entered behind the dwarf, another large round chamber, this one though wasn't like the ones above them though.

The loud roaring noise that they had all been hearing for some time was revealed as they all entered.

A luminescent moss filled what appeared to be a large underground cave that had been hollowed out by an underground river that flowed through the mountain. The river had hollowed out a softer section of the rock in this part of the mountain and a large whirlpool had been formed.

The path that the companions had been following ran around it, about twenty feet above the swirling black water. A misty spray filled the air as much the sound of the roaring of the water did. The sound wouldn't hurt them but the mist from the underground river made the narrow path that they all had to walk around extremely wet and slippery.

"This is madness," Damien shouted loudly, over the rushing whirlpool below into the dwarf's ear next to him.

Kendle shot him a sidelong glance, "it's the only way through, unless you want to go back out into that blizzard and try your luck as a human icicle."

Damien shook his head no, he knew that the dwarf was right but that didn't stop the feeling of apprehension that went through him though as he looked down at the rapidly swirling black water.

"Stay close to the wall," shouted Kendle to the rest of the group, "the path can sometimes get a little bit slippery and be careful where you place your feet, the water has thinned some of the stone in places. We will go through one at a time just in case"

Everyone nodded in agreement and following the dwarf's example, stayed as close to the wall as possible as they made their way across the worn away stone walkway.

Logan was the last to come across and it was then that

the stone decided to give way under his feet. With a loud grinding noise, the stone pathway under the sandy blonde haired thief cracked, splintered and fell away into the black water. Caliban reacting out of instinct being the next to the last across and the closest to the spythief dove towards the falling man and just before he fell completely away with the stones tumbling towards the swirling water, caught him hand in hand their fingers interlocking together in a death grip.

Not knowing exactly why he had dove to the edge of the crumbling path, Caliban looked down into the green eyes of the mans hand that he had caught and was holding on to, just inches away from his death, remembering his fathers words about if he could make any of the deaths look like an accident that he could commit, he was to do it. Screaming for Logan to hold on the white haired assassin mage acted like he was trying to find purchase on the rock with the fingers of his other hand, then as his own slate blue eyes met those of the green eyed man in his grasp again he slowly let him slip away out of his grasp.

As the others raced over regardless of the danger to lend a hand in assisting the white haired young man he let out a frantic scream, shouting "No!" as the sandy haired young man dropped away into air, plummeting downward towards the black water.

Damien saw his friend fall and started to say the words to a spell that he thought might save him but before he could finish, the young spythief's body plunged into the black swirling waters. They closed over Logan's head and he was gone.

Caliban lay there on the ledge with his hand still hanging over the edge. He kept repeating the words, no, no, no, over and over again.

As the dwarf and the blademaster came gingerly over to where Caliban was lying, they pulled him away from the broken away ledge, the assassin mage knew that he had successfully succeeded in making the party that had left from Castlekeep one member less.

A despairing black pall settled over the group as they made their way through the rest of the mountain. Damien kept asking Kendle as he fought back the tears that threatened to erupt out him, if he knew where the whirlpool let out at and if there was anyway that they could follow it to see if it was possible that Logan might have survived.

Kendle had steadfastly refused, saying that to go any deeper in the mountain would endanger them all and that there was no way that Logan could survived the rocky spin through the whirlpool swirling waters.

The saddened group finally reached the way station that Kendle told them opened up near Illsador and they entered another domed rock chamber much like the one they had spent the night before in with their heads hanging low and in joyless silence.

Travis finally turned to the young battlemage and said gently but firmly, "We cannot go back after him Damien, I feel as bad as you do about losing Logan, but there is nothing that we can do. Any deeper in the mountain leads to Malfarra and no one has ever gone near there since the dwarves left and lived to tell the tale. Going after Logan's possibly live but more than likely dead body would endanger your own well being as well as the rest of us, but if you die then the rest of the realm falls too and as much as it pains me to say this you have a duty and a responsibility to the rest of the people in the realm and that can't be put aside for the sake of only one individual."

Damien heard the words that Travis was saying and knew that the blademaster was right, he had also learnt the same under the tutelage of Tiko, but this did nothing to lessen the feelings of loss and pain that was inside of him. Whirling around angrily he stalked to the far end of the cave, away from the others to be by himself for a while, tears stinging in his dark blue eyes.

Travis watched him go, he too knew how it felt to lose somebody close to him. He had lost both of his best friends and his whole family because of his own failings in his younger life. Logan's missing seemed strange, his cutting and witty remarks about danger always seemed to lighten the mood, the lack of concern by the younger man had irritated him to the point where he had at times wanted to strangle the young thief, but now that he was gone he too found himself missing the sandy haired young man who had always seemed to be able to make light of any situation even in the direst of circumstances.

Right before the rest of the party settled into their bedrolls, Kendle went over and sat beside Damien who was staring off into nothingness. He looked into the young battlemages tear filled red-rimmed dark blue eyes as they turned towards him and said in a melancholy voice. "I'm sorry lad, so sorry I blame myself in a way, I should have made us tie up or something, anything that would have kept him from falling into that whirlpool."

Damien breathed a large sigh he could see that by the expression on the dwarfs face and knew that he was taking Logan's loss hard and said solemnly, "The gods must have wished it Kendle, or else it wouldn't have happened. Maybe if they also wish it there might be a slim chance that Logan might still be alive."

Kendle tried to smile a reassuring smile that might give Damien hope but he felt little inside himself. He hadn't told the others, but the dwarves that had been sent to Malfarra, five hundred years ago had been the very best of the best of them and none had returned. He held very little hope that a city street thief no matter how talented or cunning Logan was, could survive under the mountain alone if he was somehow still alive, especially with what lived in the dead city.

The exit to this waystation wasn't quite as snowed over as the one they had left behind yesterday and they easily dug their way out.

The first rays of sunshine that struck their eyes after being in the darkness for so long blinded Damien and the others with him. Icy snow covered everything and icicles gleamed brightly under the cold yellow sun, which even though it was bright to their eyes emitted no warmth whatsoever.

Kendle studied the terrain about them and announced that they were now less than three quarters of a day away from the Godshall.

Damien also turned to study what was called the Highland Rim. The Annulith mountains ended on the far side against what appeared to be a large plateau thrust up out of the earth by a giant hand or something, as he looked out over the vast expanse of flat almost uninhabitable land, he knew that if he stood at either end he could look down into either the Terian lands, or back behind him and almost over the mountains themselves into his own realm of Kallamar and the fourteen kingdoms. Very little lived on the expanse of flat land that marked Illsador, due to its remote and rocky location.

The young battlemage started to call Logan's attention to the sight but stopped halfway through his name as he remembered that his boyhood best friend wasn't with them any longer and was probably dead.

Alyssa saw the bright look and unfinished name both die on the battlemages face and in his eyes and went over to him and like he had done for her before they had entered the confines of the tunnels, she laid a reassuring and comforting hand on his shoulder.

Damien turned and smiled a wan smile back at her and said. "Thank you."

Kendle once again led the way but this time as he did so he complained constantly to anyone who was near him and when they weren't he continued to let out a murmured stream of curses and protests about why they shouldn't be here doing this, all to no avail.

The reasons behind his protests though, the dwarf would not make clear to Alyssa and would clam up tight every time he was questioned about it by her, at least for a while before he began grumbling anew. Finally Damien who couldn't contain his mirth any longer about the dwarf's protests told the female cleric about how Kendle had been caught inside of and had been expelled from Illsador by the Guardian dragon for attempting to steal items of value from there while on his mining quest.

Kendle threw a dark glare back over his shoulder at Damien that spoke volumes and now Alyssa also started laughing.

As the sun started to move closer to the horizon, Damien saw the massive structure begin to rise up in the distance. Illsador, or the Godshall as it was also called, was a monument to craftsmanship, erected by the god Hurgal the builder himself.

Even from this far away distance they could all see the massive pillars that marked the front of the building where all of the rulers of Kallamar had been buried since Doral Markennan himself and the place where the gods themselves walked in avatar form when they were here on Tyrus.

The Godshall itself was monumental in size and looked as if it had sprung directly up out of the rocky earth around it. The closer that they approached the larger it grew in size. Gigantic stone statues armed with large stone swords marked the arched entranceway into the hall. Legend spoke that if the Guardian dragon needed help it could will these statues to life at any time to lend it aid.

The dwarf called a halt to the group, several miles from the massive building that even from this distance seemed as if it was looming over them and said to Travis in a resolutely firm voice that there was no way that he was going to face that foul creature of a guardian at night again and that they should approach in the morning instead when it might be less dangerous.

Travis actually agreed with this and right away they set out about setting up camp, once this was done they all relaxed, everyone but Caliban.

The white haired assassin mage was feeling something that he had never felt before in his life and it was a new experience for him. Guilt filled his soul. Before he had always lived a solitary spartan like lifestyle with mostly his father for company and he showed his son little affection at all. Instead they just trained and trained, trying to turn him into the perfect killing machine. Never were there any feelings of love or friendship or anything between them other than just the fact that he knew he was his fathers own blood. He did have a friendship with Seth. They were almost as close as brothers and as he looked over to the dark haired young battlemage whose best friend he had killed under the mountain, he saw the grief that was in his eyes as he kept looking back in its direction. Caliban felt almost sorry for what he had done. None of the others in the group had blamed him at all, in fact they had all each personally thanked him for trying to rescue the other man by diving to the cliffs edge and grabbing at him regardless of his own safety and had made him feel more welcome in the small group because of it. All of them almost formed a family in a way and he felt like he was betraying the trust that they were putting in him by acting on his father's orders. His father had never treated him in such a manner until this mission itself, but his father's orders and commands were those of the throne and crown and to it he had sworn oaths of fealty and obedience.

The next morning came all to fast for Damien as they cleaned up the camp.

"Today," he thought to himself would be the day of the truth. If he was not the true heir to the throne and crown, the dragon would not let him enter Illsador," the other question he asked himself was, "whether or not it would let them live afterwards." These feelings of trepidation and anxiety filled his whole being and even intruded on his morning ritual of stretching and meditation.

Travis had reassured him that there was no cause for alarm numerous times throughout the entire morning as they closed upon the massive building. Even Kendle, who didn't look too excited at all to see the dragon again, told him that he was, as the heir, protected and would even possibly be protected by the dragon itself.

Nothing was around the outside of the Godshall as they approached but rock walls on both sides of the massive structure which added to the appearance that it looked as if it had sprung up from the earth itself. As best as Damien could tell there weren't even any seams in the rocks themselves either. Nowhere was there any signs of life or of the dragon and for a brief moment as they approached the pillared opening with its giant stone statues on both sides holding their stone swords, Damien wondered whether the guardian dragon might be away hunting or something and if they could just pass through the archway unmolested.

Instead with his every sense alert, he heard the dragon before he actually saw it.

Using its magic to camouflage itself, the great guardian dragon seemed to materialize out of the stone almost right in front of them as if it was coming out of the rock itself, its scaly body changing texture and shape as it did so, creating a shock in the small party. A moment before they were looking at solid rock, the next, the huge beast loomed over them by a good fifty feet or more. Its large leathery wings unfurled above them and a blast of air stirred up the rocky soil about their bodies and caused everyone's hair to move as if they were in a windstorm. The large creature's talons flexed and dug long gouges out of the earth about its feet the size of small trenches. It was the largest living thing

Damien had ever seen in his life. He had heard that the creature was huge but had never imagined anything as big as this. The dragon's massive wedged shaped horned head was immense and its large intelligent dinner plate like yellow eyes locked on them unblinkingly and Damien thought, its facial expression almost looked chastising in a way as it scrutinized them.

Everyone in the group froze in place as a wave of fear swept over them rendering them momentarily unable to move. The dragon itself just kept studying them with its yellow catlike eyes, then after it had looked at each one of them in turn, the great beasts head swiveled on its long neck and its large eyes locked and narrowed on Kendle, who if Damien hadn't known better, looked as if he was trying his best to hide behind Mathis' massive body.

A loud hissing sound filled the air, "Tsk, Tsk, tsk" the dragon said startling them, then shaking its head as if it was scolding a naughty or wayward child.

Its mouth as it spoke opened, revealing teeth that were huge, the size of large daggers that looked more than capable of rending flesh from bone or crushing just about anything caught between them in a single chomp.

"I thought." the dragon continued in its hissing voice. "That my first warning for you to leave here and not come back would have been enough, dwarven nephew to the Iron king." the dragon yawned menacingly revealing even more of the large sharp dagger like teeth that filled its maw.

"Most individuals take my warnings seriously and don't return when I let them live." a chiding note filled the dragon's voice but there was also a hard edge underneath it and Damien saw Kendle actually cringe. "But here you are back again?" a surprised sound now was in the dragon's voice. "I assume its not to attempt to rob from here again is it?"

Kendle had as much iron in his spine as the mountains from which he came and to see him almost cowering somewhat in fear in front of the large dragon served to cause Damien more than a little bit of trepidation and a lot of fear as he considered what he knew he had to do now.

"He is here because he accompanies me," stated the young battlemage, loudly, stepping boldly in front of the others, "not out of his choice but because I asked him to come here with me."

The guardian dragon turned its head a little and studied them all again. Then as its eyes widened slightly it spoke in a hiss, "Ahh the children of the old king have finally arrived."

Damien heard the dragon misspeak the word but overlooked it as he continued on. "Yes I have come mighty guardian," using the words that Travis had coached him in. "To reclaim the Dragon rings of kings and proclaim myself the rightful and true ruler to the rest of the realm."

The dragon eyed Damien, closer, bringing his head down so that his dinner plate sized eyes were directly in front of him, sniffed loudly, then moved his gaze over the rest of the group, pausing momentarily on Alyssa and her symbol of Dar. He sniffed at her too before rearing back up and looming over them. "I see how it is then and what is your name rightful king and true ruler? So that I will always remember it in the future and that the gods will know to whom they shall allow entrance."

Damien, wondering why the dragon had looked at Alyssa so curiously almost missed the question. Quickly he recovered and spoke his name loudly and clearly so loud that it echoed off of the stone around them.

The dragons head nodded at him, then it swung around back to Alyssa and it said in a softer voice, "Child of Dar and daughter of battle, there has only been one other of your kind in human history who was a female, she too is buried here in this hall, could you please grace me with your name also? I would like to know it."

Alyssa looked around to the others and then speaking

in much the same manner as Damien had, said her name loudly and the stone also echoed it.

The great guardian dragon bowed its wedge shaped head low before Damien almost reverently and said in a subdued manner, "You and your companions may enter son of the first king and be welcome in the hall, what you seek is inside." then it reared back and the massive stone statues suddenly came to life and pulled open the large iron doors that filled the entranceway to the Godshall.

As the group of seven moved under the dragons watchful yellow eyes, the dragon spoke as Kendle passed underneath him, "Only take that which rightfully belongs to you or is given to you, nothing else may leave the hall." the dragon then eyed Kendle with a meaningful look, which caused the dwarf to wince again guiltily under its stern gaze and he something his not being young and stupid any longer.

"There are numerous enchantments and other types of guardians throughout the hall that might not be as forgiving as I," the dragon said warningly behind them as they entered Illsador.

Huge white marble slabs tiled the floor of the ancient hall. Towering stone statues of all the gods filled the large opening, depicting a portion of what each god stood for. Pillar after pillar stood in straight lines throughout the hall, they branched off in different direction down interlocking archways.

The building appeared to Damien to be even larger on the inside than it had on the outside.

Travis somehow seemed to know where he was going inside of here and he led the way through towards a hall that had the royal symbol of Kallamar engraved in stone above its arched entranceway.

"Where," asked Mathis curiously as he starred in awe at all about him, "does all of the rest of these halls go. The building seems too large for just our kings and our gods alone."

Travis answered by explaining that the gods that they worshipped were also gods in other realities and other places and were not always known by the same names and each of the hallways was a key to those other worlds or realms. "That," he cautioned is why it's so dangerous to get lost in here, you might never find your way back out to your own realm or world again.

Damien couldn't tell where the light came from but the halls that they went down were well lit and all of them could see into each of the tombs that they passed.

Most noticeable was the intricately carved runes, glyphs and wards that surrounded each of the doorways that marked the individual hallways. Travis warned them all to stay away from them, only Damien as a member of the royal line could pass through any of the doorways without any harm coming to him.

Two large open doors marked the entrance to the Kallamarian kings tombs, the ancient symbol of the royal family crest, had been carved half on each door.

Not thinking, they all almost stepped right through the entrance way to the large room except Travis who stopped them with a slight cough, "Remember," he reminded them, "what the dragon sad about their being other guardians here besides himself and this is the home of the gods when on this planet, we need to step cautiously and be very careful from here on out" He didn't let any of them advance any further until all of them had individually met his gaze and nodded.

Behind the doors a long hall led through the rooms of tombs, inscribed in the stone on the outer walls of each was the names of the ones inside along with their living dates and any heroic deeds they might have done. The group continued deeper and deeper into the hall, every once in a while they would see other shrines or altars to one of the gods of their world. Soon they came into a section that seemed newer than the rest and Damien knew that they had reached the tomb that held his parents remains.

With his dark blue eyes he studied the room that was the tomb of his parents and felt something odd, almost as if something in the room wasn't right, as if something in there didn't belong. He wasn't sure what it was but there was a sense of magical danger and darkness coming from somewhere in the room something very powerful and very magical.

Alyssa looked over at him and saw the expression on his face and asked. "What is it, I sense it too, there is something wrong in there?" and her body shook slightly as if a chill had passed through it.

All of them peered into the tomb, but none of them stepped through the entranceway as their eyes scanned the room's interior. Other than a single body lying on one of the decorated altars and a fourth altar with nothing on it at all, except for a broken silver long sword, the tomb appeared to be completely empty.

Damien knew that his parents bodies were inside the alters themselves, their bodies, his adopted father had told him had been so desecrated by the supposed Terian assassins who had killed them that their remains were put inside of the alters rather than on top which was custom so that the sight didn't offend the gods themselves.

Only one body was lying on the top of the tombs, it was dressed in the black and gold robes of a battlemage and Damien knew who it was even before he saw the sigil of Tiko's family crest embroidered on the dead man's robes, lying in the place of honor. Colin Lightbringer, Tiko's second student who had also been killed while trying to save his parents lives had been buried with them as an honor to his dedication of service and the attempt he had made to save them that had cost him his life as well. The other altar with the broken silver sword resting on it was the tomb of the knight protector and kings champion,

Bertravis Liolbane, who it was believed had slain thirteen men by himself while trying to save the lives of the king and queen. A simple inscription had been cut into the stone on the front of the protector's tomb that read. "He died doing his duty, fighting for those that he loved."

Usually only the king and queen were the only ones entombed in the Godshall, but an exception had been made in the case of the protector and the advisor who had fought so valiantly while trying to save their lives.

Damien turned to face the rest of the group and thought for a moment that he saw a sheen of tears fill Travis' dark eyes as he looked into the tomb.

"Do you think that the room is trapped," asked Alyssa as she studied the room intently with her sky blue eyes.

"I don't see anything," answered Kendle from behind her shoulder as he looked past her and studied the room intently with his reddish brown eyes, "but I'm not certain, I sure wish Logan was here, he would know in an instant." As he said this a slight tremor went through the dwarf's strong compact body when he mentioned their missing companion, Alyssa as she had done with Damien the day before placed a comforting hand on his shoulder reassuringly and gave him a comforting squeeze.

The Dwarf was still taking the loss of Logan especially hard since he had been the one in charge of leading them through the mountains and had chosen the path, which had killed the sandy blond haired young man.

"Maybe I can tell," offered Alyssa. Saying a quick prayer to her god, she concentrated, then cast a tell traps spell and one to reveal magic at the same time.

Everything on all sides of them in the hallway burst into sparkling blue light, including all of the tombs inside of the royal chamber and at the tops of the two tombs that housed Damien's parents a brighter more powerful glow emanated from the spot where he had been told the rings were kept.

Only one thing in the room glowed red in the tell tale color that marked a magical trap. The whole body of Colin Lightbringer, the dead royal advisor and battlemage was bathed in red light from top to bottom.

"Why is his body doing that?" asked Mathis pointing to the dead battlemages form, his eyes wide and his hand tightening on the hilt of his maul, "I mean why is it glowing red while everything else is blue."

"That," Alyssa told him, pointing to the figure of the dead battlemage lying on the other tomb is what is trapped."

"So that is what we must watch out for then." said Mathis simply and directly. He had never been around much magic, having lived out most of his life out in the forests, but he knew enough what to know what to do to avoid trouble.

The rings were the brightest glowing objects in the room and were on top of the tombs that marked Damien's parent's places of rest.

"The rings are set into the top of the altar, They are connected to the guardian Dragon in some way that lets him know if they are disturbed by any other than a true or legitimate heir, so only you Damien can safely enter and retrieve them." Travis informed them.

"Really," said Kendle, in a nonchalant manner, casting a sideways glance at the blademaster. "I wasn't aware of that little tidbit of information." the dwarf whispered only loud enough for Alyssa at his side to hear.

Travis though didn't miss the way in which the dwarf had said that single word and replied. "That's probably how you ended up getting caught last time you were here." He threw a reproachful look at the dwarf. "You really should have known better than to try and raid the gods own house anyway Kendle."

Damien smiled at the exchange and almost laughed at the comment from the blademaster, gone with this adventure was a lot of the surliness that had always followed the man since he had known him and for some reason unknown to Damien it was almost as if he had undergone a startling transformation. He was smiling a lot more and had even made a few witty almost funny comments.

"I would say then," Damien stated looking into the glowing room and its glowing archway, "that this part is up to me." and before anyone could offer any mutters of protest or stop him, he simply stepped through the brightly glowing archway and entered the tomb of his parents.

None of the protective runes on the doorway flared to life or acted in any sort of way to block his entry and Damien passed through the archway unscathed.

The first thing he noticed as he made his way into the chamber that housed his parents in their eternal sleep, was that unlike his quarters back in Castlekeep after only a six year absence, there was not a single mote of dust here, anywhere in the room, even after twenty years.

Without hesitating, Damien stepped over to the tombs that held his parents bodies. Embossed on the lid of each was the royal crest, the gold ring with the dragon inside, breathing fire while in flight. The glows from the detect magic and tell traps spell that Alyssa had cast, abruptly faded as he stepped closer. Carefully, he studied the top of the each sepulcher, looking for the ring and at first he couldn't find either one. Relying on his fingers to find what his eyes might not see like he had been taught by Logan, he ran them delicately over the tops of each one and then there they were, cleverly concealed in each of the royal crests. The dragon breathing fire had gold-rimmed eyes and it was the rings themselves that were the edges of the eyes.

As Damien pried both of the rings up with a fingernail, he realized that they weren't actually gold at all, but instead they were a golden light brown and resembled the scales the scales of the guardian dragon outside of the tomb itself including little heads that seemed to be sleeping. Damien felt the blood in his veins run cold with icy fear as he looked at the rings in his palm. Everyone had told him that the Dragon rings of kings were made out of creational magic, but no one had ever told him that they were actually creational talismans themselves. But as he held the rings in his hand he could feel a sort of hidden power running through them.

Fighting the creational wizards had been why the first battlemages had been trained and he could now feel a link between the rings and his battle magic. The Dragon rings of kings were amongst the most powerful of the items ever created. Damien had thought that all of the original rings had been destroyed and that the ones he had been sent after were just copies. But now as he felt the real power radiating slightly through the rings in his palm he realized that here were two of the true talismans of the old world. The rings in the old world of the Elvynn had been used by the Elvynn rulers to communicate with the most powerful of their creational magical creatures and link them all together to help control or as the humans and other races looked at it, to enslave them. Damien wondered whether or not this was how the guardian dragon knew when Kendle had been here, he must have actually been trying to steal the rings.

A flicker of doubt moved through Damien's head as he looked down at the rings in his palm and a worm of unease coiled in his stomach. The rings were meant to be used by rulers. Other than the dragon's words about the children or child having arrived, no one had actually proven to him that he was who they said he was or thought he was. If he wasn't, he knew from his studies that the rings would kill him slowly and painfully. The guardian dragon outside had accepted him and had thought that he was the true heir. Also the wards and glyphs that barred this chamber hadn't denied him entry. Relying on that, he turned facing the others standing outside of the tomb. Before they could offer any words of protest and with a shaking hand, Damien slipped one of the golden rings over and onto his finger.

Nothing happened for a moment then a voice spoke inside of his head, "finally a battlemage has become king again."

The voice inside of Damien's head sounded just like that of the guardian dragon outside of the hall and the dragon ring on his finger seemed to tingle slightly in response with the dragons words and looked down to see its head with almost living like eyes looking back up at him for a moment before it settled back down into the place it had been before.

Feeling a triumphant rush of exhilaration and smiling at the others, Damien stepped forward towards the door of the chamber.

A.V. Wedhorn

Chapter 28
Golath

Eyelids that hadn't moved in twenty years, fluttered and red eyes opened behind the young battlemages back. Two orbs that glowed with the intensity of fiery hot coals fixed on the back of the intruder in the burial chamber leaving with the Dragon rings. The taking of the rings evoked the long dead dormant blood magic that had been used in creating the Golath lying atop the tomb. Slowly it pushed itself up off the place on which it had rested for the past twenty years. As it did so the black and gold hood over its face slid back to reveal a snowy white countenance that looked like carved alabaster. Gone was the semblance of human features on the undead creatures cold face. The cloths of its black and gold death robes hissed softly like snakes scales as they slid across the stone of its resting place and it slowly stood up on its two feet.

A Golath is a living undead construct, created through another use of creational magic called blood magic, the

A King's Quest

gods themselves might actually have been shocked to find out that there was even a Golath in their hall. Golath's are unusually deadly because they retain all of the skills that their formerly living body had and can use any and all of their abilities even though they are now dead. This one was the undead body of Colin Lightbringer, battlemage and student of Tiko, Damien's old master. Also along with being able to use all of the formers abilities, a Golath feels no pain or fatigue, nothing can tire the creature or wear it down, this makes a Golath a juggernaut of pure power about five times stronger than an ordinary human and about ten times as deadly.

Mathis was first to see the undead creature rise, having kept his eyes on the object that had glowed red since they had cast for traps. He screamed out a warning to Damien, a second too late. The undead creature struck him a powerful blow in the back and with only one punch, blasted the other battlemage completely out of the burial chamber. All watched as Damien's body flew across the hall and crashed into the far wall on the other side where he crumpled to the tile floor, unmoving and still.

Thinking that the first intruder was finished, the Golath bent over, retrieved something up off of the floor and now carrying Damien's dropped fighting staff in its fist it advanced on the rest of the small group twirling the weapon in his hands.

Alyssa, being a cleric and having learnt something about the powerful undead creatures back in Highhold the Darian fortress, felt a chill go through her as she saw it coming at them. Not actually sure what spells might work on the powerful creature she decided to rely on her god and cast a slow undead spell at the Golath. Maybe she would get lucky and the spell would buy them some time to possibly grab Damien and escape.

The undead battlemage must have sensed the magic and quickly cast up a defensive deflect magic shield of it's own that rendered her spell useless.

Seeing that whatever Alyssa had been trying to do wasn't working, Kendle and Travis now threw themselves in front of her and upon the undead battlemage with their weapons swinging. Colin Lightbringer met the attack of the blademaster and the ferocious dwarf with Damien's own fighting ironwood staff in its bone white hands.

The weapon moved with blurring speed and the undead creature cracked Kendle in the side of his head with the longer weapon before he could defend against it. The Golath's power enhanced strength sent the dwarf sprawling down the hall, pivoting and bending with the attack. The Golath ducked under and out of the way of both Travis' sword and mace. It kicked out its foot, catching him in the kneecap with a pushing motion, which stopped him before his weapons could strike out at it again. Then still spinning the Golath brought the staff back around stabbing forward in a lunging motion, catching Travis in the stomach with the weapons notched end, impaling him. The undead creatures enhanced strength sent the blademaster flying backwards through the air into a wall, his shoulder and head cracked into the stone then he too collapsed onto the earth unconscious. If the golath had released the blades hidden in the battlestaff ends the blademaster would have died right there.

Kendle had managed to roll a little with the staff's impact and came back up onto his feet ready to charge again. The undead battlemages said the words to another spell and a giant magical glowing fist burst out from his hand and flew down the hall driving itself into the dwarf's thick body. Kendle caught the blasting fist full on and was carried away with the blows force and momentum down the hall till he was completely out of sight.

Without saying a thing Mathis stepped up behind the Golath and with a mighty blow from his muscular arms that seemed to Alyssa as if it might have fell a horse, swung his

A King's Quest

massive woodsman's maul at the creatures back.

The mauls massive wedge shaped head drove into the Golath's body with a meaty thud, it should have shattered the creature's backbone with the impact and probably would have killed an ordinary man with its force, but the powerful undead golath just staggered forward stumbling slightly, then using the ironwood staff like a supporting pole, the golath planted all of his weight on the weapons end with its arms and kicked out backwards like a warhorse, driving both of his feet into the young squire in trainings chest.

Air whooshed out of the large young man's mouth in an explosive burst and he too flew backwards through the air, Mathis though didn't collide into any walls, instead he flew about twenty feet or so before he crashed onto the floor in a crumbled mass, gasping and wheezing as he tried to draw air again back into his injured chest and lungs.

Within a few seconds Braden, Alyssa and Caliban, were the only companions left standing in the hallway. The undead battlemage had cut through the others in the party like a scythe through wheat easily mowing them down and now was coming toward them and it was still completely unharmed.

Braden motioned the other two to get behind him, then he started firing arrow after arrow at the creature, they sprouted out of the undead battlemages torso like tiny little arms as he continued to advance towards them unhurriedly in much the same manner as a cat stalks a mouse. Some of the arrows that the ranger shot whistled or screamed in ear piecing shrieks while others turned to both flames and ice but none of them seemed to harm or stop the advancing Golath who continued coming forward.

Caliban watched the creature carefully as it came on, his father hadn't even warned him about this thing being here, but he knew that it was a creature of his own making. It had been placed here for the sole purpose of killing anyone who came for the rings and as it looked right now, it was including him also in that equation. Slowly he slipped his hands down into the leg sheathes at his sides and wrapped his fingers around the claw like handles of his magically enhanced fighting blades. If it wasn't stopped soon and kept coming, he would certainly find out whether or not they could cut through a Golath's flesh in order to save his own.

Braden was beginning to run low on arrows and seeing that none of the other arrows that he had shot into the creature had worked, he decided to try a different tactic and raised the sights of his bow a little higher and let loose with one of his last remaining few arrows. It struck home, hitting the evil undead creature in one of its red glowing eyes.

The Golath screamed and staggered a little, it was the first sound other than spell casting that they had heard the creature issue and this sound sounded like it was in pain.

Caliban sensing that the creature might have finally been wounded came in quickly with the glove like talon knives flashing. Moving purely on instinct the assassin mage deftly dodged both the Golath's staff that it was using and one of its swinging hands, then as he had been taught by his father, he struck at the arm with the weapon as it went by his head with both of the magically sharpened blades. The golath moved unnaturally fast and rather than having the blades pierce its arm, they sliced upwards instead along the underside and outside of its extended forearm. Where both the double blades sliced, black lines opened and drops of blackened blood poured out, then the flowing blood slowed noticeably and the wound closed leaving nothing but silver white lines on the Golath's exposed flesh.

The sight of the closing wounds caught Caliban totally unprepared and he stared at them a moment to long, just enough for the Golath's icy cold fingers of its other hand without the weapon to close about the back of his neck and lift him up into the air.

Unseen by all, Damien slowly staggered to his feet, shaking his head as he did so, trying to regain his senses. As he slowly came around he saw the creature standing in front of him holding the white haired man named Caliban high off of the ground by the back of his neck and it all came back to him. In a rush, he remembered that he had been attacked from behind by this dead former student of his own teacher.

The Golath spun and swinging the other man in his grip around in a circle as easily as one would swing a small bag of flour, hurled the white haired young man head first at the wall in front of him. The blow to the head probably would have killed the other man on impact and Caliban knew that in that instant there was nothing he could do to save himself and that he was going to die, but Damien not thinking of his own safety threw his own body in front of the others swinging one and instead of hitting the wall headfirst, Caliban had his life saved when he crashed head first into the mans chest he had came to kill as he leaped in front of him to absorb the blow.

Not waiting on Braden to continue his aerial attack, Alyssa charged in with her hammer swinging, as she watched both Damien and Caliban collapse again as the golath continued to go through the companions one by one. She asked her god for his blessing and a momentary flash of white enveloped her whole body. The Golath still using the staff as its weapon of choice blocked the hammer with its shaft where the haft and the hammer part of her weapon met, the golath released its grip on one end of the staff and a cold white hand shot out and caught Alyssa by the arm, it yanked her about off balance in midstroke. The force of his icy cold grip crushing her wrist caused Alyssa to scream in pain, the hammer fell out of her numb hand and halfway down to the ground the undead Golath known as Colin snatched it out of the air. Bringing the hammer about with one hand, he smashed it into the wall next to him, shattering her one and only weapon besides her hands and feet into dust. With the other hand still holding the struggling cleric, it lifted Alyssa high into the air over its head. Looking around with its one good eye, Alyssa saw the Golath notice the other open tomb in the hall slightly farther down. Both of them saw the powerful wards and glyphs that surrounded its entrance. Alyssa could tell from the expression that crossed the undead creatures face that it was gaining more control of its abilities after its long sleep and that now it recognized what it was seeing.

With an almost human like leer, thinking to finish off the powerful female cleric by letting the gods themselves do its work for him, the undead creature hurled the cleric of Dar towards the powerfully rune protected entrance that marked the unknown chamber farther down the hall.

Braden saw where she was going and braced for an explosion or whatever was to come when she went through entranceway but as the cleric sailed through the magically protected doorway nothing happened.

Alyssa flew almost across the entire length of the chamber then she landed hard on the stone floor and slid across the rest of its length until she crashed into what appeared to be an ancient throne with a mummified looking body sitting on it.

The female cleric lay there in the tomb for a moment until the stars blinking in front of her vision faded away, then she began looking around the room. She saw that judging by the clothes that the skeletal figure seated on the throne was wearing that she too was a female. Outside the room she saw the undead battlemage swing about and move towards the ranger Braden who was dropping his bow and empty quiver as he scrambled backwards clawing at his sheathed sword.

Mathis lay crumpled on the stone floor curled up

clutching at his chest, Travis had regained his feet and stood limply off to one side leaning against the wall, with only his mace held in is left hand, his right hand hung lifeless against his side, his shoulder was obviously broken. Damien and Caliban both seemed to be still unconscious or dazed and of Kendle, who had taken the brunt of the magical fists force blast in the Golath's initial attack and had been blown down the hall there was nothing to be seen.

"He keeps going after the weakest of us first, shouted Braden.

"I know." returned two different voices at the same time from different locations in the hall and room.

The young battlemage was getting back onto his feet and almost smiled at the sound of the other voice at the same time as his. Damien began to race through his mind, going through his own arsenal of spells, as he tried to figure out what might work against the nearly indestructible construct.

"Then he should come after me next," said Travis, panting in pain. It was obvious that he was severely injured, judging by the pained look on his face a lot more than just his shoulder, knee and arm." Then the blademaster brought his mace up and stood up unsteadily took a deep breath and braced himself, ready to meet the golath again,

"Braden if I fall," said the blademaster, his voice uncompromising in its tone and manner, "get him out of here!" he had sworn an oath, a vow that no matter what to protect Damien above and beyond everything else and all other duties and he pointed at the battlemage with his weapon. "We got what we came in here for you have the rings, there is no reason for you to die here today, you are needed," he growled eyeing Damien as he saw the protest begin to show in his face, "by a lot more people than just us in here! It is your duty to protect the people of the realm, don't forget that Damien and always do your duty just like we have done ours by getting you here!"

The Golath kept coming forward. It seemed to be a little disoriented by the arrow that was in its red eye but still it advanced.

A few steps before it reached the last three standing men in the party something odd happened and it stumbled slightly.

A meaty smack came from behind the golath and it jerked upright, its back arching as if it was in pain, then it stumbled again, off to the side for a moment revealing what had occurred.

A very battered and beaten looking Kendle Stonebreaker with blood covering half his face, stood at the other end of the hall smoking, with half of his striped reddish brown beard burnt away and also some of his plated armor missing. A maniacal grin covered the fierce dwarf's burnt and bloodied face and his eyes seemed filled with a feverish sort of crazy intensity as he slapped his thick hands together and said in a roar as he charged at the reeling Golath. "Time for round two!"

Damien screamed out a warning as the dwarf charged, Colin Lightbringer now undead spread his feet out wide and without even removing the axe head of Kendle's weapon from its back drew both of hands back. Damien recognized the power building stance immediately and knew that if the dwarf connected with what was coming, it might finish him off.

Summoning the first spell that he could think of, Damien's hand filled with five glowing magical balls, he threw all five of the magical missiles at the Golath's head. Three of the streaking missiles struck the undead construct's head, exploding in a burst of magical energy. Two of the five were deflected though by a defensive spell of some sort that the undead creature threw up. Damien wasn't sure which type of spell it was until the two missiles came streaking back in his direction along the same path that they had taken.

A King's Quest

Hastily Damien threw up his own protective magical shield spell just barely in time. The second of the two missiles shattered the hastily erected magical shield and Damien was glad that he had managed to deflect the two, or else he would be suffering the same fate as the other undead mage.

The three magical force missiles that had made it inside of the Golath's defensive spells had struck it in the head and for a moment Damien thought that he had managed to finish the creature off as its whole head seemed to explode under the magical assault.

All of the hair and skin was blasted from the undead battlemages face and what skin was left, hung in long tattered shreds, clinging to the gleaming white bone of its skull underneath.

Kendle stopped his headlong charge and looked behind him to see the roof of the tunnel behind him collapse as the Golath's purefire force spell went awry passed over his head and shattered the ceiling blocking the hallway behind him, cutting off and sealing the way that they had came from earlier. All of their heads then turned to see if the undead creature was done for. Once again the Golath's head rose again and its one red eye now locked again on Damien's own dark blue ones.

Alyssa still in the other room, shakily got back to her feet, she felt both drained and tired. She knew that during the few moments that the golath had held her arm it had stolen some of her own life force to fuel its own. A wave of nausea and dizziness swept through her body and she almost collapsed back onto the stone floor, instead she reeled awkwardly and crashed into the same throne she had hit earlier, again nothing happened when she touched it. She could see and feel the powerful magical wards and glyphs carved into the thrones stone surface and she wondered as she recovered her bearings whether or not somehow the magic in the room had faded over time.

Quickly she cast another reveal magic spell and the whole room burst into a fiery blue glow, unlike anything she had ever seen, if the magic was still as active as it appeared to be, why she wondered to herself hadn't it repelled or blocked her entry, looking around for an answer she scanned the room and then she saw what she thought might be the reason.

It was on the top of the throne, on the dead woman's robes, carved over the entrance to the chamber and glowing like a beacon on the silver hammer that the female figure sitting on the throne clutched in her long dead hands, two crossed hammers with a sword between them, made out of mythryll, the holy symbol of Dar, her own god. She thought about this a moment and came to the conclusion that this was why the magic in the room hadn't acted the way that it was supposed to, it was the only thing that made any sort of sense in her mind. At the same time that she came to this conclusion the explosion of magical missiles erupted in the outside hall. She knew by the symbols and the female figure where and into whose chamber it was that she had been thrown and quickly almost reverently she bowed her head to the female battle queen and said a quick prayer to her god.

She was in the burial chamber of the only other female to have ever been accepted by her deity, the battle queen of Kallamar, Lady Ellanine Salaris, who had her throne stolen from her by the battlemage Voriaa Sarr and who also through the help of Dar regained it almost a thousand years ago.

She knew that she was needed out in the hallway and had to return to the fight before the Golath destroyed all of her companions. She remembered now as her frozen arm began to sting, a few more of her lessons in the monastery on Golath's. Only magical weapons could hurt them and that you couldn't touch or harm one without them and that the eyes were the only way to one kill one completely with

A King's Quest

or without a magical weapon, spells were almost always ineffective and that they drew strength and regained power from those that they touched with their hands. Needing another weapon to replace her own shattered one, Alyssa quickly asked for the dead queens forgiveness as she grabbed a hold of the brightly glowing silver hammer's shaft and pulled, nothing happened, it didn't move. Letting out a scream of frustration, Alyssa put all of her weight behind it and pulled again and still nothing happened. Removing her hands from the hammers shaft she placed them on top of the dead queens own bony skeletal ones. Instantly she felt a surge of power go through her entire body in a tingling rush, then a female's voice sounded in her head, "Use it well, daughter of Dar, I pass this onto you, who is worthy, it's a gift from our god himself, after you are finished saving your friends return here and recover the champions armor also, cause you daughter of battle will need it in the future." then the female's voice inside of her head died and the hands holding the hammer fell away. The gleaming silver hammer with Dars symbol on each of its heads fell into her outstretched hands.

Gripping the weapon firmly, she hefted it up and was amazed by its lightweight and perfect balance. Alyssa saw the armor that the voice had spoken of as she gave the weapon a quick swing and knew that she would come back for it as instructed by the voice after the fight, then she turned and raced out of the room, back into the fray to help save her companions. As she did so she silently blessed Dar, for the intervention of the hammer and mentally thanked the queen who gave it to her, she knew that the chances of her being thrown where she had, had to be her god himself acting in her behalf and she was grateful, that act might help in saving all of their lives from the Golath.

As Alyssa streaked out of the battle queen's chamber in a blur of gold and black, she raised the gleaming silver hammer high over her head, shouting for the others to go for the creature's eyes or to only use magical weapons on the undead constructs body.

The golath seemed to be stumbling more now due to the magical axe embedded in the creature's spine.

Alyssa ducked low and slid under one of the Golath's waving arms and spun the flat end of the magical hammer up and around into the constructs face driving the protruding arrow sticking out from its eye socket deep into its skull. The golath rocked with the hammers impact and it dropped down to one knee, clutching at its head. A sizzling electrical hiss filled the air as the creature's hand swept out. Five globes of ball lightening streaked out from the creatures open palm. The arrow in the golath eye must have distorted its depth and distance perception, because only one of the balls streaked towards a target.

Caliban had pushed himself up onto his knees. He knew that if it hadn't been for Damien's timely interference with the Golath's earlier attack on him, he would more than likely be dead right now. He was very lucky to be alive. A loud shout caught his attention and the white haired young man swiveled his head in its direction. He saw the crackling pulsating ball of lightening streaking at him, it was only a few feet from him and he knew in that instant that it was to late for him to do anything again defensively other than to try to duck out of the way and rely on the power of the talisman armor to save him, but then Damien was there again to save him.

The dark haired battlemage had prepared several spells earlier and knew that he was the only chance that the white haired man had for survival and Damien wasn't about to let another die if he could do anything to try to save them while on this quest. Using a fully prepared shield this time, Damien launched himself into the air and threw his body into the way of the oncoming sizzling lightening ball. Caliban blinked in the resulting blinding flash of light as the battlemage and the ball of lightening exploded right in front of his eyes.

Now it was Damien who crashed bodily into Caliban and in a tangle of arms and legs they both once again fell back down onto the floor.

As the golath started to stagger once more to its feet, Alyssa rolled out of the way, Braden came in at it with his sword held high and keeping with the clerics advice, drove the tip of the steel blade directly into the creature's other flaming red eye.

The pierced Golath whipped its head about so fiercely that it yanked the sword out of Braden's grip and a sort of wail began to come out of its mouth. The keening noise grew in volume and all of the companions screamed as the horrible sound pierced their eardrums and caused them all to drop their weapons in pain and cover their ears with their hands.

A single large shadow rose up over the screaming Golath and Mathis despite the sound, seeing Braden's magical sword still stuck in the creature's eye, raised his massive woodman's maul high into the air and with a mighty swing using his powerful shoulders dropped its wedge shaped head down onto the Golath's head. The heavy weapon triangular tip split the creature's skull with the impact and the sword and maul met in the center of it. The red lights that filled the undead creature's eyes flared brightly for a moment then dimmed, as the light in them died and the Golath fell over to one side with its head split in two unmoving onto the stone floor, now truly dead at the large young mans feet.

The Golath wasn't the only thing that collapsed onto the tiled floor. The entire beaten and bloody group all sank down on to the floor too, every one of them tired, wounded and exhausted.

After a brief rest, Alyssa got back up onto her feet and went around to the others and began administering healing spells to their wounds and injuries.

Travis and Kendle seemed to be the worse out of all of them, Travis had both a sprained knee, a broken shoulder and his head had been split open. Kendle wasn't much better, with his beard half burnt off, burns all over his body from the blasting fist that had carried him down the hall and a severe head injury that had caused him to lose a significant amount of blood. They got most of her healing spells, everybody else got ointments, salves, splints and wraps. Once she was finished, Alyssa told them that she had to do something before they left and informed them of what had occurred in the other chamber with the female voice in her head.

Kendle pulled Damien off to one side as the others watched Alyssa step through the entrance to recover the armor from the ancient battle queen's burial chamber. The dwarf tugged the young battlemage down close to his mouth and whispered something into his ear, as they stood outside of his parent's chambers.

Damien listened intently and nodded his head, agreeing with the dwarf's assessment, then quickly he stepped back into his parents chambers and recovered the broken silver sword of the royal protector and champion off of the third tomb and handed it over to the dwarf, who had told him that it might come in handy later in gaining the knights support when they arrived at the Citadel, but not to mention it to Travis right away, he said he would tell the blademaster when the time was right.

Then the dwarf slipped the broken silver sword into his pack out of sight, he let his eyes linger for a moment longer on the still scarred blademaster.

Alyssa returned and held up a suit of ancient silver chain mail armor and plate combined that gleamed in the light of the hall, to everyone in the group it was apparent that the armor was not normal armor and probably possessed some sort of enchantments. Kendle went over and rubbed his fingers over its links and plate and proclaimed that it was made out of mythryll, he wasn't sure about what its abilities were though if it had any.

"So where do we go now?" asked Damien as he pointed a finger behind them.

The Golath's purefire force blast spell that had aimed at Kendle and had been deflected by Damien's own attack had collapsed the hall behind them sealing off the way they had came from.

Everyone's head turned in the direction of the dwarf and Travis asked the unspoken question that was in all of their eyes. "Do you know any other ways out of here or possibly where this hall comes out at?"

Kendle shook his head saying, "No, I mainly stuck to the large hall, looking for the artifact chamber that is supposed to hold all of the lost weapons of power, including the lost hammer of Garn that he used to create us dwarves on the anvil of life."

"Well I guess we will have to go on then till we come to a place that maybe you will recognize." Travis said looking at all of them then over to Kendle who just nodded and started off as soon as Alyssa finished slipping on the armor.

Two hours later and the group finally exited out of the many corridors and hallways that they had been traveling down. The room they entered into was larger than the massive anteroom in the front of the hall. Huge stone thrones filled the massive room. Each was ornately carved and decorated with intricate designs. Upon all carved into the front was the symbol of every deity in the realm, like in the front, tall, thick marble pillars stood throughout the room, the sunlight from the overhead windows caused them to glisten in the light. Somehow, they had ended up in the audience chamber of the gods. None though thankfully that they could see was present, no one really knew whether or not the Gods truly came here, but all of them were glad beyond belief the room was empty. Quickly they began to back out of the room and began retracing their steps when a child like voice stopped them.

"If you go that way you will never get out. The tunnel is still collapsed." As the voice spoke to them, Damien felt both of the Dragon rings stir on his fingers and grow first warm, then very hot as both heads on each of the rings encircling his fingers came to life and swiveled in the boy's direction and hissed warningly.

Printed in the United States
34994LVS00003B/28-39